Hillwilla

Hillwilla

Melanie Forde

Mountain Lake Press
Mountain Lake Park, Maryland

Hillwilla
By Melanie Forde

Published by Mountain Lake Press

Library of Congress Control Number 2013950336
ISBN 978-0-9885919-7-4
Printed in the United States of America

Design by Michael Hentges

Cover photo by the author

To Himself, for all those leaps of faith

AUTHOR'S NOTE

With the exception of White Sulphur Springs and Charleston, all of the West Virginia localities mentioned in this book are fictitious. Although "Seneca" figures in many place names in West Virginia, the state has no "Seneca County," but that mythical locale has much in common, for good and ill, with many a deeply wooded, seriously mountainous, and amazingly isolated county in southeastern West Virginia.

Contents

Hillwilla

ONE

Spit Happens

Beatrice wiped the wads of chewed-up vegetation off her face and thought of omens. Here it was, New Year's Day, and this was one of the first things to happen to her. But Beatrice told herself this would not be an omen – it would not set the tone for the entire year.

No. Getting spat on was merely serendipitous, she told herself. She just happened to get caught in the crossfire between Graf and Tess, as they duked it out over the flake of hay she had slipped into the wall rack. Graf was newly gelded and grumpy. Tess was old, arthritic and grumpy – and bigger. She lobbed off the first volley, and Graf, the lesser llama, took it full on the mouth – apart from the clumps that had landed on Beatrice. That's all there was to it: serendipity.

For other people, serendipity was about magical gifts that dropped out of the sky and into their laps and changed their lives for the better.

Stop it, Beatrice, or you'll end up a worse whiner than the biggest West Virginia godhelpus.

Beatrice Desmond had, after all, experienced benevolent serendipity – the kind that made you look forward to waking up in the morning because just maybe there was another gift under the metaphoric tree. And yes, Beatrice had experienced the kind of serendipity that made you want to stay home with the covers pulled so tightly over your head that you could hardly breathe. No one gets to the age of fifty-five without being in the wrong place at the wrong time, just when the deer dashes onto the icy highway. Just when the dear friend dies.

For the most part, Beatrice had lived a planned life, where the good things came from lots of organization and hard work, which could avert or at least minimize a lot of bad things. That was how it should be and how Beatrice's life was. But at times she couldn't help wishing for a gentle shove in a happy new direction.

This was one of those times. Graf and Tess weren't the only ones with the grumps.

At least I didn't have to spend the night in this godforsaken weather, like these poor things.

Beatrice closed the paddock gate and willed her legs to take small, flat-footed steps along the snow-packed path back to the house. At a few tricky spots she whipped her hands out of her down pockets to struggle for balance. The last thing she needed was a fall.

She turned around and looked back at the barn, where all six llamas were chowing down greedily, having worked out an appropriate pecking order in the inscrutable camelid hierarchy. "Who would take care of you, if something happened to me?" she wondered aloud.

Not for the first time, Beatrice felt a wave of relief at seeing those red walls. They were the typical dull "barn red," a paint famed for its ability to penetrate wood deeply and fortify the most decrepit of barn boards. Surely many paints of similar consistency could serve as well. Indeed she had seen dark green and gray barns in the country. But here, in Seneca County, West Virginia, barn red predominated.

She had heard myriad tales about barn red's origins. According to many, the prototypes relied heavily on ferrous oxide—rust—which was inexpensive and had the added virtue of inhibiting mold. Others claimed the original barn-red paints derived their hue from the blood of slaughtered livestock or from lead chromate—a toxic, pinkish substance that dried quickly and was protective against wet rot. In northern New England, barn red supposedly stood out even in whiteout conditions, when the farmer might become disoriented on his way to feed the animals. Perhaps because of her own New England origins, Beatrice favored that explanation, although she wondered why the farmhouse wasn't painted barn red as well. Wouldn't the farmer also be in danger of losing his way in the driving snow, as he shuffled back home after tending to his livestock? Especially if his house was white, as Beatrice's was?

She chided herself for letting her thoughts wander. All those mental side roads and detours so often got her into trouble with reductive-thinking colleagues, most of whom were men. But more and more women preferred to think one thought at a time, too. Conversation had become agenda-driven. Get to the next item on the schedule. People like that built straight driveways instead of ones that curved first north and then south, as Beatrice's did on its quarter-mile journey from road to house. Those graceful curves were one of the attractions of her little homestead.

"Where was I?" Beatrice asked herself. "Red, right." The red was welcome because it offered visual relief from the monochromatic bleakness of an Appalachian winter. Also a good part of an Appalachian fall and spring. Here, gray was the primary color. Even with full snow cover. The snow on the pasture had blue-gray streaks from the shadows of the surrounding mountains, which cast her hollow into an early twilight by 2 p.m. every day. On winter mornings, the sun didn't clear the eastern hills until nearly 9 a.m. – if it managed to penetrate the cloud cover.

What am I doing here?

In the past year, this remote homestead had lost its last vestige of charm for Beatrice. But she felt tied to it because of the llamas, which were a serious constraint on mobility. If not for them, she and Ralph would have packed their bags and headed back, in defeat, to civilization.

With his butt planted firmly in the snow, Ralph soberly observed Beatrice carrying out her barn chores. Gray with ample white flecking, he blended into the scene, as he silently stood guard. He had long ago forgotten the ignominy of being banished from the barn and pasture. The day the llamas arrived, he had dashed off, barking and wagging his tail, to greet them. But instead of returning his greeting, the strange beasts dug in their feet, fixed him in the eye, and made *that noise*. Ralph had never heard *that noise* before. It sounded like fear and menace and lunacy intertwined. He barked back more authoritatively and then sped toward them. One of the beasts lowered its head and charged toward Ralph. Ralph permitted himself a small startled yip before he headed back toward the house.

He had since come to understand that the llamas were part of the extended pack. His person liked them. Not better than she liked Ralph, of course. Like most setters, he had a big heart and was generous enough to share his human. So if she had to tend to them, he would stand guard for her. And because of his big heart, he would guard them as well against interlopers who were not part of the pack. It was very nice to be of service.

Ralph liked being a good dog.

"Good dog," Beatrice said breathlessly, as she paused in her hike from barn to house to flip Ralph's bangs with her gloved hand. She bent forward and locked eyes with him, just inches from his frosted muzzle. He fluffed out his flews to get an even deeper draught of the tea and toothpaste on her breath. And was there a bit of last night's lamb still lurking somewhere between his human's teeth? Ralph would be happy to remove it for her. But humans didn't seem to like that service. So he contented himself with breathing in Beatrice. He liked the way his human smelled and signaled his contentment by sweeping an arc in the snow with his tail.

As soon as Beatrice straightened up, Ralph sprang forward to show her the rest of the way to the back door. At least he hoped that was where she was going. Ralph would like very much to warm up by the wood stove, have a drink of water and look to see if his person had dropped any cereal on the kitchen floor.

Beatrice appeared to be veering off for the Boring Building, where she did nothing but sit at a table that was not for eating. Ralph turned around, ready to guide her there. If he were human, he would have sighed. But he was a dog, so he bounced forward.

"Oh screw it, it's supposed to be a holiday. I'll work tomorrow. C'mon Ralph, let's have another cup of tea."

Ralph went vertical, as he turned around and dashed for the back stairs with such enthusiasm that his hindquarters skidded on the icy landing. He immediately went into a sit-stay and held out a paw for her to examine.

"Did you hurt yourself, boy?" asked Beatrice, lifting the proffered paw. He calmly let her examine all four legs and declare him fit. With that assurance, the setter slammed his elbows on the landing, raised his rump in the air and made wild loops with his tail, before levitating himself through the dog panel in the back door.

Beatrice thought it would be very nice if she could park her rump before some kindly soul, proffer her limp wrist, and receive assurances that all was well. In fact, that was precisely what she needed.

TWO

Bart Sighs

"Hello?"

"Happy New Year, Daddy!"

"Martha?"

"You have some other offspring I don't know about?"

Bartholomew Desmond had been awakened from a contented nap and an even more satisfying dream in which he was an indeterminate number of decades younger than his sixty-five years. Now, what he really wanted to do was poke the fire to keep out the drafts from the nor'easter blowing outside. What he really did not want to do was talk with his only daughter and be reminded of the passage of time. Yet it wasn't her incipient crow's feet that upset him. He did find it appalling that he could be the father of a woman on the brink of middle age, but what upset him was the internal transformation in his once-sweet, perpetually laughing, ginger-haired girl.

"Oh, I'm out of it. Just dozing off a little before the fire. Sorry. And Happy New Year to you, too."

"Are you feeling okay? You taking your blood pressure meds? I hope you haven't been out shoveling. Have you been being good?"

Of course, I've been out shoveling. Who else is going to do it? And why should anyone else do it? It's my house, isn't it? It's my problem if I need to go somewhere. And if you're so bloody concerned, Martha, you could haul your tight little ass over here and man a shovel yourself.

What Bart did say was, "Of course I'm taking the pills. Of course I'm taking care of myself. I appreciate your concern, but I'm not senile or an invalid, and I expect to make it all the way through the year just begun. So don't worry. How bad is the snow out your way?"

"We have almost a foot already. But it looks like it's petering out. And I didn't say you were an invalid. I just worry. You're all I've got, Daddy. Who else am I gonna worry about?"

"Well, you've got your aunt. I'm sure she'd like to hear from you, find out how you're doing."

"Beatrice? Fat chance!"

Bart sighed, loud enough for Martha to hear. For a change, he did not fill the awkward silence with soothing words. He looked longingly at the dying fire and sighed again, softly this time.

Why do some women have to be so unpleasant?

"Oh, I know you think I'm being petty. You always take your little sister's side. Even against me. But after what she did to me, I don't want to have anything to do with her again. I really needed a hand five years ago, and she just couldn't be bothered..."

And there it was again, the old lament about the inheritance.

Tune up the bagpipes. The dirge begins anew.

It was all about the small fortune that fell out of the skies, courtesy of ancient Aunt Adelaide who had trekked off to Australia—to Adelaide, as a matter of fact—and lost contact with the whole fam damily back in the States. Everyone had thought she was long dead, but she made it to the plummy age of ninety-five, living in a Sydney nursing home. She had married well and generated prodigious progeny, none of whom danced sufficient attendance on her in her widowed dotage. To punish them, she bequeathed the bulk of her estate to an animal welfare organization and left the rest, one hundred fifty thousand dollars, to her American relatives. The money was to be divided equally among Nephew Bart, Niece Beatrice and Great-Niece Martha.

Bart, whose determination to overcome the genteel poverty of his and Beatrice's childhood resulted in prudent investments, had no particular need for an extra fifty thousand. It certainly would have been nice, but he owned the slate roof over his head and the half-acre of well-landscaped Dover soil on which the old, well-appointed house sat so gracefully. He didn't need or want much more than that—and peace. It wasn't as if the money would go to underwrite a scuba-diving excursion to Aruba. Bart had no particular interest in ever leaving Massachusetts again.

So when Martha complained about the woes of starting up her new interior design firm, Bart promptly offered his daughter his share of the manna. She hadn't even gotten around to asking him, although Bart knew she would. Making the offer was easier than listening to the oft-repeated complaints about the plumbing problems in her smartly situated but ancient-of-days Boston office building. And when those tales of woe subsided, Martha would wind herself up for more tales of the alimony she had to pay to get out of her miserably disappointing second marriage.

"... almost near a nervous breakdown, with all that stress. And Beatrice knew that. She knew the extra money would have given me the cushion I needed. I could have avoided the second mortgage I'm paying just to furnish the office, to make it look presentable. You always told me that the face you present to the public is so important, Daddy. You understand that. And maybe I wouldn't be working every freakin' holiday to pay for all the expenses. You know I'm calling you from the office right now, Daddy, and..."

Had he ever lectured his daughter about putting on a good face for the public? Bart couldn't remember. Maybe he had. After her mother died of breast cancer, he was on autopilot for much of poor Martha's childhood.

Working my ass off, raising a little girl, what did I know? I muddled along and probably resorted to all sorts of stuffy platitudes to appear paternal.

It wasn't that he didn't love his daughter. There were times he truly adored her. He just knew he had not the dimmest notion of how to raise a child. Like the solid, responsible man that he was, he just kept showing up, day after day, at work and at home.

I did the best I could. No, I faked it. But that's pretty much what life boils down to—faking it, as conscientiously as possible.

"... does she do with it? Buys some dirt-bag place in Appalachia. She's gonna be a farmer in her second childhood? Give me a break!"

The fire was out. Bart was going to object and say that Beatrice had always loved the country, loved to play in the dirt as a child, loved animals. He was going to object and say that it was Beatrice's money, and if she wanted to throw it out the window of a train pulling into South Station, well, that was her prerogative. But he didn't. He sighed again.

Just as Martha seemed to be working up a new stanza, Bart heard an annoying click in his ear and was informed she had to take another call. "I'm sorry, Daddy, but it might be that new client on Beacon Hill I'm trying to land. Gotta go. Happy New Year and be well!"

The phone went dead before Bart had a chance to return the good wishes. There was a time when he fumed over call waiting. He had always found it the height of rudeness to jettison one partner in conversation on the chance of making a more satisfying connection with that metallic click on the line. Bart likened call waiting to being on a date and then jumping up from the table to snag the better-looking woman who had just strolled into the restaurant—while the forsaken date was left to pick up the tab. Somewhere along the line, he had ceased to care about the decline of manners and decency. As long as he could putter around his garden and take his aging black Lab for a walk, the rest of the world could kiss his white Irish ass. Not that he would ever share that misanthropic sentiment with anyone else, except maybe with Bea. He would smile and nod amiably when needed and let the world think he was a doddering old fudd. As long as the world left him in peace.

Bart rose gently from his button-down leather easy chair and creaked over to the fireplace to wad up newspapers and resurrect the embers. Addie, lying just off the apron, thumped her black tail heavily in sleep. Bart smiled.

THREE

Post-Holiday Blues

Evie Rudner swirled her nearly empty Manhattan dejectedly. "This is definitely not a glass half full."

Her lunch companion was her secretary, Shirley McClintock, still a sparkly southern belle despite the march of time. Shirley was also one of the few women who could snap her fingers to catch a server's attention without giving offense. Motioning toward Evie's glass to signal the need for a refill, she flashed the waiter a thousand-watt smile.

"Goddamned holidays. Next year, remind me to make vacation plans for, I dunno, the Seychelles, so I can miss all that Christmas cheer," Evie said.

"Next year, don't trek off to West Virginia for Thanksgiving. You've been in a pet ever since."

Shirley made no pretense of submissiveness toward her boss. She knew how much Evie valued her. Evie, despite her love affair with all things high tech, was old school about secretaries. She needed a live human being, not voice mail, to keep the Forces of Chaos from storming her castle, at least on the job. Shirley was an excellent portcullis.

She was also that rare creature who actually preferred the term "secretary" to "administrative assistant." A gifted liar, dripping molasses with every prevarication, she left the thwarted caller or visitor almost cheerful despite failing to gain access to the boss. No one suspected a petite, champagne-haired Georgia peach like Shirley would lie. From her exposure to legions of southern novelists, Shirley had absorbed awesome creativity when it came to concocting, at the last minute, whatever excuse Evie needed to end an unwanted encounter.

Evie considered Shirley a friend, not just another employee in her public relations firm – even if Shirley referred to Evie only as "Boss" or, in the presence of others, "Miss Rudner."

Miss Rudner had indeed been "in a pet" since visiting her longtime friend Beatrice in West Virginia. Evie was not someone given to brooding. But she had not been able to shake the darkness infusing that trip, not even after she had returned to her bright, tastefully decorated townhouse in McLean, Virginia.

"Goddamned right! That visit fucked me over."

"Did you kiss your momma with that potty mouth?" Shirley often chided the Boss about her occasionally foul language. But the scoldings usually made Evie even more inclined to scatological excess, at least in Shirley's presence.

This time, Evie ignored the challenge. "Beatrice has always had a dark side, but she was darker than usual."

"Honey, I don't know why anybody would want to live in the mountains, anyway. Give me the sunny seashore, where I can bake all of life's cares away."

Evie snorted. "And ogle buff cabana boys?"

"They ogle me."

"I've no doubt," sighed Evie, staring at Shirley's impressive, but still tasteful, décolletage. "No, I can't even blame the bleak backwoods scenery. Beatrice has lived there some years now. I thought she was reasonably happy. But she used to have a lifeline. Her best friend, Kate, wasn't all that far away. But now there's no Kate."

"The loss of a loved one leaves scars. As I recall, you were quite undone yourself by your friend's death."

Although Evie tried to keep her personal life separate from her office life, everyone knew she had been rattled by Kate Stuart's death, months earlier. She had dropped her usual focus on business concerns to dash off to Staunton, on short notice, for Kate's memorial service. Kate, Beatrice, and Evie had seen each other through the rollercoaster years when they were all trying to launch careers in the Washington, D.C., area. They had covered each other's backs through the ups and downs of romantic relationships. And long after, they stayed connected, even though their paths diverged, with Evie remaining resolutely single and happily obsessed with her business, while Kate managed somehow to have it all: a successful legal practice; a sturdy, attractive husband; and two cheerful, smart sons on a nauseatingly healthy Staunton farm.

Then there was Beatrice's strange and isolated path.

"Yeah, and Beatrice knew Kate even longer than I did. They were college roommates, for Christ's sake. When Kate died, I felt like I buried my youth."

"You are only as old as you feel. And since I plan to live forever, I'm decades away from starting middle age."

Evie rolled her eyes. The secretary currently devouring her Cobb salad was a few years older but truly felt like the belle of the ball.

"Don't you *ever* get depressed?" asked Evie sullenly and snapped a chunk of her satay off the skewer.

"In a previous life, I did so many good deeds that I am now reaping my karmic reward," Shirley replied nonchalantly, while dousing her salad with blue cheese dressing.

Karma and reincarnation occasionally surfaced in Shirley's anecdotes. Evie was never sure whether Shirley was serious or merely spinning one of her creative fabrications. Evie, however, had little tolerance for any kind of metaphysical indulgence. Raised to honor both her Jewish and Presbyterian roots, she preferred to believe death was final. No reincarnation. No afterlife. No deities with a game plan. To Evie, life should be lived as comfortably as possible, without giving or taking grief. Playing more or less by the rules made sense, not for moral reasons but merely to minimize the potential for conflict and secure harmony for the maximum number of people.

Her beliefs, or lack of them, made Beatrice an odd choice for a friend. Beatrice believed in something she called the Cosmic Chuckle, wreaked by bored gods. Maybe it was a skewed relic of Catholic guilt. Or maybe it was just the way Beatrice's life played out.

All Evie knew for sure was that her friend was driven. As someone who took genuine joy in her own work, Evie admired Beatrice's work ethic and basic toughness – even if all that grit had not yielded any noteworthy material success. But whatever was driving Beatrice, it wasn't necessarily propelling her toward something positive. Often, it was simply driving her away – from pain, from disappointment, from life.

"Y'all still with us?" Shirley asked.

"Yeah, sorry. You just got me thinking about that damned visit. I started worrying about Beatrice all over again. And, as you know, I most definitely do not enjoy worrying."

"Oh, life has a way of working out. Your friend has probably made new friends out there in back of beyond. And they'll see her through whatever it is."

"What friends? She doesn't have any that I can see. The locals don't give her much to choose from, of course. I saw a guy come out of this trailer that served as a diner, and I swear he was a troll. Or a white trash version of the Taliban. Beard down to here." Evie leaned back and drew a horizontal line across her navel. "Quite a catch, that one. Picking his teeth with a dirty thumbnail, while he readjusted the family jewels with the other hand."

"Bless his heart. He probably just needs a little feminine intervention to promote proper grooming. Many men are diamonds in the rough, filled with potential."

"Hey! Focus! We're not talking about your dating options, Shirl. We're talking about a woman who lived like a hermit even before she headed for the hills. And after surviving that asshole of a husband, Beatrice isn't bloody likely to see any man, much less one of those hillbillies, as the light at the end of the tunnel."

"Language!" Shirley intoned, waggling a manicured index finger.

Ignoring the teasing, Evie continued. "Best thing that bastard ever did was croak himself. Instead of celebrating, Beatrice retreated more, at least at first. As bad as that spell was, though, I think this is worse. I don't think I've ever seen her so withdrawn as since Kate's death. And Kate didn't do her any favor by bequeathing her all those goddamned llamas."

"Well, isn't this just the most fun business lunch? I do believe you've been working too hard lately. Kick back a little. I can hold down the fort. Find yourself a nice beau. Just make sure he's rich, Boss, so you can retire in style."

"Don't get any ideas. And don't even think about retiring yourself. You're sticking with me to the end. And that won't come until I start drooling over my accounts receivable. Then I'll just sell the whole goddamned PR agency and have pots and pots of money to afford the Old Farts Home.

And then, my dear Shirley, I shall have lots of action, from what I hear." Evie smacked her lips and winked.

Daubing delicately at her peach-colored lips with a napkin, Shirley batted her eyelashes innocently and added, "It isn't the size of the walker. It's the size of the man in the walker."

"What the fuck does that mean?" Evie threw up both hands in exasperation. Nevertheless, a smile formed on her lips, as she realized gratefully that she suddenly felt better.

FOUR

Overwhelmed

Padding into the kitchen in search of his glasses, Arthur Stuart cursed when he collided with the barn cat. She had been weaving in and out between his ankles and chirruping reminders of the overdue state of her dinner. Only dimly aware of the feline cajolery, Arthur tripped, spinning the cat into her water dish, which burped water over one of Arthur's socks.

"Goddamned cat! Go do something useful and catch a mouse." He shooed the large gray tabby out the kitchen door.

As he bent over to pull off the wet sock, his glasses, perched atop his head, pivoted down low on his nose. "What the…? Oh, there they are." He tried to push them into the proper position on the bridge of his nose with his right hand while limply holding the wet sock with his left. But his right hand was still in possession of the book he was reading when he lost his glasses.

Unable to accomplish that task, he dropped both sock and book into the puddle left by the cat.

"Son of a bitch!"

He slammed his hand on the kitchen counter. The impact knocked over a half-filled wine glass, which splintered into a hundred shards, while a rivulet of merlot dribbled from the counter.

"Noooo! Not Kate's crystal!" Arthur moaned, as he grabbed for a paper towel to scoop up the mess. As he pawed at the glass spikes with the clumped up, wine-stained paper towel, one of the splinters stabbed into his naked big toe. "Mother-humping, cock-sucking sonofabitch of a miserable bastard!"

At this point the kitchen phone rang. Grasping it, Arthur yelled "Go away!" into the mouthpiece and hung up.

He sat down at the small antique oak table, where he and Kate had shared many a breakfast. With difficulty, he levered the injured foot onto the opposite knee and extracted the glass spear. He daubed at the blood with a linen napkin that was lying on the table.

"Oh, Christ, I've got blood on it. Kate will kill me."

And then he realized Kate wouldn't kill him. He could break all the crystal he liked, stain all the napkins he could find, and Kate wouldn't care. His wife of thirty-some years was dead. "Nearly ten months gone," he murmured. "And here I am with this mess."

Squeezing his toe with the linen napkin, Arthur shook his head and thought about the past miserable year. He was never good about figuring out his feelings. He had let Kate handle that for him, like so much else. But he knew he felt angry—and sad and depressed and empty and most of all overwhelmed.

The phone rang, and this time he was glad of the interruption and managed a polite hello.

"Are you all right, Arthur? It's Beatrice."

"Was that you I yelled at before? Sorry. I just tripped over the goddamned cat as she lobbied for dinner. I broke a glass and made a mess."

"I can call back if you need to tend to things."

"No, no, it will keep. Only a minor mess, no big disaster. I already picked up most of it."

"Have you eaten dinner yet, Arthur?"

"It's too early. Oh, Jesus, it's already seven. Well, I'll nuke something when I get off the phone."

"And while you're at it, feed the cat."

"Yeah, yeah, yeah. Christ, Beatrice, you're as bad as Kate."

"I'll take that as a compliment. She wanted me to check in on you."

Silence.

"Well, I called to wish you a Happy New Year, even if January is half over already. The new year *will* be an improvement over the old one, you hear me?"

"It would be hard for it to be worse."

"I know. But the law of averages should work in your favor. And any time you feel the need of a nose kiss from one of the llamas, you haul your ass out here for a visit. They miss you."

"I doubt it. I was never all that hands-on with them. It was Kate they would cluster around the fence to greet every morning. She had a real gift with them, with all animals."

"Not too shabby with people, either."

"No."

As Beatrice continued, Arthur's thoughts drifted to happier times, to a house full of people, all sorts of people. Some of them he couldn't stand. Lots of them couldn't stand each other. But they were all crazy about Kate. She got along with everybody and actually liked their differences. Differences fascinated her. She could be friends with a Presbyterian determinist and an atheist activist, with a flaming feminist and a good ole boy chauvinist. The discourse would always be civil and respectful, as long as Kate was around.

Was there anyone Kate wouldn't tolerate?

Arthur decided she would probably close her door to anyone who was cruel to animals or children, in that order.

At times, he had wished his wife were less accommodating. He was most comfortable around Dixiecrats like himself—men, mostly—men who hunted, belonged to a church, had graduated from a good school, preferably the University of Virginia, took proper care of their families, and did something useful for a living.

Despite occasional WASP stuffiness, Arthur was as likely to respect carpenters as lawyers like himself, auto mechanics as well as doctors. As long as they were useful. He despised people lacking a proper work ethic, whether they were the idle rich or the welfare poor. Although he tithed to his church and believed—good Democrat that he was—that there were times when people needed a helping hand, it grated on him to think his donations might be going to at least some people whose need was born more of laziness than the vagaries of fate.

Beatrice had once accused him of being a closet Republican, like herself. No, there was nothing closeted about Beatrice's political views. She had a hard view of the world and an even harder view of government. Less was better, in her opinion.

"Come over to the dark side," she had teased him once, when he expressed doubts about the wealthy, seemingly unemployed liberal senatorial candidate who claimed to know what was best for the working poor.

The teasing comment had annoyed Arthur. But he ended up voting for the candidate's Republican opponent. And never confessed that to anyone. Not even to Kate.

Beatrice could be annoying. Like now, when she was pushing him to eat dinner at regular hours, take proper care of the cat—or even think about the llamas that used to be his and Kate's. He didn't want to visit them or visit Beatrice.

Why couldn't the friends of one's spouse be just like one's spouse? Then it would be easy to get along with everybody.

But he had chosen to marry Kate, and sameness was simply not in her nature. So he agreed—at times grudgingly—to put up with her many, often irritating friends.

Beatrice was far more tolerable than most of the circus. She and Kate had history, and Arthur respected history. He respected their friendship and was genuinely glad it made Kate happy. But that didn't mean he could always understand the relationship.

"...and when I gave her grain this morning, she turned up her nose at it," Beatrice said, intruding on Arthur's thoughts. "Do you by any chance recall Reine being fussy during her last pregnancy?"

Arthur didn't have a clue. He remembered smiling as Reine's baby, just minutes after dropping onto the soft grass, tottered up on its impossibly long, splayed-out legs. He remembered Kate hugging him and squealing with delight when the baby wobbled over to Reine's tummy and started making loud, sucking noises while simultaneously humming.

"No, I would never even have known Reine was pregnant."

"Hmm, that probably means she carried without any fussiness."

Wearily feeling the male need to solve this apparent problem for Beatrice, Arthur suggested she contact Kate's old llama vet. "Roger might remember. And he might even be willing to come out your way from Staunton, if you'll pay the travel fee."

"Yeah, that's an idea. Thanks. I'm probably being antsy for nothing. I feel a little overwhelmed sometimes, taking on Kate's little herd. And me such a novice."

"She insisted they go to you," he reminded Beatrice sharply. He was tiring of her problems and annoyed that she should feel overwhelmed.

He knew a thing or two about feeling overwhelmed.

Arthur eased the conversation to an end. As the receiver was nearly back in the cradle, he heard Beatrice's dismembered voice saying, "And feed the cat!"

He also heard a mewling at the kitchen door. As he let the cat inside, he didn't know whether he was more annoyed at Beatrice or at himself.

FIVE

Things That Go Bump in the Night

Roger Satterthwaite, DVM, of Staunton, Virginia, had little interest in making a more than two-hour trek over mountains, in winter, to revisit a herd he only dimly remembered or to reacquaint himself with a woman he remembered not at all. Beatrice Desmond assured him that she had been on hand for several of his calls at the Stuart farm outside Staunton. Realizing the veterinarian had no logical interest in developing a client in West Virginia, Beatrice hoped a passing acquaintance might at least lever some information out of Dr. Satterthwaite.

But she sheepishly realized she had far too little information for anyone, even someone familiar with the pregnant llama in question, to venture a diagnosis over the phone. The good doctor muttered the usual platitudes about the client being the best judge of her animal's behavior and urged her to seek advice locally.

"Well, that's the problem. No one around here has any familiarity at all with llamas."

Dr. Satterthwaite glanced at his vet tech, who was gesticulating with animation about the furry backlog in his waiting room. Good manners prevented him from being rude, but he was desperate to extricate himself from this persistent caller.

Then he remembered that large Davis woman. She had worked for one of his colleagues as a vet tech and loved to accompany him on calls to local llama farms. She had good hands and a good eye and was eager to learn. And then she went off to Virginia Tech and became a vet herself. The word was that she had gone back to her native West Virginia to set up a mobile practice, not too far from the state line. Perhaps Miss Desmond might look for a new listing for a Dr. Davis? Relieved that he had come up with a face-saving solution, Satterthwaite signed off and hurried back to his patients.

Neither Google nor the phone company knew of a local vet by the name of Davis. Beatrice was reluctant to call the horse vet she had been using for her little herd, lest she burn that bridge prematurely. But Ralph's vet, who handled dogs and cats exclusively, would have nothing to lose by helping to locate a farm vet.

An hour after she had left a message with Dr. Sharp's assistant, the dog vet called back. "My office manager knows the woman you're thinking of. She only just set up shop, maybe thirty miles from you. I don't have a number, but she works out of her home in Grenwick. And there certainly won't be more than one of her. Her name is LaTanya Davis."

Beatrice thanked her and tried directory assistance one more time. There was indeed a new residential listing. She punched in the number. A gruff voice answered on the first ring. "Davis. What can I do you for?"

"Is this Dr. LaTanya Davis, the veterinarian?"

"Well, sorta. But I don't hold to my momma's weird imagination no more. You can call me Eltie. Like the initials? You got a sick sheep or something?"

Beatrice did not find the down-home patois encouraging but persevered. "Well, I've got a pregnant llama who is giving me some worries. I'm not very experienced with..."

"A llama? Hot damn! I thought I'd never see one of them again since I moved back to West By-God! I love working with those beasts. Where on earth are you?"

Beatrice explained where she lived and that she suddenly inherited the little herd when her dear friend died last year. She said she had been a kind of godmother at her friend's farm, but her experience with large animals was extremely limited. Basically, she said apologetically, she had just followed along after Kate and done as Kate instructed. Once, she and Ralph had watched over the Staunton farm when Kate and Arthur took a Florida vacation. Neither of their sons had been able to housesit. But it was spring, and Beatrice didn't need even to serve up hay. None of the animals was sick or pregnant, and the most she did for them was change their water and turn the barn fans on and off.

Eltie Davis interrupted Beatrice's recitation of her incompetence, asked a few pointed questions about Reine's behavior, and then riffled through some paper near the phone. "Yup, I've got a farm call not too far from you tomorrow. You gonna be around, say, three-ish?"

Beatrice assured Dr. Davis she would be home. As soon as the call was over, a relieved Beatrice poured a celebratory bourbon. The wan sun had already dropped below the western hills, but there was an hour of daylight yet, and that made her hand hesitate as she reached for the icemaker. "Screw it. I need this." She plunked four cubes into the glass and retreated to the den. Ralph padded after her.

It was completely dark when Beatrice awoke. No lights were on. The fire in the woodstove had gone out. After turning on the lamp by her easy chair, she was horrified to see the fifth of bourbon more than half gone. Her head already felt like it was stuffed with cotton wool. And she felt a blistering thirst. She went into the kitchen, poured herself a large tumbler of water, and popped a vitamin C and two aspirin. She had the presence of mind to lock the doors and then went upstairs to bed.

Sleep it off, you idiot.

She woke with a start. The clock read 3 a.m. Had something bumped against the door? It was another half hour before Beatrice could heft herself out of bed. By this time, an iron vise had taken hold of her skull, and her stomach was fluttering. "C'mon, Ralph, let's check," she grunted.

No sound came from Ralph's crate. It was empty.

That's funny.

Thinking the dog had remained downstairs after falling asleep by her easy chair, Beatrice checked the den. No Ralph. And then it hit her. He must have taken himself outside, through the dog panel in the storm door, to do his business for the night. When she closed the main door, she had locked Ralph out. The temperature was in the single digits.

Her heart was racing as she pulled on her parka and boots. Grabbing the flashlight and fighting back panic, she called his name as the Maglite beam bobbed back and forth along the frigid terrain. "Ralph, sweetie, where are you?"

Skidding on an icy patch, Beatrice went down heavily on one knee, her bad knee. As she arose, it gave a sharp protest. So did her head, which reeled with dizziness and sent ominous signals to her stomach. On all fours now, she threw up.

Oh, Christ, what an idiot you are. What have you done? Poor Ralph!

Miserably, she limped around to the front of the house, still within the confines of the Invisible Fence, which Ralph respected. No sign of him. She went back inside and turned on the floodlights, posted on all four corners of the small house. Beatrice rarely turned them on. She preferred the peace of country darkness. But now she was glad she had them. One of the floodlights cast some illumination on the barn, about a hundred feet from the northeast corner of the house. She caught the glow of several pairs of eyes clustered at the entrance.

Oh, no, don't tell me there's a coyote or bear inside.

There wasn't. Inside was Ralph, huddled shivering in a corner, curled into a pile of hay that had fallen from a nearby wall feeder. Unthinking, Beatrice shone the light in his eyes. Thudding heavily against the hay, his tail stirred up a cloud of dust that danced in the beam of the flashlight. She gimped with more speed toward the barn.

After realizing his human was not going to let him into the warm house, Ralph had done the sensible thing. He had bolted through the Invisible Fence and suffered a nasty electric shock in the process. Then he sought the warmth of the large hairy beasts. Fortunately, the large hairy beasts had not chased the dog out of their home. But they were clearly unsettled by his presence.

Beatrice was unsettled herself to realize the dog was not rising to greet her. She switched on the barn lights and veered off to her tack room before going to Ralph in the far corner. She retrieved an old blanket from the cabinet that housed incidentals like nail clippers and extra halters. When she reached Ralph, she wrapped the blanket around him and tucked it in under his fur. He wagged his tail again and licked her chin as she bent over him. But he was shivering. She yanked off the blanket, opened her down parka, and wrapped it around the dog. Then, curling up next to him in the hay, she pulled the blanket around them both. It wasn't too long before the setter raised his head and licked her face again. The shivering had decreased. "Oh, Ralph, I'm so sorry!"

They both arose, with Beatrice reclaiming her parka while removing Ralph's shock collar. "C'mon, boy. You won't get zapped." Warily, Ralph followed her back to the house. He stopped briefly to sniff nervously the spot where Beatrice had been sick but promptly headed up the back stairs, through the dog panel and into the warm kitchen.

Although Ralph had stopped shivering and slurped from his water bowl, Beatrice wasn't taking any chances. She lit the wood stove and motioned for him to lie down on the adjacent pillow. She settled into her chair and reached down periodically to scrabble the top of Ralph's head. Within half an hour, Ralph was snoring contentedly.

SIX

Goblins

Ralph was not much given to analysis. Few of his species were. But he instinctively knew something was wrong with his human, and his very survival depended on making it right again. Those icy hours alone in the dark had taught him that. He also knew that good dogs could make their humans laugh. It's what good dogs do. And his human had told him often enough that he was a good dog. But she didn't laugh much anymore. Maybe if he kept a very close watch on her, he could figure things out. Ralph had been bred to retrieve. Perhaps he could retrieve laughter for his human.

The hangover was trivial compared with the guilt and shame. Ralph seemed fine physically, ate breakfast with his usual gusto, moved with his usual careless grace. But he was watchful. And that made Beatrice feel even worse, the way he dogged her every footstep.

Probably afraid I'm going to banish him to the cold. What an idiot I am!

Guilt was a powerful motivator. She had one more translation to knock off by the close of business, several articles to edit by the end of the week, and a stack of submissions to review as soon as possible. Wolfgang was waiting at the institute for her recommendations.

Beatrice's association with his journal, a think-tank quarterly little read outside NATO circles, had been a long one. She had started as a humble translator, earning peanuts and commuting to the job in the D.C. suburbs. A succession of personnel crises improved her earning power, as she learned layout and editing tasks. The computer era allowed her to telecommute, and she moved to a stone house in the rolling ex-urban hills of Purcellville, west of Leesburg. By that time, Wolfgang had become institute director and depended on her more and more. As long as she was willing to meet impossible deadlines and lend a hand to myriad tasks, Wolfgang couldn't care less if she was one door down the hall or fifty miles away, as long as she was instantly accessible by phone or fax or e-mail.

Beatrice would never get rich from the job, but the income covered her modest lifestyle. Although the work was not all that fulfilling, she derived considerable satisfaction from her versatility and usefulness—and from being the institute's only nonclerical employee without a doctorate or military brass. What she liked most about the job were the translations; only a small part of her tasks these days but a satisfying one. Fluency in German and Russian was accorded minimal respect in the new century. The hot languages were Arabic, Farsi, and Chinese, of course. But Beatrice had not fallen out of love with the cultural and grammatical idiosyncrasies of German and Russian.

With the new vet arriving at three, Beatrice, despite the traumatic events of the wee hours, applied nose to grindstone. She was glad for the deadlines. They gave her an excuse to delay any detailed examination of her descent into that bottle of Jack Daniel's. Her current lonely lifestyle was all too conducive to full-blown alcoholism, and she feared and acknowledged a genetic predisposition to that unhappy state.

For ten years, her father had wrapped himself in a muzzy fog of alcohol every evening after coming home from the shipyard. He had good reason for trying to obliterate the synapses that allowed for memories. But that justification provided meager solace for his two motherless children.

Bart, already a teenager by the time their mother killed herself, bore the brunt of the responsibility in the first few years of their father's decline. When Bart went off to college, on scholarship, the heavy burden fell on Beatrice's skinny shoulders.

Bart stayed in touch, worried about her, occasionally mouthed off at their father. But essentially it was up to Beatrice to raise herself. She was more than up to the challenge. At times, she even relished it and savored the unusual degree of independence she enjoyed, in comparison with her classmates.

By the time she went away to college, also on scholarship, her father had pulled himself out of the toxic fog. Just like that. Part of her was relieved. Part of her resented his sudden intrusion into her life and his attempts to exercise parental authority. Part of her was disappointed that he no longer needed caretaking. Suddenly she was out of a job and felt unnecessary—and uneasy. She did not like feeling redundant and, over the decades to come, would expend far too much energy making sure she would never be redundant again.

She and Ralph put in a full morning in the Boring Building, the cabin that served as her office. Shortly after noon, she forced down a bowl of oatmeal, mixed with honey and topped with banana chunks, in the hope that the carbs, calories, and potassium would make a dent in her hangover.

Then it was time for a brisk walk with Ralph, partly to have a better opportunity to check him out properly and partly to oxygenate her bloodstream. After that, she would still have time to corral and halter Reine.

Beatrice dreaded the vet visit, dreaded the possibility of perhaps learning the bad news that she would be unable to meet the challenges of tending properly to Kate's beloved llamas. She dreaded dealing with this new, unknown person. So many of her encounters with the locals had been disappointing, even jarring.

Dread had become a common companion over the past year. Almost every morning when she awoke, there it was, like a leering goblin squatting on her chest.

The Ford F-250 diesel rumbled up Beatrice's driveway only twenty minutes late. Beatrice and Ralph went out to greet Dr. Davis. The first glimpse was a surprise. From Dr. Satterthwaite's brief bio, Beatrice had expected a youngster, maybe thirty at most. Not too many folks beyond the younger years went back to school. The first thing Beatrice noted, when her guest extricated herself from the cab, after rummaging through the rubble in the passenger seat, was a very long, very gray braid. Much grayer than her own mostly dark, tousled mop of short hair. And when she looked up, way up, to scan the veterinarian's face, she saw more than a few lines. But they probably had more to do with sun exposure and cigarettes than age. From the open truck door, Beatrice could smell the staleness from years of cigarette smoke. Mid-forties was the age she finally assigned to her guest.

Eltie first extended a large, gloved hand then retracted it to pull off the glove with her teeth. Beatrice did likewise and rather liked the gesture. Naked hands said "I come in peace" a lot more clearly than gloved hands, she thought. Then the vet shot down onto her haunches and regarded Ralph, who was on a sit-stay.

"Well, what have we here?" Eltie said. "I believe we have a bird dog." Ralph was still sitting, still watching, but when his guest gave his left ear a scrabble with her still-gloveless hand, he wriggled into her. Licking her face, he wagged his tail at such a high tempo he nearly bowled her over.

Ralph likes her. A good sign.

Thinking she should not miss the opportunity to ask about Ralph's exposure to the cold, Beatrice gave the vet an edited version. She said only that Ralph had broken through the Invisible Fence and was gone from the house for a few hours in the nasty cold. She described how she had found him shivering in the barn and how quickly he had appeared to warm up.

During the recitation, Eltie remained on her haunches, as she looked into Ralph's eyes, pulled down an eyelid, flipped up a flew, felt around his ribcage. "They certainly can get hypothermic quickly on a night like last night, especially if they don't have a small space—like one of those igloo houses—to retain body heat. But he seems okay. The hay probably helped."

As she straightened up, she regarded Beatrice with intensity.

"I was so worried. I thought I'd lost him."

Eltie maintained the intense gaze, and then her face assumed a more sociable, if less readable, expression. "Bless your heart! It looks like you had yourself a helluva night."

Beatrice's cheeks burned with shame. On the surface, this woman was merely sympathizing with her client's angst over the dog's close call. But Beatrice knew the vet knew. For one thing, she had lived in Seneca County long enough to know that "Bless your heart!" was a euphemism for "You blithering idiot!" For another, Dr. Davis could probably smell the bourbon still being excreted through Beatrice's pores. Or maybe it was the bloodshot eyes and pale complexion. In any event, Dr. Satterthwaite was right: Dr. Davis had a good eye. And out of the corner of her own eye, Beatrice thought she saw one of the resident goblins dancing a merry little jig.

SEVEN

That Seneca County Chip

"Why Ralph?" Eltie shouted over the sound of running water, as she washed her hands in the utility room.

From the adjacent kitchen, where she was filling the teakettle, Beatrice called back, "What do you mean?"

Drying her hands on paper towels, Eltie padded into the kitchen in her wool socks. Interposed between his mistress and the visitor, Ralph raised his head from the floor in greeting. Eltie bent down and cupped his muzzle briefly. "Looks to me like he's a pure breed. And they usually have names like Lord Farthingale of Cheltenham. But Ralph? How come?"

Motioning for Eltie to sit down at the breakfast nook, Beatrice fired up the kettle and then joined her at the table. Ralph relocated next to her chair and slapped a proprietary paw on her knee. "It has to do with how he chose me," she said, absent-mindedly scratching the paw on her lap. "The best animals are the ones that choose us, don't you think?"

Eltie looked skeptical.

"I was visiting his kennel and mom-dog was nursing the pups. Lots of grunting and of course I wanted to take all of them home. This guy broke away from his littermates and waddled over to me. He wiggled his way halfway up my shin, got a startled look on his face, and then ralphed up his breakfast on my sneaker. He lapped it up, wiggled some more, and went back to mom. I was honored, and to honor him, I took him home and called him Ralph."

Eltie erupted in a full throated laugh. "Better than Puke, I guess," she snorted. "But a good name for a good ole boy."

Beatrice's discomfort with the visit was easing, as was her hangover. The examination had not produced anything conclusive. She was no closer to figuring out what was wrong with Reine, but at least there was no bad news. And if she had come up short from Eltie's initial assessment of this new come-here client, Eltie had fared better in Beatrice's assessment. She decided the new vet was someone she could work with. So if something was indeed wrong with the pregnant Reine, there would at least be someone competent only a short distance away.

By the time the two women had reached the paddock where Reine was eyeing them warily, the vet had switched her focus from Beatrice to the llama. Eltie was all business and exhibited a confident manner that had a calming effect on both client and patient. Dr. Satterthwaite had been right about her good hands as well. Eltie had a way of touching the animals that told them she was no threat but most definitely in charge. After leading Reine into the chute, a procedure that normally would have the llama dancing with tension, Beatrice could feel the animal's muscles actually relax while Eltie ran her hands over Reine's flank. The llama stood stoically for the ultrasound and tensed only briefly when the portable machine emitted a few soft beeps.

The baby kicked. A good sign. Reine appeared to flinch.

"This ain't a first pregnancy, you say? Odd."

"Why odd?" Beatrice had asked.

"Well, sometimes the little girls, they just don't rightly know what's going on inside of them. I mean, it's not like anyone asked them if they wanted to get preggers. And sometimes the first-timers are just not happy campers with all the changes going on. Some humans are like that, too, you know."

"I know," Beatrice said stiffly, avoiding eye contact.

Now sitting at the little kitchen table, Beatrice thought back to the paddock conversation and realized how often Eltie switched her speech patterns. There were times when the tall woman sounded like her main occupation was poaching 'sang and ramps to sell to the Charleston herb collector who would periodically drive into Seneca County and buy up all the ill-gotten gain for a tiny fraction of what it was worth. Then, during the examination, Eltie had asked her to push the animal's flank closer to the ultrasound machine. The vet had said "poosh" in the local manner. Complimenting the llama on her compliance, she had said, "That's a 'noice' girl" – another example of the weird blend of displaced Cockney and Scotch-Irish layered on top of southernspeak.

In the next minute, Eltie would spout forth a string of multisyllabic words in a well-enunciated staccato. She wasn't trying to impress her new client with her erudition. Both the good ole gal and the educated professional lingo seemed within her comfort zone. The zigs and zags between the two speech patterns were initially unnerving, but Beatrice adjusted and decided she liked the layers. It probably meant Eltie no longer fit quite precisely anywhere—just like Beatrice herself with her long Boston "a's" and hard piedmont "r's." She now sounded like a foreigner whether she was running errands in Seneca County or visiting Bart in the Boston burbs. She bet Eltie knew something of feeling foreign, too.

The conversation turned to speculation about whether this would be the winter everyone dreaded, after so many mild ones. Weather was a safe topic for two people with so few common points of interest. But even that chatter began to dwindle uneasily.

Eltie stood up abruptly. "Thanks for the tea and the use of the phone." After the examination, she had checked her answering machine and learned the next appointment had canceled. Because of that Beatrice had offered a tea break to kill time until the vet's next scheduled farm call, also in the area. Or that was part of the reason. She felt a little less overwhelmed and a little more competent about the tasks ahead while in the presence of this confident woman.

"So just keep an eye on her?" she asked.

"I'm only a phone call away, Hon. If something bad is gonna happen, Reine and her cria ain't likely to circle the drain in more time than it takes me to get here."

Beatrice had her doubts but nodded slowly and began walking Eltie to her truck. As they rounded a curve, Eltie pointed at the large gazebo-like structure in one corner of the snowy pasture. "A sun-shade so they won't get heat stress, right?"

"Yes, Kate—their original owner—was a fanatic about heat stress. It was one lesson that took, even if we're a lot cooler than Staunton, where the herd comes from."

"Great idea. And nice work. Who did it for you?"

"Ben Buckhalter, the same contractor who built the barn. I love that guy. He really worked *with* my ideas and did a whole lot of Bobcatting to get a drivable approach to the hay mow out back."

"Get out!"

"What?"

"You got yourself a good contractor from the git-go. Ben's kin."

"Well, I guess I shouldn't be surprised," Beatrice began. She was about to say something complimentary, but Eltie stopped her short with a dark look.

"Oh, yeah, all that inbreeding here in Seneca County."

"No. That's not what I meant…"

"See, no webs." Eltie waggled her fingers.

Beatrice sucked exasperation in through clenched teeth. "You can knock the chip off your shoulder. I was going to say competence obviously runs in your family. Thanks for coming out."

Beatrice pivoted crisply and plodded back to the kitchen. Eltie stood dumbfounded for a second before slouching into her truck and easing it down the snowy drive.

Beatrice willed herself not to turn around.

Damn, I burned that bridge.

But she'd had too many experiences with the Seneca County chip, when a pleasant conversation would suddenly turn dark. West Virginians were always inferring insults about their isolation, their educational or economic status, their IQ – their "inbreeding." There was no shortage of West Virginia jokes. Many did indeed come from mean-spirited outlanders. But plenty were hatched by West Virginians themselves, who would cheerfully regale each other with the latest. Those jokes were rarely shared with the come-heres. And if they were, there was absolutely no correct way to respond.

Beatrice had never knowingly said anything hurtful but found the constant need for vigilance and censorship exhausting. Every now and then it wore her down, and shedding her native politeness she gave vent to her frustration. As she had just done with Eltie. The hangover certainly didn't help.

Damn. That was one bridge I really needed.

EIGHT

Six Degrees of Separation

"Un-Bee-Fucking-Lievable!" shouted the disjointed voice on the other end of the line.

The ringing phone had jarred Beatrice out of the first stages of nodding off over her second bourbon of the night. It was only eight-thirty, but she had spent a long day in the Boring Building and was looking forward to an early night. She had debated about answering and now regretted picking up the receiver. Only one person would open a phone conversation that way, and Beatrice wasn't sure she had the energy for Evie Rudner at the moment.

"Tell me absolutely everything you know about Tanner Fordyce," Evie demanded.

"Who?"

"Oh, Christ in a wheelbarrow! You are just hopeless! Hopeless! Tanner Fordyce? Hello? The rich bastard who lives in your godforsaken part of the woods? The adventurer, entrepreneur, philanthropist?"

Something about the name did ring a dim bell in Beatrice's head, but she was sure it had nothing to do with her godforsaken neck of the woods. "Oh, wait," she said. "Isn't he the guy who raises bloodhounds? Didn't Kate know him?"

"Bloodhounds? That's what you remember? Hell, Kate knew goddamned everybody, so I wouldn't be surprised if she knew him, too. As for the dogs, yeah, he has something to do with dog shows, but I haven't gotten that far yet."

"What do you mean, you haven't gotten that far?"

"In his book, dumbass! His freaking book. It's an exercise in egomania, all the more so since he was not about to use a ghostwriter. But when a guy has lived the kind of life Fordyce has, the end result is a pretty damned interesting autobiography. And I've landed it."

Still shaking the cobwebs out of her brain, Beatrice was trying to piece together the backstory. Evie was not a publisher, so… "What are *you* doing with his book?"

"His publisher—strictly small time—wants *me* to handle the hype for the book's coming-out party over the next year. Thanks to your big brother."

"Now I'm really confused. What's Bart got to do with it?"

"Apparently he and the small-time publisher are old classmates. They had some reunion for Boston Yalies recently, and they got chatting over drinks. The publisher mentioned this new author who was buried somewhere in Appalachia. So, naturally, Bart said that's where you were buried, too. The publisher asked where and was gob-smacked to learn you and Fordyce are both planted in the same web-toed county. How's that for serendipity?"

"Creepy. Talk about six degrees of separation. But I've never heard any mention of him locally."

"When's the last time you actually talked to a local?"

"Yeah, yeah, yeah. But you still haven't told me how *you* got in the picture."

"Like I said: Bart. God bless his Irish Catholic ass! He asked his old Eli homey if a publicist had been assigned to the Swashbuckler's book yet. Apparently not. Apparently the publisher is too small. So Bart starts singing my praises and says how I'm familiar with the area where the rich old fart lives. Can you believe that? What a sweetheart my boy is!"

"*Your* boy?"

"Oh don't go getting all Drusilla on me. Besides, you know I've always had an eye for that particular Caligula—and for the pot of money he's probably sitting on."

"Ewww! Bart as Caligula? What a concept. Glad it's been a while since dinner."

Beatrice did indeed know about Evie's interest and doubted that financial incentives played much of a role. Years ago, Evie had accompanied Beatrice on a trip up north. Both friends stayed in Dover with Bart and Martha, and Beatrice was shocked to see Evie flirting with her reserved, sweet brother. In her opinion, those two couldn't be more different.

Like someone gawping at a car accident, Beatrice watched a clearly flattered Bart wobble ever so slightly out of his shell during the visit. Remarkable – and not merely because Bart was only recently widowed at the time. He was just not the sort of man drawn to high-energy extroverts. His wife, Betty, had been solid, reliable, quiet, genuinely nice, and genuinely boring. Evie, on the other hand, had many vices, but being boring was not one of them.

Nothing ever happened between brother and friend. Of that Beatrice was reasonably certain. Evie would probably have told her every creepy detail if it had. But Beatrice knew Bart and Evie had become regular correspondents somewhere along the line. From her own experience, she knew both were adept at the nearly lost art of writing letters. Sure, it was Bart's style to focus on his dog's latest antics or the thrill of seeing the first crocus in March, while Evie would pepper her letters with gossip about outrageous colleagues or clients. But in their own way over the years, each was cautiously and glacially revealing him/herself to the other.

Just recently, Beatrice had begun receiving e-mails from her big brother and suspected Evie was responsible for that astonishing show of technological progress. E-mail exchanges between brother and friend might be ramping up the intensity of their mostly written friendship.

"Well, clearly you'll be of no use to help me break the ice with this Fordyce character. Naturally, I could let the new bitch Adriana – yes, I kid you not, Adriana! – handle this essentially small-potatoes job. The guy is so saleable even she couldn't mess it up, although the little princess would probably have a nervous breakdown once she realized her cell phone wouldn't work out there. But it's a great excuse to see you again. So. Can I stay with you when I set up my first meet with the Swashbuckler? I can't imagine there's any local motel that wouldn't scare the crap out of me. And I promise to cook for you, to earn my keep."

"Of course, you can stay here. I welcome your company – and your cooking."

Neither Beatrice nor Evie fit the stereotype of apron-clad homemaker, yet both were enthusiastic cooks. Beatrice remembered fondly the months when Evie had stayed at her Virginia apartment decades ago. Years out of college, Evie had saved up to go back to school and get her MBA. Although a creative type, she had a hard, practical core. A business degree, she decided, would help achieve her dream of launching her own PR company one day. The PR company for which Evie worked at the time did not share that belief, and Evie's leap of faith cost her serious downtime. For part of that period, she used Beatrice's apartment as a safe haven, while she beat the bushes for new employment. Cooking was a way of coping with one sour job interview after another.

The two women traded off their culinary adventures. Beatrice, still commuting to her think-tank job, limited her efforts in the kitchen to the weekends, but she looked forward to the aromas of Indonesian or Afghan cuisine wafting down the apartment stairwell when she returned home from work on weekdays. Somewhere along the way, though, Beatrice had lost her enthusiasm for the kitchen. It would be fun to revive those experiences, if only for a few days.

"Super! Can I come down a week from Thursday? And maybe stay until Monday morning? I think I can spare that much time away. The Swashbuckler is having some shindig over the weekend, and I suppose I need to be there. And then I'll have to stake out some interview time with him. Will that work for you?"

"Yes, ma'am. Bring wine."

"Manischewitz, right?"

It was an old joke between them. Evie still had a soft spot for cloyingly sweet Concord wines, the only alcohol her Jewish father would drink, much to the annoyance of her Scottish mother, who recognized the virtues of single malts. Although no connoisseur, Beatrice had a somewhat broader approach to wine and enjoyed teasing her friend. At the same time, she made sure to have the ghastly sweet stuff on hand whenever Evie visited.

"You can take the girl out of Brooklyn, but…"

"That's Arlington, thank you very much. My parents, unlike yours, were *high*-class refugees."

Evie was the only one of Beatrice's friends who shared her dicey economic beginnings. Kate had probably never known a financial concern in her life, and at times that had created an enormous gulf between them. Evie could be a royal pain in the ass, but she knew what it was like to worry about keeping a roof over her head. That shared knowledge was an important bonding element for the two women. Besides, Evie could lift the spirits of the most woebegone. She sometimes made Beatrice want to slap her, but she also made Beatrice laugh. A lot.

A week from Thursday was something Beatrice could look forward to. Something she could hold on to.

NINE
Getting a Grip

The early bedtime Beatrice had anticipated did not quite work out as planned. After the chat with Evie, she poured herself a third bourbon to celebrate the imminent visit. That was followed by a fourth, most of which soured in her glass, as Beatrice slumped semi-comatose in her easy chair.

When she awoke at 1 a.m., she swore at the clock. She still had to let Ralph out and check on Reine before closing up for the night. Determined not to repeat her earlier neglect of the poor dog, she made sure Ralph was securely tucked away in his crate before she locked up and shut off the lights.

By that time, however, she was wide awake and experiencing the familiar surge in her pulse, as her body struggled to cope with the wide fluctuations in blood sugar levels triggered by the flood of alcohol. Just in case her stomach was planning on announcing its disgruntlement, she decided she should sit up for a while, reading in bed and sipping from a tall glass of water. It took two more hours before sleep was possible. And when it came it was thin and readily disrupted.

At one point, she became uncomfortably aware of the sound of the furnace fan, which seemed to be vibrating excessively. Immediately, she began running mental lists. There was no local HVAC company to call. The locals tended to their own heating needs. More often than not, that meant spending weekend after weekend felling and splitting wood, enough to feed the woodstove and last through winter. None of the locals owned a "fancy" propane furnace, like Beatrice had, to say nothing of the luxury of air conditioning.

She wondered how much enlightenment she could wring from her twenty-year-old home handyman book. Could she troubleshoot some furnace problems herself? Could Ben Buckhalter or his occasional sidekick, "Uncle" Virgil, be of help? Perhaps they could at least recommend someone who knew about propane furnaces?

Unbidden, a tear of frustration rolled down Beatrice's cheek. Once again, she was feeling overwhelmed.

Undone by a stupid furnace fan. And you don't even know for sure anything is wrong. Get a grip!

Wobbling in and out of sleep, she repeatedly woke up almost every time the furnace clicked on. Her eyes ratcheted fully open with one particularly loud click. And she became suddenly aware of her stomach.

Oh, no! Am I going to be sick?

But it wasn't nausea she experienced. It was a vague pressure. She patted her belly to calm it and felt its familiar, comforting roundness. It was just as round and firm and full as it had been yesterday. But something was wrong, she knew. There was an eerie stillness about it. Odd, she thought, that silence was something that could be palpated. Not fully conscious, she just lay there staring at the gray ceiling and hoping that her mounting fears would prove unjustified, that all her fears would go away.

Instead, pain kicked in. Mostly it was a dull cramping but with the occasional, disconcertingly sharp edge. She knew what was wrong, even before the wetness began to spread beneath her.

Even then, she just lay there. To do otherwise, to call out for Bill, to hear the sound of her own scared, suddenly high-pitched voice, would make this nightmare real. It would mean the child she had tried so hard to conceive had left without a goodbye, had stolen silently away in the middle of the night.

As the cramping intensified, she lurched out of bed. Staggering toward the bathroom, she trailed behind her the evidence of the great sadness that had crept into her life.

The pain in her gut was now competing with the protest emanating from her troubled right knee, which she had bumped against the bathroom door. She released a little cry—more out of frustration than pain—and realized that the bathroom was all wrong. It didn't have the "harvest gold" tile of an earlier decade. It was tiny, much too small to accommodate two adults.

Her muffled whimper startled Ralph, who emitted a soft yodel, ending in a question mark.

Still disoriented, she gripped the door for support and pieced together the events of the past few minutes. She was not in the bathroom of the Virginia house she had shared with Bill nearly twenty years ago. She was not having a miscarriage. There was no blood on the floor. There was no husband. There was no baby. No family. She was alone, in West Virginia, far removed from anyone who gave a rat's ass whether she lived or died or drank herself into another hellacious hangover.

From the bedroom, Ralph chirruped with another soft question of concern. "It's all right, boy, go back to sleep. I'm okay."

Beatrice snorted at that assertion. Her heart was racing, but this time she doubted it had anything to do with her blood alcohol level. The dream memory had simply been so vivid.

Nevertheless, it took her a while to realize nothing needed doing. There was no need to call 911. There was no need to mourn anew. That was over and done with. Still, she was surprised to find her cheeks chilled from tears. She was grateful there were no witnesses – this time. All was calm. All was quiet, except for the sound of the damned furnace.

That's what you get for obsessing over Reine's pregnancy. Thumping her flank to listen for return thumps. That's all it was: a little trip down memory lane. A very potholed, crooked lane leading to your own ill-starred pregnancy. Get a grip, Beatrice! It's over! It's all fucking over!

She shook her head roughly to clear it, to purge the demons.

Heading back to the bedroom, Beatrice briefly considered pouring yet another bourbon to anesthetize the memories away. But the slight wobble in her gut warned her that would be a bad idea. Instead, she turned on the light and headed downstairs.

It took her a while to find the handyman book. She carried it back upstairs and propped up the pillows for a read. Settling into the bed, with the heavy book on her belly, she thumbed through the index until she found "furnaces, troubleshooting."

It wasn't exactly soothing reading, but it restored an illusion of control. Perhaps she could tackle this one problem by herself.

Such a small problem, by comparison.

TEN

Awkwardly Bridging the Cultural Divide

Two days later, normalcy, more or less, prevailed in Beatrice's dining room, where she was consulting a fat German dictionary, until a muffled gasp of surprise emanated from the kitchen. She hastily tapped the sought-for word into her laptop translation, clicked SAVE, and headed for the kitchen to investigate.

There she saw four disembodied legs on the floor. Two were clad in heavy denim and shod in beat-up, steel-toed work boots. Two were feathered with white and gray fur.

"Hey, Ralph! Leave Uncle Virgil alone!" Beatrice ordered.

Predictably, Ralph bumped his head on the top of the cabinet opening as he extricated the front half of his body from under the sink.

"Aw, he just surprised me. He weren't bothering me none, Miz Desmond," Virgil's still-muffled voice explained. "We was just pondering what all to do next."

Beatrice realized those sentences probably represented the largest number of words Virgil Arbuthnot had ever uttered at any one time around her. She wondered if Ralph's presence made him more comfortable and thus loquacious or whether it was the invisibility afforded by the under-sink cabinet. The handyman had enormous difficulty making eye contact, at least with her, and tended to stammer when he did.

Beatrice had inherited "Uncle Virgil," which is how she thought of him, shortly after her move to the mountains five years ago. She found him through Ben Buckhalter, the all-purpose agricultural contractor who had saved her driveway from washout, dug a small pond to handle seasonal runoff from the mountain above her house, and most recently built all the facilities for the llamas.

"Uncle Virgil" was the way Ben referred to the handyman, although the avuncular relationship was not substantiated by DNA. Virgil was the uncle of Ben's wife's sister-in-law. Wizened by years of hard outdoor labor, Virgil was of indeterminate age, perhaps not much older than Beatrice herself. Until a few years ago, he was a regular in Ben's work crew, but severe arthritis forced him to cut back on his labors.

His working relationship with Beatrice began when she realized, pre-llamas, that she and her lawn tractor could not possibly keep up with the mowing demands of the farm's open areas. Ben had suggested hiring Virgil to make hay on about seven acres of mostly flat meadow. Beatrice and Virgil worked out an arrangement where they would split the modest proceeds from the hay he baled and sold. She thought that was unfair. "But you're doing all the work," she protested. "But it's your land," Virgil had countered, with finality.

So twice a year, after each cutting, Virgil would show up and laboriously count out her share on the kitchen table, to the penny. Now that she had llamas, Virgil was working only four acres, giving her half the hay and selling the rest himself and keeping the cash. Beatrice figured he was getting the worst part of the deal, but he stubbornly dismissed her suggestion that he accept additional remuneration.

Although she saw Virgil maybe half a dozen times a year, with odd plumbing and carpentry and gutter-cleaning tasks added to his list of (paid) jobs, she knew next to nothing about his life, though not for lack of interest or effort on her part. She surmised only that he was close to Ben and occasionally lived with Ben's immediate family. That seemed to be the case today, since Ben had dropped him off at Beatrice's house late morning and was scheduled to retrieve him later this afternoon.

Beatrice returned to the dining room to work and oversee Virgil's efforts. She had no trust issues with him working, unattended, in her house while she was in her office. But there were several different tasks on the day's list, both indoors and outdoors, and each required explanation. She figured it would be easier if she were on hand to answer questions as they arose.

It would be a long day – a long day of doing the little dance they did: each respectful of the other but each profoundly uncomfortable with the other.

When Virgil finished installing the new kitchen drain, and before he retrieved the ladder to reaffix the strip of vinyl siding blasted off in a windstorm a few weeks earlier, she offered him, as always, a cup of coffee or tea. As always, he declined.

Never, in the five years she had lived here, had any workman accepted an offer of a hot beverage, soda, or even water, to say nothing of the occasional proffered brownie. Never had any workman even availed himself of her bathroom facilities. During the barn job, which went on for a month from sunup to sundown, she assumed nearby trees were well watered. But other calls of nature were apparently suppressed. Stern mountain pride.

Ben, at least, would occasionally park his tall self on a kitchen chair and chat. The conversation always began with the task du jour but often strayed to bits of local gossip, to the occasional but guarded autobiographical snippet, plus lots of philosophizing about life in general. Both partners in conversation held a flinty view of the world and had ill-disguised contempt for laziness and irresponsibility.

By mid-afternoon, the skies had darkened sufficiently that Beatrice turned on the dining room and kitchen lights. Outside, snow was falling upwards, whipped by blasts of wind, ricocheting off the hills surrounding her hollow. When the wind slacked off, the snowflakes trained horizontally, first from the west, then from the north. Within any given half hour, those flakes would head in all four directions of the compass. Little of the squall was likely to settle on the ground. But she worried about Virgil's arthritic hands, as he installed a new gate hook in her catch-pen.

Shortly after the lights went on, Ralph, previously napping on the oversized pillow near the dining room table, whipped up his head and sucked his flews in and out. Stretching, he eased off the pillow and plodded sleepily toward the utility room, where Virgil was standing.

When Beatrice arrived in the kitchen, she also saw Virgil in the utility room, rubbing warmth into his reddened hands. She wondered how long he'd been there.

He touched index finger to visor and said, "All finished."

"Okay, let me get my checkbook. Have a seat, Virgil." she said, motioning him to the chairs.

Not moving, Virgil called after her, "You maybe wanna keep an eye on that crack in the catch-pen post. It's gonna need one of them gate hooks, the bolted kind that goes all the way through the post."

Beatrice suppressed a sigh.

Why couldn't you just install one today?

Maybe he didn't have one. But more likely, he was reluctant to violate the mountain maxim, "If it ain't broke, don't fix it." Besides, opting for the long bolt would have required initiative – and perhaps a consultation with Beatrice. She was glad Uncle Virgil's "nephew" had no shortage of initiative and wasn't shy about consulting with her, even if it occasionally meant bearing bad tidings.

Patience, Beatrice, patience.

She reminded herself, yet again, that Virgil was a hard-working gem, perfectly suited to the small tasks that were too numerous or required too much muscle for her to handle by herself.

At the kitchen table she wrote out a check for the agreed sum and took it to the handyman, still firmly planted in the other room. Just to be contrary, she extended her hand in thanks – in full knowledge of his reluctance to shake on the deal just concluded.

But, goddammit, that's what you do.

As always, he offered a limp hand in response and withdrew it the instant after contact.

"I'll just be waiting on Ben out back."

"No, you won't, Virgil. It's snowing, cold and windy out there. Come into the kitchen, take off your jacket, and have a seat."

"No, ma'am, I'm just fine." But he did at least edge a foot out of the utility room.

"Oh for heaven's sake! Sit!" Beatrice snapped in exasperation and pointed to a chair. Virgil scuttled over and sat down heavily.

At that same instant, Ralph, monitoring the exchange, precipitously parked his butt on the floor. Beatrice clapped a hand over her mouth in a futile effort to stifle a giggle. Virgil and Ralph exchanged quizzical glances. Beatrice shook her head in embarrassment. A sheepish grin broadened Virgil's face. Ralph thumped his tail appreciatively.

"I'm pouring myself a cup of tea. Would you care for one, too?" she asked, knowing what the answer would be.

"No, ma'am. I'm just fine as is."

Beatrice poured her tea and headed back to work. "I'll be here in the dining room if you need me," she said, while she sucked in a big breath and prayed Ben would not be delayed.

ELEVEN

Five Degrees of Separation

Far too many minutes later, Ralph harrumphed from his dining room pillow. Beatrice could just make out the sound of snow-muffled tires on her driveway. Responding to the thump on her back door, she shouted, "Come on in, Ben."

By the time she reached the kitchen, Ben's large frame filled the doorway, and Virgil was hurriedly pulling on his jacket. "Hey, Beatrice!" Ben called. Then: "Wait a minute, Uncle Virgil. I've got to give Beatrice something."

As Ben's frozen fingers fumbled with the zipper on a vinyl carry-case, Virgil peered anxiously out the door.

"That Clara you got in the truck?" he asked.

Engrossed in retrieving something from the case, Ben muttered into his chest, "Yeah, she was curious to see the llamas and wanted . . . " He stopped abruptly.

Beatrice jumped in. "I'd be happy to introduce them to her. Clara's your niece, right?" she said, already yanking a parka off the coat pegs by the back door.

"Aw, no, don't trouble yourself. She saw them as we were pulling up the drive."

"I doubt that. With this wind, I'm sure they've tucked inside the barn and are seriously chowing down on hay."

"Well, one of them poked his head out of the barn."

Beatrice shot Ben a skeptical look. "I promise I won't hold you up. But she's come all this way. Why not let me take her down to the barn for just a few minutes? Come along if you like. Or keep warm if you prefer."

Ben shrugged amiably and followed her. Virgil hesitantly brought up the rear. Beatrice waved at the passenger huddled in a quilted jacket. The girl waved back shyly. Opening the passenger door, Ben said, "Clara, this is Miz Desmond. Wanna see the llamas?"

Clara nodded enthusiastically and began sliding out but then stopped warily.

"Hi, Clara," Beatrice said. "They've got a bad case of cabin fever with this weather and could stand seeing a new face."

Clara climbed out of the truck. Standing before Beatrice, she looked about thirteen or fourteen. Tall and skinny. A little shy. But there was a quickness about her eyes. She looked appraisingly at Beatrice before averting her eyes again. Beatrice proffered her hand. Clara promptly grasped it firmly for a few seconds before breaking off the connection.

The group trudged down the hill to the barn. Ralph trailed them to about ten feet away from the Invisible Fence and plunked down in the dusting of new snow. Before the humans reached the paddock gate, all six llamas were clustered on the other side. Virgil remained on the house side of the gate, as Beatrice ushered Ben and Clara into the paddock. The herd scattered a bit but remained intensely interested in the visitors.

"Ooh," Clara said softly. Ears tilted forward with curiosity, Barrie, a densely coated white and gray llama, inched toward the girl.

"It's okay," Beatrice assured her. "She's just curious about you. She's very friendly and polite."

Now about three feet away from Clara, Barrie lowered her wooly head and gently edged a soft, charcoal gray nose toward her face.

"She'd like to sniff your nose. It's how they say hello. Then she'll let you stroke her neck."

Clara stood transfixed. Beatrice assessed the reaction as enchantment, not fear. In the background, Ben beamed.

Barrie softly touched her nose to Clara's. Beatrice admired how the girl stood her ground, even though her eyes were squinted. When Barrie puffed gently into Clara's nostrils, however, Clara gave a little squeal, and the llama started back.

"Did I do something wrong?" she asked, disappointed.

"No, no. You're just a new smell, and she needs to get used to it."

Sure enough, Barrie eased closer again. This time, she did not make direct contact but from a few inches away puffed at various spots on Clara's face.

"Ooh, that tickles," Clara giggled. "Can I pet her now?"

"Sure."

Clara slowly moved her hand to the llama's wooly neck and began stroking it wonderingly. Barrie stood calmly, her full attention on the girl, but her long ears assumed a more relaxed, vertical tilt. Clara removed one mitten and eased her fingers deeply into the wool. "It's so soft! And warm. Can you make yarn out of it?"

"I'm only just learning to, but yes. And I think her wool, in particular, will make very nice yarn."

"I do, too!" Clara said with authority. Meanwhile, Vike had circled around in back of the three humans and sniffed hesitantly at the back of Clara's stocking cap. "Hey, brown llama! Whatcha doing?" Clara turned her head toward the newcomer, who sniffed her ear. Clara giggled.

"What's this one called?" she asked, still stroking Barrie.

"That's Vike, short for Viscount. He's one of my boys, a gelding."

"And this beautiful white one?" Clara tilted her still-mittened hand toward Barrie.

"That's Barrie, short for Baroness. She's my youngest girl."

Clara's enthusiasm was so infectious that Beatrice considered haltering up Vike for a little walk. But she noticed the two men shifting from one foot to the other.

"I don't want to hold you guys up. Maybe when the weather's better, you could come back, Clara, and we could take a couple of the llamas for a hike."

Clara whipped around to her uncle. "Could I, Ben?"

"We'll see," he said cautiously, but with a smile.

"I hope you do. I don't get much of a chance to show these guys off. I expect they get bored with just me and Ralph around."

The group headed back to the house. Clara looked back over her shoulder and waved a loose mitten at the llamas, clustered at the paddock gate. Then she turned her attention to Ralph, who had stuck his nose into her butt. "Well, aren't you a pushy puppy?" Clara laughed and gave Ralph's head a vigorous scratching. His tail revved up like a helicopter about to go airborne.

Clara and Virgil piled into Ben's truck. Ben was about to slide behind the wheel, when he remembered something, "Oh, the list. I almost forgot what I had for you."

He raised an index finger, signaling to his passengers that he'd be right back.

Once in Beatrice's kitchen, he pulled a printout from his case, which he'd left on the kitchen table. "My cousin Eltie said she was out here a while back. You wanted some info about local goat producers?"

Beatrice looked perplexed but then remembered a brief exchange in which she had asked the vet how she could prepare herself for the possibility that Reine might be short on milk. It was just one of many questions on her checklist. Eltie had said goat milk was a good substitute, if needed, and Beatrice could probably find local sources.

But Eltie had said nothing about tracking down those sources herself. The list of local goat farmers, with their phone numbers, was certainly welcome but quite unexpected. Beatrice recognized it as a peace offering.

Apparently I didn't burn that bridge, after all.

"Thank you, Ben. That was very nice of her."

She scanned his face to look for any sign that he was aware of the tense exchange that had concluded his cousin's farm call. She saw no indication of suppressed irony. But she also knew Ben well enough to suspect he was adept at concealing negative thoughts and emotions when necessary.

"Sure. Well, I'd best be going. I've got to stop by the Fordyce place briefly and want to get back down that mountain before the temperature drops much more."

"The Fordyce place?"

"Yeah, you know him?"

"Unbelievable!" Beatrice replied, only just managing to edit out the syllables Evie would have added.

Seeing Ben's confusion, she added quickly. "No, no, it's just weird. An old friend of mine from D.C. is coming down for a few days to see him. A work thing. What a strange coincidence."

TWELVE

Bunnies and Banshees and Bears, Oh My!

Rabbits! So many rabbits! They peek out from under the sharp tangle of briers on the creek path. There, on the right: two of them, sitting like plump dumplings, completely unconcealed by the briers. On the left are two more, brazenly showing their startlingly white tails, which stand out crisply against the muzzy multitude of grays. Gray ears. Gray flanks. Gray grass. So easy to track. By focusing his attention on those twitching white puffs, Ralph can predict the direction in which the rabbits will dart.

He lowers his head and goes into stalk mode: left front paw curling softly off the grass at the precise moment as his right rear paw. Head and tail define a perfectly horizontal line. Softly, slowly, Ralph inches forward. Not a leaf crackles. Not one twig rolls. Never has he stalked prey so soundlessly, so efficiently.

Ralph pauses. His human does not like him to chase rabbits. Eating rabbits is forbidden. But his human is not here. Surely his human would not be happy to see so many rabbits littering the creek path. Surely there are limits to how many rabbits even a human could tolerate.

Ralph is a good dog. But he is a dog. And there are certain things a dog must do. Stalk. Hunt. Translate a dizzying array of smells.

Ralph smells the blood pumping through the rabbits. He imagines their soft flesh yielding to his teeth. One sharp jerk of the neck and the rabbit will be dinner—a much better dinner than those monotonous gray lumps his human shakes into his bowl twice a day.

A jagged noise jolts Ralph's focus. Three geese! Ralph hates geese. They are raucous, hateful things that mock him. When he closes on them easily on the grass, they elude him by waddling into the creek. But when Ralph slips into the water after them, they do the unthinkable. They lift up, ponderously, and take to the air. It is not fair.

Ralph turns back to the rabbits. He can chase the geese off later. The rabbits' scent calls to him. He knows he can overtake not just one but many of them, so stealthy is his stalking, so primed are his muscles for the killing spring. Ralph the Rabbit Slayer. Litter after litter of pups will learn of his skill. Veteran hunting dogs will cock their heads in awe at his prowess.

Inch by silent inch, he comes within striking distance of the first two rabbits. Digging his rear claws into the soft soil, he readies for the pounce.

In one exquisitely fluid motion, Ralph goes briefly airborne. Then, just as his front paws hit the dirt, on either side of his quarry … *that noise* shatters the stillness, and the rabbits are gone.

Ralph winces. He squeezes his eyes shut and shakes his long ears, in hope of emptying *that noise* out of his head. But it is futile.

When he reopened his eyes, Ralph could not see very well. His third eyelid remained closed over each eye and only sluggishly responded to the brain's order to retract. When his eyes fully opened, he was shocked at how dark it had become. Ralph saw only the bars of his crate. He smelled no rabbits. Inhaling cautiously, he breathed in Beatrice, the synthetic fibers of the bedroom rug, the acrid tang of shower cleaner in the adjacent bathroom, the lingering aroma of last night's leftovers downstairs.

Then *that noise* intruded again, overriding his cataloging of olfactory input. Sleepily lurching out of the crate, Ralph bumped his shoulder blades on the opening. He barked authoritatively in the direction of the bedroom door then turned his head and directed a deep bark at the bed where Beatrice lay still. Did she really not hear *that noise*?

Barking, Ralph tumbled down the stairs and headed for the back door. He paused briefly, cocking an ear for his human. Sure enough, clunks and thuds came from upstairs. It seemed to take forever, but finally his human showed up at the back door. He hopped a few times to encourage her to open it. Succeeding, he charged outside.

Fumbling for the big flashlight, Beatrice flipped on the outdoor lights and slipped on the rubber shoes she kept in the utility room. She was thankful for the recent thaw. At least she would not have to negotiate her way through snow or ice.

The llamas trumpeted again, an eerie call that reminded Beatrice of donkeys braying, roosters crowing, and banshees wailing. Ralph, positioned as close to the barn as he could get without receiving a shock, barked again. Beatrice jolted stiffly down the slope to where the setter was sitting alertly, now silent. More trumpeting. She shone the flashlight into the dark pasture and caught the glint of llama eyes. The herd was clustered together, all pointing in the same direction.

Beatrice shuddered. This was not a false alarm, not one of those times when a neurotic Reine was startled by a deer and shouted her distress. Beatrice wished she had remembered to retrieve the .38 from her nightstand, if only to fire a shot into the ground on the chance that the noise would scare off a predator. She clumped over the hard grass into the barn, turned on its dim lights, and headed for the tack room. There, she kept an old blackthorn shillelagh. It had been in the family for generations. Sometimes she took it with her on dog walks. Maybe she could bounce it off a coyote's nose. A feeble course of action, she realized, but better than nothing.

Keeping to the fence line, Beatrice systematically zigzagged the beam over the landscape, in the direction where six llama noses pointed. With every shadow shifting in the wan light, she felt an atavistic shiver, the same vulnerability that must have haunted ancient caves long after the torches had gone cold and unseen creatures of fang and talon yawped in the blackness.

She heard a rustle in the far corner of the pasture. Movement flickered in the flashlight beam. She was too far away to see clearly but instinctively bellowed, "Yah! Go away!" in the hope the unknown thing would be more scared of her than she of it.

From her rear, an intensely focused Ralph barked twice, with low, deep authority. "Good dog," she murmured gratefully.

Yelling intermittently, Beatrice willed her feet to move toward the corner. Glinting dimly in the flashlight beam, the woven wire looked askew. She tried to inhale some courage and then exhaled deeply, generating a vapor cloud that temporarily obscured her view. And then she saw the five-foot span of fence, crumpled to half its normal height. Several broken lengths of no-longer-woven wire spiked off at odd and dangerous angles.

"Shit!"

Although an errant deer hoof would occasionally ding the topmost wire after a less-than-balletic leap, no deer could have done this kind of damage. And just as Beatrice came to that queasy conclusion, the brush crackled loudly about thirty feet ahead on the other side of the crumpled fence. She flicked the flashlight beam up from the fence line and caught two red pinpoints in the blackness. The disembodied eyes appeared to be roughly at the same level as hers.

"Yah, bear!" Beatrice yelled, her voice cracking. From the distance, Ralph echoed a baritone protest.

The glowing red eyes suddenly extinguished. The bear had apparently shrugged down on all fours. It began crashing heavily through the brush beyond the crumpled fence. In her flashlight beam, Beatrice saw the silver-rimed tips of shrubbery give way to something very large and very black, moving purposefully away from her.

"Yah! Git!"

Beatrice exhaled in jagged puffs. The bear was gone. The llamas were safe. But the relief was short-lived, as she realized she needed to prevent the llamas from escaping or getting gored by the bear's handiwork on the fence. It was an impossible task in the dark. Wearily, Beatrice clumped back toward the clustered llamas and began herding them toward the paddock in front of the barn. One by one, she closed the gates separating barn and paddock from the main pasture. The llamas would have to make do with this limited space for the rest of the night, at very least. She would worry about fence repairs tomorrow.

"Tomorrow" was only a few hours away. She wondered if sleep would come and ease her jangled nerves in those few hours.

As she turned off the barn lights, Ralph gave forth with a high-pitched, worried bark. "It's okay, boy, I'm coming. Everything's okay."

Is it?

THIRTEEN

Beatrice Answers the Phone

It's going to be that kind of day, Beatrice thought, as the telephone rang for the second time in her first hour out of bed. She had just come in from the pasture and was stamping the snow off her boots, when she heard the crisp syllables of Ben's wife, Amanda, on the answering machine.

"Wait, don't hang up. I'm here," Beatrice shouted into the phone, as she fumbled with her gloves. "Amanda, are you still there?"

"Yes, Beatrice, I'm still here," Amanda replied, in the maddeningly precise tones one uses with slow children or Alzheimer's sufferers.

"How are you doing, Amanda?"

"Oh, I'm all right."

The flow of conversation was never smooth with Amanda. Beatrice wondered if she was that way with everyone or whether it was yet another one of those come-here/born-here disconnects. It was all the more perplexing because Amanda Buckhalter was not exactly the stereotype of an Appalachian hillbilly. True, she had married early, not to Ben. Hubby number one was a drunken batterer, but the stereotypes stopped there. Amanda had managed to extricate herself from the misery of her late teens and early twenties without incurring more misery. One reason why she managed that feat was because the marriage produced no progeny.

The only reason Beatrice knew all this back history was Food Festival, the closest grocery store. The employees of Food Festival had better things to do than ring up purchases or replace the milk gallons two days past their expiration date. From what she could see, the employees went to Food Festival every day to gossip. One day, as she was trying to get the attention of one of the hair-netted ladies behind the lunchmeat counter, Beatrice heard chapter and verse about Amanda Buckhalter. She was not interested in eavesdropping, but Elva and Mildred, as their nametags identified them, had no interest in dropping their conversation to address the needs of a customer, especially one they didn't know. And once she heard the name Buckhalter—well, Beatrice was human, after all.

According to Elva and Mildred, Amanda had borrowed money from an out-of-state aunt to get her tubes tied, after she miscarried because of a beating at the hands of her first husband. Amanda, the Food Festival ladies concluded, was determined never to conceive another child with the abuser. Beatrice walked away before she asked for shaved Virginia ham. She lost her appetite, because she suspected Elva and Mildred were probably chewing on more than a kernel of truth about poor Amanda.

But poor Amanda had gone on to get an associate's degree at a community college forty miles away. She parlayed the business and computer skills she learned at school into a bookkeeping job at the local gravel quarry. And those skills would later prove invaluable to Ben, when his new wife took over the administrative tasks for his contracting business. Those details Beatrice had learned over the course of various conversations with a proud Ben.

He and Amanda had no children.

With what she knew about Ben's wife, Beatrice was predisposed to like her. But there seemed to be no way around the younger woman's brittle reserve. So rather than try and start a conversation with some observation about winter's frigid return, she waited—more than a comfortable number of seconds—for Amanda to come to the reason for the phone call.

Finally: "Ben wanted to know if you would be around this afternoon. He can do the fence repairs then."

"Oh, Ben will do the job? I thought Virgil was coming."

"No."

Beatrice had called Virgil to fix the bear damage. He was supposed to come out a day after the call. The next day he left a message to cancel, without rescheduling or explaining. Amanda obviously had no intention of providing any further details or telling her why a busy contractor would handle such a picayune job.

"Uh … okay. What time?"

"Three-ish."

"Well, thanks for calling. I'll see him then."

"Oh, he may have Clara with him. Will that be all right with you?"

"Sure. I'll have her help me grain the llamas."

Silence.

Beatrice knew she had said the wrong thing. Her intention was to smooth over Amanda's apparent concern that Clara's inclusion in Ben's visit would somehow be inconvenient. Amanda was not smoothed over. Instead, she was probably thinking that Beatrice was interested in exploiting Clara as farm labor.

After exchanging stiff goodbyes with Amanda, a relieved Beatrice turned to her chore list. It was growing by leaps and bounds, but at least Ben's visit would free her from checking on her makeshift repairs at regular intervals to make sure none of the llamas had strangled on the plastic-coated wire she had laboriously woven into the gap in the fence. Somehow, she was supposed to knock off a translation while doing a thorough housecleaning and booze run and being on hand for Ben's appearance. Thank goodness she had done a major grocery shopping yesterday at a far more distant – and festive – establishment than Food Festival.

Her chore list had grown because of the first phone call of the morning.

It was Evie, full of apologies: "I really, really hate to do this to you. But could I possibly arrive on your doorstep today? The weather forecast is just ghastly for tomorrow. I even looked into the possibility of taking the train from Union Station. Do you have any idea how long that takes? And then there would be the problem of slogging through the snow from White Sulphur Springs to your place. Is there any chance for today? Please, please, do not kill yourself with housecleaning and cooking. Hell, I wish I could bring Jadwiga with me. Except she'd probably never come back to me. She's always talking about how she misses the countryside outside Cracow. The way that woman talks, you'd think Poland was an endless stretch of pristine meadows and woodland. You'd never think the commissars spent decades spewing heavy metals into the atmosphere and ground water. But delusional though she may be, that little Polack can clean. But where was I? Oh, yeah. Don't bother cleaning. But if it's okay, I could leave in, oh, maybe two hours. That would put me at your place before dark. First, I'll have to gas up the Subaru, of course. And give Shirley, God bless that Georgia peach of a secretary, a long list of instructions. But before dark should work. Will it work for you?"

"How many cups of coffee have you had, Evie?"

"Cups? Pots, is more like it. But your mockery puts off the central question. Or is that the central answer?"

"The central answer is a definite yes. I've been keeping an eye on tomorrow's weather, and you're smart to get a jump on it. You'll be more than welcome today. Just promise me you'll take a couple of hundred deep breaths before you get in your Subaru."

"Ommm… See, I'm relaxed already. By the way, I've got dish for you. In fact, it's sort of related to you," Evie giggled.

She giggled?

"Is that what they call the 'teaser' in your business?"

"I will spill all the details when I see you. Toodles!"

Beatrice ignored her friend's pleas to refrain from a cleaning frenzy. The vacuum cleaner was in overdrive later that afternoon and nearly drowned out the sound of the third phone call of the day, more calls than Beatrice had received in the entire previous week. She picked up in the kitchen a heartbeat before the answering machine kicked on.

"Is this Beatrice Desmond?"

"Yes."

"Please hold for a call from Ms. Martha Desmond."

"Whaat?" Beatrice said to the canned Vivaldi that suddenly vibrated into her right ear. Ten seconds elapsed. Then twenty. Then a knock sounded from the back door. Then a bark erupted from Ralph.

Then Beatrice slammed down the receiver. "Give me a fucking break!"

She ran to the back door and saw Ben through the door's eyebrow. He was wearing a goofy grin.

"Oh, damn, I'm sorry. That wasn't for you. That was about an idiot phone call – the business version of drunk-dialing. Oh, God, I hope Clara didn't hear me."

"Naw, she's getting something in the truck. 'Business drunk-dialing?'"

"You pick up the phone and some VIP's assistant tells you the VIP is calling and you should hold until the VIP gets around to focusing on you, to prove how important the Very Important Person must be."

"Or how insecure the Very Insecure Person must be?"

"Bless you, Ben."

FOURTEEN
Head-Spinning Developments

Accustomed to solitude, Beatrice had too many people competing for attention inside her brain: the friend who would arrive within a few hours, the contractor standing in front of her, his missing "uncle," his suddenly ubiquitous niece and, from out of the blue, her own niece.

Beatrice tuned back in to Ben's pained explanation about Uncle Virgil, who had slipped on the ice, triggering new inflammation in his arthritic spine and badly spraining his right wrist and left knee. He had hoped anti-inflammatories would get him back to work but was currently spending a lot of time lying in as close to a fetal position as he could manage, apparently in Ben and Amanda's spare bedroom. Meanwhile, Ben and some of his crew were helping to clear out Virgil's backlog of odd jobs by tackling them in and around their own jobs.

"I'm sorry to hear of Virgil's troubles, but I'm glad you're here. Let me show you the problem."

"Naw, I could see it from the drive. Must have been a big bear. I guess that brief thaw got him out and about. I expect he's holed back up now and won't be bothering you for a while."

Ben retreated to his truck, where Clara had just pulled a toboggan from the bed. "I didn't want to risk getting the truck stuck in your pasture," he explained over his shoulder.

Beatrice watched as uncle and niece unloaded fence material onto the ground and then rolled it onto Clara's ankles, as she braced her feet against the toboggan's front curve. Digging her mittened fists into the snow on either side of the sled, she scooted forward and was soon gaining speed down the slope toward the barn. Beatrice admired how the girl bobbed from side to side while balancing the heavy roll and keeping it from spilling into the snow. Ben, checking his tool belt and adjusting the prudent suspenders that kept his jeans in place, trudged after his niece.

Satisfied that the pair knew what they were doing and would not let the llamas escape, Beatrice went back inside. She planned to load up the grain buckets for the llamas, but the phone was ringing again.

"Beatrice? It's Martha. Belated Happy New Year!"

What? No assistant to make the call?

Beatrice congratulated herself for hanging up earlier. "Right back at you, Martha. How nice to hear from you."

"I know, it's been just forever. But starting up a new business is so time consuming. Especially when you have to take every tedious little job that comes your way, just to make ends meet."

Beatrice interpreted that as a reference to her failure to fork over her share of Aunt Addie's legacy. Even if Martha was making an effort, Beatrice decided to let the silence hang.

"Are you still there? I tried calling earlier, but we were apparently disconnected."

"I had a caller waiting."

"Wow, how times change! You are the last person on earth I would expect to have call waiting."

Beatrice decided an explanation would be pointless.

"Well, I just wanted to touch base. I was thinking of you because I saw an old friend of yours. Evie Rudner? Yes, indeed, she showed up at a gathering Daddy was having with some of his old classmates. And get this, you'll never believe it. He's the one who brought her to the dinner party. I guess she was in Boston on business. Probably just paid him a courtesy call. Did you ask her to check in on him, by any chance?"

"No, I had no idea she was going to Boston."

"Well, that's weird. I wonder why they got together, then."

"Martha, they're old friends. They've been keeping in touch for years. I imagine if she was up there on business, Bart asked her along as his date."

"Date?" Martha sounded apoplectic.

"It has been known to happen."

"But Daddy? He's a widower. And what could she possibly see in him?

Beatrice chuckled. "His roguish charm?"

"Hmmph. More likely his stock portfolio."

"Martha, you can't be serious. Evie has pots and pots of money. She's had her own company for years and has been very successful. And I believe she has made a few shrewd investments over the years."

"Well, folks like her are known for their skill at handling money," Martha sniffed.

"You mean PR folks?"

"Well, if you say she's okay, I feel better. But I just worry about a younger woman taking advantage of Daddy." Martha ignored Beatrice's gibe – or was unaware of it.

You just worry about any woman staking a claim to your inheritance.

"She's only a few years younger and looks great for her age. Besides, I imagine if things got serious, she'd ask Bart to sign a prenup."

"Really?" Martha sounded both shocked and intrigued. "She has that much money?"

"I have no idea how well-heeled Evie is. But a gold digger she most definitely is not."

"Oh, I didn't mean to imply that. And I'm sorry if I've misjudged your friend. But a girl has to look out for her dad, after all. Maybe you could broker a meeting between me and her? You know, if she's going to be a fixture in Daddy's life? I'd like to get to know her."

Beatrice rolled her eyes. The "gold digger" had suddenly morphed into a potential backer. "I think I'll leave that up to Bart."

"If you think that's best, but let me know if there's anything I can do."

"Like what?" She had no clue what plans her niece might be hatching. She hoped Martha would keep her nose out of whatever was going on between Bart and Evie. Before Martha could craft an uncommunicative reply, the usually annoying crackle sounded over the line. Saved by call waiting, Beatrice thought.

"Gotta go. I've been waiting to hear from a contractor. Now don't be a stranger, hear?"

Beatrice stared into the receiver in her hand. So much to process. So little time.

As various scenarios spun through her mind, she discerned a vague tapping from the back door. It was Clara, her knock muffled by mittens.

"C'mon inside, Clara."

The girl hesitated. "Ben said he'll be through in maybe half an hour.

He said I should see if I could help you grain the llamas?"

"Sure. Let's go to the garage. I keep the grain there instead of the barn, so I don't have to worry about the bear bothering the llamas."

Clara shivered. "I'm scared of bears."

As they entered the garage, Clara gasped, "Oh, I almost forgot. I wanted to ask you something." She stopped to investigate the deep pockets in her parka. "It's here somewhere," she said through teeth clenched over her mittens, as her naked hands pulled out a packet of gum, a bracelet, a hair clip and, finally, a plastic baggie.

She extracted what appeared to be a lumpy length of wool. "Why does it look clunky like that?" Clara asked.

Beatrice took the misshapen yarn in hand. "Did you spin this?"

"Yeah, it's my first try. One of my cousin Eltie's customers has sheep. She gave me some wool and showed me how to use a drop spindle. But look how uneven it is. It's like rope. How could anyone make anything with that?" The teenager looked both earnest and dejected.

"Damn, I have never been able to figure out how to work a drop spindle. But your first attempt looks about the same as mine, which I did on a spinning wheel. And that's a lot easier."

"You have a spinning wheel?"

"Yeah, wanna see it?"

Later, when Ben rapped on the door, woman and girl were playing with the spinning wheel in Beatrice's den. More than half an hour had passed, apparently.

Beatrice got up and waved Ben inside. Clara yelled to him, "Ben, you'll never guess! Miz Desmond offered to teach me how to spin. Is it okay? Can I?"

Before Ben could answer, Beatrice interjected, "It would be more like the blind leading the blind, but I'd be happy to have the chance to develop some fiber skills. I know a little about knitting, and maybe Clara could help me process wool from the llamas."

Clara, nodding vigorously, looked from Beatrice to Ben, who said, predictably, "We'll see."

FIFTEEN

Hard Places, Hard Times

"No, Ben. We just can't."

Amanda's voice was low, and Ben knew there was no negotiating room. Sitting opposite her at the dining room table, he slumped forward and hung his long arms off his knees. He shook his head slowly. "It's just that Mike's in a real bind. Clara won't be able to live with him while he's in Virginia. I really want us to take her in. The less time she spends with that mother of hers, the better."

"You can't solve your brother's problems. He knew what he was getting into when he married that piece of trash, Charyce. As for Clara, well, you know how fond I am of her, but we have our own problems."

Ben doubted his wife's fondness for Clara. Although Amanda always treated her decently, he suspected she thought of the child as a threat—as a bud about to open just when the bloom of Amanda's youth was beginning to fade. It saddened Ben that so many women saw their younger sisters and daughters and nieces with bitterness. It likewise saddened him that bitterness colored so much of Amanda's outlook, even if she tried her best to hide it.

"We only just took in Uncle Virgil," Amanda continued. "There is no room for Clara. Sure, on the occasional weekend, she can sleep on the couch. But live with us? I don't see why Mike won't take her."

"He'd love to take her. But the custody arrangement means Clara has to stay in West Virginia unless Charyce expressly gives her okay. And you know the chances of that happening."

His brother Mike was a master carpenter. An artist, really. But there wasn't much call for artists in Seneca County. He had no difficulty finding work, but window framing was not what Mike wanted to do. What he wanted to do was make acoustic guitars. His craftsmanship was much admired by a few studio musicians in Branson, Nashville, and on the

West Coast, but he didn't have the facilities to fill orders consistently. If he could just build up a stake, he could afford the time and the space to devote to his craft.

A few months ago, Mike had seen the chance to stash major money away. A friend recommended him to a Virginia developer building high-end residential clusters in an affluent section of the Shenandoah Valley. Each of the executive retirement villas and vacation houses would be one of a kind, with made-to-order cabinetry and carved banisters and sliding wooden partitions, features requiring skills that went beyond those of the average carpenter. The developer was ready to pay a small fortune for an artisan with Mike's gifts. The only problem was Mike had to relocate to Harrisonburg for the next few years. Harrisonburg was a good three hours away from Seneca County.

When Mike and Charyce divorced, they technically shared custody of Clara. Charyce, a waitress at a karaoke bar, drew a small amount of child support. Ben assumed the child support was the main reason for Charyce's part-time interest in Clara. Clara lived mostly with Mike, in the small cabin he had built with Ben's help. Charyce lived in one of the county's few apartment buildings, located near the courthouse. She had a one-bedroom unit, and Clara, when she stayed with her mother, slept on a foldout couch in the living room.

But lately, Charyce's fortunes were looking up. Never lacking for boyfriends, she had attracted a more financially stable love interest than usual. Rodney Madsen owned a tractor dealership in an adjacent, more affluent county. He had a nice middle-class house near a nice middle-class school. He had given Charyce a nice, if not extravagant, diamond ring, and the wedding was already scheduled in a nice Methodist church. No doubt about it, Rodney was nice. But something about him made Ben nervous. Ben wasn't thrilled about Clara being in her mother's care, and he was even less thrilled about his niece living with Charyce and Rodney.

Clara was Ben's goddaughter. He took his responsibilities seriously. Maybe it was his Catholic upbringing. His mother, a Baltimore Moriarty who happily relocated to the alien landscape of West Virginia to marry Carl Buckhalter, put her foot down when it came to embracing an alien religion. There would be no Protestants in Mary Moriarty's family. After his conversion, Carl never set foot in a church again, Catholic or Protestant, except to attend a wedding, funeral, or baptism – and then only at Mary's prodding. But Ben and Mike went through the entire drill, from baptism to full church weddings. Because they were devoted to their tiny, feisty mother, they accepted their religious indoctrination with light hearts, if not spiritual conviction.

Standing over a tiny infant, whose limbs jolted into spasms when the priest thumbed oil onto her forehead, fueled a different kind of conversion in Ben. Clara was so little. She looked so vulnerable suspended over the hard marble font that Ben, ritualistically promising to stand up for the child, found he really meant the words.

And now he saw her suspended over another hard place.

Alas, there was another godparent-godchild connection to consider. Uncle Virgil was not a blood relative to Amanda, but he was her godfather. He drove her to the emergency room twice when she was still in her disastrous first marriage. He never asked any questions, dispensed any advice, or made Amanda feel any more ashamed than she already felt. When she was a child, he would treat her to an ice cream cone and listen complacently as she spun out her dreams and plans. Unlike her parents, he never rolled his eyes or laughed or criticized. Virgil was a simple soul. He was happy to accept her just as she was, and that was often comfort enough for a lonely little girl or a restive teenager or a woman terrified of losing the last of her dreams to middle age. He had always been a rock-solid presence in her life, even if now he had fallen on hard times.

Virgil had gone through a lot of hard times: work injuries, car accidents, illnesses. His wife left him for another man. His only son died in the first Gulf war. And now that Uncle Virgil was in a hard place again, Amanda was not about to desert him. Amanda Buckhalter may have lost her sense of fun and many of her dreams, but she had not lost her sense of loyalty.

She and Ben lived in a new, well-kept double-wide that would put some clapboard colonials to shame. But there was no denying its small size. Ben had refashioned two of the closet-sized bedrooms into a "master" bedroom for him and Amanda. When Mike was working on projects in Virginia, Clara often stayed in the closet-like guest room. But that space was now occupied by the ailing Virgil. It appeared unlikely he would be able to continue his arrangement with an elderly widow, who rented out the upper floor of her house to Virgil at a very modest rate in exchange for handyman chores. But even that modest rate was beyond Virgil's means as he faced weeks of unemployment – months if his back required surgery.

Alone in the dining room, Ben tipped back the last of his now-warm bottle of beer. Not for the first time, he considered how much of life was about timing. If only he had started his farmhouse reconstruction project earlier. Many years ago, he had inherited his grandmother's house on Gurney Mountain. Gramma Buckhalter owned three hundred acres on the mountain. For decades after her husband died, she lived there in rugged isolation, tended scores of sheep, and turned down all the buyout offers from the Colorado company scouting for ski resort sites.

Before he died, Grampa Buckhalter, no slouch when it came to building skills, expanded the nineteenth-century farmhouse, dowsed out a deep, abundant well, installed indoor plumbing, and wired the house for electricity. Unfortunately, the location was far removed from any power lines, so the lights shone only when the generator ran.

Ben recognized the homestead's potential but had difficulty finding the time to work on it. It didn't help that access to Gurney Mountain was horrendous – a dirt track that required four-wheel drive in summer rains, to say nothing of winter snows. So Ben let his legacy lie dormant for years. He did the minimum to keep the old house from falling apart. But a while ago, that Colorado company began building a ski resort down slope from the Buckhalter farmstead. The developer had already put in a road system connecting the resort to the county highway at the foot of the mountain. Power lines had gone up, and Ben could now afford to link the farmstead to the grid. He had begun fitting in as many weekends and summer evenings as he could to transform the old farmhouse into a worthy home for him and Amanda. It would have three thousand square feet, more than enough to accommodate the two of them, along with Uncle Virgil and Clara.

But Ben was at least a year away from realizing that dream. And Clara needed a soft place to land – now.

SIXTEEN

Barszcz *and Preparation H*

The huge soup pot dwarfed the two women. Evie, the shorter of the two, had to stand on tiptoe to get a good view of the contents. She and Beatrice peered at it gingerly, as if the roiling magenta liquid was a batch of C-4 explosive. Evie tentatively held a long wooden spoon over the pot.

"Jadwiga warned me not to overheat it, or the beets would get mushy. Think it's done?"

Beatrice shrugged. "I don't think we could undercook it. There's no meat in it, and in this weather it must have stayed plenty chilled on the drive out."

"I would have packed it in icepacks and put it in a cooler, but the little Polack had to make so damn much of the stuff it wouldn't fit in anything I had."

"Taste it," Beatrice urged.

"You first."

"Oh, for Christ's sake!" Beatrice snatched the wooden spoon and dipped it in the brew. "Hey, it's good," she announced. "Maybe not my first choice for breakfast but damned good."

"Jadwiga swears *barszcz* is the best hangover cure in the world. Electrolytes and vitamin B, she says. Of course, with her accent, who knows? She knew you'd be a bad influence on me and I'd need a home remedy.

"Hey, I think the potatoes are done. Why don't you take them out of the oven? Jadwiga says you can't eat *barszcz* without a big dollop of mashed potatoes in every bowl. That makes it *'czysty' barszcz.* That's 'genuine borsht' to you. I understood the adjective because of the old folk's tales about being called a *'czysty zyd.'* Roughly translated, that means a 'real kike.' I learned that line early on."

"Heard when the Cossacks were bearing down on you in South Arlington?" On occasion, Evie overemphasized her Jewish roots. Beatrice assumed it had as much to do with confusion about her mixed ethnic identity. Or maybe it was survivor guilt, since the Rudners had been smart enough and gutsy enough to cross the Atlantic decades before Hitler started exterminating the Jews of Poland.

"*Czysty* Mick! That's what you are. Bigot, bigot, bigot!"

"Hey, one of my best friends is Jewish. Well, sorta. It would help if she didn't look like she just emigrated from Edinburgh." Evie's dark red hair and blue eyes were a maternal legacy, one that rankled. Evie had little affection for her mother's relatives, who objected strenuously to her parents' interfaith marriage.

The two women started laughing. The exchange of ethnic insults was an old routine, made funnier in the presence of Polish culinary mysteries. The ridiculous aprons helped, too. Beatrice was wearing a gaudy green one, featuring a leering Leprechaun demanding, "Kiss me, I'm Irish." It was a gift from Evie, who chose it precisely because of its tastelessness. Evie wore a black apron, bearing a white pentacle in the center. It was a gift from Beatrice, playing on the contempt her friend had for all things New Age. Above the pentacle was a quip Evie found irresistible, for obvious reasons: "Eve was framed."

They regrouped to the small kitchen table. Like eager children, they leaned over steaming bowls of the beet soup, with a large mound of mashed potatoes floating in each. Ralph had already settled down beside Evie and draped his long throat over her ankle. He knew a sucker when he saw one. Once again, Beatrice thought what a good judge of character her dog was. And then she found herself separating off and observing the scene. That maddened her. Especially because her observations sabotaged the warm feelings she had been enjoying.

Her friend looked old, tired. Sure, part of it was the hangover. Part of it was morning. Women of a certain age do not look well in the morning. Evie's eyes were puffy. Her skin looked sallow and lacking in elasticity. Her too-thin shoulders were slightly stooped forward. Evie the powerhouse actually looked frail. The woman bent over the soup bowl was wearing all of her years, and that saddened Beatrice. No, it scared her. Mortality is hard enough to grasp in oneself. It is harder to accept in the people one loves, she thought, especially because all of her loved ones were contemporaries or even older. It was one thing to choose an isolated lifestyle, as Beatrice so obviously had by moving to such a remote location. But the unchosen isolation that would result from losing her friends would make life unbearable. It was nearly unbearable that she had already lost Kate, a surrogate sister and an individual whose very presence was life-affirming for everyone around her. It was terrifying that more losses would follow.

Those were odd thoughts for someone who had survived devastating losses in her childhood. And even a gentlewoman farmer knows the old saying, "If you have livestock, sooner or later you'll have dead stock." But intellectually grasping reality is not the same as emotionally incorporating it. Beatrice thought denial was not necessarily the evil psychotherapists denounce. If, through every waking moment, we were fully cognizant of our fragility and the legion of ways in which the lives of our loved ones will end, we would be too paralyzed to do anything. Understanding the virtues of denial, she thought the old advice about living every day like it was your last was ridiculous.

The beady-eyed expression on Evie's face snapped Beatrice out of her gloomy ruminations. The jaunty tilt of her friend's head was reminiscent of the twenty-something-year-old Evie, brimming with defiance and irreverence and vitality. "You have yet to show the slightest interest in the tantalizing tidbit I alluded to over the phone," Evie goaded.

"Umm, let's see. You and Bart have decided to go public as an official couple?"

Evie's face crumpled like that of a petulant toddler. "Crap! Who ratted me out? Oh, wait, I know. It was that cuh..." Evie stopped. "Sorry, I know Martha is blood. But if anyone deserves the c-word, it's her. So the little bitch is already beating the bushes in search of information. But I must say, I'm surprised she turned to you. I thought you were still persona non grata."

"I did, too. But apparently, the idea that you might muscle in on her filial inheritance made her forget about the inheritance *she* tried to muscle in on."

"Ooooh, I could have a lot of fun playing gold digger. But aren't I just a tad too old for that role?"

"I think Martha's already casting you in a new role, as patroness, thanks to me. I got a little pissy about her insinuations and hinted that you had more money than God. As if I have any remote idea of what your financial situation is. I went so far as to say that if you guys got around to considering marriage, you'd probably ask Bart to sign a prenup."

"You didn't! Oh, that's rich. I'll have to figure out a way of exploiting that idea to mess with Martha's head."

"Yeah, well, you don't want to mess with it too much if you *are* serious about whatever it is you have going on with my big brother. Martha may drive him nuts, but she is his daughter."

"Oh, relax. I don't want to cause Bart the slightest discomfort. And when you get right down to it, I don't really think I want to marry him."

"So what do you want?"

"Oh, Beatrice, what the hell do I know?"

Beatrice knew Evangeline Rudner loathed introspection. When it came to career and finances, Evie was a long-range planner who figured every angle. Figuring out her feelings, or even defining her values, was another matter. It wasn't that Evie suppressed her emotions. It wasn't that Evie lacked principles. She just had no interest in examining them. At times, she seemed to think that was Beatrice's job: articulating what was going on in Evie's internal life—but only up to a point. Evie once accused Beatrice of being an "annoying scab-picker." Of course, she was right.

Evie lifted the stainless steel teakettle from the trivet between the plates and stared at her image. "Jesus H. Christ! Look at those bags!" she exclaimed, probing beneath her right eye with her free hand. "Where's your Preparation H!"

"What?"

"Hemorrhoid cream. Any brand will do. If I'm going to look halfway decent by tomorrow's affair, you'd better have a good supply."

"What *are* you talking about?"

"Honestly, Beatrice, I sometimes wonder if you even have double-X chromosomes. You schmear Prep-H beneath the eyes, and it shrinks the bags."

"I bought some for the llamas a while back. Kate used to keep it on hand to help alleviate hair loss from irritation on their noses."

"Waaay too much information. But find that tube. I'm desperate."

Desperate to shift the focus of the conversation, Beatrice thought, as she padded off to the medicine cabinet.

SEVENTEEN

The Advantages of Invisibility

Standing before the bathroom mirror, Clara fidgeted with her bow tie. She had thought only women were plagued by fashion priorities incompatible with physical needs: high heels that hurt your ankles, curlers and wands that yanked and burned your scalp, mascara that flaked into itchy eyes, waistbands that restricted breathing. But now she realized men had to put up with similar nonsense. She never knew any male who wore a bow tie, of course. Bow ties were hardly standard fare in Seneca County. Regular ties were rarities enough. She yanked at the thing again, in hope of easing the feeling of imminent asphyxiation. She succeeded, but the stupid thing now bobbled untidily.

The bow had been provided and tied on by Tanner Fordyce's snippy and brusque-handed assistant, Ms. Krupp. Clara was one of a half dozen locals who had hired on as servers, working the latest Fordyce party. For lack of any local catering service, Ms. Krupp was forced to improvise. Most of the current batch of servers had worked at earlier events staged by Tanner. They were the ones who survived Ms. Krupp's winnowing process. Although she was relieved to find that theft of the silverware was not much of a risk among the local hires, their demeanor left something to be desired. Some were just so terminally clumsy they were a danger to the many *objets* in Tanner's sprawling lodge. Some wore such surly expressions that the guests became uncomfortable.

Clara was one of two new hires. She briefly considered consulting with the other newbie about bow-tie etiquette. But she saw that her momma had devised her own way. Clara wondered what Miz Krupp would have to say about Charyce Trask's fashion statement. Instead of affixing the black ribbon around the neck of her white shirt and under the collar, Charyce had tied it around her naked neck, inside the collar, which was unbuttoned. The next two buttonholes below the clavicles were empty as well, to reveal Charyce's cleavage. Clara noticed that all three buttons were missing. She sighed.

Miz Krupp would not trust Clara with food. Her job was to "bus," a term the girl did not understand but figured out it meant retrieving empty glasses and plates and silverware and taking them back to the kitchen. Someone else had the job of loading the dishwashers.

Even rich people can be gross.

Clara noted lipstick smears and greasy fingerprints on the glasses – or "stemware," as Miz Krupp called them. Otherwise, she paid little attention to the guests. Her job was not to interact with them. Her job, as Miz Krupp specified, was to be "invisible." Clara was good at that. She had developed a knack for invisibility around her mother and her mother's boyfriends.

She did notice several large bloodhounds and even managed to sneak a piece of cracker to one of them, who rewarded her with a long string of drool from a pendulous flew. It narrowly missed sliming her freshly pressed black jeans. She stifled a giggle, scratched the beast on its head, and watched wistfully as the dog clumped off down a long dark hallway.

Clara next noticed a change in her mother's attire. Miz Krupp's ever-watchful eye had spotted Charyce's deviant bow-tie arrangement. The tie now closed the collar, but beneath the neck the shirt gaped lasciviously for lack of buttons. Although less bosom showed than before, the peep-show effect was far more risqué and therefore ogled by several male guests. Clara thought again how crude rich people could be. She couldn't help being amused that her mother had bested Miz Krupp, although she imagined Charyce would not be asked back for any future parties. She hoped she herself would not be blackballed, too. She would probably be safe, because she and her mother had different last names. Despite her mother's goading, Clara stubbornly remained a Buckhalter.

During one of her bus runs, Clara noticed one of the female guests sticking out like a sore thumb. The woman was not merely alone, there was a well-defined space all around her in the otherwise crowded great room. She wondered if the woman smelled bad, though she certainly looked clean enough. A well-cut mop of thick dark hair. Gracefully draped black trousers, probably expensive. A light gray overblouse. A long, bold, silver necklace and matching earrings. The clothing was old fashioned, to

Clara's way of thinking. But she envied the woman for how comfortable the outfit must be. And she liked the necklace. She found herself staring at it too hard, and the woman caught her eye.

Then Clara realized she knew the woman.

Miz Desmond cleans up pretty good.

The girl had no explanation for that empty space surrounding Miz Desmond, who nodded her head in greeting and smiled feebly. Clara grinned briefly then returned to clearing one of the tables. For some reason she felt embarrassed. She wasn't sure whether it was for herself or for Miz Desmond.

Clara's embarrassment was replaced by relief when, out of the corner of her eye, she saw someone finally talking to Miz Desmond, who no longer looked so stiff. That someone was a short woman in a black dress. To Clara's eye, the woman had pulled off something unlikely: She managed to look stylish, attractive even, without dressing inappropriately for her age.

The mature women Clara knew were mostly fat and wore dowdy clothes designed to cover up love handles and bloated bellies. A few others, of trimmer proportions, revealed more than anyone in his right mind would want to see. Their clothes were too tight, too short, too gaudy. Her mother fell into that category.

Clara didn't want to be fat and frumpy one day. But she didn't want to look trashy, either. Apparently there were alternatives, after all.

It was a while before the youngster laid eyes on the main attraction. She had apparently missed his initial entrance, but from the kitchen she heard a sonorous male voice that initially brought a hush to the crowded great room. Then the level of laughter increased, laughter that Clara thought sounded nervous and self-conscious.

Do grown-ups really enjoy stuff like this?

She thought she knew one grown-up who did not.

Clara didn't have to ask anyone if Mr. Fordyce was the boss. It was obvious by the way people clustered about him. He stood well above his admirers. Tall to begin with, he had positioned himself on the stone apron of a cold fireplace. None of his partners in conversation, Clara noted, ventured to step up onto the apron with him. It was odd, because he appeared friendly enough. He flashed a big smile with white, even teeth. And he laughed a friendly laugh at things people around him were saying.

The next time Clara had the opportunity to look at where Mr. Fordyce was standing, someone had finally joined him on the apron. It was the same short woman in the black dress who had talked to Miz Desmond. She was chatting face to face with Mr. Fordyce. He was significantly taller, but she seemed completely at ease with the height difference. Instead of craning her neck up, she tilted her head to the side when looking up at him. It was slightly flirtatious, Clara thought, because the woman had to look up through her eyelashes. But Clara noted no other signs of flirting – no pressing into the tall man, no playing with her hair, no wetting of her lips. The woman did occasionally place a light fingertip on the man's wrist, as if she was making a point. She seemed to have his full attention. She seemed to radiate a kind of energy Clara wasn't used to seeing in women. The lady in the black dress might be middle-aged and then some, but she had power. Not the sexual power of her momma. Something different. Clara stored the impression away to think about later.

One of the nice things about being invisible is learning so much from people without ever having to reveal anything about yourself. Clara would have a lot to think about after this party and a lot to write in the diary she maintained so meticulously.

EIGHTEEN

A Port in a Storm

The world is too much with us, now and then, even for dogs. It was one of those nights for Gertrude. Her hip hurt, and she had a minor case of dyspepsia from eating junk food. And it was so noisy. Gertrude didn't like it when people laughed without really feeling happy. When a dog smiles, the smile is genuine. And so Gertrude, figuring her hostess obligations were duly met, plodded down the semi-dark hallway to her sanctuary, the Man's study.

And just when she thought she had made a clean getaway, her sensitive nose was bombarded with a new cloud of scents. Human. Female. Adult. Some animal dander. What now? But Gertrude was raised to be polite, so she turned her massive head and allowed her tail to make a languid half-circle.

"Are you all right, dog?" asked the source of the smells. "Hip hurts, huh?"

The woman, with some difficulty, knelt down on one knee and offered a hand for Gertrude to smell. Gertrude half-heartedly obliged, inhaling stinky human perfume and a full menu of foodstuffs. Then there was the smell of a dog, clearly one of lower stature than a bloodhound. And another animal smell: lightly musky, with a soupcon of acidity and an odd hint of melon. Gertrude sniffed more intently, folding her flews into the woman's now supine hand.

"That's Ralph," offered Beatrice. "And maybe the llamas?" She reached forward and fondled a long, velvety ear. Gertrude responded with a slow loop of the tail. After a minute, Beatrice straightened and said, "Nice to meet you, girl."

Gertrude resumed her slow walk down the hall. When she realized the Woman was not following, the bloodhound turned her head, raised it slightly and yodeled softly. The Woman had apparently been well trained: She followed Gertrude's lead.

Gertrude led her into a large, wood-paneled study lit by a single, green desk lamp and padded to one of two large dog beds, a kind of hammock stretched over four sturdy posts more than a foot high. She settled into the canvas, which sagged to within six inches of the floor. Beatrice sat down beside the unusual bed. She couldn't resist palming the dog's bony underside.

Gertrude sounded the letter "o" in a mellow contralto, and Beatrice responded obediently by spreading one of the hound's ears over her left hand while slowly massaging it with right thumb and forefinger. The dog sighed and settled her head onto her chunky front paws. "It's tough getting old, isn't it, girl?" said the Woman. Gertrude sighed in contentment. Within a few minutes, she began breathing deeply. Beatrice continued the massage and told the sleeping dog, in a whisper, "What a good girl. What a good girl."

Gertrude began snoring softly.

And just as she was about to locate a lost little girl in the woods, with the anticipation of being showered with praise and affection, Gertrude had her dream shattered – in reaction to a door slamming.

"That insufferable boor!" She recognized the Man's voice. Clearly in a snit. Should she heft herself out of her bed and offer solace? Humans could be such work.

Gertrude compromised by baying gently in the Man's direction. "It's okay, girl," said the Woman, too loudly. She was still sitting, tailor-style, on the floor nearby.

"Who's there?" demanded the Man sternly.

"Sorry, I just followed the dog down the hall. She seemed to be in some discomfort, and I wanted to make sure she was okay. I guess it's just arthritis." Beatrice rose awkwardly and walked a few steps in the man's direction.

"The bane of the large dog," said the man stiffly. He turned on a floor lamp and eyed the trespasser intently. "One of my guests, I assume? Are you quite comfortable?"

The tone was formal, cold and aristocratic, and showed not the slightest concern for Beatrice's comfort. As someone intensely territorial about her own turf, she understood.

"I apologize. I really didn't mean to trespass. I must confess I used the dog as an excuse to get a breather. I'm not much of a party animal, I'm afraid. Besides, this one is a very soothing influence." Beatrice nodded toward the dog, whose peaked eyebrows twitched from one human to the other, as if she were watching a tennis match.

"Trudy is an old soul," said Tanner, somewhat more warmly. "But she's picky about the company she keeps. So just how have you won over the grand dame?"

He walked toward hound and woman. As he did, the curiosity on his face morphed into a more exultant expression. "Well, if it isn't the elusive Miss Desmond." Standing just out of reach, he offered his hand to Beatrice.

"The effusive Mr. Fordyce, I presume," said Beatrice, who stood her ground and extended her hand.

Tanner erupted in a short laugh, walked forward and clasped Beatrice's hand firmly. "I am pleased to meet the Hermit of Seneca County. From what I hear, hardly any of the locals have laid eyes on you. Are you deliberately cultivating an air of mystery? Or are you merely shy?"

"Neither. I'm determinedly misanthropic."

"Have you not learned that honesty is a punishable offense? What in Heaven's name are you doing at a party like this? There isn't an honest person in the house, myself included."

"If you know so much about me, you know I'm hosting your new publicist, and she brought me along. Evie is an old and very dear friend." Beatrice was annoyed with herself for sounding so defensive.

"Evie Rudner doesn't strike me as someone who has ever needed a chaperone. She probably came out of the womb wheeling and dealing."

"As I said, Evie is a friend." Beatrice's voice was tight.

"Consider me chastised. Care for a drink? I need one before going back into the fray."

"I never drink at parties. Besides, I've got to drive down that rutted series of switchbacks you call a driveway."

Gertrude groaned her way off the dog bed and sidled up to Beatrice. Nosing the woman's hand, the dog thumped her tail heavily against Beatrice's thigh.

"That shameless display of flirting is Gertrude's way of reprimanding me for my errant behavior. She knows all my secrets, loves me anyway but gives me little slack. God, she's a hard-hearted wench." Tanner bent forward and raised the dog's head in one hand.

Gertrude lifted her prominent eyebrows in sad adoration of her wayward human. Beatrice furrowed her eyebrows in suspicion. Tanner's patrician accent had taken a sudden dive. The final endearment for the dog was uttered by an entirely different voice. Nasal. Flannel-mouthed. Neither of the "r's" was vocalized. The vowels were all over-emphasized. And the "God" sounded more like "Gwad."

It was entirely possible that Tanner merely had a good ear for dialects. But Beatrice figured he would have saved that talent for, say, replicating the constipated Hanoverian diction of the royals. She supposed Tanner had had ample exposure to a diverse set of characters, and duplicating their speech patterns would certainly amuse his homeboys in the Hamptons or Palm Beach.

But a Boston working stiff? Beatrice didn't buy it. She scrutinized her host from a new perspective. The thick mane of white hair was a genetic blessing not limited to any single socioeconomic or ethnic caste. Nor was his height. Money could have straightened his teeth or his nose. Discipline and a personal trainer could override the worst genes to keep him trim. And those pale blue eyes could be shanty Irish as well as boarding-school English. Tanner Fordyce might call to mind George Sanders, that sardonically patrician actor of the 1940s and 1950s, but Beatrice now suspected Tanner's image was no more authentic than one of George's fictional roles.

"Does your birth certificate say Dorchester or Savin Hill – or maybe Quincy?" Beatrice asked.

Tanner didn't miss a beat. "Revere," he said, dropping the second "r" and adding a third syllable. "And no, you shall not find that factoid in my autobiography."

"Does Evie know your book is fiction?"

"Ms. Rudner has no need to know. I successfully reinvented myself. Why not invent my autobiography? It will be our little secret, yours and mine."

Beatrice snorted a mirthless laugh and then, in vintage blue-collar Boston-speak, added, "Yeah, good luck with that, fella!"

NINETEEN

Chevy Strategy

"The bastard conned me? I bought the whole goddamned shtick! Damn, I must be losing my edge." Evie tamped an unlit cigarette on Beatrice's dashboard. First one end, then the other, over and over.

Beatrice curled her hands more tightly around the steering wheel. She needed all her focus to manage the horror show of a driveway that snaked one mile down the mountain from the Fordyce fortress to the county highway. There wasn't much ice, but pockets of fog obscured the next sudden switchback. Beatrice had started out in second gear but was now in first, in the low mode of four-wheel drive.

She caught only snippets of her friend's ranting. She understood Evie was in a difficult position. She had a responsibility to the publisher. She had a responsibility to Fordyce. And she had a hard-earned reputation on the line. Evie had buffed up more than a few shady images but had never engaged in outright lying. And Tanner Fordyce's autobiography was clearly a lie.

"... so stupid, because the real story is probably even more interesting, even more saleable. What a jerk!"

Beatrice finally reached the main road and, breathing a sigh of relief as she shifted out of four-wheel drive and up to third gear, she was now able to listen.

"... so I guess we can assume his City of Revere birth certificate doesn't list him as Tanner Fordyce? What is he, Billy O'Shaughnessy?"

"Haven't a clue. He reverted to archetypal, tight-lipped WASP, when he realized he wasn't going to charm me into silence. Can't you just back out of the whole deal, since Fordyce misrepresented himself?"

"Yeah, probably, but that will really screw the publisher. He's a small outfit struggling to compete with the big boys. And he's your brother's friend, and that's another reason not to leave him in the lurch."

Beatrice made a mental note of Evie's concern for Bart. Evie didn't often let personal ties complicate her business decisions. "So do you run with the autobiography as it is? I mean, it's not like it's illegal to lie about your own past, is it?"

"Not illegal but embarrassing if a publisher represents something as the truth and then it turns out to be a crock of shit. And any future reveal wouldn't do my image-maker reputation any good. If he's blathering about his Revere roots with a total stranger like you, the guy doesn't exactly have a gift for secrecy."

"How do we know what he told me is true?"

"What does your gut tell you?"

Beatrice stared into the fog ahead and pulled up the image of how Tanner looked, as he assumed his working-class Boston persona. She shook her head. "My gut tells me Billy O'Shaughnessy."

"Shit!"

The rest of the drive was uncommonly quiet. Evie was not normally someone comfortable with long pauses in conversation. But her mind was in overdrive. By the time Beatrice's truck started climbing up the driveway toward home, Evie had a plan: "The world's fastest rewrite. The bastard."

"Is that even possible? Aren't there all sorts of deadlines?"

"Deadlines, shmeadlines. I can do impossible. And he can goddamned well do impossible, too. I'll make goddamned sure of that. I wonder how much of his little tale is true. I'll get a research nerd working on that. And we probably need a ghost. We probably need..." Evie turned her head slowly toward Beatrice and chuckled menacingly.

"Oh, no! No, you don't! I'm a translator, an editor—not a ghostwriter."

"And how many times have you rewritten something one of Wolfgang's PhD puffballs wrote to make it readable, to tailor it to an audience that doesn't share the puffball's affinity for buzzwords? That sounds like a ghostwriter to me. Besides, you've already established rapport with His Lordship."

"Rapport?" Beatrice squeaked. "The guy's a jerk."

"He's a jerk who felt comfortable enough with you to spill his guts. Now that I think of it, people are always spilling their guts to you. Who knew you were so maternal? It's like they all want to fess up to Mommy."

"If this is your way of fattening me up for the kill, you need to finesse your technique, Rudner."

"And Mommy will probably come cheap, too."

"Oh, it just gets better and better."

Pulling up the drive, Beatrice shuddered at the black sentinel highlighted in the Chevy's high beams. For an instant she thought the bear was back—and way too close to the barn. But she quickly realized the figure sitting unmoving on the slope leading from house to barn was Ralph. Something was obviously wrong. Normally, he would resemble a canine pogo stick at the first sight of her truck. But he was not budging from his alert-sit position. He moved his head from the barn to Beatrice and back to the barn.

Beatrice had left the main door open, with the storm door, containing the dog panel, locked and offering minimal protection. Had there been an intruder? But Ralph seemed disinterested in the house. The barn was his focus. Beatrice, still in her party shoes, wobbled closer to the setter. An eerie humming was coming from the barn. Ralph finally broke his sit, wiggled up to Beatrice, and circled around Evie, who was bringing up the rear. Then he dashed back to the butt print he had left in the snow.

The humming was coming from Reine. It was not the contented murmuring that llama moms sometimes broadcast to their offspring. Reine's song conveyed petulance and would not have been unusual if, say, the herd was being rounded up for shots or toenail trimming. But there was no apparent cause for petulance. More alarmingly, the other llamas were clustered together, apart from Reine. And they were staring hard at her.

In the next hour, Beatrice would exhaust her limited vetting skills. No temperature. No apparent wounds. No limping. No discharge from any orifice. Gums and inner eyelids were neither too pale nor too red, as far as she could determine. She even felt a reassuring thump from Reine's flank. The baby was still alive. Reine submitted to Beatrice's amateurish examination with unusual docility. Beatrice couldn't figure out if that was good or bad. But she knew it was bad that the llama continued her humming, off and on, and that the llama's muscles felt tight, tense, stressed.

Evie, who had changed into jeans, appeared in the barn with a thermos of steaming tea. "Bless you," said Beatrice. She released Reine from her halter and watched with worry as the other herd members cleared a path for the fretful pregnant camelid.

Beatrice flipped over an empty galvanized trough and thumped it with her palm. "Park it, lady."

Evie eased onto the trough, produced two mugs from the deep pockets of her parka, and began pouring. "Better pack them up pronto for the dry cleaner," Evie said, pointing at Beatrice's silk trousers, stained from snow and mud and crusted with stone dust and bits of hay.

"Great idea – if there were any dry cleaners within a fifty-mile radius."

"Swell."

The two women sipped their tea in glum silence.

"Did you figure out what's wrong?"

"Haven't a clue."

"Swell."

TWENTY

Rules of the Game

He didn't understand the rules of the game. He didn't understand the smells emanating from the small cylinder spinning across the kitchen table. But the two humans were playing some game. And Ralph liked games. He cocked his head and focused his most endearing "Please, may I play, too?" look on one woman and then the next.

Beatrice and Evie ignored the setter, who eventually settled onto the pillow in comforting proximity to the wood stove, which crackled energetically.

"So, I figure this burg has no shortage of meth cookers? Wanna score?" asked Evie, as she idly flicked the empty pill bottle back across the table at Beatrice, who merely rolled her eyes and then rolled the orange bottle back at her.

"Please tell me you have more bourbon stashed away somewhere, at least? Since I've run out of Zoloft, I can't be held accountable for my actions. Especially since the goddamned mountains have apparently swallowed the sun. Gawd, how do you stand it? What a week!"

It had indeed been a memorable week. First the derailed Fordyce project. Then the weather, with the power outages lasting for hours every day. Evie was well and truly stuck in Appalachia. The roads were impossible. The day following the Fordyce fete dumped a foot of new snow. Then came an ice storm. Then came a thaw. Then came rain, which promptly froze over. Now they were back in thaw mode, but the warmer temperatures did nothing to lighten the landscape. Evie never realized there were so many shades of gray.

Between power outages, she helped Beatrice fill buckets of water, so they could flush toilets and wash dishes whenever Mother Nature extinguished the lights once again. Evie marveled at just how dark it was inside Beatrice's house without electricity. But the darkness of a country night didn't bother her as much as the darkness of an overcast mountain day. Without some form of illumination, whether from Beatrice's gas lantern, battery lamp, or electric lights, it would have been impossible to read a book inside the house at high noon.

"We're inside a cloud. What can I say?" Beatrice had explained.

And then there was the constant dampness. Even when it wasn't actively snowing, sleeting, or raining, the out of doors was saturated in an icy fog. Evie couldn't get close enough to that woodstove.

Unfortunately, Beatrice kept trekking outside to check on Reine. And Ralph felt the need to dash back and forth through the dog door to keep regular tabs on both women: Beatrice in the barn and Evie in the kitchen. His commuting made for a constant draft from the flapping panel. Evie shuddered and warmed her hands around her coffee mug.

Beatrice didn't mind Evie's grumpiness all that much. She left her friend alone for large chunks of the day. When the electricity gods cooperated, Beatrice sequestered herself in the Boring Building to see to her own deadlines. That left Evie free to implant the kitchen phone into her ear. She was still mourning the uselessness of her cell phone but was coping admirably with the landline. She spent hours every day on the Fordyce recovery effort, while regularly checking in with the ever-reliable Shirley to keep tabs on the daily administrivia back at the office.

The daytime separation kept Beatrice from overdosing on her friend's ill humor. Beatrice realized it was nice having a friend around, even a grumpy one. On winter days like these, the isolation of the mountains was the most trying, even for a hermit like herself. Besides, Evie distracted her from her worries about Reine, who seemed better but was still not quite right. For days there had been no shot at a farm call from Eltie. Beatrice's driveway was an abomination. Virgil, who could normally be tapped to borrow a tractor from one of his many contacts to plow her out, remained out of commission.

The latest thaw held promise, however. Beatrice planned to tamp down the slush with her truck in four-wheel drive. She figured she wouldn't get stuck going down the hill to the road. And depending how that run went, Eltie's truck just might be able to make it uphill.

A few hours later, Beatrice had her answer, as she dripped her way into the utility room, where she was gratified to see the lights back on. As she declared victory, she noticed her hands were shaking. She had used up a lot of psychic energy, willing the truck not to go off into a snow bank—or worse, plunge down the slope angling off the driveway and into a bog.

"Sounds like a reason to celebrate if ever I heard one," yelled Evie from the kitchen, where she had finally extracted the phone from her ear. "I found your backup bottle of Jack Black."

"Oh, why not," said Beatrice, walking into the kitchen as Evie pushed a rocks glass into her hand.

The pillow up against the side window softened the bumps, while still allowing Clara to feel the cool comfort from the frigid glass. It soothed her inflamed cheek, as she drifted back to her dreams.

She didn't even realize that Eltie had stopped the truck. "You stay put, now. No need to get cold. I don't think I'll be too long," Eltie said and closed the driver's side door. As her cousin rummaged around in the large tool box in the bed, Clara dozed off again.

Beatrice was at the vet's side and grabbing for some of her gear, so Eltie could sling the portable ultrasound device over one shoulder. "Glad to see the electricity is back on or this would be useless," she said.

As the two women headed for the barn, Beatrice noticed the fogged-up passenger window. "Is that Clara?"

"Yeah, she didn't get much sleep last night. Family emergency. Figured she could catch up on the ride."

"But she'll freeze! She can take a nap on my couch."

Beatrice had turned back to the truck, and as she was about to tap on the passenger window, Eltie shouted, with an odd tightness in her voice, "No!"

Beatrice promptly deduced the reason for Eltie's tenseness. Clara was sporting a nasty welt on her right cheek. Looking from the child to Eltie, who had rushed to the truck, Beatrice touched her own cheek and raised her eyebrows at the vet.

"A bad accident," Eltie said a bit too casually, without meeting the older woman's eyes.

"Uh, huh. Well, let's get her inside where it's warm."

Clara, still foggy with sleep and swathed in an army blanket, plodded after Beatrice and promptly plunked down on the living room sofa. Beatrice barely had time to place a throw pillow under the girl's head before Clara snapped her eyes shut and curled into a fetal position. Sleep-deprived or not, this was a very different teenager from the inquisitive, plucky kid Beatrice had seen earlier. As Beatrice fussed about the living room, Eltie shadowed behind, saying nothing. Explaining nothing.

An hour later, Beatrice learned that neither the ultrasound nor Eltie's examination revealed any reason for Reine's distress. That also meant, of course, that Beatrice had no remedy for that distress.

As she helped the vet pack up her gear, Evie exploded into the barn. She ignored Beatrice and fixed Eltie with a hard look. Before Beatrice could provide any introductions, Evie was in the tall woman's face—no mean trick considering the height difference. "How the hell did that little girl get a bruise like that? Has she seen a doctor?"

Eltie stepped back and stiffly repeated the vague accident line.

"Sounds like the kind of accident the cops should know about. Or maybe Family Services."

Eltie tried to explain that Clara was safe now. She was safe with her cousin.

"For how long?" Evie demanded. "How long before she goes back to whatever accident-prone environment caused that welt?"

Eltie muttered something about the uselessness of the local authorities. Evie was unimpressed. "And you!" she said, turning her frustration on Beatrice. "This is okay with you?"

Beatrice raised her hands helplessly, her eyes looking down. She could not meet Evie's outraged stare.

Once again, she had no answer.

TWENTY-ONE

Hatching a Plan

"I will dismember him," promised Ben in a low growl, as he burnished the kitchen table with this thumb.

"Just ain't right," Virgil said, his head down, shaking slightly.

"And that mother! What for all that's holy is wrong with her? She's always been a piece of work, but even white trash like her should know to put her kid first."

"Lord have mercy," Virgil agreed, still shaking his head, still avoiding eye contact.

Amanda cleared her throat. Then she offered, in a quiet, reasonable tone, "This is Mike's problem, Ben. It's up to him to decide what to do about Clara."

Virgil slumped a little closer to the table. Ben squeezed his eyes shut for a minute then headed out of the kitchen. The outside door slammed behind him.

Virgil turned to his goddaughter and pleaded, "Amanda, I can get me one of them air mattresses. Clara can take the cot in the guestroom. She should be with folks what loves her. Please, Amanda. It'll work out."

Amanda pushed herself back from the table with stiff elbows, inhaled deeply and said quietly, "No. No. No. That won't happen. You're not a youngster anymore, Uncle Virgil. We have to take proper care of you."

Defeated, Virgil turned his attention to the table top again. The pair sat in silence.

Five miles away, Clara, sacked out on Eltie's sofa, just couldn't seem to get enough sleep. But jarring images kept disrupting the peace of that sleep. Her mother refusing to believe her, accusing her of messing everything up, screaming at her, taking a fist to her, and then another. That long scary walk in the dark, in the snow. And then, when she finally made it to Ben's house, things didn't turn out the way she had hoped. Ben got so angry. Was she the reason why? Did she do something wrong? It seemed like she made Uncle Virgil sad, too. And then there was Amanda. Quiet, tight-lipped, disapproving Amanda.

Clara didn't stay long at Ben's house. Shortly after her arrival, she was in Ben's truck, en route to her cousin's house. Her godfather explained that Eltie had more room. He said Eltie had the medical knowhow to take proper care of Clara's bruised face. He sounded embarrassed, sad, confused. And that scared Clara all over again.

At least she received a warm welcome when she arrived at Eltie's. Her cousin's friend Vaughn was particularly nice. Thanks to her, the past few days had been tolerable, if confusing.

Vaughn had parked a steaming mug of hot chocolate on the side table by the sofa. She couldn't resist reaching out and smoothing the hair on the girl's head and snugging the Afghan under the girl's chin. As she did, Clara opened her eyes and managed a wan smile. "Oh, I'm sorry to wake you, honey. Brought you come cocoa. It's in an insulated mug, so it'll keep warm. No hurry, but it's there when you want it, sweetie." The woman leaned over and planted a light, dry kiss on the girl's forehead. As she did, a wisp of pale blonde hair fell across Clara's face.

Clara wrinkled her nose at the tickle, smiled again and muttered, "Thank you, ma'am." The teenager was not normally one to tolerate much physical intimacy, especially from a relative stranger. But Vaughn was different somehow.

"Goodness, child, will you never call me by my Christian name? It's Vaughn, dear. Please call me Vaughn." Her tone was light, perhaps sad, but utterly without reproach.

"Sorry, ma'am – I mean, Vaughn."

From the kitchen, Eltie raised her voice. Clara caught only a few words. Cuss words. But she had already figured her cousin was talking on the phone with Ben. About her. It gave her the unsettling feeling that something momentous, something affecting her future, was being hashed out. But she couldn't bring herself even to eavesdrop. Or do more than smell the chocolate. She drifted back into sleep.

He was sitting by the sofa. Rodney. Her mother's boyfriend. The unfocused glassiness of his eyes shone in the dark. He seemed to be rocking back and forth. When she looked closer, she saw his hand between his legs. When she looked again, she saw what it was holding.

Clara's eyes snapped open. She saw Vaughn knitting quietly on the chair beside the sofa. Clara felt a wave of relief to realize it was just a dream. "I think maybe I'll have some cocoa now," she said.

"Hope you like it, dear," said Vaughn, smiling into the knitting on her lap.

The conversation continued in the kitchen. But now Eltie lowered her voice. She had signaled Vaughn to stick by Clara and make sure the girl didn't hear what was said over the phone.

"Just yesterday, Ben, the bitch waltzed in here like she owned the place. Didn't even knock. And she started making threats. If I woulda been here, Charyce woulda found out what it felt like to get her face bashed in. Get a little of her own medicine.

"But Vaughn couldn't be rude to anyone. She even served her coffee, for pity's sake. And all the while, Charyce is smirking at her, like she's got the goods on her. But bless her, Vaughn stood her ground and would not let that piece of trailer trash take Clara out of the house. You know Charyce has no interest in being a mother. She's just afraid of losing child support. And I suspect the marriage is off, if Clara ain't part of the package."

There was a long pause. "Yeah, Ben, I know. I know exactly what's going on. Your suspicions were dead on. And I'd like nothing better than to put that pervert in a deep dark hole. But Charyce is gonna go down swinging before that happens. The threats she was making were not pretty. Vaughn and I are the perverts, according to her. For all I know that will actually carry weight with the idiots that serve as the local justice system."

Another long pause. "Relax, Ben, Vaughn and I will be glad to keep Clara for a while yet. But it's not a permanent solution. I could give a horse's patootey about what people think. I don't care what trash Charyce dishes out about us." The tall woman's voice grew softer. Whispering into the phone, she added, "Vaughn would love nothing more than to mother Clara. But I don't think she's tough enough to stand up to the scrutiny we can expect, if we try to get custody."

Another pause. "But that's another year away, Ben. And do you know for sure that Amanda will agree to it even then, even after you've fotched up the old Gurney Mountain homestead? I'm sorry, honey, but your wife just don't strike me as all that eager to become a mother to anyone.

"But I got a plan that just might work. At least until Mike has a chance to rescind the current custody agreement, requiring Clara to stay in the state. Although I'm not too sure that uprooting her to Virginia is such a hot idea anyway, what with him working around the clock. Let me tell you the imaginative foster situation I've got in mind. If it works, Clara will be safe and still close to the family members who truly care for her."

After Eltie hung up the phone, she lingered in the kitchen. She heard laughter from the living room, where Vaughn had turned on the television. She had found an old Mel Brooks movie on one of the satellite channels. And the silliness was evoking giggles from Clara. The naughtier jokes made Vaughn blush and cover her mouth. And that only made Clara erupt in new laughter and generally act a bit more like herself.

Bless her.

Eltie thanked Providence yet again for bringing such a partner as Vaughn into her life.

Five miles away, Ben was now chopping wood. The activity was cathartic. Eltie's idea might just work. Ben was not happy about airing dirty family laundry, but this was one time when mountaineer pride would do no one any good. Least of all Clara. As the wood chips flew this way and that, he realized he would have to pack away the chip he wore on his shoulder. He had learned to keep it from weighing him down too much or from alienating come-here clients who did not know about local ways. But like most of his kin, he had nurtured that chip. It was an integral part of his personality. With discomforting reluctance, Ben realized it would not serve him well now. Now, he would have to reach out to someone with not the remotest idea of the blood ties, the fierce loyalties, the family tragedies, the old feuds, the hidden pain, the human weaknesses, the dark secrets that marked Appalachian life.

Or so he thought.

TWENTY-TWO

Opening Salvos

Tanner Fordyce had deigned to descend from his mountaintop retreat to launch his first working session with his new "ghostwriter." He didn't much like being deprived of the home-court advantage. But he had to acknowledge that a lesser vehicle would have little hope of making the ascent up his own daunting access road. So Mohammed Fordyce would come to Beatrice Desmond's mountain.

As he dismounted from his Hummer, he surveyed the scene with a flinty eye, assessing the net worth of the property and looking for telltale signs of frailties. The property was far better maintained than the typical homestead in this corner of Seneca County. The fences and gates looked more than capable of keeping the small herd of llamas in bounds. The animals themselves looked healthy. The house was ridiculously small but well-tended. He assumed the woman owner must not be quite the hermit he had heard. There must be a boyfriend or even an ex-husband lending muscle to the homestead. Why the unknown lover was so invisible raised all sorts of interesting questions.

Is she embarrassed about him? Is there some legal reason for his absence? Perhaps he's married. Yes, that seems likely. He's unable to extricate himself from marriage to his wealthy wife and so a dejected Beatrice headed for the wilderness to ease her heartache, kept alive by the lover's rare, guilty visits.

There were some holes in his theory, but Tanner was confident his stereotype was essentially true.

He began having second thoughts, as he regarded the woman trudging to his car, a gray dog loping by her side. Dressed in jeans, boots, an old army jacket, and a fedora, she looked like she was in her comfort zone – not at all the way she had seemed at the party. This was not the picture of dejection. This was not a frail woman or a woman dependent on anyone.

She must be a lesbian, Tanner decided. He managed to break out of his reverie, flash a brilliant smile and call, "Beatrice, *ciao bella*!" pronouncing her name the Italian way.

He was pleased to see her annoyance at the greeting.

Definitely a lesbian.

The woman thrust her hand forward to shake his firmly. "Tanner," she nodded. "Thank you for being willing to trek out here for our meeting."

Ralph produced an authoritative bark and then sniffed around the visitor's knees and crotch. To Tanner's credit, Beatrice thought, he didn't flinch at the setter's inspection.

An indignant baying came from the Hummer. Ralph jumped back, barked several times, and then inched forward to sniff around the vehicle.

"I hope you don't mind. Gertrude was feeling despondent this gray morning." He began opening the door.

"Hold it!" Beatrice barked. "Put a lead on her first."

Taken aback, Tanner said with annoyance, "I don't happen to have one." But he kept the door closed.

"Fortunately, I have several," Beatrice said, raising an index finger as she turned back to the house with Ralph in tow.

Once inside, she slipped Ralph's choker over his head and clipped on the leash. Dancing in anticipation of a walk, Ralph kept closely behind his human, as she thrashed about the hall closet in search of an extra lead. "Self-entitled bastard," she grumbled. Ralph softened his eyes and blinked repeatedly at her. This had become the dog's way of short-circuiting his mistress's anger. It didn't always work, but it did today. Beatrice bent forward, tugged on one of the setter's long ears and said, "Oh, not you, poop-head. It's the male in the driveway who seems to think he can lift his leg wherever he wants."

Although Beatrice had a few qualms about inflicting a strange dog on Ralph, she suspected he would have no problems with the aged, laid-back Gertrude. The latter might have a few problems with Ralph's ebullience, but the old girl was unlikely to do anything more than snarl to make the younger dog honor her space. She was mainly annoyed by this Richie Rich's utter disregard for her space. Territorial on the best of days, Beatrice was not inclined to extend Fordyce any slack, given her own reluctance to work with him in the first place.

Outside, Tanner leaned sullenly against the Hummer, with his arms folded across his chest. When he heard the back door slam, he straightened.

I'll be damned if I'll look like some schoolboy slouching in fear at the prissy schoolmarm.

He spread his lips in a false smile.

The canine introduction went well – on Beatrice's terms. Much to Tanner's surprise, she led him off to another building he had not noticed before. Beatrice was not ready to admit the interloper to her home. The meeting would take place in her office, where she had readied coffee and tea and fixings for lunch.

As they walked, Tanner complimented his hostess on her property. She sucked in her breath sharply.

Oh, Christ, what'd I say to piss her off now?

This was a decidedly testy female, one who was not rendered malleable by his considerable charm.

Then he realized Beatrice had stopped. Her eyes were squeezed shut, as she placed a cautious hand over her right knee, slightly flexed. "An old knee problem," she said by way of explanation.

Instinctively, he reached for her left elbow and was vaguely surprised that she didn't pull away from his touch. She even leaned in toward him for the first few hobbles. When she resumed a somewhat normal pace, she seemed embarrassed. "It's just some debris under the kneecap. But I swear, sometimes it feels like I'm getting Black and Deckered."

"You mean, the old IRA trick to punish the worst informants? The lucky ones just got shot in the kneecap; the unlucky ones got a drill?"

"Yup."

"Perhaps I should include a chapter about the time I ran afoul of two IRA arms smugglers. It was in Tripoli."

"Since my research didn't pull up any reference to a Libyan sojourn, I'm gonna assume we're talking Tripoli, Iowa, right?"

"Mr. Google does not know everything about my life, Miss Desmond," Tanner said haughtily.

"Nope. Mr. Google doesn't know about Revere, for example. But I do, don't I?" Beatrice turned toward him with a wolfish grin.

TWENTY-THREE

Changing Names, Changing Lives

It was a long day. Nonetheless, Beatrice began to feel hopeful about the project, hopeful she could actually work with Fordyce – productively. He had indeed had an interesting life, one that evinced courage, flair, intelligence, resourcefulness. He had made shrewd investments, in the States and abroad. He had done his share of good deeds, personally overseeing supply transports to worthy groups, such as Doctors Without Borders. He was instrumental in saving two hapless Peace Corps volunteers who had gotten on the wrong side of Bangladeshi villagers, who somehow conjured the notion that the Americans were poisoning their wells. Ample research also corroborated Tanner's tales about rehabilitating some of the child soldiers recruited into the madness of various civil wars in West Africa.

Although he did his share of large-game and bird hunting – on safari in Kenya and South Africa, in New Zealand, New England, and right here in West Virginia – he donated generously to various wildlife-conservation organizations and helped establish and underwrite Seneca County's new animal shelter. And as a prominent member of the American Bloodhound Club, he had opposed some fads that might jeopardize the breed's hardiness and good temperament.

With all the verifiable swashbuckling and do-gooding in his curriculum vitae, Beatrice could not fathom why he still felt the need to exaggerate or outright lie about other – unverifiable – exploits. In the course of their long day, he laughingly admitted that he had, indeed, never been to Tripoli. Not in Iowa or in Libya. He appeared genuinely impressed to learn she did not have confirmation of that gap in his resume, that she had gone with her gut and bluffed him. "I would not care to play poker with you, Beatrice," he said, once again deploying the annoying Italian *BAY-ah-TREECH-eh*.

Getting the details of his less-than-patrician background was going to prove extremely challenging. Thanks to the capable research grunt Evie had lent to the task – a twenty-something girl working part time, while she readied her master's thesis on late-nineteenth-century Irish literature, of all things – Beatrice had learned a few sparse details of the life that began in Revere, Massachusetts.

She still did not know how the working-class lad had raised the capital to make investments that would ultimately make him wealthy. Those investments had underwritten Tanner's globe-trotting adventures and put him in close proximity to the many influential people he had charmed. Beatrice did not know the financial back story yet, but she did know the name on his birth certificate. It was not Tanner Fordyce.

It was not Billy O'Shaughnessy, either. But she and Evie had rightly intuited the first name, and she had sniffed out the globe-trotter's bog-trotting roots. He was born William Francis Berrigan but legally chucked the Berrigan before bulling his way into Harvard, somewhat after the usual age of matriculation. He kept the William, officially, but came by the Tanner honestly, Beatrice concluded.

Before he launched his Ivy League career, he had worked in a leather-tanning factory, well south of New England. Beatrice wondered if anyone in Tanner Fordyce's current circle knew his first name had smelly origins. In some corners of Asia, at least in bygone eras, people who worked animal skins into leather acquired a miasma that could not be cleansed from their pores. They numbered among the outcasts of society.

Feeling like an outcast herself, Beatrice could not help developing a grudging admiration for the subject of her new opus. Tanner Fordyce was a mover and shaker today. She wondered what that meteoric rise up the social ladder had cost him.

There was much about Tanner Fordyce to feed her curiosity. But she would have preferred to do her digging from a distance. For every legitimate piece of bio she dug out of Tanner, he would toss out four or five misleading cues to coax his biographer off the true scent. Tanner might be a skilled hunter, but he also knew how to think like prey.

Beatrice wondered if he was consciously aware of that parallel. She had grave doubts about Evie's optimistic assessment of her allegedly maternal ability to elicit confessions from this particular subject. She had the feeling she would need to share a few vulnerabilities of her own before getting him to open up. But she had little interest in doing so.

She also remained uncomfortable about having Tanner on her property, even if he had been generous with compliments about the place. Beatrice could not help experiencing a swell of pride, when he appeared genuinely impressed at her ability to keep such a "yar" homestead. But then he indulged in one of his flights of vaguely taunting rhetoric. Referring again to her "hermit" ways, he noted that her self-imposed isolation was in keeping with the ways of the locals. But she would never fit in as a fellow hillbilly. No, Tanner declared, she and her home were too upscale for that.

"I believe you are more of a Hill Wilhelmina. Maybe a Hillwilla."

When Beatrice sighed and shook her head, Tanner snickered gleefully. He could torture her with a truly annoying name.

That last bit of banter played out as the Swashbuckler and his reluctant Boswell were finishing up at the Boring Building. Itching for a drink, Beatrice tapped a foot as she waited for Tanner to coax a comatose Gertrude up from the braided rug by the office door. She looked longingly toward her house and envisioned the ugly Hummer pulling away from that sanctuary and heading down the driveway. But her reverie was quickly interrupted by the sight of another vehicle slowly moving up the lane toward her. A familiar red F-250.

That's funny. What's Ben doing here?

"Just close the door after you," she said, turning back to Tanner, who was still cajoling the sleepy Gertrude outside. "I'll lock up later. Gotta see what's up with Ben."

She hurried toward the house, with Ralph sprinting ahead, barking cheerfully. Ben had already gotten out of his truck and raised his arm in greeting while waiting patiently for Beatrice, walking with her stilted gait. Ben and Ralph had exchanged greetings by the time Beatrice reached the truck.

"Hope you don't mind me dropping by. Just finished up a day's work at that big gray barn down the road."

"No problem. Good to see you, Ben. Let me just finish some business, and I'll be right with you."

She turned back to look for her first guests, one of whom erupted with a low bay and a slow loop of the tail. It took a few moments for Gertrude to reach Ben, who had dropped to a squat at the bloodhound's approach. The dog regarded him adoringly, eye to eye, and Ben responded by scratching her wrinkled neck firmly with both hands. She moaned blissfully.

"Do you see this? Do you?" Tanner asked Beatrice, in mock exasperation. "Nearly a decade together and she's off with the first bloke reeking of Milk Bones." To Ben he said, "I think I shall sue you for alienation of affections, Ben."

Tanner thrust out his right hand, and Ben, rising with some difficulty as he extricated himself from the large dog, grinned affably but was unable to suppress a slight roll of his eyes.

"You guys know each other, I take it?" asked Beatrice.

"Ben Buckhalter built a veritable palace for the hounds. Even Gertrude approves, although she still prefers the lodge's comforts over the kennel and the company of the rambunctious pack."

Tanner, clearly interested in the reason for Ben's visit, showed no inclination to leave.

Could Ben be the married, scandalously younger lover?

Tanner ditched his previous lesbian idea. Leaning his tall frame against the Hummer, he crossed his ankles, amused to see Ben shuffle from one foot to the other in obvious discomfort.

Beatrice noticed his discomfort, too. Turning to Tanner, she said abruptly, "So. We're on for another session next Wednesday at nine? Take it easy on the roads. Still some slippery stuff out there." At that, she beckoned Ralph and Ben to follow her into the kitchen.

Tanner sniffed at his dismissal and took a few beats before altering his posture. As the trio walked toward the house, Tanner checked for telltale signs of intimacy in their movements but saw none. Disappointed, he opened the vehicle's door for Gertrude and couldn't resist calling out, "*Ciao*, Hillwilla!"

From the back, Tanner could see Beatrice's shoulders stiffen.

TWENTY-FOUR

The Other Shoe Drops

Even by Seneca County standards, Ben took quite a while to get to the point. He mentioned the road conditions, the first signs of winter relenting, the supply problems he was having with the nearby barn job.

Native courtesy and five years of schooling in local ways had rendered Beatrice complicit in the meaningless chatter. But her conversational skills were limited, and she was already tired from sparring with Tanner. Finally, she let her end of the conversation drop and allowed an uncomfortable silence to descend. But she couldn't resist the schoolmarmish tactic of raising her eyebrows ever so slightly, while peering amicably but quizzically at Ben, as if to coax the words out of a shy schoolboy.

It worked.

"We were hoping… Well, Clara and me, that is. We were hoping maybe to take you up on your offer to show Clara how to spin up the llamas?"

Already nodding, Beatrice began to respond with an enthusiastic affirmative, but Ben dropped his gaze and kept on talking.

"If you have the time, that is. If it would work for you. We could work out a payment, or maybe Clara could help around the farm. She could even come every day after school and muck out the barn or brush the llamas or whatever needs doing."

Ben finally paused for breath. Beatrice assured him she would be delighted to share what little she knew about processing llama fiber. And she assured him that no payment or work would be necessary. "I like Clara. I think it would be fun."

She was about to add something about time constraints, in view of the Fordyce project, coming on top of her regular workload. But Ben interrupted her with such force that she wondered what subtext she was missing.

"No, ma'am. That would not sit well with me. Not with Clara, either.

If you're not comfortable with a paying arrangement, Clara would be happy to help with farm chores. In fact, she needs to come up with a 4-H project at school. So working with the llamas would be a good way to kill two birds with one stone."

"Well, I don't know, Ben. She's so young—still growing—and the llamas are pretty big. I'd worry about her getting hurt." Beatrice did not add that she was also worried about liability issues. Ben was not the sort to sue her if his niece got knocked down by a romping llama. But Beatrice had heard less-than-pleasant things about Clara's mother. And various dire scenarios flashed through her brain.

"Don't you worry about that, Beatrice. Clara is a tough kid with a good work ethic. She'll be just fine. You've already seen her give me a hand with chores. She's a quick learner and will come in real handy."

Beatrice was still engrossed in dark thoughts. Something that started out as a light offer, involving the occasional get-together with a bright, pleasant girl, was turning into a time-consuming project fraught with complications. Ben was being uncharacteristically pushy, for all his polite demeanor. He was clearly uncomfortable. She was unnerved by the unusually long periods of no eye contact. She was troubled by his use of "ma'am." Had he ever called her "ma'am"?

Clearly Clara was in trouble. The child's swollen cheek and depressed behavior had telegraphed that reality days earlier. Beatrice supposed the llama-fiber "lessons" and farm chores were a way of putting some distance, however temporary, between the girl and the trouble. But a few visits a week certainly wouldn't solve whatever problems Clara had. And what problems would land on Beatrice's doorstep as a result? Would Clara start acting out? Would whoever was responsible for Clara's welt create problems for Beatrice?

By now her thoughts were racing—so much so she was no longer focused on what Ben was saying. She pulled herself away from her mental inventory of possible consequences when she realized one of his sentences had ended in an upward tone.

"Will I be here tomorrow afternoon? Umm, sure. But I don't know whether..." she stammered.

Ben steamrollered right over the pause. "Great, Clara will come by after school. She can hop the school bus that comes down your road."

"School bus? When? What about getting her back home?"

"Oh, don't you worry. One of us will take care of it." With that, Ben slapped his forehead, a gesture so artificial Beatrice was embarrassed for him. "Oh, I'm so sorry, Beatrice. I just realized I left my chainsaw in the Aldermans' field. I'll need it for another fencing job tomorrow. Better run before it's too dark to find it. Don't know where my head is, I surely don't," he said with a hollow chuckle.

Beatrice knew where his head was. Ben was too much the craftsman to leave any piece of equipment lying out in a snowy field. And a day spent with Tanner Fordyce's artful lies made Ben's clumsy attempts at dissembling all the more blatant. But she was so dumbstruck by the whole conversation she did not know how to respond. Before she realized it, Ben was heading for his truck. He held up his hand in a gesture that could have equally been a farewell or a warning not to pursue him.

"What in God's name just happened?" she wondered in a soft murmur.

Angry with herself, Beatrice started making mental lists. Could she knock off the next day's long translation before Clara arrived, whenever that would be?

Realizing she had no idea what the school hours even were, she grabbed for her laptop. After a frustrating hour of slogging through Seneca County Board of Education sites for any clue, she surmised the earliest any school bus was likely to wend her way was three-thirty, probably later. That at least would give her time to do the translation, but she was unlikely to have the opportunity to get in any research on the Fordyce project. She needed to be in top form for that task, to spot anomalies that would help filter out the many lies in his CV.

With a sigh, Beatrice decided to download, for the next day, some of the copy Wolfgang needed edited in the next week. She could look for the familiar, talented writers who usually required little editing—and thus less of her scattered attention as she waited for her young charge. Simply waiting, without a task, was unthinkable.

Having a basic game plan for the coming workday, Beatrice suddenly panicked over what exactly she was supposed to do with Clara. She could hardly be expected to come up with a crafts curriculum on such short notice. Did she even have any clean fiber around?

Does a thirteen-year-old need to carbo-load after school? Do I have any snacks on hand? O. My. God! Am I supposed to throw in dinner, too?

But first, she searched two closets to find the bags of washed fleece she had tucked away months earlier. Then she started taking inventory in the kitchen. Because it was winter, the larder was well stocked, so she should be able to improvise. But spontaneity did not number among Beatrice's strengths. She jotted down likely snacks and likely dinners to prepare for two.

And then she wasted half an hour ranting. Once again, she grew angrier at herself than at Ben, not only because she had allowed herself to get sucked into this situation. She was also annoyed at her obsessive-compulsive streak, which led to micro-managing, particularly when she felt out of her comfort zone. Beatrice did not feel comfortable around children. Perhaps it was the loss of so much of her own childhood. Perhaps it was the loss of her child many years earlier. What could she possibly talk about with a thirteen-year-old? She knew her own grasp of fiber arts, the ostensible reason for the visit, was woefully limited. That would necessitate finding some other common ground with Clara, and what in heaven's name would that possibly be?

Beatrice felt overwhelmed, inadequate, tired, angry ... and hungry. It was nearly nine-thirty. She had remembered to feed Ralph in the midst of her planning. But her dinner remained to be cooked. Or ignored. She poured herself a long-delayed bourbon. With Ralph padding wearily behind her, she went into the den, plunked down in the easy chair, and alternated between sipping from her drink and resting the icy glass on her aching knee. Within thirty minutes woman and dog were snoring softly, only slightly out of sync.

TWENTY-FIVE

How the Inch Became a Mile

Clara was grateful to be on autopilot. All day at school she was unable to focus on the tasks at hand and worried about the events of early evening. In Seneca County parlance, evening began sometime after three-thirty, right about the time the school bus would jostle down the one-lane road where Beatrice Desmond lived.

But now that time had come, and the teenager felt a measure of relief. It was just like those days when she had a tough test at school. She would worry and worry ahead of time. But once in the classroom, she would feel absolved, her mind clear.

None of which meant Clara was comfortable when she jumped off the bus and trudged up Beatrice's drive. Clara suspected the woman was less than enthusiastic about her arrival, which was why Ben and Amanda had instructed her to ingratiate herself and be on her best behavior.

Normally, the potential for failure and rejection would have generated rebellion in the young teen. But Clara understood the deal involving Miz Desmond had somehow become the only alternative to returning home to Momma and Rodney. She inferred she was buying time until she could live with her father. So she would play along, however clumsily.

On seeing Clara's pained smile at the door, Beatrice was not surprised. She figured the girl was as much a victim of manipulation as she was. But she was not about to make her pay for her caretakers' ham-handedness.

Keeping to the ruse of a fiber lesson, Beatrice brought Clara to the barn, to get a feel for a representative fleece – on the hoof. Beatrice chose Barrie for the test subject. The three-year-old was a gentle soul who responded biddably to humankind, even if she would rarely seek out contact herself. Barrie spent most of her life on the outskirts of the herd, where she seemed quite content.

Both Clara and Beatrice temporarily forgot the awkwardness of the occasion, as Barrie nuzzled them and hummed tentatively. Her wool was exquisitely soft and silky. Tucked deep into the fleece, a naked hand felt an immediate surge of humid warmth, even on a cold February day. Barrie did not look remotely discomforted by the cold. She had developed a layer of lard to get through the winter with ease. Beatrice patted the llama's flank appreciatively. Clara followed with an affectionate pat.

Beatrice spouted forth with the few factoids she had learned about the lightness and warmth of llama wool. Then teacher and student marched back to the house, where Beatrice had laid out exemplars of llama wool in its rawest form, with dirt clods and the odd dead bug; after washing, while still littered with dried vegetation; after combing and picking; and then after spinning (the sole skein that Beatrice had actually processed all by herself). Beatrice continued the tutorial, addressing the processing stages. Clara was only half listening, but she was fascinated by the fiber itself, which she scrutinized, stroked, separated, and even sniffed.

Asked if she wanted to pick through some washed llama wool, Clara agreed, with more politeness than enthusiasm. But as the pair settled into their labors, the girl became absorbed by the task. Not much talking took place as the two, sitting on the den floor, huddled over the newspaper, where they flicked the debris and most obvious guard hairs, while they dropped the picked-over fiber into a paper bag. It was a comfortable silence.

Admiring the girl's quick hands, Beatrice asked if she had done any farm work before. "Not really, but sometimes I help my cousin on farm calls. I bottle-fed a lamb once," Clara said, without moving her eyes off the wool on the table.

"Good entry for your resume," Beatrice nodded. "Did that help you get the job at the Fordyce party?"

"No. Momma found out a waitress canceled at the last minute. And I lied about my age. Old Lady Krupp knew it, but she was desperate." Clara looked up quickly to see if the disrespectful reference bothered Beatrice. It didn't. Beatrice was focused on fiber.

"Hmm, I wondered how a kid your age landed a gig like that."

"What's a gig?"

"I guess you'd call it a one-shot job."

The work continued for a while longer, until a loud growl disrupted the peace. It did not come from Ralph. It came from Clara, who clapped a hand over her stomach and blushed.

"Oh, for heaven's sake, look at the time!" Beatrice said. "Eltie was supposed to pick you up half an hour ago. Why don't we get dinner going? If she comes in the meantime, she can just join us."

In the kitchen, Beatrice thrust a paring knife into Clara's hand and told her to chop mushrooms. Befuddled, the girl said, "I've never seen raw mushrooms before."

Despite the need for several instructional interruptions, Clara was more help than hindrance. She expressed interest in the ingredients, particularly in one tub produced from the refrigerator. Beatrice knew she was on shaky ground with pesto, but the homegrown and homemade pesto was already defrosted, and she didn't want it to go to waste.

Clara looked predictably cowed, as she peered into the tub's slimy green contents. She made a face but said nothing. Beatrice cautioned, "Yup, it looks weird. But if we avoided everything that's different, life would get pretty boring."

When Clara did not look convinced, Beatrice added matter-of-factly, "All I ask is that you try it. If you don't like it, you don't have to eat it. Of course, that won't do your growling tummy much good." Beatrice dumped the chopped mushrooms and other veggies into the olive oil already sizzling in the skillet.

Clara did not know how to take that. Her mother would rant and rave if Clara turned her nose up at nuked frozen food. A contest of wills invariably ensued. But Beatrice didn't seem to care. She merely made a logical point. Besides, Clara was hungry, and the sizzling skillet smelled good. Maybe the green sludge would be edible.

As the pair carried their bowls of pesto pasta to the kitchen table, Ralph harrumphed and a knock soon sounded at the door. "What did I tell you?" Beatrice asked.

Eltie came in, carrying a small suitcase and looking flushed. She shot forth with a volley of apologies about a mare about to foal, a partner out of town on a family emergency, a long, cold night ahead of her—and could Beatrice please let Clara stay over with her, just this once, it's a last-minute thing, and nobody else is available, and she'd be ever so grateful because this one favor would really save her hide, and she's so embarrassed even to put Beatrice in this position but would owe her big time and…

Beatrice interrupted the litany to ask Clara, gaping wide-eyed at her frazzled cousin, to excuse the two women and continue eating her dinner. Beatrice grabbed the tall vet by the elbow and pushed her into the den.

In a hoarse whisper, Beatrice said, "Why are you lying? This is no last-minute emergency. How dumb do you think I am?"

"Aw, Christ, Beatrice, I'm sorry. We're just desperate. We need to get Clara out of Dodge. For reasons I'll explain later, she can't stay at Ben's or with me right now, much as both of us would like to have her. And it would be just as well if that bitch Charyce didn't know where Clara is. Her father is trying to get back here from a job in Virginia, but that's a few days yet. I know it's a big thing to ask, but if you could just take her tonight?"

"You're damn right it's a big thing to ask. Do you even know if I have a spare bedroom?"

"Oh, the couch would be just fine."

"That's not the point!" Beatrice roared, stomping her foot and immediately wincing and covering her right knee with her right palm. "I barely know any of you. But as bad as that is, what's worse is how you all thought you could just manipulate me. Did you ever even think of asking me outright? Bloody goddamned insulting!"

Eltie fidgeted with her braid and avoided eye contact. After a pause, she said softly, "You're right."

"Ya think? All right, look, I get that the kid's in trouble. I can take her in for tonight, maybe for the whole weekend. But you make goddamned sure you or Ben pick her up before dark on Sunday. You got it? And you make goddamned sure you keep solidly between me and whatever trouble's chasing Clara. I don't want her mother showing up on my doorstep. Got that, too?"

"Oh, thank you, Beatrice. If we could have the weekend, that will be all we need. Thank you so much!"

"This is only a stopgap measure. Nothing permanent. Got it?"

"Got it."

TWENTY-SIX

Serendipity—Or Another Cosmic Chuckle?

"Shut up, Amanda! Shut the hell up! I've had it!"

The uncharacteristic outburst echoed leadenly through the Buckhalter kitchen, where four huddled around the small table. Virgil flinched and suddenly became engrossed in smoothing out a broken thumbnail. Biting her lip, Amanda pointedly ignored the single tear making its glacial progress down one cheek. Eltie glowered briefly at Ben then grimaced at Amanda's prim portrayal of a martyr. Ben, having recovered his temper, cupped his wife's hand softly, but she retracted her arm with cobra-like speed and folded her hands tightly on her lap.

"Aw, I'm sorry, honey. But this is my goddaughter. We can't just farm her out to some stranger, who has every right to be mad at us. Clara needs us, and I'm darn well gonna be there for her. I wish you could be happy about this. But it's gonna happen whether you're happy or not. Clara's coming here to stay for as long as she needs."

Amanda rose stiffly and walked out of the kitchen. Without turning in her direction, Ben called out, "It *is* gonna happen, Amanda."

A conversation with his brother had stiffened Ben's resolve to stand up to his wife. Mike had tried to extricate himself from his contractual obligations in Virginia. But his employers were not sympathetic. Perhaps if Mike had told the full story to his immediate supervisor, an affable bear of a man who proudly displayed photos of his four daughters, the answer would have been different. But Mike was mountain born and bred, for all his ability to deal with come-here clients and impress bosses on the other side of the Alleghenies. Mike referred only to a vague family emergency. The suits were unimpressed and gave him an option: Mike could cope with that emergency on his off-hours while abiding by his contractual obligations. Or he could lose his job and immerse himself in family affairs back in West Virginia. One boss hinted at the possibility of a lawsuit for breach of contract.

Mike was not so naïve as to believe the lawsuit threat. But he had no doubt his job was on the line, and with it his best chance of earning enough money to build that home for him and Clara. And so he appealed for help from his big brother and extended family.

Ben sympathized but could not entirely suppress angry feelings toward Mike. Although he had long since made peace with his and Amanda's childless future, Ben knew he would not have shied away from any sacrifice to keep a daughter safe and happy, all the more so if she were such a shiny and hardy gemstone as Clara. Wouldn't it be better to work a less substantial job near home, a job affording far more time with his daughter, even if it meant they had to live cheek to jowl in a tiny cabin?

Ben figured he could set up a privacy screen for Uncle Virgil in the east corner of the living room, where the older man could have a proper bed for his ailing back. Virgil was certainly willing. Clara could take the tiny bedroom. And they would all manage to share the one bathroom. Hadn't he and Mike and their parents and great aunt managed in far less comfort when they were growing up?

There was no guarantee Charyce would cooperate, of course. She certainly had threatened mayhem for Eltie and Vaughn to prevent them from serving as Clara's guardians. Perhaps Charyce really did view Eltie and Vaughn's lifestyle as perverted—while refusing to believe there was anything repellant about Rodney's professed fondness for Clara. Undisguised loathing between Charyce and Eltie was no doubt a factor, too.

But Ben guessed Charyce would tolerate Clara living with him, especially since he and Mike were willing to abet the fiction of Charyce's continued de facto custody over Clara—with that handy monthly child-support payment. Besides, Charyce would certainly welcome being freed from keeping regular hours to supervise her daughter. The fly in the ointment was Rodney. Would his marriage proposal stand if Clara was not with Charyce?

The chirping phone jarred Ben out of his ruminations. He sucked in a puff of air and held it as he saw Beatrice's name and number materialize on Caller ID. That showdown with Amanda might be coming earlier than Ben had thought.

Beatrice didn't sound friendly, but her tone was more subdued than angry. She was calling to offer a reprieve to the extended Buckhalter family. An old knee problem, she said, had flared, and she could frankly use Clara's help for a few more days. Getting down the hill to the barn was a little tricky, and the girl had eagerly volunteered to take on the haying tasks for the next few days.

"It's still just a temporary arrangement, Ben. But Clara probably needs more stuff than Eltie brought in the bag. We'll play it by ear for the next few days, okay?"

Ben assured her it was most definitely okay, and someone would drop by that evening to bring another bag for Clara.

"Jesus H. Christ!" Beatrice hung up the phone and crutched toward her recliner. "You didn't hear that," she told her Clara, who was doing a bad job of stifling a giggle.

Clara was far more comfortable with Beatrice's new propensity for creative swearing than with her earlier demeanor. She also noticed how creative Beatrice had been in her conversation with Ben, who hadn't heard the whole story of what happened that Saturday. It had begun with Ralph barking furiously. Clara responded by scrambling down the hill to the barn.

What she saw there scared her to the bone: Beatrice limply hanging onto the llama chute. As bad as she looked, she sounded worse, like she had a rope around her neck, with someone slowly cinching it in. With an eerily tight calmness, Beatrice asked Clara to fetch the aluminum crutches in the bedroom closet.

It was a long, slow, scary journey back to the house. As Clara helped Beatrice crutch her way up the snow-covered hill, during the many stops en route she tried to piece together what had happened in the barn. Even after they finally reached the house, after Beatrice had filled an ice bag and settled into her recliner, Clara had heard only the sparsest of details.

The full story apparently began with a skittish Reine. The humming and pacing spells, followed by completely normal behavior, had become so common that Beatrice almost ignored the latest manifestation of the animal's troubles. She knew the limitations of her diagnostic skills, but a highly tuned sense of responsibility propelled her. And so she tugged a haltered, prancing Reine into the chute.

As usual, Beatrice could find nothing amiss. Reine tolerated the thermometer and gum check, but when human hands began palpating her furry flanks, she bucked. Beatrice managed to calm her by firmly stroking her neck with a fist. But as she stepped back to approach Reine's flank once again, the llama wound up her left hind leg for a righteous kick.

Stupidly, Beatrice bolted out of the way. Stupidly, because the kick would probably have connected with the metal chute. Stupidly, because even if Beatrice's shin had been in harm's way, a kick from a three-hundred-fifty-pound llama would cause a nasty bruise but probably nothing worse. Llamas were not half-ton horses. Yet humans often have as much difficulty as llamas in suppressing defensive instincts. So Beatrice jumped.

Unfortunately, she was off balance when she jumped—a rookie mistake. Kate had often lectured on the importance of maintaining balance when working with any animal, even dogs. Kate was a natural athlete. Beatrice was a natural klutz. The klutz's left mud boot caught on the chute in midfall, which spun her around and smashed the outside of her right knee into one of the horizontal metal bars. When she hit the ground, Beatrice was briefly aware of an odd angle to the right leg. She squeezed her eyes closed. When she reopened them and looked at the injured leg again, it was straight. But it hurt. Like hell.

Her first priority was to release Reine. Using the chute as support, Beatrice worked her way to the front of the llama, laboriously unbuckled the halter, and released the chute's neck vise. Reine clattered awkwardly backward and danced out of her restraint and then out of the barn.

Beatrice's initial relief was short-lived. The knee was pulsing pain. A wave of nausea seized her. She knew she could not walk off this injury. Beatrice did not possess much physical courage, but her native toughness had seen her through various ailments. This time, however, toughness would not be enough. The realization made her feel queasy—and broken and something akin to ashamed.

"Oh Christ, oh Christ, oh Christ, oh Christ!" she intoned, clinging to the chute. And then she yelled and yelled and yelled for Clara.

TWENTY-SEVEN

Observation, Rumination

It made a satisfying squeak when Ralph's canines rubbed against its nubbly sides. Its smell was enticing. Not quite food. But interesting. As slayer of all things furred and pulsing warmth, little things with sharp teeth and high-pitched squeals, Ralph knew the toy was not prey. But it moved like prey, skittering in odd directions designed to elude his hunting instincts. Ralph appreciated the toy because he could stalk it, chase it, toss it up in the air, and catch it behind all four canines, as he stretched his neck upward, making a perfectly vertical line from chin to breast. That was the victory gargle, the gesture he made when prey was firmly in his grasp.

It had been a long time since he had seen the toy, although he had smelled it, hidden behind doors that were barred to good dogs.

His human used to take the toy out from behind the doors and throw it in the air. She would laugh, as Ralph jumped and ran. But that had not happened for a long time. Being a dog, Ralph had no idea how long. He just knew he missed the toy.

Now, here it was again. The young human female was making the toy do little bounces on the hardwood floor. She had good technique; she made it more interesting than his human did. And she did not seem to tire of the game. But Ralph was distracted by other things.

His human smelled funny. Not, good-funny. The smells were not quite sick, but wrong. She moved very little. And when she did, she moved with a second, strange pair of legs that made scary noises. Sometimes, when she put the legs aside, they fell down and made very loud, even scarier noises.

Worst of all was the way his human sounded. Her voice was low and dull, with none of the changes in tone that meant approval or affection or play or fun. Ralph did not like it when his human yelled, but yelling would have been better than this.

So while the girl made the toy do interesting, jittery movements, Ralph lay watchfully, his two front paws stretched out straight in front, his ear cocked for his human. Eventually, the girl gave up the effort to entice him. Eventually, Ralph laid his noble head between his paws and closed his eyes, but his eyebrows twitched whenever he heard a noise from his human.

When it was time for him to do his business for the night, his human did not take him outside; the girl accompanied him instead. She seemed unsure of herself. Ralph had learned that little ones, human or canine, often needed extra attention. He trailed after her in the dark, but eventually the call of nature grew too strong. So he lifted his leg, whereupon the girl started back to the house. Ralph followed.

When they were back inside, his human was not in sight. But he could smell her upstairs, where he scrambled to make sure she was all right. The light was still on. She was sitting up, reading, in bed. He sniffed her to verify she was not in distress. She absent-mindedly scrabbled his head. That was a normal reaction. He tucked himself into his crate, scratched up the Ralph scents on his pillow, circled exactly three times, and curled into a tight ball.

From downstairs, Clara called up to make sure Ralph was inside and asked if she should close the door. Beatrice assured her the dog was already in his crate and told her to shut off the downstairs lights and go to bed.

Clara did as requested then climbed the stairs slowly. Eltie had arrived that afternoon with more of her belongings. The teenager regarded them, scattered around Beatrice's tiny guest room.

Is this now my life?

A wave of homesickness slammed into her, but she wasn't sure what home she was sick for. Could she be yearning for a home she had never experienced?

As she trudged into the small bathroom to brush her teeth, her throat tightened, and tears welled up in her eyes. She shut the door quietly and sat down on the closed toilet lid to cry just a little. The bathroom felt alien. There were no carpets, like Clara was used to. Her bare feet were cold on the naked tiles. Beatrice's toothpaste tasted funny. The shower worked differently from the showers at Momma's, Ben's, and Eltie's. The towels were a different texture and size. The colors were unfamiliar. Clara even found herself resenting Beatrice's requirement to keep the toilet lid closed, so Ralph would not slurp from the bowl.

And Ralph – even the dog didn't seem to like her. Clara loved animals, and her day might have been halfway tolerable if she could have curled up next to his big, warm body. But he spurned her. When she tried her best to interest Ralph in the Kong toy, nothing worked. He kept his eyes firmly on Beatrice, who had retreated so far inside herself she wasn't of comfort to anyone – dog or girl.

Everything was unfamiliar. And unfamiliar felt scary. The homesickness welled up anew. Clara began feeling something close to panic. Where would she live? Who would take care of her? Would anyone ever want her?

Her mother had always acted like Clara was an inconvenience. But now that Clara couldn't live there, surely she should have been able to count on her father. But he apparently didn't want her, either.

Okay. As much as Daddy acts like he loves me, he never really has been around all that much anyway.

Uncle Ben had always been a presence in her life. But now he was packing her off, too. Clara realized it probably was because of Amanda, who didn't seem to like anyone much. But if Ben really liked his goddaughter, wouldn't he have taken her in?

She couldn't really fault Eltie for not wanting her. Eltie was a relative you visited every now and then. She had never been a substitute mother. Besides, she was a little scary – big and loud and different, although she could be fun. Vaughn was really nice. Too bad Vaughn couldn't take care of Clara, but then she didn't really know Vaughn all that well.

Not much more than she knew Beatrice, really. So here she was, living with a stranger – a stranger who didn't want her. Clara wasn't stupid. She could see what any dummy could see: Ben and Eltie were trying to trick Beatrice. Fortunately, the woman didn't seem to blame her. Beatrice was polite, at least, and could even be interesting at times. But she was so different from anyone else Clara knew.

Forcing the panic down, she gulped hard to choke off the last tear. Making a silent list of her woes had always had a vaguely soothing effect. It gave her permission to feel lousy; it made sense of feeling lousy. But feeling sorry for herself had never cheered her. Ever practical, she commanded herself to focus on more useful subjects.

Clara had no idea how long she would be staying with Beatrice, but she suspected it could be a while. For now, at least, she needed the woman to be her caretaker. She knew she could not yet fend for herself. She knew the world could be a dangerous place, and she was years away from acquiring the skills needed to cope with those dangers.

It had been scary to see Beatrice hurt. What if she had to go to the hospital? What would happen then? At the same time, Clara saw the injury as an opportunity. It made Beatrice need Clara, too. Being needed by someone wasn't as good as being loved and wanted by someone, but it was something.

As she tucked herself into the strange bed in the strange bedroom, Clara decided she would make herself absolutely indispensable to the woman down the hall. She thought perhaps she might start by fixing a big breakfast the next morning. That thought had an oddly calming effect on her stomach, which had been jumping with nervousness only a few minutes earlier. The knowledge that she had a plan—that she had a job, that she had some control over her unpredictable circumstances—was comforting. A thin sleep overtook Clara and her newfound but tenuous sense of control.

TWENTY-EIGHT

Counting Blessings and Breaths

When you feel down, count your blessings. Beatrice had so often heard people, even people she greatly respected, utter that apothegm with the same confidence with which pharmaceutical reps tout the virtues of Zoloft or Prozac. Apparently, vast numbers of people had experienced the recommendation's anti-depressive efficacy.

But Beatrice felt utterly alienated from the worldview that encouraged such notions. And she resented the implication that, if the prescription did not work, then the patient was a whining, narcissistic ingrate.

Beatrice was certainly aware of the blessings in her life. And she was not lacking in gratitude for them. Well, not exactly. She saw no reason to be grateful (to whom? to what?) for the good things that had come about by her own dogged, hard work. That was how the lion's share of blessings had entered her life. But she was grateful she was equipped with the perseverance, the work ethic, the stamina, the vision that made her capable of bringing the Good into her life.

Nor was she so self-absorbed, even at her most melancholy, that she did not understand that others – so many others – were far worse off. But she could not fathom how focusing on the Bengali cripple, whose mother had deliberately broken his back to improve his odds as a beggar, could possibly hearten anyone. If it was selfish ever to feel miserable when one had a roof over one's head and sufficient food, was it not downright smug to cheer up at the thought of hungry and homeless war refugees? Besides, the miseries of others were a further reminder of another apothegm in which Beatrice *did* believe: Life is never so bad it can't get worse.

Beatrice would readily admit – to herself, at least – that her fear of the Cosmic Chuckle was a sign of less-than-radiant mental health. Trotting out one's blessings to stroke and cosset was an invitation for the Cosmic Chuckle to whisk those blessings far, far away. They could disappear in a nanosecond, just as Hanorah Desmond had quite literally vanished overnight from Beatrice's childhood, and just as Walt Desmond had disappeared into the bottle for so many of his daughter's formative years.

So, as Beatrice lay abed, unable to sleep because of the throbbing in her right knee and her racing thoughts, she was not grateful for the roof over her head. She was not grateful for the paycheck due to arrive at the post office in another week. Nor was she grateful for the seemingly willing young assistant down the hall. Instead, she wondered how the hell she would get to her P.O. box to retrieve the check, to say nothing of how she would get to the bank to deposit it. And unless she got the money to the bank in timely fashion, she wouldn't be able to pay the mortgage to keep that roof over her head. As for the child down the hall, the benefits, she thought, were more than outweighed by the complications.

What Beatrice really wanted right now was a good, stiff drink. But that meant hefting herself onto crutches and gimping downstairs to the kitchen – and then figuring out a way to transport the drink to wherever she planned to drink it. She was already suppressing the urge to pee because of the rigors of traveling just a few feet to the bathroom, with no stairs involved.

So she lay in bed and considered her options. The only way out of trouble, Beatrice knew, was to put one foot in front of the other. In literal terms, that was a bit tricky. Nevertheless, coming up with a plan was her way of beating back that terrifying sense of being out of control, of being at the mercy of the Fates.

Three days had passed as a cripple. The swelling was down but not by much, and Beatrice knew she had a problem above and beyond earlier knee problems that had also required a crutch or two. She had scored one bit of luck Monday during her reluctant call to the orthopedist, whom she had seen once within the past year for a painful cortisone shot to her arthritic wrist. Because she was an established patient, and because the orthopedist had a cancellation, Beatrice would be able to see him the next day. Negotiating the thirty miles to his office would be daunting, however. But just before making that phone call, she had sucked up her courage and made a trial drive over the frozen but only partly snow-covered meadow between the driveway and her office. She discovered if she pivoted her foot at the ankle, taking care to avoid any torque to the right knee, she could move from accelerator to brake. The amount of force needed for both pedals was doable – so long as panic stops were unnecessary.

The child down the hall, although not old enough to play chauffeur, was old enough to fend for herself, if Beatrice's odyssey lasted beyond the arrival of the school bus. In addition to haying the llamas in the morning, Clara could give Ralph a potty break and, if necessary, feed him dinner.

At least Beatrice thought she could depend on Clara for those chores. The sleepless woman was painfully aware, however, that Clara's disposition had taken a turn for the worse in the past few days. Naturally, the girl was reeling from whatever dramatic events had necessitated her removal from her mother's custody. Clara's relatives had still not seen fit to detail those events for Beatrice. And Beatrice, preoccupied with her own sudden misfortune, had lost the energy and will to pursue the issue.

But she also knew she herself had played a role in Clara's withdrawal. The accident had done nothing to improve the girl's sense of security. Nor had Beatrice's resulting depression. Intellectually, the woman realized the child was trying to help with that ridiculous pancake breakfast she had whipped up Sunday morning. Any other time, even without an appetite for more than a small bowl of cereal, Beatrice would have gamely chowed down and expressed appreciation. But her body was still in upheaval from the accident, and she was afraid that a single mouthful of syrupy pancake would have had volcanic consequences. In addition, her sense of territoriality was appalled at the mess in the kitchen.

Beatrice had rejected the breakfast with a stiff politeness that instantly dulled Clara's large blue eyes. As the girl silently went about wrapping up the pancakes and cleaning up the kitchen, Beatrice had a new reason to feel pain: guilt. She had no energy to soothe the teenager's pain, however. And so the two roommates retreated deep within themselves. The atmosphere weighed so heavily even Ralph lost the bounce in his step.

From his crate, Ralph breathed deeply and rhythmically in his sleep. The sounds had a calming effect on Beatrice, whose heart had begun to work like a trip-hammer at the thought of the challenges that lay just a few hours ahead. Only half-aware, she tried to attune the pace of her breathing to his. She didn't succeed, but the effort allowed her to exhale some of the tension built up over the course of the day. Her pulse slowed to a gerbil rate. And that small effort made her feel more in control of her life.

"Dear, sweet Ralph," she whispered. Still asleep, the dog thumped his tail in contentment. The unconscious canine reaction engendered a conscious human reaction: a soft laugh. It was only a small chuckle, but it was the first time in days Beatrice had exercised those particular muscles. The laugh was followed by an involuntary sigh—another exhalation of tension and sadness.

"What a wonderful work of creation you are," she said softly. Another thump from the crate. Another slight chuckle from the bed.

Well, it seemed there was one blessing that made Beatrice feel a bit lighter. Light enough to extinguish the bedside lamp, to forget about the bourbon bottle downstairs, even to forget about her bladder. In the dark, listening to Ralph's reliable, soothing breathing, she began counting each breath. As she did, the mind chatter slowed. As she did, the pain from her swollen knee eased. As she did, the worries about the next day dulled, because she knew that between now and then one of life's greatest blessings of all would embrace her: sleep.

TWENTY-NINE

Boston Bruisers

Work, Beatrice mused, if not exactly a blessing, was often a welcome distraction. Since her medical odyssey had totally consumed Tuesday, she needed to jump on an editing deadline first thing Wednesday morning. Fortunately, Tanner had called to say he would be unable to make their planned Wednesday session until early afternoon. Once she sent her editing off into the computer ether, Beatrice would have to focus on what she hoped to accomplish with Tanner that afternoon.

Those tasks she understood. Mercifully, they left very little time to focus on her crippled status and how the hell she was supposed to cope with the farm, the llamas, and even the poor dog in the weeks that lay ahead. Oh, yes, and then there was Clara. But that was yet another problem for which Beatrice had little energy, to say nothing of any solution.

With right leg propped up on an adjacent dining room chair, ice bag on knee, Beatrice tapped furiously on the laptop's keyboard. Ralph lay on the floor, near his human but keeping a wary eye out for those crutches leaning up against the table. Although he was gradually reclaiming his cheerful disposition, he remained unnerved by the crutches, especially their propensity to spring to life and clatter onto the hardwood floor from wherever Beatrice had positioned them.

Which is exactly what happened when Ralph, hearing something outside, barked an alert, startling Beatrice. When she twisted around to peer out the nearest window, she jolted the table, animating the crutches. They missed Ralph, who was already halfway to the kitchen door. But they landed just out of Beatrice's reach. As she hefted her weight from one chair to the next, to get closer to the fallen aluminum soldiers, someone knocked.

"Goddammit, keep your shirt on, I'm coming!" she yelled. She assumed it was Tanner but was too weary and hurt and angry to care about alienating her visitor. She clumped into the kitchen, where Ralph was wiggling hospitably over the prospect of company. "Why didn't I teach you how to work a doorknob?" she mumbled.

"Sorry, Tanner, it takes me a while."

The expression on his face instantly changed from haughty impatience to shock. "Good God, what happened? You are one sorry looking Hillwilla."

"Gotta love that silver-tongued Irish charm," Beatrice grumbled. "Come into the dining room, so I can collect my stuff, and then I'll ask you to drive all three of us over to my office, so we can get started."

"Of course." Tanner Fordyce actually sounded nonplussed.

Acutely aware of every square inch of floor space these days, Beatrice was grateful Tanner had not brought Gertrude on this visit. She was also grateful that the slow retreat of the snow had not seduced Tanner into choosing one of his sports cars for the trip. The Hummer would accommodate her leg's minimal flexion with room left over for crutches and dog.

Tanner waited until they relocated to the office, with Beatrice settled at her desk, before attempting to satisfy his curiosity. "So what does the other guy look like? And do you need me to tune him up for you?" Tanner inquired in Revere-speak.

Beatrice erupted in appreciative laughter. She couldn't help finding his kneejerk protectiveness, however jocular, endearing. It made her feel less alone, less overwhelmed. She gazed up at his mirth-filled face, which now looked downright boyish. The intensity of her gaze dimmed his smile to an expression of concern and curiosity. Beatrice suddenly felt embarrassed, averted her eyes, and blushed. As often happened when she felt uncomfortable, she distanced herself from the scene and retreated into her mind, which was now replaying a quirky vignette from high school. Tanner's Beantown bruiser comment had resurrected Joey Della Chiesa, one of several affably rowdy classmates, perpetually posturing in tough-guy stance: slightly bent forward, legs spread apart, chin tucked into chest, eyes avoiding direct contact, unless a stare-down was the prelude to some ridiculous scuffle.

Despite being a star student and "good girl," Beatrice managed to avoid the curse of full-blown geekhood by appearing to prefer solitude – by rejecting others before they could reject her. Her aloof and seemingly self-assured attitude had earned her a modicum of respect from so-called tough guys like Joey.

The respect grew after she bailed him out of a jam in history class. At the insistence of his dogged mother, Joey had squeaked his way into a college-prep class, where he promptly found himself in over his head. The teacher, who had better things to do in the evenings than grade papers, gave multiple choice tests and had the students correct each other's papers, as she rattled off the appropriate letter of the alphabet for each answer. The teacher was such a creature of habit that she always told the kids to pass their papers to the student in front. Joey Della Chiesa sat in back of Beatrice. Beatrice always corrected Joey's papers.

Early on in that course, Joey, whom Beatrice knew not at all, whispered into her ear as he leaned forward to pass along his test, "Please, Beatrice, ya gotta help me out! I'm gonna flunk, and my mother will kill me." Normally harboring a prissy contempt for cheating in any form, Beatrice recognized how much it must have cost Joey to make that plea. Besides, she knew a few tough guys in her neighborhood who would twist themselves into knots to avoid angering their far tougher mothers.

So she erasered away a few of the penciled circles and added a few of her own. But only a few. Joey got a D-plus. He was not thankful, at first. But gradually his test scores rose to a B-minus. To safeguard herself and her supplicant, she had to make his progress believable. Ironically, Beatrice noted that Joey actually did make some improvement during that term, although not quite to the B-minus level.

Joey returned the favor weeks later, when Beatrice took a shortcut after school and ended up in the proverbial dark alley. About a half-dozen tough guys, including one notorious psycho, confronted her. The latter tried to grab her, but she veered away and snarled, "Back off!" The psycho was about to wheel on her, when a reedy male voice piped up from the shadows, "Aw, leave her alone, she's okay." It was Joey, who had the street smarts to follow up that comment with an immediate request to bum a cigarette from the psycho. Having the attention span of a gnat, the psycho suddenly forgot Beatrice and launched into a long, obscenity-filled complaint about Joey's mooching. She raised both eyebrows in an expression of gratitude and walked, not too quickly, out of the alley. But she took note of the grin that spread across Joey's lips, even as he kept his head down, affecting grudging submission to the psycho's harangue.

Had Tanner been Revere's answer to Joey Della Chiesa, Beatrice wondered? Only stodgy people do not reinvent themselves at some point in the first fifty years of life. It was certainly possible. Whatever else he was, Tanner was far from stodgy.

"Earth to Beatrice!" Tanner said, rousing her from her memories.

Her eyes fluttered upward, to where Tanner was now half-sitting on the edge of her desk. Slowly she scanned his face. And suddenly, uncharacteristically, she found herself jabbering. With considerable detail, she filled Tanner in on recent events. She told him how she had broken her leg. She told him about her odyssey to reach the doctor. She told him the doctor's finding: She had a depression fracture at the very top of her tibia. She told Tanner how the X-ray had missed the fracture, but the MRI zeroed in on it – just as it highlighted the utter lack of joint space between patella and femur. She told him she was not supposed to bear any weight on that leg for six weeks. Almost hyperventilating by now, she told him that once the leg healed she would need a knee replacement.

Beatrice didn't tell Tanner how she felt about all this or how she planned to cope.

He didn't ask. After a pause, he reacted: "You drove yourself to the doctor with a broken leg? Why in God's name didn't you call me?"

Now it was Beatrice's turn to be nonplussed. She might have understood if he had chided her for not calling "someone." But he was shocked – even offended – that she had not called him.

Who'd a thunk?

From his perch at the corner of her desk, Tanner leaned in, gripped her by both shoulders, and gave them a brief, firm shake, while saying in a low voice, "Next time, Beatrice, call me. *Capisce*?"

THIRTY

Words for Every Occasion

The slight stoop to Clara's posture had less to do with worries about slipping in the snow than analyzing the snow's quality. She had considerable opportunity to examine the changing texture of her footing, because she had hopped off the school bus at the Boggs place, a mile before Beatrice's house. Since taking the new route, Clara had made the acquaintance of Joanie Boggs, who lived on Beatrice's road.

Joanie would not have been Clara's first choice as a friend. She was not the sharpest tool in the chest, as Clara's father might say. But Joanie had barn cats. And one of the cats had just had a litter, which Clara was eager to see. Besides, Joanie might have useful information about the come-here down the road.

Clara was disappointed on two counts. Joanie had gasped when she learned Clara was staying with that Desmond woman. Rather than serve as a source of information herself, Joanie tried to pump Clara. Instinctively, Clara responded vaguely. She surmised the Boggs family knew next to nothing about Beatrice, except that she was "snooty" and "weird."

The second disappointment came when Clara visited the litter. The mom-cat was a scruffy thing. Its eyes were crusted with discharge, and its temperament had soured from motherhood. The cat growled, as the two girls leaned in for a closer look at the kittens. Even without the baneful warning, Clara would have backed off. The newborns repelled her with their bulging, closed eyes; their flattened, almost naked ears; and the hideous pinkness of their twitching noses. They looked and squeaked like tiny, extraterrestrial rats.

Appalled when Joanie began cooing, in a falsetto, at the squirming things, Clara could not extricate herself fast enough from the barn, the cats, and her schoolmate. Besides, even though it was doubtful Beatrice knew the schedule, Clara wanted to make sure she was not too late. Perhaps she was supposed to check in with her new guardian before visiting a friend? Her mother certainly had no problems with Clara's comings and goings. But Beatrice was not her mother. So Clara figured as long as she beat the second school bus, the one that transported the kids involved in extra-curricular activities, she would be on safe ground.

That was assuming the snowy ground didn't upend her, as she trudged along the side of the road. The snow wasn't exactly slippery, Clara thought. After weeks of squalls almost every day, after weeks of being whipped by the wind, after a few days of above-freezing temperatures, the snowpack acquired an almost greasy look. The girl had read somewhere that Eskimos (few Seneca County children had ever heard the politically correct "Inuit") had nine different words for snow. She wondered if that was true. She wondered if an Eskimo would immediately recognize the current texture and pronounce sagely, "Oh, that's *quagtiakut*."

Clara wondered how she would describe her *quagtiakut* to someone unfamiliar with snow's diversity. She plodded on, head down, for quite some distance before crafting a likely answer. The texture, she realized, was like the first stages of cookie dough, just as you muscled the packed brown sugar into the softened butter: equally granular and greasy.

Because she was lost in thought, and because the cookie dough muffled tire sounds, Clara failed to move fast enough to avoid a spray of snow, sand, and salt, as a blue sedan clipped around a blind curve and sped in the opposite direction from Beatrice's farm. From the shoulder, Clara turned to glare at the departing car. It looked a lot like her mother's Ford, she thought. If maternal feelings had suddenly overwhelmed Momma, she certainly didn't wait around at Beatrice's to retrieve her only daughter. Clara decided nothing good could come from Momma visiting Beatrice. Dread gurgled in her abdomen, as she continued her walk down the road.

Looking like a framed letter A in the open doorway, Beatrice perched on her crutches and called out to Tanner as he headed for his Hummer, "You have no idea how glad I am that you were here today. I owe you, big time."

Tanner's entire face broadened into a slightly wicked grin. He doffed an invisible hat and replied, "*De rien. Avec plaisir, Madame.*"

Ever the showoff, Beatrice thought uncharitably, but she grinned back and managed a little wave by hugging one crutch into an armpit. The guy had a talent for annoying her with false tones—not too surprising, given the many falsehoods defining his persona. But as much as his verbal ooze could get under her skin, Beatrice had every reason to rejoice in his language skills this afternoon. It was one thing when she was the target of Tanner's annoying verbiage. It was quite another when he aimed his words at Charyce Trask.

Clara's mother had indeed burst onto the farmstead about thirty minutes earlier. The forcefulness of that entrance was undercut by the unfortunate incident on the driveway, where Charyce, driving too fast, had spun out on an icy patch and ended up perpendicular to her intended direction. When she tried to close the ninety-degree angle and head back uphill, her rear tires churned up ice and gravel. Frustrated, Charyce slammed the shift lever into reverse, stood on the accelerator and executed another spin, this time heading downhill, away from Beatrice's house. Undeterred, Charyce pulled the emergency brake, shut off the engine and hiked up the remaining hundred feet of driveway. Although not lacking in vigor, the hike was short on dignity, because Charyce forgot she was wearing the high heels chosen for her upcoming shift at the bar.

The driveway drama was not lost on Beatrice and Tanner, who had only just returned from their short working session at the office. Startled by Ralph's barking, Tanner went to the door to investigate; Beatrice clumped behind him. They watched the last spin-out wordlessly. As Charyce huffed and wobbled over the ice patches, Tanner said he vaguely recognized the intruder. Beatrice confirmed the identification.

"Motivated little piece, isn't she?" he sneered.

The little piece barged through the open doorway with such intensity that Tanner had to press his back against the wall to avoid a collision. Beatrice, however, maintained her three-point stance without a wobble. A darkness fell over her face.

"How dare you try to snatch my only child away from me!" thundered Charyce by way of an opener. The soliloquy went on and on, with all three people clustered near the doorway: The two women faced off against each other, while Tanner leaned with seeming nonchalance against a wall. The younger woman ranted about what "my lawyer said," accused

Beatrice of violating child labor laws, hinted at some unnatural motives for taking in Clara, and threatened to file kidnapping charges or at very least a civil suit. She tossed out various legal malapropisms and exercised more four-syllable words than she had probably used in her nearly four decades on the planet. The scene might have been funny, except for the pure malice in Charyce's demeanor.

Steadily holding her adversary's eye and listening to every word, Beatrice was on alert for any threat about taking Clara off the premises. She wondered if that was Charyce's intent or whether a shakedown was in the offing. Beatrice was far too busy listening and observing to counter the woman's list of charges or to make any attempt to defend herself.

The angry silence was not what Charyce expected. She had come prepared for a lengthy shouting match, in which she would have a clear advantage. Not sure how to proceed, she paused just a few seconds.

During that pause, Tanner, still leaning on the sidelines, raised a hand like a meek schoolboy. "Ms. Trask? Do you by chance know who I am?"

Charyce whipped her head around and looked the man up and down, with hostility initially, then in cool appraisal, and finally in recognition.

"Oh, yes. Aren't you Mr. Fordyce?" She could not resist cocking her head flirtatiously.

"That I am. And if you know my name, you also know I have more money than God. I also have more attorneys than God, and I assure you, Ms. Trask, not a one of them attended law school in West-By-God Virginia. If you pursue your legal threats—or any other threats against Miss Desmond—I shall place those JDs at her disposal. They will create so many obstacles that your case will be tied up in court until you are a grandmother. Just think of all the billable hours your lawyer will chalk up as he struggles to surmount those obstacles. Do you have the money to pay for those billable hours, Ms. Trask? Can you afford all the court fees? Will your employer give you the time off to be deposed, appear in court, answer countercharges? Think long and hard about whom you threaten, Ms. Trask. You do not want me as an enemy."

Throughout his speech, Tanner's tone was almost cordial. As Charyce thought of a response, Beatrice thumped her way forward, uncomfortably close to the younger woman. "Get out," Beatrice growled softly. "Get out and never come back."

Charyce blinked, literally and metaphorically. She looked from Beatrice to Tanner, as if expecting male rescue. Seeing only his vulpine smile, she turned on her high heels and wobbled indignantly down the driveway.

THIRTY-ONE

The Quieting Effects of Mozzarella

"Was that my momma's car I saw on the road?" Clara asked nervously, as she unloaded her book bag on the kitchen counter.

Beatrice, hopping from stove to refrigerator while supporting herself with one wrist moving along the counter, extracted a plastic bag filled with chocolate chip cookies. "Help yourself," she said, offering the bag to the girl. "I made and froze a big batch before the accident and decided to defrost some for us tonight. It just felt like a cookie night."

"Funny, I was just thinking about chocolate chip cookies."

"Yeah? Great minds think alike."

Despite her new limitations, Beatrice insisted on making dinner. Clara, who had no shortage of experience cooking for herself and sometimes for her mother, too, did not feel nurtured. Recalling how Beatrice rejected her pancake breakfast, Clara figured the woman was too picky to trust her.

Still, Clara took some comfort from the pre-dinner drill. Her new guardian might have rejected her cooking, but she did let Clara help with the preparations. She called Clara her "sous-chef," and Clara was starting to like some of the weird things they hatched up in the oven or on the stove, even if that first entrée of slimy green pasta still grossed her out.

Besides, the time spent chopping and sautéing was as pleasant as life could get under Beatrice's roof. Girl and woman were strangers thrown together by circumstances not of their choosing. They were still stiff with each another. Little comfortable chit-chat played out between them, to say nothing of meaningful conversation. But a certain camaraderie had developed over the kitchen counter, even if the conversation focused merely on how long to steam the broccoli or how to minimize the blood spatter from extracting pomegranate seeds. Once, while slicing mushrooms, Clara related something that happened at school. Once, while rolling out dough for calzone, Beatrice shared an anecdote about the Italian neighbors of her childhood.

The pre-dinner drills were comfortable, because they reminded Clara of happy times spent with her father. On occasion, those times did indeed involve cooking. Mike, who had lived more years as a bachelor than a married man, was in no danger of starving in a stocked kitchen. His cooking skills left something to be desired, but his interest in food had not wavered since leaving the glorious aromas in his mother's kitchen. He and his daughter enjoyed trying new recipes, even when they failed.

And there were other times, such as when her father solicited help with his work. He let his daughter do more than fetch tools. Sometimes he let her do a little fine sanding. Sometimes he let her stain trim. Whatever the task, the conversation flowed. Clara chatted about playmates, TV shows, school, her hopes, her fears. Mike talked about the childhood stunts he pulled with his brother. He talked about his parents, only one of whom Clara remembered: Meemaw. He talked about the facial features, talents, and interests Clara supposedly shared with a long-dead great-aunt or great-grandfather.

While cooking or sanding with Mike, Clara felt part of something worthy, something bigger than herself. Clara felt loved.

Though Clara hardly felt loved in Beatrice's kitchen, she felt useful and therefore welcome. And that was something.

"Was Momma here?" Clara persisted, while slipping Ralph a cookie piece, minus chips.

"Oh, yeah, she wanted to check on how you were doing. Hand me the French knife, will you? It's the one that looks like a right triangle."

Passing the knife to Beatrice, while remembering at the last minute to present the handle first, Clara steered the woman back on course. "How come she didn't wait for me to come home, so she could see for herself?"

"Oh, wait. Can you fetch the grater from the drawer, please? Yeah, that one, the second one from the top," Beatrice requested, stalling for time to think. "She had some earlier appointment that ran late. And you were a bit later than usual. Otherwise she would have had some time with you before she had to get to her job."

Beatrice knew her scenario was lame. Clara also knew it but was thankful whatever had happened between her mother and Beatrice must not have been that bad. Beatrice did not seem worried or angry. She had not packed Clara's bags or locked her out of the house. It looked like Clara would be eating dinner here and sleeping here.

The conversation lapsed awkwardly. The only sounds came from the grater occasionally clanking against the bowl. Beatrice found herself wishing that mozzarella did not have sound-baffling properties.

Rescue came in the form of a chirruping phone. She nodded to Clara to answer.

"Someone from Mr. Fordyce's place," Clara explained, covering the phone's mouthpiece, as Beatrice crutched forward.

That someone was Tanner's driver. Beatrice was unaware Tanner had a driver or why he would need a driver, but that was how Cal Blake introduced himself. Cal said he was at Beatrice's disposal to drive her to medical appointments or the grocery store. If she liked, they could set up a regular weekly appointment to run errands while her leg healed.

Her first instinct was to thank him very much and dismiss the idea. She was vaguely offended by this assault on her independence. Besides, "Cal Blake" could be an ax murderer, for all she knew—though he would have to be an incredibly well-informed ax murderer.

Common sense prevailed, and she accepted. Right now she was not independent. She could not afford to be. And at least Cal would be getting paid for his service, so she would not need to feel guilty about putting him out. Oddly, she did not feel guilty that Tanner was the one paying.

Hey, he's the one who said he has more money than God.

She briefly considered asking Clara to take the weekly, chauffeured rides to the supermarket but concluded it would be too complicated, requiring too many explanations about even the most basic items on the grocery list. Would the child know a scallion from a leek? A zucchini from a cucumber?

Obviously, Beatrice would exhaust herself hobbling down multiple supermarket aisles. The only alternative was to use one of those electric carts major supermarkets provided for the handicapped, the disabled, the ambulation-challenged, or whatever the Political Correctness Police called people like Beatrice. The thought depressed her enormously. She had suddenly become handicapped. The fact that this status was temporary provided little comfort.

What's wrong with me? Someone has done something nice, something practical for me and I'm whining? How depressing.

Still, she was relieved not to have to thrash about in search of transportation. Although the larder was always well stocked, especially in winter, she was running out of perishables such as fresh vegetables and milk. The prospect of making phone calls to seek favors from people like Eltie or Ben was daunting.

Beatrice was easily daunted these days. She had exhausted herself with just a few phone calls to her insurance company and various medical-supply companies in search of an even more pressing form of transportation, a wheelchair. She realized that a fifty-something woman, even one used to a physically taxing lifestyle, was pushing the envelope by relying on crutches for all her movements around the house. The phone work turned up an outfit that would deliver a wheelchair to her door.

She could handle this, she reminded herself. She was resourceful, after all. She had managed tough times before. Back then, of course, she had friends who rallied round her. But her friends were far, far away now. Kate was dead, and Evie might as well be in China.

And whose fault is that? Except for Kate, who couldn't help the aneurysm that blew out her brain, they didn't leave you. You left them, dumbass, for this country adventure, which has proved far more challenging than you anticipated. What were you thinking?

Seeing Clara staring nervously at her, Beatrice realized she had been doing an excellent impression of catatonia for about fifteen minutes after hanging up the phone. She felt a brief surge of resentment at the social pressure requiring her to snap out of it and stop scaring a thirteen-year-old, but a healthier part of her brain recognized that the responsibilities generated by Clara's presence might just be important to her survival – or at least her sanity.

So Beatrice snapped out of it. The grater started clanking again. The paring knife made reassuring chopping noises. And after a loud fart from Ralph, followed by laughing groans from both humans, the conversation, however halting, resumed.

THIRTY-TWO

Dark and Festering Closets

Because it was winter in West Virginia, the windows stayed closed. They closed out not only the snow and cold but also the sounds of the outdoors. Now that Beatrice was no longer able to plunge herself into the midst of those sounds, their absence stifled her. A seasoned walker, she knew that winter, for all its snow-muffling, was hardly silent. She ached to hear the soothing rattle of the beech, which would not surrender its papery leaves even in the coldest weather. As she settled the bed linens about her neck, she tried to imagine the strident *cheee* of the red-tailed hawk, circling over her pasture in search of some hapless rodent.

But all Beatrice heard was the ka-klunk of the pressure tank refilling with well water after the recent toilet flush. She doubted that noise would have inspired Emily Dickinson to put pen to paper.

Feeling claustrophobic and spectacularly sorry for herself, Beatrice stared at the ceiling, visible by the dim light of her alarm clock. An hour passed, but sleep failed her.

She lacked the energy to maneuver her leg into a more comfortable position or turn on the light so she might seek escape in one of the novels on her bedside table. Instead, she tried to concentrate on her breathing but only became irritated at its irregularity. Then she turned her attention to the dog's soft breathing. As so often happened, Ralph, even in sleep, had a gentling effect on his human. She finally stumbled into an on-again, off-again slumber.

When she next opened her eyes, she was aware of a bad smell. Was it propane? Weeks earlier, after consulting her handyman book, she had concluded that her furnace, despite a noisy fan, was working just fine. Had she been wrong?

Then she realized it wasn't propane she smelled. It was the natural gas that fed the kitchen stove. A sick feeling came over her. She knew she would have to check the kitchen—she knew there was something very bad in the kitchen.

And just like that, there she was, in the kitchen. And she was not alone. She tried to keep her eyes on familiar things: the refrigerator drawing she had crayoned of a big black dog; the crack in the glass door of one cabinet, which her tall father had smacked with his head, because her mother had mistakenly left the door open. Her parents had laughed that the crayon dog had such a big nose. They had laughed about the cracked cabinet.

Beatrice didn't feel like laughing now. She forced her eyes to shift down, to see the legs sprawled on the kitchen floor. She recognized her mother's ratty slippers. She recognized the cheap Sears watch on the hand that was dangling over the edge of the open oven door.

By now, Beatrice was coughing. The smell was bad. She covered her nose with her hand and shut off the oven. And then she saw her mother's face. It was so healthy looking, with those rosy cheeks. Her mother looked healthier than she had looked in months. Peaceful, too. She could almost imagine her mother had just found a funny new place to take a nap.

Deep down, Beatrice knew her mother wasn't napping. She even sensed that the rosy glow of her mother's cheeks wasn't healthy at all. But still she tried to nudge her mother awake: "Mommy? Wake up! Get up off the floor! Please wake up, Mommy. Getup, getup, getup, getup…"

She heard a cough. Maybe it was her mother, about to wake up after all. But, no, the cough had come from herself—though she wasn't sure whether it came from the little girl who had breathed in too much natural gas or the mature woman whose sinuses were draining.

Beatrice felt a familiar dull ache around her eyes and coughed herself awake. She realized she was not in Massachusetts. It was just a dream. Well, not quite. It was a pretty accurate replay, one that often visited her sleep in her youth. It had surfaced far less frequently in later years. But when it struck, it still struck hard, as Beatrice's skyrocketing pulse rate attested.

She exhaled deeply, in hope of thereby exorcising the old, sad tableau. She punched her pillow, readjusted the covers, and focused once again on that gray, blissfully unscary ceiling. Once again she listened for Ralph's breathing. Eventually, his sleep rhythm worked its magic. Bit by bit, she felt the tension drain out of her.

And everything was peaceful again – until the damn phone shattered the silence. Her arm flailed around to quash the dreadful noise. When she finally succeeded in putting the receiver to her ear, she heard clipped military tones from a male voice of indeterminate age. The voice repeated over and over again: "There has been an accident, ma'am."

Well, of course, there's been an accident. I broke my damn leg!

Beatrice, too polite to say that into the phone, said only, "I know."

That wasn't enough for the robotic voice, however. "I'm afraid you'll need to identify the remains."

"I can't drive," she objected, hoping the voice would go away. But the next thing she knew, she was standing next to a state trooper. Just by leaning on his arm, she was somehow able to walk on her broken leg. She felt no discomfort except for the cold. The room was so cold. The trooper wanted to show her something. She was afraid if he raised his arm to point, she would fall and break her leg again. The trooper told her she could stand just fine. He gently pulled her fingers off his arm.

"No, don't go!" she pleaded.

The trooper was gone. The only thing in the room was a metal gurney. It wasn't empty. When she pulled back the sheet, she saw Bill's face. He was pale, but Bill was always pale. She knew he was going to sit up and tell her how stupid she was for standing on a broken leg. She knew he was going to tell her how stupid she was for breaking the leg in the first place. She didn't want to hear it. But she couldn't walk. She could stand on the broken leg; she just couldn't move it.

She wanted to be anywhere in the world but where she was. Bill was going to sit up soon, and she just couldn't stand it. If he sat up and talked, Beatrice knew every bone in her body would shatter.

"Is this your husband, ma'am?" The robotic voice had returned from somewhere behind her.

"I don't want to be here," she answered.

"But you know you can't leave until your husband sits up and speaks and every bone in your body shatters," the voice explained, dully.

Suddenly, Beatrice knew precisely what she should do. She would not identify the body. She would not wait for Bill to sit up. Instead, she would sit up. And as soon as she did, the body on the gurney would vanish.

And so, with some effort, Beatrice hoisted herself into a sitting position in her bed, in Seneca County, West Virginia, some fifteen years after her husband had run his car into a tree. And she was right. There was no body. There was no gurney or state trooper or robotic voice.

In the first two years after Bill's death, ruled a likely suicide, Beatrice had often relived the part where she had to identify the body. The actual identification was remarkably painless. It certainly helped that Bill's face was unblemished, apart from a small, cherry-like stain on his chin. She later learned that the cherry stain marked where the steering wheel had shoved Bill's chin up and into his brain stem. She recalled thinking—quite calmly—that the blemish was the same color as her dead mother's rosy cheeks.

No, the tough part had been the irrational fear that this was all some sick ruse, some new manifestation of the mental illness that had been claiming more and more of Bill's brain. Either that or he had just taken one Vicodin too many. In any event, she worried he would come to and start ranting at her. It suddenly occurred to Beatrice that her greatest fear in the identification process was neither the reality of Bill's death nor the hurtful words Bill might say if he regained consciousness. What she feared most was the embarrassment if that state trooper heard the resurrected Bill's diatribe.

"How dumb was that?" Beatrice said out loud.

Of course, she had felt loss and sadness and guilt. And a lot of pain. As she sat up in bed in the dark, she remembered how she had thought it quite possible the pain could break her, almost literally. But it neither broke her nor made her any stronger, contrary to that old saw. It merely eased with time. And the dreams, just like the dreams about her mother, had faded. Until tonight.

Although exhausted, Beatrice had had enough of her fractured dream-memories. She reached for the light, grabbed a book and started reading—a spooky suspense thriller. "Piece of cake," Beatrice said aloud. "Let's go take a look inside somebody else's dark and festering closets for a change."

THIRTY-THREE

Within Fifty Yards of Upchuck

By morning, a sleep-deprived Beatrice was still not completely beyond the grip of nightmares. Although depressed by the misfortunes of the past year, she didn't think the dreams' leitmotif of suicide constituted some subliminal warning. But she did wonder if her subconscious self was sounding another kind of alarm. People she cared about had a way of exiting her life in uniquely painful ways. And now two new people had entered her life – in ways that were not entirely comfortable. Beatrice suspected Clara's and Tanner's intrusions had something to do with the troubling dreams.

There wasn't much she could do about Clara, because she needed the girl's help. But maybe there was something she could do about Tanner. Fortified by her morning tea, Beatrice sucked in her breath and punched Evie's office number into the phone.

Shirley's honeyed tones told her Miss Rudner had headed off for a meeting. Could she take a message? As Beatrice reconsidered the wisdom of this phone call, Shirley switched gears and announced she might be able to catch Miss Rudner after all.

After a few minutes, Evie's voice surfaced on the other end of the phone. "Everything okay?" she asked breathlessly. "I think you've called me at work maybe twice in twenty years."

Beatrice assured her friend everything was fine and then spent a few minutes dodging the central issue.

Evie called Shirley into the office. She said she didn't want to be interrupted and asked her secretary to stall the client awaiting her.

When an embarrassed Beatrice began protesting that she could call back, Evie snapped in a low voice, "The client's an asshole who needs constant handholding. I was gonna short-sheet the meeting anyway. Do him good to wait. Now cut the crap and tell me what's really going on."

"Look, Evie, I don't think this Fordyce project is going to work. For every fact I ferret out about Tanner's life, I turn up half a dozen new dodges. I don't think we have the right chemistry. I'm not the right person. I don't think I can do it. I don't think I'm objective enough. And with the broken leg and Clara and all, I've already got a lot on my plate."

Hearing stillness on the other end of the line, Beatrice stammered, "I'm sorry, but do you possibly think you could find someone else?"

After another long pause, Evie said, "You're dithering. You don't dither. Sonofabitch, you're scared! Tell Mother what has you so fucking rattled."

"I'm not rattled," Beatrice said defensively.

"Liar, liar, pants on fire! For Christ's sake, you know I make a piss-poor shrink. And your tossing the Fordyce project sure as hell would screw me up. Jesus, you're normally Miss Responsible. You can't just up and leave now, Beatrice. What the hell are you running from?" Evie sounded both concerned and frustrated.

"No, no, you're right. I made a commitment to you and should see it through," Beatrice responded dully.

Another pause. Then: "Oh. My. God! You're running from him! Tanner got under your skin somehow. Well, now I'm all interested. What's going on?"

"Don't be ridiculous. Nothing's going on. I just had a bad night. Didn't get enough sleep. Feel overwhelmed. I'll get over it. Sorry I bothered you."

As Beatrice's brain desperately scrounged for some trivia to divert her old friend's attention, Evie interrupted, "Oh, wait a minute, Beatrice. What's that, Shirley?"

Beatrice heard the phone mouthpiece muffled. The next sound was a tinny bell, followed by a throaty laugh from Evie.

"Did you hear that?" Evie asked. "That was Shirley's goddamned kitchen timer. Seriously. She keeps one on her desk. Shortly before you called, I told her to concoct some excuse to end the client meeting as soon as possible. So to remind herself, she cranked up the kitchen timer as I headed out the door to meet the guy."

"Well, go take the meeting now. I've returned to my senses. We're good."

"Nah, I don't feel like it now. I sent Shirley off to reschedule. Can't wait to hear the yarn she spins to get rid of him. Stick around. Gonna put you on hold."

Wishing she could hang up, Beatrice listened to Diana Krall purring out a Cole Porter classic on Evie's music-on-hold system. Even canned, the song reflected her exquisite taste.

After several minutes, Evie's laughter replaced Diana's dulcet alto tones. "I knew it. It was 'Biddle, Benson and Burkhardt' again."

"What?"

"Biddle, Benson and Burkhardt is the imaginary client Shirley invented years ago. Well, she told the real client I had been diverted by yet another BB&B emergency. It seems Russ, one of my account execs, was pitching an idea at Mr. Biddle but got so nervous that young Russ 'upchucked' – Shirley's word – all over the conference table. Unfortunately, the incident sent Mr. Biddle into a sinking spell. He has a bad heart, you know. So I was called in to apply smelling salts, do CPR, mop up the vomit or something – all while finishing Russ's presentation, I guess."

"The real client bought it?"

"Who would make up a lie like that? I mean, other than Shirley? I swear to Christ the woman gets so wrapped up in her fabrications she actually believes them."

Beatrice heard an Old South accent intoning, from a distance, "I am not a fabricator. I am a gifted storyteller, blessed with more than a smidge of dramatic flair."

"More than a smidge, indeed," said Evie, flipping her phone to speaker mode. "Tell Beatrice and me how you decided to put puke into that particular story, Shirley. I want to understand your process."

"Do you know how boring it is to announce the same old emergency call from Biddle, Benson and Burkhardt? I need my creative space, too. Besides, no one wants to be within fifty yards of upchuck. I figured your Mr. Cranmore would just scoot on out the door rather than have his olfactory senses perturbed."

"She does have a point, Evie."

"Why thank you, Miss Desmond. Your friend is quite perspicacious, Miss Rudner."

"And you are quite scary, Shirley!"

"You're welcome," she responded, seemingly without sarcasm.

"Before you go, Shirley, can you explain to Beatrice and me just why it's always Biddle, Benson and Burkhardt? Who the hell are they anyway?"

"A silk-stocking law firm. I was a quite well-regarded litigator there in my previous life. And poor Mr. Biddle did indeed have a troubled heart."

"Of course, he did," Evie said flatly. "Thank you Shirley."

"You're more than welcome."

Flipping off the phone speaker as Shirley tottered out the door in her platform stilettos, Evie mumbled into the mouthpiece, "I haven't a clue whether her tongue is planted firmly in cheek. Or she just might be serious. All I know is, if that southern archangel ever decides to embrace the Dark Side, this boss is well and truly screwed."

The conversation veered off into equally lighthearted subjects before ending. Evie had either forgotten Beatrice's earlier, panicky query or chose not to revisit it. Having little patience for analyzing motives and emotions, she apparently had faith in Beatrice's reaffirmed commitment to the Fordyce project.

As for Beatrice, embarrassed both by her own panic attack and its possible implications, she was grateful for the intercession of Shirley, Biddle, Benson and Burkhardt. Even if she was back in the soup with Tanner Fordyce, she was grateful she had been saved by the bell—even a tinny bell on a kitchen timer.

THIRTY-FOUR

Extraordinarily Rare

Now that regular thaws were eroding the icecap, the consistency of the snow seemed to change from hour to hour. As Clara trudged up the long driveway, she veered off to the side, where the snow was thin and crusty. Cracking it with just a nudge of her toe, Clara thought it akin to a glaze of confectioner's sugar: fragile but not quite crumbly. She wondered what Beatrice would think of that. The two of them had developed a game of describing the snow's changing texture as accurately as possible.

"Try to describe it in a way that would make sense to someone who has never seen snow before," Beatrice had said. Food analogies often proved the most serviceable.

Clara thought the game made the woman feel better about having so little exposure to the outdoors. The girl liked the challenge to her own powers of communication. And she liked the praise a particularly deft description earned, especially because Beatrice was not a spendthrift with praise. So when Clara came up with the analogy of hard sauce – the Christmas pudding topper made from brown sugar, butter, and brandy – Beatrice's reaction meant she had come up with a real winner: "Oh, that's just perfect! Yes, snow really does acquire that thick, granular feel sometimes, doesn't it?"

Clara let herself into the house. On the kitchen counter lay a note, a request to turn the oven on to three-hundred-fifty degrees at five forty-five if Beatrice wasn't back yet, a reminder of the cookies up for grabs in the fridge, and an exhortation to watch for signs of distress in Reine when she grained the llamas.

Beatrice was in her office, as usual, with Ralph, who didn't even yodel a hello as Clara walked up the drive. The teenager felt glum. She didn't mind the chores. She liked the llamas. But it was so lonely to come "home" to an empty house, though Clara was certainly used to the phenomenon.

Rarely was her mother home when the school day ended. But it was worse here. When she and Beatrice cooked together and talked, life didn't feel so uprooted. But in this silent kitchen, Clara's sense of loss echoed off the walls.

Besides, she had something to share. She wished some of her family members were around. Well, maybe not her mother, who rarely focused on any of Clara's anecdotes about school. Even her father, although always happy to have Clara around, was often too preoccupied with some chore to pay much attention to his daughter's chatter. Ben was a good audience, however, and she imagined he would be delighted to listen to what she had to say today.

Ben had taken her out twice since Clara relocated to Beatrice's, once for the whole day. They drove over to Marlboro County, site of the nearest movie theater, to watch the latest Pixar release. Clara had complained she was too mature for such childish fare, but she fell in love with the animation, the characters, the plot. She and Ben dissected the characters' motives over a pizza blowout. After that came a trip to an old-fashioned ice-cream parlor in Marlboro Old Town. It was a wonderful day Clara wished would never end.

She had yet to see her mother or father since the move. Eltie had stopped by just once, in between farm calls.

Clara found it ironic that her most frequent visitor was not a family member at all. Vaughn would show up in the late afternoon several times a week. She always brought food, sometimes an entire meal. Vaughn was an old-school cook: southern dishes, sinful desserts. She would usually make her appearance before Beatrice returned from the office, during the silent kitchen hours Clara had come to dread.

Beatrice also seemed happy about Vaughn's visits. After the first few drop-offs (ham and biscuits, lasagna, black-bottom pie, and cornbread), Beatrice urged Clara to write a heartfelt thank-you. A note of gratitude struck Clara as quaint. She had never written one. With family, you just thanked them when you saw them. And Vaughn was sort of like family.

But Beatrice was adamant. "Letters may strike you as old-fashioned, but you should never take a kindness for granted. People who do kind things are rarer than you might think. They should be treasured. Writing a note is the least we can do."

So woman and girl sat at the kitchen table with two yellow legal pads and jotted down their thoughts about Vaughn's visits. Unable to resist playing editor, Beatrice chopped here and added there, but Clara's words were still recognizable as her own. The note included one paragraph by each author in her own inked penmanship.

Several visits later, Vaughn said, "Do you know how long it's been since I received a thank-you note, child? Well, I can tell you it's been quite a long time. And it meant a lot to me, dear, especially the part about enjoying my company."

Fearing the little woman might cry, Clara squirmed in her chair. But she was glad she had written the note.

Vaughn had appreciated being appreciated, even by a kid writing a few words, Clara thought, as she finished up the llama chores. Appreciation was something she badly wanted herself. So she steeled herself to go in search of it.

Beatrice's office was a no-man's land. Clara had seldom been there. It had an atmosphere of tension, time constraints, organized chaos—with papers scattered not only about Beatrice's desk but also on the floor. There was some inscrutable system to all of it, apparently. If Clara accidentally dislocated one of the papers lying on the floor, for example, Beatrice would squawk in distress. The Boring Building was not a fun place, and Clara had no guarantee of being welcome there. Once, even after Beatrice had specifically asked Clara to bring something up to the office, the girl was put off by the woman's clipped tones. Beatrice apologized, saying she was hard-pressed to meet a deadline. It was clear, however, she wanted Clara gone as soon as possible.

But here she was, knocking, uninvited, on the office door. Ralph barked twice then wiggled forward with a sloppy greeting. Beatrice, on the other hand, did not even turn her head Clara's way but kept focused on the computer screen. She raised an index finger to counsel silence, until the sentence in her head crawled across her computer screen.

"Okay, what's up? Anything wrong with Reine?"

Clara suppressed a sigh.

Of course, you would think of the llamas. You wouldn't think maybe something was wrong with me.

Actually, Clara planned to use the llamas as the pretext for her visit. Reine had been fine, if disagreeable aloofness could be considered fine. But Tess had acted oddly – nice oddly. The llama had walked softly up to Clara, sniffed politely and then, when Clara stroked the fat old girl's wooly neck, Tess had lightly rested her large head on Clara's shoulder. And sighed. The llama showed none of the signs of distress Beatrice had taught Clara to monitor. The ears were forward. There was no "stress wrinkle" beneath the eyes. The tail was not twitching. But the gesture was odd for Tess.

Clara told all this to Beatrice, who listened intently. After mulling over the described events, Beatrice offered, "Maybe she just likes you."

Clara felt absurdly flattered, which emboldened her.

"Beatrice can I show you something?"

"Sure."

Clara extracted from her pocket folded pieces of paper. She handed them over without comment, but Beatrice immediately noticed the large, red A-plus scrawled on the first page. Beatrice looked at the girl expectantly.

"You done good! Before I read it, tell me about the assignment."

Clara said the class was supposed to write journal entries. Most of the kids had written about boyfriends or football games or Christmas vacation. A few of the "drama queens," as she called them, had described their anxiety about passing an exam or going on a first date. Clara said she didn't want to share anything personal. She figured she'd have to make something up. But then she seized on the idea of writing a journal from someone else's perspective. That would be Reine. Clara, writing as if she were the pregnant llama, expressed her resentment at having humans poke and prod her, complained about winter's claustrophobia when the snowcap penned the herd inside the barn, and grumped about the kicking inside her belly.

Beatrice said not a word as she pored over the two pages. She seemed completely absorbed by the words on those pages – Clara's words.

"Clara, this is … stunning. Such empathy is extraordinarily rare for someone so young. And your descriptions are dead on. I can see Reine in your words. It's just wonderful."

Clara beamed.

THIRTY-FIVE

Lost in Thought

As she waited for Tanner to show up for what had become a weekly appointment, Beatrice looked over the copy she had made of Clara's A-plus paper. She was touched at Clara's reaction to praise—and to Beatrice's request for a copy. The girl did not seem to realize her own intelligence. Perhaps that was to be expected, given the less-than-loving mother she had. But Beatrice was surprised nonetheless, because Clara came across as far more mature and self-possessed than most youngsters her age.

She recalled her own childhood and reckoned most adults would have said the same of her. But that maturity offered no protection against a host of insecurities. Doubts about her own intellectual powers might not have numbered among Beatrice's demons, but insufficient nurturing and a surfeit of negative feedback will leave their mark on any child.

Beatrice recognized she was on dangerous ground, however, if she began seeing herself in Clara. That would help no one. She had no desire to be a mother at this stage of life, and she suspected Clara's emotional needs would be far greater than even a far more maternal woman could meet. Still, she found herself feeling compassion for the girl, admiring her, and coming perilously close to feeling a bond.

An exchange of baying interrupted her thoughts.

Swell. Tanner brought Gertrude.

Beatrice was fond of the hound, as was Ralph. But it was hard enough to wheel herself around the small cabin without a rangy, one-hundred-twenty-pound dog taking up precious floor space.

A few minutes lapsed, and neither the dogs nor Tanner showed up at her office door. Rolling herself to the front window, she saw Tanner shaking with laughter, as he watched the dogs chase each other.

When he finally walked in, he was still chuckling. "In most regards," he began, "dogs are morally superior to humankind. They have the best human traits, including the willingness to lay down their lives for a loved one. And they lack most of man's pettiness."

"What prompted this philosophical insight?"

"The scene outside. For all of their virtues, dogs are natural-born thieves. I brought two supposedly indestructible ring-toys, one for each dog. Same exact toy. But for a dog, the best toy is the one another dog has. So for the next five minutes, I watched them repeatedly steal each other's prize. I finally lost track of which ring was the coveted one."

"Dogs are wonderful," Beatrice said, smiling.

"That they are."

"Speaking of wonderful things, check this out." Beatrice handed the copy of Clara's paper to Tanner.

"By your young charge, I assume?"

"Just read it."

Tanner settled on the executive chair, unused as long as Beatrice was in the wheelchair. He slouched forward, elbows on knees, with the stapled papers in both hands. Twice he sniffed, nodding his head backward. Beatrice couldn't tell whether he was stifling a laugh, nodding in appreciation, or sniffing in derision. His face revealed nothing. That unnerved Beatrice. She needed him to validate her opinion about Clara's work and badly wanted to share some of her concerns about Clara. She suddenly realized she valued Tanner's opinions – probably about a lot more than Clara.

He handed the paper back to Beatrice with the same unreadable expression. He stood up and looked out the window.

"I hate this," Tanner finally said.

"You hate Clara's paper?"

"What I hate is waste. I knew the girl was smart. But from this paper, she's clearly gifted. What are the odds her gifts will ever bear fruit? The public schools are bad enough. In fact, I'm surprised that her teacher recognized this essay's insights and creativity. If the girl had parental encouragement, she might have a chance, even with this county's low educational standards. Since the loving mountaineer family has farmed her out to a total stranger, I think we can assume encouragement is not much available. I gather her trashy mother is the reason for that move? What a horror show!"

"I don't know the details. After the kid got her face pummeled, her uncle and cousin took her away from Mommie Dearest. The mother's boyfriend was somehow involved. I shudder to think how."

"I've got a pretty good idea," Tanner said, working his jaw muscles. "So what's with the father? Can't he put his sorry ass on the line for his daughter?"

"Something about work obligations in Virginia. Something about the custody agreement preventing Clara from moving out of state," Beatrice said, shrugging.

"And he's supposed to be the healthy parent? One day the cretin will realize what he missed out on. And it will be too late."

Gone was the patrician detachment. Beatrice didn't necessarily think this was the "real" Tanner, but the angry, sad man in her office was revealing a persona new to her. And she thought this persona might just fit into Revere's blue-collar milieu, unlike the silverback who had held court from the apron of his imposing stone hearth weeks earlier.

"Have a care, Hillwilla. Those synapses are smoldering."

Raising her eyes from the assessment process going on inside her brain, Beatrice met Tanner's slightly defensive stare. As she did, inspiration hit: "Are you flashing back to your own childhood, or do you know something about fatherhood yourself?"

Beatrice instantly regretted the exultant tone to her voice. By the flash of anger that briefly glittered in Tanner's pale blue eyes, she knew she had hit pay dirt. It was ridiculous, she thought, that she had already put in so much time on this man's autobiography without being able to pin him down about such basic vitals as marital history. He would only allude vaguely to an early, failed marriage, with the comment that he had no intention of violating his ex-wife's privacy by writing about it. He would not say when he married, whom he married, how long they were married, or if there were any children. He would not budge and would usually divert her with some other aspect of his life that needed further exploration.

Availing herself of several Web sites that assisted genealogical searches, for a small fee, Beatrice had tried to ferret out the information herself. She found three Boston-area marriage certificates for three William Berrigans in the era when Tanner would have been in his twenties. Each of the grooms had been born in the same year as Tanner, but other particulars were off. Since the young Tanner started his travels at an early age, including some interesting summer jobs while at Harvard, Beatrice realized she could not assume the Boston area was the venue for his ill-starred wedding. She abandoned her search.

But now she wondered again about one of the three certificates, the only one from Revere. What was the bride's name? Something Irish. Did that mean a Gaelic name? No, no, that didn't sound right.

For a few minutes, Beatrice disconnected and became lost in her own thoughts.

Oh crap, it happened again.

She snapped back – uncomfortably aware of Tanner's disapproving and slightly alarmed stare.

"Care to tell me what just occurred?" he asked.

And then it came to her. It wasn't the name that was unusually Irish. It was the bride's place of birth. "Millstreet, County Cork!" she said.

Once again, she was dead on target. This time, there was no anger in Tanner's eyes, but sadness clouded them.

THIRTY-SIX

An Ish Day

For the next hour, Beatrice and Tanner haggled. He argued certain things about his life must remain private. She pointed out that writing an autobiography was not a stellar way to safeguard privacy.

Finally, Tanner agreed to a chapter about his former wife but only if "Patty" gave her prior consent. For now, he would say nothing about the marriage.

Beatrice fretted over how long it would take Tanner to consult with his ex-wife. He offered no time frame for the event and was maddeningly indifferent to the looming deadline.

Their tenuous rapport in danger of fraying, Tanner concocted a halfway-plausible excuse for cutting their meeting short. He retrieved Gertrude's ring-toy, scratched Ralph on the head, and whistled at the hound to follow him out.

Slow to respond at first, Gertrude broke into a Wile E. Coyote trot. Beatrice could almost hear the piano keys plunking out each exaggeratedly arched canine footfall. The large dog kept her head tucked into her chest, while her eyebrow whiskers twitched left and right. Her pendulous flews concealed the object she was stealing, but the two humans had no doubt what it was. In a practiced motion, Tanner stooped slightly, pulled back the loose folds on Gertrude's nape with his left hand, while his right hand disappeared inside the dog's mouth and fished out Ralph's ring-toy, covered with saliva. He held the sloppy trophy off to his right side, where Ralph suddenly and silently appeared, swiftly closed a soft mouth on the ring, and trotted to the back of the cabin – reprising Gertrude's earlier twinkle-toed gait. Tanner pivoted sharply to block Gertrude from following the setter.

The two humans shook their heads in amusement – and relief. They were glad the canine thievery had broken the tension, so the meeting would end on a light note.

As she watched Tanner's tall frame disappear in the swale between office and home, Beatrice felt tired. The Fordyce project was getting more and more complicated. So was her connection to Fordyce. She was starting to doubt she could pull together anything worth reading. Meanwhile, her regular job was suffering—the job that paid the mortgage—and this was just one more reminder how little in Beatrice's life was flowing smoothly.

She suddenly noticed she had forgotten to flip the calendar page from February to March. The calendar's compilers seemed to think March marked a radical climatic change. Apparently it did for the North Carolina garden that was the focus of all twelve photographs in the wall hanging. Beatrice had liked the clever concept when she ordered the calendar online. Shot from different angles, the same well-landscaped garden progressed gradually through the seasons, as it was visited by different flora and fauna.

Taken on an overcast day, the February photograph displayed a wrought-iron bench, dusted with snow and nestled beneath the naked branches of a dogwood, artfully pruned to encourage graceful curves. The photographed garden scene had blended smoothly with the wild white spaces outside Beatrice's window.

The real-life scene currently framed by her window, however, had little in common with that North Carolina garden in March, where daffodils and hyacinths exploded in yellow and white and provided a vivid contrast with a fat, rufous-sided towhee pecking at the dull green grass. The calendar colors were gentle compared with the retina-searing greens that would follow in April and May. Nevertheless, they covered far more of the spectrum than Beatrice's terrain, which had lost most of its snow but still offered a bleak choice of colors. The whites and grays of January had given way to subdued yellows and browns: yellow grass, pockmarked by brown mounds of earth churned up by groundhogs and moles in search of thawed roots that would provide some meager hydration and nourishment. The birds visiting the three-dimensional yard, as opposed to the two-dimensional one above her desk, were far from spring plumage. In their dull greenish-yellowish feathers, the goldfinches frenetically searching for seeds were about as colorful as the dead plants they probed.

There was much about March that merited the qualifying "ish," Beatrice thought. The first half was winterish; the second half springish. The temperature ranged between coldish and warmish, unless the wind was howling through the hollows.

Beatrice had frittered away an hour since Tanner's departure and had accomplished nothing. Unable to gear up just yet to edit the article Wolfgang needed by close of business, she thought she would ease her way back to the tasks at hand by checking e-mail first.

Repeatedly clicking DELETE without opening the trash in her inbox, Beatrice nearly missed an item she had been awaiting for a week. One of Wolfgang's PhD puffballs, active in Harvard alumni affairs, had responded to her request and ferreted out copies of the Harvard yearbook and the Harvard directory for the year when Tanner got his BA, plus the freshman register of four years earlier. The alumnus had already sent them off to Beatrice by snail mail. As she dashed off a thank-you by e-mail, she wondered if the postal gift would give her any useful grist, any reason to anticipate a turn for the better in the Fordyce project.

As she clicked on the SEND icon, the numeral 1 appeared beside the inbox. Grateful for another opportunity to delay tackling her editing deadline, Beatrice promptly navigated to the incoming message. She was surprised to see Tanner's name as the author.

She was even more surprised by the content of Tanner's message. He said he had alerted his ex-wife to Beatrice's interest in including a chapter on the marriage. He provided Patricia Scanlon's address and phone number—and his conditions: If Patty was amenable to an interview, then Beatrice had his blessing; if his ex-wife was not receptive, the subject of his failed marriage would be off-limits. Forever.

It was good news in terms of moving forward with the autobiography. But Beatrice also knew her chat with Patricia Scanlon would require the right touch. Somehow, she would have to come across as trustworthy, while asking nosy questions. She had no idea what kind of relationship had been birthed by the divorce. Animosity could make Patty eager to dish. But if the parting had been more sad than acrimonious, the former wife could be reluctant to pick at old scabs. Then again, some exes retained strong loyalty toward one another. Given Tanner's stated concern for Patty's feelings, Beatrice suspected loyalty played some part in the emotional dynamic between the two Revere natives.

In other words, Tanner was likely to hear chapter and verse from his ex about Beatrice's initial conversation with her. In other words, Beatrice needed to fine-tune her approach. While keeping an eye on the book's priorities and the personal information readers would expect, she had to factor in the conflicting priorities of the two subjects at hand.

She didn't have the energy for that just now. So she let her eyes wander back to the e-mail inbox, where she noticed for the first time that the helpful Harvard alumnus's message contained an attachment. Double clicking on it, she saw several scanned pages from the Harvard directory. Under the Fs were Tanner's address and phone number. He had apparently lived off campus. Was that a sign of an outcast, Beatrice wondered? Then she remembered he was older than most of his classmates. Perhaps he simply felt too mature for campus life.

The helpful alumnus also included the appropriate page under the Bs, because Beatrice had also expressed interest in finding a William Berrigan. There was no listing. The name change, as her earlier research indicated, was already a done deal.

Inexplicably, the attachment included other directory pages, seemingly at random. Beatrice scanned down the various listings and wondered why the alumnus had sent them. Then she noticed a listing for "Bohr, Prof. Teddy S." She remembered from decades earlier how some of her dorm mates would get their hands on the Harvard directory to look for the bogus names. She rather liked the tediously boring professor. It became a game to look for the pun on each of the attached pages. Yup, under S there was "Sorgen, E. Norma." Under W was "Wicke, Tyne E." Under D was "Dingh, Lakhshmi." Beatrice wondered if the phallic preoccupation of the Harvard students of her and Tanner's eras continued into the twenty-first century, decades since women supposedly started roaring.

Of course, it has.

She conceded that some of the entries were clever—or at least clever-ish.

THIRTY-SEVEN

Problems in the Nest

The scouts, up north for a while now, chirped warnings to the other boys: "Steer clear of this nest site. It's mine!" Or so Ben imagined. All he could hear was the dull, raspy *fizzbee, fizzbee,* from the male phoebes. Already, some of them were frenetically poking around in the brush for just the right twig or piece of moss to deposit in the chosen location.

Ben was sitting inside his truck with binoculars perched on the dash. On the seat beside him were a power-return tape measure and sheets of graph paper, which he had been using to chart the layout of the fencing and gates he would soon install in the Cutlip pasture. He had done the layout days earlier, but if anyone wondered why his truck was there, he had a reasonable cover story.

Ben loved birding and had compiled a respectable life list. But not one of his crew knew about his hobby, and he planned to keep it that way. Seneca County men might shoot ruffed grouse and wild turkey to put on the table. But they certainly didn't look at them through binoculars or spotting scopes.

Mike, of course, knew about Ben's secret because he, too, had learned the difference between a phoebe and a peewee at an early age. Their mother was fanatical about birding. When the boys were old enough to trot along beside her—but not old enough to be mortified—Mary Moriarty Buckhalter would pack them up, along with a picnic lunch, and head off for her favorite birding site, where field and woods and creek came together. It was part of several hundred acres held by an absentee landowner who belonged to Mary's church. She had asked his permission to trespass, and he happily agreed, as long as she avoided buck season.

For Mary, this was the best part about living in Seneca County, a birder's paradise. Her enthusiasm was infectious. For Mike, the excursions were a happy excuse to wobble along the slime-slick creek rocks in search of blue fossils that polished up like gemstones. For Ben, the birds themselves were reward enough.

Today's excursion to the Cutlip pasture was Ben's self-prescribed therapy to chase away the blues lingering after his visit with Clara. An occasional outing to a movie or ice cream shop, he realized, was a half-assed way to make a child feel loved and secure, when she had just learned she was not the top priority for a single member of her extended family. In their earlier outings, Clara had acted eager to please, desperate to prolong her time with Ben. This time was different. Ben was shocked when Clara didn't want to check out his neighbor's new filly, because she needed to go "home" and study for an upcoming math test. "Home?" he asked wistfully. "Is that how you think of Beatrice's place, honey?" Staring out the passenger window, she replied, "I don't guess I can call your place home, can I?"

Now he was the one staring out the truck window, but having difficulty concentrating on the avian adventures outside. He was focused on heavier fare, like why some children had to endure such a difficult start in life. He and Mike had been so lucky. Why couldn't they pass along their carefree childhood to the next generation? Their father kept a sturdy roof over their heads and plenty of food on the table.

As for Ma, well, she was The Phenomenal Nails. That was what Ben and Mike called her for a while when they were in their teens. They had bragged to their buddies that their mother was tough as nails. At five feet, two inches, she reduced their two-hundred-fifty-pound football coach to a fidgety five-year-old, after he tried to bully Ben into playing with a blown-out bursa in his knee. She rarely raised her voice. She just had a way of holding your eye that was other-worldly.

Ma was also fun. She had incredibly accurate aim with a pressurized can of whipped cream. Her Halloween party was the talk of Ben's sixth grade buddies, who had initially affected ennui as, blindfolded, they followed Ma's creepily whispered instructions to sample the peeled grape eyeballs and spaghetti brains of lost souls. But by the time she unleashed the hay-stuffed witch, speeding down a zip-line from the second floor of the Buckhalter house, while Ma's visiting sister, hiding beneath an upstairs window, let loose with a banshee wail, even the toughest tweens squealed like piglets.

Ben wished Clara could have experienced a party like that. But then he recalled his last birding expedition with his mother, the annual Christmas bird count, that Audubon-sponsored snapshot of bird populations all over the country. She had insisted on participating, even though she was dying of emphysema. Ben reluctantly camped out with her in his truck, parked at one of the designated observation sites. He kept the engine running and the heater on and wouldn't let her leave the vehicle. He plied her with hot tea from a thermos.

Probably because of the engine noise, their count was disappointing, and they had a lot of free time between bird sightings. Mary wanted to spend the time with talk—about maternal guilt. "What the heck do you have to feel guilty about, Ma?" he asked.

"What a lousy model your Pop and I were for you boys. No emotion. No connection."

"What are you talking about?"

"I loved your father, Benjy, truly I did. But I was never in love with him. Truth be told, I felt sorry for him at first. There he was so alone and out of place at that Baltimore factory, the same place where my Da worked.

"Carl was just one of so many West Virginians who headed north and east in search of work they couldn't find back home. They all had that stricken look. They pined for their mountains, their clear, swift-running streams. They longed for green spaces and quiet.

"The city folk were none too kind about Carl's ill-fitting clothes and clumsy backwoods ways. So Carl willingly put up with the Moriarty clan, with all our rowdiness, because we didn't laugh at him. We stuffed him with food and gave him back a sense of kin. I thought of him as a sweet, stray puppy." A coughing fit interrupted Mary's story.

Ben pointed out that his father never seemed much like a vulnerable pup to him. Pop was strong and strong-minded, sure of what life was all about.

"Bullshit!" interrupted Mary, whose language was becoming more abrupt as her time was running out. "He was a good provider. But Carl was sure of only two things. That he would never, ever leave home again. And that he wanted nothing to do with anything or anyone different from him. He hated blacks and city folk. He hated Republicans, come-heres, people with money. He hated Jews, and he was none too fond of my Papist ways.

"I knew all that when I married him. But I figured I could change him, at least soften him. I couldn't. Oh, don't get me wrong. I was no victim. I saw him as someone who'd never leave me, never raise a hand to me. What did it matter, I thought, if we never really connected?

"But those first ten years, those years when I thought we'd never have kids, were so hard. I felt so alone. I was so starved for the touch of his hand."

Ben twitched in his seat. His discomfort prompted a wheezy cackle from his mother. "Oh, Jesus, Mary and Joseph! I'm not talking sex. I came from a touchy family. You know how your aunts are. Rose, May, and me, our Ma and Da—we talked all at once, about everything. When we made a point, we'd punch an arm. We'd swat a thigh after a good joke. We'd cry at each other's tragedies, big and small. We'd yell at each other when we were mad. And we'd forgive each other anything.

"That's what family should be. Not that polite, wordless distance between Carl and me. Him on his recliner. Me on the far end of the couch. The TV on. And that filtered down to you and Mikey. Carl didn't want me to 'fuss over' you boys, as he called it. It would make you soft, he said. So after a while I distanced myself some from you boys, too. Stupid me.

"So, look who you two married! You boys were so starved for emotion that Charyce's sexpot bitchiness and Amanda's never-ending personal dramas actually looked appealing."

Mary had reached over the stick shift and squeezed Ben's knee. Hard. "I'm so sorry, honey."

Looking out the window of a different truck, years after that conversation, Ben wondered how many of the male phoebes' clumsy pre-nests would survive. He knew that, in a few weeks, the ladies would wing up north and bank smartly into the Cutlip barn for an inspection. He knew some of the female phoebes would stab in disgust at their mates' nests. They would not merely reject the sites; they would dismantle the construction twiglet by twiglet and painstakingly transport the building materials to another, better site, while Mr. Phoebe chirped his frustration.

Ben felt frustrated, too. His mother had deconstructed his childhood. His wife had thwarted his plans for saving Clara. Clara had stonewalled his efforts to make nice. Ben felt as useless as those avian scouts soon would.

THIRTY-EIGHT

Happy Hour

The spring peepers did not have their usual cheering effect on Eltie, even though their song was sufficiently ebullient to permeate closed windows and doors. As a veterinarian, Eltie felt reverence for the life force in all animals – particularly for seemingly fragile creatures that were nonetheless capable not only of surviving an Appalachian winter but defying it. More than two months before the last frost, more than one month before the last shovelable snow, the little amphibians were celebrating the sudden and gloriously balmy weather.

They were calling for mates even as the numbers in Eltie's digital thermometer flashed a steady decline. The thermometer would read twenty degrees within a few hours of the next dawn. The vet knew the tiny tree frogs were perfectly capable of hunkering down in the duff through winter. They would enter a dormant state, in which glucose, produced in the liver, would keep vital organs from freezing. But Eltie found herself fretting over how much of that nourishment was being expended in the raucous chorus outside. It depressed her to think of thousands of little semi-frozen frogs, haphazardly diving back under the leaves to wait for the next warm spell, in the hope sufficient numbers of worms and other invertebrate delicacies would wriggle far enough toward the sun to become breakfast.

Frogs hope?

Eltie recalled more than a few lectures against anthropomorphizing. "Indulge your fantasies on your own time, if you must, Ms. Davis," one particularly misogynistic professor had sneered, "but the bloat twisting Rover's gut won't wait for you to stop compromising your diagnostic responsibility with your bathetic female intuition."

Bastard!

Well into his sixties at the time, her perpetually annoyed professor longed for the days when females were rare in his classes.

Memories of the contempt she experienced in vet school – because of her gender, because of her West Virginia accent, because of her age, because of her large frame – added to Eltie's weariness. She knew, of course, neither those memories nor the imperiled peepers were the primary reason for her funk. That would be Clara.

"Shit!" Eltie groused softly and then looked quickly around to see if Vaughn was within hearing distance. Vaughn disapproved of coarse speech, just as she disapproved of Eltie forgetting to stow her work boots on the rubber mat by the back door. Eltie had again forgotten, which explained the ejaculation when she saw her scuffed-up size-tens lying akimbo beneath the coffee table. In her stocking feet, she padded across the living room to remove the evidence. She might have gotten away clean, except Gracie clattered along beside her. For a little dog, the Boston terrier made a ridiculous amount of noise.

Eltie chided herself for her grumpiness. She was enormously fond of Gracie, even though a Boston terrier was not her first choice as dog of the manor. But it was the first choice of Vaughn, who confessed to feeling intimidated by the large dogs that ranked high in Eltie's affections. Pleasing Vaughn was not normally a problem. But it had been a tough day, and she didn't feel like tucking her boots away or censoring her language.

Thanks to Gracie, Vaughn, peering out from the kitchen, saw the boots in Eltie's hand. The small woman merely smiled at her partner. As Eltie headed back to the living room, Vaughn pressed a full glass of wine into her hand. "I think you need this," she said.

Eltie took the glass and padded into the kitchen, where she took up a stool and gratefully watched the dinner preparations. Gracie clattered onto the tiled floor in bright expectation of some tasty morsel falling off the kitchen counter.

"Our little family," Eltie said, tugging gently on the dog's pointy ears. "Helluva lot lighter on the soul than the family with shared DNA."

"Difficult visit with Clara?" Vaughn asked, as she stirred the onions sautéing over a low flame.

Eltie didn't know where to begin. There had been no "scene," as Meemaw Buckhalter would have said. Clara had not been overtly rude. But there was something sullen about her. Eltie wished she could write it off to the terrible teens. Except Clara was hardly a typical teen, any more than she had been a typical ten-year-old or typical toddler. Clara had always been exceptional: bright, enthusiastic, with a strong work ethic and unusual empathy for adults and playmates alike.

As she explained these impressions to Vaughn, Eltie realized that expectations of Clara had always been high. The child had very little opportunity to be just a child. "Maybe that's why all of us have let her end up in this mess. We expect she'll be able to handle it the way adults have to handle tough times," she said.

"Clara seemed to be handling things all right when I saw her yesterday."

"Really? Well, I don't expect she's mad at you. That and she's a sucker for your pecan cookies."

Vaughn smiled at the flattery but objected. "Why would she be mad at you? You didn't strike her or inflict Rodney Madsen on her."

"No, but I was someone else who let her down," Eltie began but then realized she was on dangerous ground. Clara would, after all, be living here right now if it weren't for Vaughn. No, Eltie corrected herself, it was not because of Vaughn; it was because of what she and Vaughn had together. And that had to take priority over the needs of a second cousin, twice removed, no matter how endearing and worthy the girl was.

"You did not let her down, sweetie. Why, you're the one who figured out a solution. You're the one who found Clara a safe harbor."

"Safe harbor in a strange land," Eltie argued. "Strange woman."

"Beatrice seems perfectly nice to me," Vaughn said distractedly, as she checked a three-by-five recipe card."

"I think she's a drunk. I've smelled whiskey on her breath a few times. The first time I met her she looked like she had a major hangover."

"Well, she's certainly been sober every time I've stopped by. And very polite and well spoken, too."

Eltie wondered if her partner was deliberately obfuscating in an effort to whitewash Eltie's guilt, or whether she truly did believe Beatrice was a worthy guardian. In either event, she was annoyed. "Well-spoken – or just plain phony?"

"Oh, sweetie, you think anyone who wasn't born in Seneca County is suspect. As I recall, you had your suspicions about me, too, at first, with my Eastern Shore ways."

Eltie braced, wondering if this was a complaint about the truly snotty way she had treated Vaughn at first. Vaughn certainly was different, but her refinement was not the problem. It was the evolution she had brought about in Eltie, a woman who had spent her first thirty-odd years sidestepping any meaningful connection, with men or women.

"But then my irresistible charm kicked in," Vaughn added flirtatiously, while focusing on the roux just starting to bubble.

The potential for conflict dissipated; Eltie suddenly felt relieved. Maybe it was the wine. More likely it was Vaughn. Eltie didn't buy Vaughn's version of Clara's alleged rescue. But the fact that Vaughn seemed to believe it eased some of the guilt. Having someone who saw you as noble made you feel just a little bit noble. Being loved, after all, meant you must be doing something right.

"Is the pregnant llama doing okay?" Vaughn asked.

"Aw, hell, I don't know. Beatrice says the llama is acting off. But I can't find nothing wrong. I don't figure the woman has much savvy when it comes to livestock. Then again, lots of owners are in tune with their critters. Especially female owners. And sometimes that instinct nips major problems in the bud."

Take that, Professor Edgarton!

"Maybe Beatrice's instincts will nip some of Clara's problems, too."

"You really think so?"

"She just might be what Clara needs right now. Someone different. Someone smart. Someone older. Someone who knows a thing or two about life."

"How do you figure?"

"I have good instincts, too, sweetie. And they tell me Beatrice has had more than her share of troubles and seen her way through them – for the most part, at least. That's a useful thing for Clara to see right now."

Eltie was skeptical. But she could live with her doubts, which suddenly didn't weigh quite so heavily on her.

THIRTY-NINE

Whack-a-Maul

Arthur Stuart jammed the wadded handkerchief into a back pocket of his jeans and repositioned his glasses from top of head to bridge of nose. His brow was a bit drier, but his eyes still stung from the salt in his own sweat. There was a dusting of fresh snow on the greening paddock, devoid of animals now except for the gray tabby perched on a fencepost. With front paws tucked against her soft belly, she shivered briefly, hinting that she and her human would be much more comfortable inside, in front of a cheerful hearth fire.

The cold bite of the random flakes felt good to Arthur, who bent over to insert another metal wedge into the crack just starting on the six-foot length of red oak. He knew he should be researching an upcoming case at his law office. At very least, he should be hunting for the missing utility bills his accountant needed before tax time got any closer.

Instead, Arthur grasped the maul. With one hand he swung it over his right shoulder and, with the down stroke, hit the wedge cleanly, coaxing a highly satisfying crack from the wood. The rail was now hanging on by a shred, which Arthur deftly dismembered with a short whack from an ax. Scooping up the rail with one gloved hand, he tossed it onto the other dozen rails he had split that Saturday afternoon.

Arthur had no plan for the split rails. Perhaps he would build an accent fence for the lilies he was thinking of planting south of the garage when the weather got better.

Unlike some recently widowed men, Arthur was not sinking into physical decline. He had a big frame, a certain amount of vanity, and a lot of discipline. All of which meant he was damned if he was going to be fat as well as sad.

Besides, physical work was one of the few things that made him feel better. He still savored the feeling of hard labor. Nor had he lost his love of gardening. And he still enjoyed keeping his and Kate's farm well-tended.

He would not let his fifty-six-year-old body go to seed. He wasn't so sure about his fifty-six-year-old mind.

It surprised Arthur how grief could still surprise him. Unsettled dreams plagued his sleep. It wasn't as if he had circled the date on the calendar and told himself to obsess about the anniversary of Kate's death. In fact, he would have been hard-pressed to remember the precise date, if it had not entailed some irony: the first day of spring, with all its implications of rebirth and new life. "Shoulda been the Ides of March, instead," Arthur grumbled, as he rolled another bole into place.

The previous night's dream had replayed only part of the reality of that first vernal day forty-nine weeks earlier. Once again, his brain suffered him the sight of his stricken wife, lying on the ground. At least the ground one year ago was soft and green. In the dream, as in real life, he briefly thought Kate had decided to take a nap on the grass, because there was no sign of accident, no bruising. Arthur tried to tell himself there was nothing unusual about the dramatic positioning of her limbs (the result of multiple seizures just before death). Arthur tried to tell himself there was nothing strange about his wife's head, although some swelling was evident from the subarachnoid hemorrhage—which, ironically, eased once Kate's heart stopped pumping.

In the dream, as in real life, Arthur did what everyone does in such ghastly circumstances: He called to Kate, bent down, nudged her shoulder then shook her. He shook her far more roughly than he would ever risk shaking her had she been merely sleeping. He wanted to shake Death out of her. And then he sat back on his heels in the certainty that Kate was long gone. He did not cry. He did not call her name. He hugged his knees while rocking slightly to and fro and gazed, unfocused, into the far pasture.

Arthur had no idea how long he did that, but when he again looked down at his wife, he suddenly became repelled. That thing was not his Kate but dead meat. He still felt vaguely guilty about how badly he wanted to put distance between himself and the body. But he knew that vultures could get at her before the EMTs arrived. So he picked her up and carried her inside. Even though he found her before rigor mortis had set in, he was surprised at how difficult it was for him – almost seventy pounds heavier than his lithe, athletic wife – to pick her up. Dead weight, he thought grimly. After he deposited the body on the sofa, an item of furniture that would end up at the county landfill before the week was over, and after he called 911, Arthur headed for the downstairs bathroom and threw up.

The previous night's dream had reprised in exacting detail all of those unlovely events. But the dream added a proximate cause to the circumstances of Kate's death. In the dream, Kate was chasing llamas in the pasture. Graf, the herd sire, had jumped a fence to get at the girls. Dream-Kate was dashing to close a high gate that would have a greater likelihood of keeping the intact male from the llama ladies. The exertion caused the ballooned artery to rupture, or so went the plot line in Arthur's dream.

In reality, Kate's death had no such logic. Graf had indeed run out of his paddock and into the girls' paddock. But that happened one month after Kate was in the grave. The randy llama did not need to jump any fences, after a distracted Arthur failed to latch not just one gate, but two. Arthur meant to ship the llamas off to Beatrice's farm much earlier, but he had a million other details to handle. And so, Beatrice would get one more llama than anticipated: the fetus growing inside Reine.

Leaning on the maul, Arthur thought once again of the utter illogic of every aspect of Kate's death. Sure, his wife was no longer young, but one look at her and you could see her physiological age was almost a decade younger than what the calendar said. Except of course for that aneurysm.

Even that was illogical. There was no family history of aneurysms. Kate was a natural athlete who took excellent care of herself. She never had high blood pressure. She never smoked. She never drank more than the occasional glass of wine. And she certainly never used illegal stimulants like cocaine. Even the migraines from which she had suffered for decades had no correlation to the little brain balloon that killed her.

The migraines merely prompted a new doctor, certain he could come up with more effective treatment than his predecessors, to look more closely at Kate's brain. An MRI revealed an unruptured aneurysm – of nasty size and nastier location. Nevertheless, the neurologist with whom Kate consulted had cheerfully predicted a thirty-five-percent likelihood that surgical "clipping" would solve the problem, with surmountable side effects. Kate didn't like the odds. She really didn't like the strong possibility of catastrophic consequences. After learning she probably had been harboring the aneurysm for years without symptoms, she decided to take her chances.

Arthur knew none of this until two weeks before Kate's death. Beatrice, however, had been aware of the diagnosis since the day Kate received the MRI results, months earlier. Beatrice had accompanied Kate to the appointment with the neurologist.

Arthur couldn't forgive Beatrice for that. She should have told him. He would have had more time to use his lawyer's logic on Kate. He would have persuaded her to have the surgery, and he would have seen to it that his wife got well. Kate would be alive today. He wouldn't be out here scratching the wood chips clinging to his sweaty skin. He would be arguing with Kate over where to position the lily bed.

Intellectually, he knew his logic would have had no impact on Kate, who had the strongest will of anyone he had ever known. Intellectually, Arthur also knew Beatrice faced a tough dilemma: honor the trust Kate had placed in her and thereby abet Kate's appalling choice to exclude her whole family from the decision-making process; or rat Kate out and most likely lose her closest friendship, one dating back almost forty years, with the strong possibility Kate would be just as dead anyway. But Arthur resented Beatrice nonetheless, partly because he knew the dilemma was nowhere near as difficult for her as it would have been for him. Beatrice was one of those black-and-white people. He might admire individuals who always seemed certain of their course of action, but he often found them annoying.

Arthur crashed the maul into the first wedge on the new bole. For just an instant, he imagined he was smashing Beatrice's head then shuddered at the uncharacteristically savage thought. One blown-out brain was quite enough. Besides, Arthur dimly recognized that Beatrice was merely a convenient focus for his anger. The one he was really furious with was Kate – for excluding him, for leaving him.

FORTY

Tough Cookies

The call to Patty Scanlon was long overdue, Beatrice admitted. She told herself she needed to catch up on the backlog in her day job. She told herself the pressure was off, because Evie and Bart's publisher friend had worked out an arrangement to postpone the publication deadline. But none of that was why Beatrice kept putting off the call.

She was afraid she would learn something about Tanner that could jeopardize the personal dynamic developing between them. She also didn't like going into a possible confrontation with so little information. Beatrice had no idea if Patty had been coerced into cooperating or would be a willing partner in conversation. Beatrice knew only she was inserting herself into a relationship about which she was completely ignorant.

She had steeled herself to make the call as soon as the workday began, but it took three cups of tea before she tapped out the number.

A vigorous, deep voice answered, and Beatrice wasn't sure whether a woman or a man was on the other end of the line. "May I speak with Patricia Scanlon?" she asked.

"This is Patty."

Beatrice noticed no brogue, but even the first few words revealed a heavy Boston accent. She identified herself, somewhat clumsily, and gave a brief explanation of her reason for calling, a reason she hoped was old news. Patty gave no hint of recognition, so Beatrice plodded on, fleshing out the details.

"So how's the leg doing?" Patty interrupted.

Startled, Beatrice said she was just fine, thanks, and pressed on with her agenda.

"So how many weeks of non-weight-bearing ya got left?" Patty interrupted again. Before Beatrice could answer, Patty added that she was a physical therapist, and the drill on tibial depression fractures varied widely.

"Umm, another week, and then if I get the okay from the orthopedist, I can progress to a single crutch."

"Not a walker?" Patty asked, pronouncing the word, "walk-uh."

Beatrice decided the medical chit-chat was a useful way of breaking the ice. She explained she was alternating between a wheelchair and crutches, so a single crutch should be a snap. She couldn't help bristling a bit at the assumption she would be shuffling around with a walker.

"You're a whole lot better off than most women your age, if you can handle crutches. How much you weigh?"

This is getting ridiculous.

Yet Beatrice answered and received the assurance that a thin frame should make her recovery easier. She interrupted Patty before the physical therapist could share more of her wisdom. "Can I get you to fill in some of the blanks for the autobiography? The publisher thinks we can't omit something as important as Tanner's only marriage. Maybe we could start with dates – when you first met Tanner? When you guys got married?"

Beatrice figured it was easier to blame someone else and look like the poor serf doing the scut work. There was a pause, which she let hang in the air.

"I was five years out of nursing school, and Will had just finished his freshman year at Harvard."

"I know Tanner, or Will, was a bit older when he started college, but I'm confused about the dates on the marriage certificate, which was the only way I found out there was a marriage."

"Will is playing things close to the chest again, hey? Yah, and probably talking outta both sides of his mouth, too. Oh don't get me wrong, he's been decent to me and… Even after the divorce, he's stepped up more than a few times. But Himself can be a piece a work."

Beatrice made note of the disjointed sentence. But Patty seemed to be on a roll, and Beatrice didn't want to impede the flow of words.

"Don't trust the certificate. Goddamned clerk was half in the bag when we got the license. Screwed up the dates, and we didn't even notice. I'm six years older than Will. Does that make me a cougar?"

Beatrice chuckled and tried to get Patty to focus on the other question, about when the couple met – a question all the more interesting given the age difference.

But Patty's roll came to a halt. "Lookit, I'm not all that comfortable talking about ancient history over the phone, to someone I never laid eyes on. I'm not saying I won't answer your questions. But I'd like to see you first. Get to know you a bit. And then if we get along okay, well, we can have a little chat. How about you come up here for a sit-down?"

Beatrice, given her less-than-ambulatory state, did not relish the prospect of travel, especially since there was a chance Patty could decide against cooperating anyway. But she had to concede the awkwardness of asking nosy questions over the phone.

"Since we just got an extension on the deadline, I guess I could do that. But I couldn't make it for another two weeks. I'd want to be at least somewhat comfortable gimping on one leg."

Patty said she would need that time to work around the few physical therapy clients she still saw. She explained she was semi-retired but liked to keep her hand in.

The two women exchanged contact details, dates that might work. Beatrice was ready to get off the line, but Patty apparently wanted to linger. As uncomfortable as she was, Beatrice did not want to miss out on any useful information. She waited for Patty's lead.

"So how's Trudy doing?"

"Looks like she's hurting some from arthritis, but that happens to the best of us."

"Ya got that right. Will says Trudy likes you. That's saying something. She's picky, that one."

"He said a lot of bloodhounds can be shy."

"Oh, what a bullshit artist he is. You'd think he invented the breed. He never laid eyes on a bloodhound until he met me. My folks had a series of great hounds, and they were all as friendly as can be. But Trudy always had attitude, even if she's a great old gal. Me, I blame the attitude on the Fordyce factor."

"She certainly has dignity," Beatrice said neutrally, not knowing whether it was dangerous to join in mocking Tanner or whether it would be dangerous to disagree. "I think she thoroughly intimidated my setter at first, but she and Ralph seem to get along now."

Patty wanted to know what kind of setter Ralph was and whether Beatrice hunted with him. She sounded disappointed when she learned neither Ralph nor Beatrice had ever been on a hunting expedition. Then she explained that her bloodhounds – she had "just" two now – were involved in rescue work, mostly for lost campers and hikers. There weren't very many of them in the Boston area, but her "boys" sometimes went off to the Berkshires to help some "goddamned city fool who doesn't know jack about the woods." Patty added she no longer joined in the searches but kept up with the dogs' training and helped oversee the training of other bloodhounds.

Beatrice was beginning to like Patty, even if the woman's abrupt turnabouts could be discomfiting – like when she said, out of the blue, "I think Will likes you."

"What makes you say that?"

"Well, I could be wrong, but he has bitched a lot about you. Will usually blows off people he finds annoying. So even though you annoy the hell out of him, he must find you interesting. Which probably means he can't figure you out. Will figures he's smarter than everybody else. Bastard's probably right most of the time. But not so much with you.

"Now if you were under thirty-five, you could be a bitch on wheels and he'd be interested. Will's not the most enlightened guy, as you've probably noticed. So, what are your intentions?"

Beatrice erupted in laughter. "To finish this writing job without committing homicide or suicide."

"Too bad. He could use a tough cookie to keep him on his toes. Will hasn't been around any tough cookies in a while."

"Since you guys divorced?"

"Goddamned right."

FORTY-ONE

The Weird Sisters

"Shirley, would you come in here a minute?" Evie yelled at the open door to her office.

"'Her voice was ever soft, gentle, and low, an excellent thing in woman,'" chided Shirley, as she appeared in the doorway a few seconds later. The tiny woman was wearing a Bluetooth headset, rakishly framed by subtly blond feathers of well-coiffed hair. An iPad was tucked in the crook of her left arm, while a felt-tipped pen was interlaced through the fingers of her right hand, and the top of a Post-It pad peeked out from the breast pocket of her fitted blazer.

A woman for all seasons, all eventualities, Evie thought admiringly.

"I'm on speaker phone with my friend Beatrice. We're discussing the human condition and need your input. Two questions. First: When's the last time you had sex?"

Shirley closed her eyes in thought before replying, in faux befuddlement, "What decade is this?"

"Gotcha," said Evie. "Next question: When's the last time you had chocolate?"

"What time is it now?" Shirley replied without missing a beat.

"*Quod erat demonstrandum*," shouted Evie toward the phone on her desk, as she released Shirley with a friendly wave. "As I said, chocolate is not a substitute for sex. Sex is a poor substitute for chocolate. Are you aware that women in Ivory Coast retreat to sexually segregated villages after producing the requisite number of progeny to guarantee support in their old age? They spend their remaining decades lounging around, happily celibate, while plucking berries off the nearest cacao bush."

"Rudner's fractured anthropology lessons," said Beatrice. "And are you aware that new unrest has erupted in Ivory Coast, and the rebels have seized the main port for cocoa exports?"

"Omigod! What are we doing mucking around in the Muslim world? Send the Marines to Ivory Coast! Stat! I mean, what's the point of having all those buff young men in uniform if we can't protect vital resources?"

The subject had come up a few minutes earlier, just after Beatrice explored plans to fly to New England to interview Patty Scanlon. Even before checking with Brother Bart, whose house would serve as a comfortable base of operations, Beatrice wanted to see if the airfare could be comped. She was willing to eat the price of the ticket if necessary but had some other ideas that would jack up the price of the business trip. So she wanted to economize where she could.

As soon as Beatrice mentioned the upcoming trip, Evie jumped at the idea of meeting up with her and Bart. At that point sex had reared its ugly head.

It was not that Beatrice was a prude – at least not too much of a prude. She had no idea how far Evie and Bart's relationship had progressed. Nor did she want to know the details. But as soon as Evie declared her interest in staying at Bart's, Beatrice wondered about a possible problem.

"Well, I'm just wondering," she told Evie. "Would things get complicated if I brought Clara up with me? She'll be on Easter break soon, and I was thinking of taking her to Boston. I could use her help getting around while I'm still using a crutch. She's too young to leave alone, and besides it would probably do her good to see the world beyond West Virginia. I'd pay for her ticket myself; write it off as a business expense with the IRS."

"So, what's the problem?"

"Sleeping arrangements."

"Huh? Bart's house is big as a barn. He can certainly put all of us up."

"Are you being deliberately obtuse? Since you're forcing me to spell it out, I'm wondering if I'd catch flak if I exposed Clara to … cohabitation."

Evie burst with laughter. "Once again, I am cast in the role of corrupting influence. What are you, the Taliban? I need my own space, dumbass, and have no desire to crowd my toiletries into Bart's Spartan bedroom. Besides – and no disrespect to your brother – I wouldn't exactly be heartbroken if I never did the deed again."

"You send confusing signals to your fans. I'll bet some of your colleagues think you're shagging legions of young male interns on Capitol Hill."

"Yeah, well, I never miss the chance to keep people guessing. But really, Beatrice, there's a reason we dry up after fifty, despite what those dreadful women's magazines say."

"And that reason is…?"

"So we have a good excuse not to keep having sex, silly girl! I mean, how many times do we have to fake orgasms? How many times do we have to pretend we're hot to trot, when all we really want is to retreat to our own comfortable, solitary beds and sleep through the night without getting jostled by thrashing arms or jolted awake by raucous snores?"

Beatrice started to feel a bit sorry for Bart. She suspected that many post-menopausal women, though not aspiring to the libidinous escapades portrayed in *Cosmopolitan*, did not share Evie's opinion. For the sake of argument, Beatrice raised that possibility over the phone.

It was then Evie brought Shirley into the equation.

After the secretary made her exit, the talk returned to Clara's participation. Beatrice wondered whether the presence of a teenager would prove too much of a damper on the get-together. On the other hand, she added, the girl would soon celebrate a birthday, which was another reason for not abandoning her.

Evie agreed.

"All the more reason to bring her, Beatrice. She's a nice kid, and she could benefit from seeing us in action. Let her know not all women are sluts like her mother or fat, dumb, toothless hags like her grandmother probably is."

"Uh-oh, you aren't gonna start singing 'I am Woman, Hear Me Roar,' are you?" Despite her own weariness with the restrictive stereotypes much of the world—female, as well as male—tried to impose on women, Beatrice could also tire of Evie's vocal feminism. Evie never passed up the opportunity to participate in a pro-choice march in D.C. Nor would she skip a chance to vote for a candidate supporting female quotas in business, even if she herself put competence ahead of gender in her own hiring priorities. Beatrice, on the other hand, supported neither side in the abortion debate. And she believed women politicians were no less likely than their male counterparts to go on the take, betray their constituents, or wage war. Beatrice was an equal-opportunity misanthrope.

“Hey, listen, I don’t have many maternal instincts, but it sure sounds like that kid could use a good role model. Who does she have for examples? That horror show of a mother? The dyke aunt or whatever the vet is? And then there’s you, utterly lacking in any fashion sense.”

“Is ‘dyke’ the politically correct term these days?”

“Who cares? I’m sure the vet is just a dandy role model—so dandy she can’t be bothered taking care of a young relative who gets beat up at home.”

Beatrice had grown well aware that a judgmental streak could suddenly surface in the midst of Evie’s otherwise laissez-faire approach to her fellow humans. She also knew, however, that Evie had no shortage of compassion and had long contributed to a wide variety of charities—not merely to get the tax break or to showcase political correctness. Beatrice doubted Clara had ever encountered anyone like Evie and suspected more exposure would indeed be educational.

“What about taking a side trip to that fancy-schmancy college you and Kate went to?” Evie continued. “The campus isn’t far from Bart’s place in Dover, is it? Wouldn’t it be a kick for an Appalachian kid to break into that place? I’ll bet Wellesley has more poor urban kids from Anacostia than girls from White Trash West Virginia.”

Beatrice found herself bristling at the contempt shown for West Virginia. She wondered if she was acquiring her own Seneca County chip on the shoulder: It was okay for her to gripe about local ways; it was quite another for an outlander to put down her adopted state. Nevertheless, she saw some merit in Evie’s suggestion.

“Clara’s so bright it would be nice for her to see some of the rewards for working hard at school,” Beatrice mused. “And the campus will be exploding with daffodils.”

“Oh goodie, road trip! And along the way, we get to play God with an impressionable young mind. Sounds like just the kind of break I need. So, what dates you got in mind? ‘When shall we three meet again?’”

FORTY-TWO

Straining at the Poop Pile

It all depended on Reine. There was no way Beatrice could clear the decks for any trip if the llama had yet to deliver. If Arthur's recollection of the date of the accidental breeding was accurate, Reine could pop any day now. Beatrice looked at her list of things to do. Even if Reine cooperated, a lot of work remained to prepare for a trip up north.

Beatrice did not look forward to researching the cheapest and most convenient airline deals. Then there was the rental car to consider, because she didn't want to importune her brother by borrowing his wheels. The risk of putting a dent in her brother's shiny new Mercedes made her cringe. The odds of an accident were significant, not merely because of Beatrice's orthopedic problems. The icy switchbacks of Seneca County were child's play compared with just about any driving situation on the mildest spring day in the Boston area.

Metropolitan Boston's traffic planners had long ago designed rotaries, supposedly to facilitate movement through intersections without the cost of installing traffic lights. Merging into a Boston rotary was much like cutting across traffic in downtown Calcutta, where anything less than split-second timing would mean a collision with several cars, overloaded jitneys, bicycle cabs, and cows. As in Calcutta, the Boston driver could not afford any hesitation, as he thrust his vehicle into the fray. The other drivers could smell fear through the exhaust fumes. And they would seize on it, flipping the bird out the window with their left hand while with the right hand jerking the car into the path of the timid—all while screaming colorful obscenities. Having long since lost the aggression levels needed to drive in Boston, Beatrice shuddered.

She quickly diverted her attention to more manageable items on the list. "Eltie/Llamas" was one heading. Even if Reine's cria was on the ground and nursing heartily, Beatrice would feel better if someone checked in on the little herd. She figured Eltie owed her that much.

There was also the matter of "Hay." Because the pasture was a month away from providing adequate nutrition, supplemental feeding would be necessary, even for a few days. She recalled Ben offering to arrange delivery of a huge round bale, which could be dumped in the middle of the pasture, where it would last for weeks. Ben made the offer to free the crippled Beatrice from the daily haying chores involved with square bales, but she rejected the idea – not merely because she had Clara's help. She hated the waste involved. Weather would render a significant part of a ton bale inedible. But as a stopgap measure, the round bale now made sense.

Clearly, she needed to call both Ben and Eltie to request favors. That did not sit well with Beatrice's independent streak, but she was far too pragmatic not to tap those resources. During those phone conversations, she would also need to address another list item: "Clara/Permission." She could hardly drag a minor off to New England without getting the approval of some family member. But who? She had never even met Clara's father and had no address or phone number for him. Nothing good could come from any further contact with Clara's mother, and Beatrice figured that Charyce – at least in a moral, if not legal sense – had forfeited her right to weigh in on Clara's Easter break activities. Ben was probably the best choice.

Once again Beatrice shuddered. He was certainly an amiable guy, but entering into that conversation could be like venturing into a minefield. She had no intention of letting any family member pay for Clara's airfare. Even though Beatrice had been manipulated into providing an emergency home for the youngster, she felt increasingly guilty about all the free labor Clara was providing. Even now, as Beatrice made her plans in the late afternoon, the child was manning a shovel in the pasture and tossing llama "beans" into a cart.

When Beatrice had first broached the subject of weekly manure pickup, Clara's eyes widened in horror. The average thirteen-year-old girl, who has not grown up on a farm, has a natural aversion to poop, even if llamas have the tidiest toilet habits of any livestock. Never would they mess inside the barn, not even in mid-blizzard. And they tended toward concentrated, collective dung piles, which made pickup easier. Easier, but still physically taxing and not exactly pleasant. Although Clara was an exceptional child in many ways, manure day triggered heavy sighs and glum facial expressions. From her kitchen window, Beatrice often noted how the girl would dramatically suck in her breath just before addressing the manure. But Clara addressed it nonetheless—sometimes with good humor, particularly if Barrie or old Tess rewarded her efforts with a tentative nose kiss.

Beatrice had recently learned about Clara's early-April birthday. The Boston trip could be a nice reward for her hard work and a birthday treat. But Ben's mountaineer pride could complicate things. He might view a free plane ticket for Clara as an insult, implying that the extended Buckhalter clan was too impoverished or too indifferent to Clara's needs to provide for her—even if, Beatrice thought bitterly, there was an element of truth in those perceptions.

Ben might also worry about exposing the child to urban values at odds with Seneca County culture. More probably, Beatrice speculated, Ben would worry about Clara embarrassing herself—and, by extension, all of the Buckhalters and maybe all of West Virginia—by sticking out like a sore thumb up there in Yankeeland. Thinking back on her own humble origins, Beatrice snorted at the irony.

After working out the financial game plan with Evie, Beatrice had decided she should talk with Clara before anyone else about the proposed Boston junket. The girl had been tossed this way and that in recent weeks, with no say about where she lived and precious little say about how she spent her time. Clara had the right to say no. If she did not want to join Beatrice, then she could hole up with some family member for a few days. But Beatrice was hopeful she could make the trip appealing.

She doubted Clara had ever been on a plane, and even in the current era of TSA pat-downs and tiny bags of peanuts for in-flight sustenance, most middle-school kids would probably view their first plane trip as a worthy adventure in and of itself.

In addition, Clara had a wide-ranging curiosity about the larger world. Beatrice suspected Boston would have exotic cachet for the girl, cachet that would overcome any fears about feeling out of place. Besides, Beatrice had no doubts her big brother could work his charm on Clara and make her feel at home. He had raised Martha almost single-handedly and genuinely liked having a daughter, unlike so many men who felt cheated if they had not produced a son. Bart had developed considerable skill at making life comfortable and fun for Martha. Even though she had turned into an obnoxious forty-year-old, she had been an engaging teenager, closely bonded with her dad.

Further down the list, Beatrice saw "Ralph" and sighed. She hated to kennel the dog but figured he could tolerate the loneliness for less than a week – at the perfectly respectable boarding facility in Marlboro.

She began a new list, arranging the timing of the phone calls and conversations that lay between her and Boston. Engrossed in establishing precise priorities, she did not hear the utility door open. She jumped when Clara appeared beside her in the kitchen. The girl had padded in softly, carrying the boots she had removed before entering.

"Beatrice, I think something's wrong with Reine," Clara said nervously.

"Define 'wrong.'"

"She's at the poop pile like she needs to pee, but nothing's coming out. She'll go away and then come right back and try again. And she's humming again."

"Shit!"

Beatrice knew straining at the dung pile was one sign of the onset of labor. Every single one of her camelid books cheerfully talked about the huge percentage of llamas that delivered between nine and eleven in the morning, after no more than an hour of active labor. In some feat of evolutionary adaptation, the critters had synchronized their body clocks to make sure newborn crias would dry off long before the sun set and the temperature dropped. Those same books also said troublesome deliveries often came in the evening hours. If you see your llama straining at the dung pile in late afternoon, the authors warned, call your vet.

"Shit," Beatrice repeated.

FORTY-THREE

Plop Went the Wee One

Beatrice barked instructions to Clara – to call Eltie, to bring the cordless phone, to separate Reine from the rest of the herd – while Beatrice fired up the lawn tractor as her means of transportation to the delivery room. As always happened when in crisis mode, a part of her protectively isolated herself from the scene. That alter ego found sardonic humor in Beatrice's impression of someone who knew what she was doing.

In truth, she was scared down to her brittle bones. She was scared of failing the llama that had been entrusted to her. She was scared that, by extension, she would fail Kate. She was scared she or Clara would get hurt in the rescue effort. More than anything, Beatrice wished she were not here in this place, at this time.

It didn't help that Eltie was unreachable. According to Vaughn, the vet was on a farm call in an area with no cell phone coverage. Vaughn promised to keep calling the farm's landline to alert Eltie to the troubled labor. As soon as she knew anything, Vaughn would call Beatrice's landline – hence the cordless phone.

By the time Beatrice, crutches crossed over her lap, rode down the hill to the barn, Clara had already herded Reine into a stall and shooed the rest of the llamas into the pasture.

Halter in hand, Clara ran to open the gate for Beatrice. The girl had never haltered a llama, and Beatrice had not been in a position to teach her how. That time had come.

Reine could be skittish about halters, but her current posture – head slightly down and eyes glazed – suggested her sole focus was on internal developments, with no energy left for resistance. Beatrice crutched her way into the stall with Clara beside her. Leaning against the wall, she demonstrated how to slide the halter over an imaginary llama's nose then told Clara to stand at Reine's left shoulder.

"I don't think I can do it," Clara stammered.

"Yes, you can," Beatrice said, gently but firmly. "Her mind is on more important things than you. Do it now, while her head's down and within easy reach. You can do it."

The girl walked close to the llama then turned her head, doubtful and wide-eyed.

"Breathe out. Breathe in, and the next time you breathe out, slip the halter on."

Clara breathed out, jaggedly, but the next exhale was steady. Reine let her slip the halter over the end of the nose but jerked up as the halter cleared mid-nose. Clara held on and with some clumsiness brought the webbed cotton tongue around the right side of the llama's head and into the buckle at the left jaw joint. With a big sigh, Clara looked back at Beatrice.

"Good girl! Now I need you to snap the lead on the halter and move her into the chute."

Clara needed to tug a bit to get Reine moving, but the animal complied, humming fretfully.

Beatrice clumped behind the pair until they reached the chute. Reine stopped short. "Get into the chute yourself, Clara. You can duck out the side once she gets far enough in."

Clara stepped halfway in and tugged on the rope, but Reine wouldn't budge.

Although she had not reached that magic date when she was allowed finally to bear partial weight on her injured leg, Beatrice decided to take the risk. "Get ready to move her neck into the V at the front of the chute. I'm gonna goose her backside."

Leaning on the left crutch and gingerly planting her right foot on the ground, Beatrice raised the other crutch and tapped Reine's right hamstring. The llama hopped forward just enough to nose through the V. Needing no instruction, Clara wound the rope around one of the chute's front posts to prevent her from backing out. After ducking under the horizontal side bar, she loosely tied off the lead rope and closed the V to hold Reine's neck in a wedge that permitted some movement but was still too narrow for the head to retract.

"Excellent girl!" Beatrice exclaimed.

Asking Clara to retrieve a satchel from the tack room, Beatrice, aided only by the left crutch, moved warily into the rear of the chute. When Clara returned, Beatrice pulled a roll of vet tape out of the bag. As she bit off its plastic covering, she realized the limitations of having only one hand free.

"Clara, I'm gonna take hold of Reine's tail with one hand, and I'll need you to wrap this tape around it."

Clara complied wordlessly, but her hands shook as she wound the sticky tape around the furry tail. The taping was less than artful but allowed Beatrice a clear view of what was going on sub-tail, where she saw a dark blob protruding. She guessed it was a nose covered with gloppy membrane. If she was right, that was good news. It wasn't a foot. No breech birth.

As Beatrice pondered her next course of action, Reine groaned softly, spread her rear legs, and the cria's entire head, veiled in that weird membrane, pushed out, along with what looked like the toes of the left foot. A few more grunts and pushes expelled only another inch or so of head and left foot.

"Uh-oh," said Beatrice.

Clara came around the back to have a look. "Is that the baby's head?"

Before Beatrice could answer, the cordless phone rang. Reine startled slightly, so Beatrice rubbed her flank in reassurance. Clara snatched the phone and passed it to Beatrice.

"Eltie, thank God!"

Beatrice's relief was short-lived. Eltie was an hour away, and if labor did not progress, Beatrice would have to intervene. The first order of business, Eltie explained, was to clear the membrane from the baby's nose so it could breathe.

"I can do that," Beatrice told herself mentally and then twitched when she realized she had said the words aloud. Donning a pair of cheap latex gloves from the satchel, she sluiced down the baby's head with her right hand. The glop peeled off easily. The cria made a soft choking sound but then seemed to take normal breaths.

Eltie told her they could now wait maybe fifteen minutes for labor to progress normally. She assured Beatrice she would stay on the line to talk her through whatever needed doing.

Later, Beatrice and Clara would have very little memory of what transpired during those fifteen minutes, but they agreed it was the longest quarter hour they could recall. Moving even more slowly than the time was Reine's baby, whose head bobbled sickeningly from its mother's birth canal.

It was Eltie who called "Time." She suspected the baby's right elbow was caught on the pelvic girdle. Beatrice needed to insert her hands into the birth canal and extricate the right leg.

Suppressing a wave of nausea, Beatrice dribbled K-Y jelly on her gloved right hand and edged her fingers around the tight space between baby and birth canal – all the while praying she was not hurting Reine too much. To Beatrice's amazement, the llama did nothing more than groan a few times but kept still. She hadn't a clue what she was doing but suddenly felt the space become much tighter. On both sides of her hand, she touched hard bone. She pushed into the wedge counterclockwise, then clockwise, then counterclockwise. Reine groaned. Beatrice groaned in sympathy. The next sound was a sucking noise, as the right foot and left elbow slipped out. The right elbow was still stuck inside.

All the while, Clara was giving Eltie a play-by-play. "Eltie says you gotta grab both feet and give a firm, slow pull, in line with the baby's spine."

Beatrice made a grab for her discarded crutch. She hoped she could somehow prop herself up by the armpits to have two hands free. Before she could execute this maneuver, Clara came up beside her. "I can do it," the girl said quietly.

Both shocked and grateful, Beatrice took the phone, wobbled out of the chute, and watched, fascinated, as Clara, setting her jaw, grabbed both of the cria's feet and pulled. Reine gave a long, low moan then dug in with all four feet. Next came an incredibly loud sucking noise, and the entire baby shot out and plopped onto the ground. Reine gave a heavy sigh. The baby squeaked weakly.

Beatrice gasped, "What an excellent, excellent girl – both of you!" She rubbed Reine's flank then turned to Clara and said, "That was the bravest thing I've ever seen."

As Clara liberated the new mom from the chute, Beatrice suddenly remembered Eltie. She apprised the vet of the happy outcome, thanked her for her help, and signed off. The two midwives were now free to admire the little bag of bones, already shifting into a decent kush and wobbling its long neck erect for a few seconds.

"It's a boy," Beatrice said.

"Do you have a name?" Clara asked.

"I had planned to stick with the royal names. But that just wouldn't be right. Only one name for him now."

"What's that?"

"Why, Miss Buckhalter, his name will, of course, be Buck."

FORTY-FOUR

Rolling Thunder

Perched tailor-style on Beatrice's couch, Clara bobbed her head slightly to the beat emanating from her ear buds, as she penciled in Ts or Fs on the printout of a take-home geography test. She was allowed to check the textbook for answers, but it lay unused beside her right thigh—the test was ridiculously easy.

"Who wouldn't know Charleston is the state capital?" she said, shaking her head.

Normally, she would have been annoyed or even insulted at seeing yet another test that posed no challenge. Of course she knew which states bordered West Virginia. She snorted as she scrawled a large F next to the query as to whether Alabama was one of them.

But Clara took it in stride today. She was still riding the high from yesterday's experience with Reine and the adorable, fuzzy little Buck. That was one challenge Clara had handled well and, according to Beatrice, bravely.

She turned up the volume on the music player, as a favorite song began. The device was woefully outdated, but Clara had managed to upload some decent CDs, courtesy of the public library. Despite the music, she was dimly aware of the crackle of gravel on the drive and assumed Beatrice and Ralph were returning from the Boring Building a bit earlier than usual.

If the hot boy-band had not been blasting its vocals into her ear, Clara might have noticed that the gravel was crackling in a different location from where Beatrice normally parked.

She didn't notice anything amiss until the shoes. Bent over the papers on her lap, Clara wondered why on earth a cripple like Beatrice would wear four-inch heels with a one-inch platform at the soles. Then it occurred to her she had never seen Beatrice's bare legs. As Clara's eyes slowly traced upward, focusing on the legs before her, it was quite a while before the skirt hem came into view.

The legs looked familiar.

"What are you doing here, Momma?"

Charyce Trask settled beside her daughter on the couch, her half-naked right thigh against Clara's denim-clad left thigh. Charyce reached her right arm around Clara's far shoulder to pull the youngster toward her. The gesture was awkward. Clara stiffened slightly but let her mother's head rest briefly on her shoulder.

"Oh, honey!" Charyce exhaled dramatically. "I miss you so much. I know that woman doesn't want me here. But a momma just gotta see her only born child. I been so durn sad. All the time."

Charyce nuzzled Clara's meager shoulder again. Clara said nothing. Nose still muffled in her daughter's sweater, Charyce raised her brows to take in a sliver of Clara's impassive face.

Then she leaned away from her daughter and bent forward, over hands folded in lap, like some medieval penitent. Looking at her hands, Charyce continued, "I know what I done was wrong. I never shoulda hit you like that, honey. I just lost it when you said what you did about Rodney. He's a good man, Clara, really he is. He has so much stress with the job. A lot to handle with all them people workin' for him, with all them taxes to pay, all them sales to make. It makes him feel peaceful-like to watch a sweet young thing like you sleep, without a care in the world. Rodney said it was like watching the baby Jesus Hisself."

Charyce extracted a Kleenex from her jacket pocket and, as she daubed at her eyes, risked another furtive glance at her daughter. Clara was looking forward, into space.

Charyce pressed ahead. "We want you to come back home. My home – yours and mine, I mean. And, if you like, Rodney won't stay over 'til we get married. Which will be soon, if only you agree to all of us being family. Can you do that for me, honey? Can you tell your father and uncle how much you want to be family with Rodney and me? Once we get married?"

Silence.

"Rodney is a Christian man, and he don't want to risk coming between a momma and her baby girl. So if you say no, he'll give up his own happiness.

He'll give up on marrying me. You see how good he is. But he really wants to be a father to you and a husband to me. If only you say yes. Can you do that for me, honey?"

Clara twisted a reddish brown curl around the pencil in her right hand. "Momma, Rodney wasn't just looking at me. He was … creepy, and he scared me. He wasn't acting like my father."

"You're wrong, Clara," Charyce said in a tight voice.

"I don't want to be around Rodney. And I don't want to live with you," Clara added, with a soft shiver in the second sentence.

At that, Charyce rose abruptly to hover over her daughter. She narrowed her eyes.

Reflexively, Clara edged sideways on the sofa then stood and moved more than an arm's length away. She had long learned to put distance between herself and her mother when Charyce got wound up.

Suddenly, Ralph appeared in the living room. He sniffed the air briefly then nosed Clara's hand, hanging by her side. He looked toward Charyce, holding his tail stiffly at half-mast.

Oblivious to the dog, Charyce bellowed, "You're spoiling everything! You know how much money Rodney has? Rodney ain't much in bed, and if I never have to mess with that limp little weenie again, well, that'll be fine by me. But his bank account sure ain't little. He's big at the bank. And I aim to get me a big piece a that. I aim to get halfa that big old house and halfa that big old business. And he's just dumb enough to give it to me – if he gets what he wants. And I guess that's you. So you're gonna do what needs doing. If Rodney wants you to jerk him off every morning and blow him every night, that's what you're gonna do!"

By then Clara had raised her hands to her ears, her face crimson from fighting back tears.

Charyce's head snaked toward her daughter. "You think I care?" she shrieked. "You hear me, brat?"

During the outburst, Ralph had silently inched between girl and woman. His tail remained stiff, while his head was now level with his ropey shoulders. Raising his eyes, not his head, he looked up at Charyce, exposing his upper teeth in an eerie imitation of a mirthless human smile.

Noticing the dog for the first time, Charyce locked angry eyes on him.

But Ralph held her gaze and emitted a long, low growl.

Charyce tottered backward, and as she did she spotted a heavy crystal vase on an end table. Shifting her eyes from the dog to Clara and back again, she reached out and wrapped her right fist around the vase's narrow neck … and raised her arm.

From her vantage point, Beatrice could not tell whether Charyce planned to smash the vase over Ralph's head or pitch it at Clara. She had rolled up in her wheelchair, muffled by the carpeted floor. She had stopped a few feet behind Charyce and for several stunned moments eavesdropped on her tirade.

Beatrice had forgotten all about her plan to visit the half-bath off the utility room but was glad the crutches she would have needed to negotiate that narrow space lay across the wheelchair's arms.

She was also glad they were the old wooden versions. She had been alternating between them and the aluminum ones to minimize the unique strains each put on different body parts. The aluminum crutches were lightweight; the wooden ones were not.

She grabbed the lower end of one crutch, leaned her upper body forward and to the right, then swung a wide, swift arc with her chosen weapon. The broad part of the crutch smashed against the side of Charyce's right knee, upending her.

As Charyce crumpled to the floor, she let loose the vase she was holding. It hit the coffee table, splintering apart. Ralph and Clara jumped back, narrowly avoiding the flying shards that caught the late afternoon light.

After the pieces settled, the only sound in the room was a soft "unhhhh" coming from the floor, where Charyce, after slamming down on her right hip, lay on her back while grasping her right knee with both hands.

"Help me," she groaned. "Please."

FORTY-FIVE

The Postmortem

Physical courage did not rank high among Beatrice's virtues. Equipped with a petite frame and lacking any natural athleticism, she had learned, even when young, supple, and fully ambulatory that it was wise to walk, if not run, away from potential physical confrontations. She had experienced a few trouncings in the rough-and-tumble neighborhood of her childhood, a neighborhood where leather wrist guards were, for a while, high fashion for teenage girls—a statement of bravado and a practical precaution if the wearer ran the risk of engaging in a knife fight. Beatrice did not number among the girls sporting that particular fashion statement.

There were some painful exceptions involving matters of high principle. But Beatrice knew that, more often than not, there was nothing shameful about avoiding or escaping from a battle she was sure to lose. Running away was not quite the same as surrender or, worse, collaboration, although it did nothing to prevent future flight-or-fight quandaries. Fortunately, society expected less of girls in that regard. More fortunately, the average neighborhood bully had a short attention span.

Given her unflinching awareness of her weaknesses in battle, Beatrice would later flinch, thinking back to the bizarre scene that had played out in her living room that overcast March afternoon.

In her recollections of that drama, Beatrice realized courage had very little to do with it. Her adrenaline levels were already off the charts before she had driven up to the house, put the shift lever in reverse, pulled the emergency brake, and shut off the engine. She could not miss Charyce's crappy little Ford. So she was expecting, at very least, yelling and threats.

As she hauled the folded wheelchair out of the truck's cab, Beatrice remembered the high-tech recording doo-dad in her canvas shoulder bag. She had bought it for her sessions with Tanner, although more often than not she preferred a yellow legal pad and roller-ball pen. But she had thought it might come in handy for this occasion. Before entering the house, she turned the recorder on.

By the time she rolled into the living room, Beatrice was fully wired—physiologically and technologically—but still reasonably calm. Maintaining that calm had been difficult, as she heard the disgusting tirade coming from Charyce. But calm she was … until the intruder grabbed the crystal vase.

Beatrice didn't know whether she was protecting Ralph or Clara. In her value system both were equally worthy, and neither was able to fend for himself or herself. Both were in her care. In the moment, Beatrice was hardly capable of parsing the moral issues involved. At that point in time, the only reality for Beatrice was rage. Not the screaming, hyper variety. Her rage had an icy, Celtic edge. Her face was not flushed but white with grim determination.

As highly charged dramas often do, everything moved in slow motion, and Beatrice dimly perceived she had ample time to consider her options. She would remember, later, that she had discounted the effectiveness of trying to reason with Charyce. She had recognized the advantage of taking the intruder by surprise, which is why she took care with her rolled approach on the carpet. She also had deduced her vulnerability would increase—and her likely effectiveness decrease—if she tried to stand and, say, bop Charyce over the head. Besides, those exposed backs of the knees just sang out to her.

The slo-mo, dispassionate concentration also helped Beatrice craft an action plan after she whacked Charyce with the crutch. Serendipity played a role, too. As she wheeled away from Charyce's collapse, Beatrice noticed the retractable ice cleat on the rubber bottom of the splintered-but-still-useful crutch had popped out. She admired the short, stout metal spike and contemplated its multiple uses. Flipping the crutch so the spike was farthest away from her hand, she wheeled forward again and calmly pushed the crutch toward the supine Charyce. She recognized that, in her crippled state, she could not withstand even an injured woman's attempt to grab for the crutch and gain the upper hand. So she positioned the spike over Charyce's throat and shoved it just hard enough to induce fear of a clumsy tracheotomy.

Holding the crutch in this menacing position, Beatrice calmly outlined Charyce's options. She revealed she had recorded every foul word screamed from Charyce's mouth. Such evidence of child endangerment and abuse would not play well with a family court judge. Charyce would lose custodial rights to Clara and, in the process, her monthly child-support payments. If Charyce had second thoughts about conceding defeat on that score, she should be aware that her recorded words established that she had not been the de facto custodial parent for some time – a period during which she fraudulently continued to cash those checks. Beatrice made it clear she would place all the damning facts at the disposal of Mike Buckhalter and his lawyer.

In her slow-motion strategy session, Beatrice had calculated that Charyce would be more compliant if allowed a way out. That would be her access to Rodney's wealth. There was a chance, after all, Charyce could still snag the pervert even without Clara as a dowry. But if Rodney knew what Charyce really thought of him, he would drop her faster than his limp, little weenie would shrivel in a cold shower. Beatrice actually said something like that to the splayed-out, crutch-pinioned Charyce. If Charyce ever bothered Clara or Beatrice or anyone or anything connected with them again, Rodney would get the recording.

It occurred to Beatrice there was one major flaw in her strategy. What would she do if Charyce, a younger, fitter woman, snatched the recorder away from her?

Like most bullies, however, Charyce had no experience with getting pummeled. Once she was truly hurt, the fight went out of her.

As Beatrice cautiously withdrew the crutch, Charyce made no move to rise, much less pose any physical threat. The older woman started to lose some of her edge but summoned sufficient authority to tell Charyce to vacate the premises.

"I don't think I can walk," the younger woman whimpered.

For some unknown reason, that pretension to victimhood got Beatrice's adrenaline pumping all over again. "I suggest you figure out a way. Now!"

Charyce, gasping little puffs of pain, rolled onto her left side and then her left knee. With her right leg off to the side, she pushed away from the floor with her fists until she was more or less standing, bent over, on one leg. Pushing on her left thigh with both hands, she slowly straightened her back.

As soon as she went vertical, Ralph, who had put himself on an alert sit-stay, moved fluidly onto all four paws … and growled.

Charyce reacted with another whimper and began gimping toward the front door. Her pace picked up as Ralph padded after her, with Beatrice rolling somewhat behind. Clara remained fixed on the same spot on the carpet, where she had jumped to avoid the shards.

Beatrice watched from the door until Charyce's car backed away and after far too many maneuvers moved forward down the long driveway. Only then did Beatrice reach out to Ralph for a mutually reassuring scratch to his still-raised hackles. The dog's ears relaxed, and his tail came up and made a few, hesitant passes.

"Good dog. What a good dog," Beatrice whispered, as Ralph's tail began making its usual gentle loops.

Beatrice wheeled her way back to the living room. A stooped Clara was plucking vase shards from the carpet and depositing them into a paper bag. Beatrice moved to where she had dropped the intact crutch.

Hoisting herself up onto the single crutch, she said softly, "Put the bag down, Clara. I don't want you to cut yourself. We'll get out the vacuum later."

"I'm sorry about the vase," Clara said shakily.

"I don't give a good goddamn about the vase," Beatrice said with a sigh and beckoned the girl.

Clara put the bag on the coffee table and, swallowing hard, moved toward Beatrice. Leaning heavily on the crutch anchored in her left armpit, Beatrice reached out with her right arm and pulled the girl to her in a slightly unstable embrace. It took Clara a minute to unstiffen. Then she hung her head over Beatrice's shoulder and sucked in air. And sucked in air. And finally exhaled in sobs.

FORTY-SIX

You Ain't Heard Weird Yet

"I'm going to be a perfectly dreadful role model for you, Clara," Beatrice cautioned, after settling awkwardly into the aisle seat, with her single crutch not quite tucked under her legs. "When the stewardess gets it in gear, I am going to order a double bourbon, just one. This is not something one should do in the early afternoon. But I am not a fan of flying."

Clara, occupying the window seat, reluctantly turned away from the spectacle of luggage trolleys and taxiing planes. She regarded her companion thoughtfully and, after a pause, said, "I won't tell."

Beatrice laughed and handed the teenager a large bar of dark Belgian chocolate.

Clara took the bribe but tucked it into her tote. "For later. Right now, I don't want to miss a minute of what's going on." On her lap were several maps, one charting the air route from Roanoke, where they were about to take off for Charlotte before going on to Boston. She also had a conventional road map, on which she had made some marks with a highlighter. With a finger, she followed the I-81 corridor snaking up through Virginia, West Virginia, Maryland, and into Pennsylvania.

"The farthest north I've ever been is the West Virginia-Maryland border," she said breathlessly. "Meemaw was gonna take me to Baltimore once, but she got too sick. This will be a new record. And I've never been south of Virginia, either. Does it count if we never leave the airport in North Carolina?"

"Counts in my book."

"How many states have you been to?"

"Oh, I guess all of the East Coast states, mostly by car. I've had a few flights out west, though."

"Yeah, but that's a whole lot more than me."

Throughout the afternoon, Clara was sometimes mute with rapture over the remarkably 3-D clouds outside her plastic porthole. At other times she erupted in chatter, sharing an observation about the awesomeness of flying or questioning Beatrice about upcoming events.

Beatrice was happy to see the girl's enthusiasm. It was hard to believe this was the same Clara who had been robotically plucking glass shards from the carpet just a few days earlier. Beatrice had always believed in the curative powers of a road trip, even if this journey was unsettlingly far above the interstate highway system. Despite the weekly grocery outings, courtesy of Tanner's chauffeur, the walls had been closing in on Beatrice. It felt restorative to see more of the world again.

During Clara's awestruck silent spells, Beatrice reviewed everything that had happened the previous week. There had been many such reviews in the preceding days, but the distance afforded by the airplane and the pleasant muzziness of her drink ensured a calmer perspective on the recent past. The main emotion Beatrice now felt was relief, intermingled with some awe over how much had been accomplished, for the good.

One such accomplishment was informing Eltie and Ben of Charyce's visit. Another dreaded but successfully completed task was the call to the lawyer Beatrice had previously entrusted with mundane real estate matters. He proved sympathetic and attentive. She provided him, as well as Ben, a copy of the damning recording but resisted his recommendation to get the police involved. Her instinct told her it was important to leave Charyce an exit strategy. She placated the attorney by e-mailing him a comprehensive account of the attempted assault and her defensive response.

Eltie and Ben were overcome by shock, regret, and gratitude – so much gratitude that they were eager to facilitate Beatrice's travel plans and agreed the trip would indeed be good for Clara. The shock over Charyce's violent visit preempted the concern they would later feel about the cost of Clara's airfare. Meanwhile, Ben addressed Beatrice's worries about feeding the llamas. The day before her flight, he deposited an enormous round bale in her pasture. He flatly refused reimbursement.

Reine was proving to be an attentive mother, and Buck was plumping nicely. Both animals appeared entirely normal, despite their travail, but Eltie said she would stop by a few times to check on them and take in Beatrice's mail. Eltie also offered to put up Ralph at her house, but Beatrice worried about problems with Gracie, the yappy Boston terrier, and fretted even more about the lack of fencing in Eltie's yard. With Clara's help, she took Ralph to his regular dog vet, who had excellent boarding facilities and an even more excellent chain-link fence.

So much time spent on reflections, and the Charyce drama's aftermath, meant Beatrice did not have a chance to plot out her interview with Patty Scanlon. But she figured she could accomplish that as soon as she had settled in at Bart's, with the help of all the information on her laptop, which she reluctantly brought along. It was hardly lightweight, but she could manage it in her partial-weight-bearing state, because Clara was on hand to roll both of their stowable bags, crammed to bursting. Boston could offer up three season's worth of weather in the first week of April. It might snow. It might be a muggy eighty degrees. It might even be spring. Packing was a challenge.

Nor did Beatrice have the time to pick out a gift for her host. She hoped to snag that opportunity when they arrived in Massachusetts and secured their car rental. She was actually looking forward to driving, even in Boston. Since she had started bearing some weight on her injured leg, it finally seemed to be getting stronger. Working the accelerator and brake was no longer painful. Because the rental would almost certainly have an automatic transmission, her uninjured leg would be free for emergency braking—a distinct possibility in metropolitan Boston.

For the first time in weeks, she felt capable, hopeful.

Nevertheless, her sense of competence wilted toward the end of the flight. Her leg had begun to hurt. She dreaded the upcoming slog through Logan Airport and was having second thoughts about negotiating her way, in the dark, toward the city via the unfamiliar Big Dig arteries.

Hobbling off the plane, Beatrice was so focused on staying vertical and avoiding collisions that she paid no attention to the honking of the public address system. Fortunately, Clara, determined not to miss one sight or sound of this experience, heard the nasal voice urging Beatrice Desmond to meet her party at baggage claim.

And her party was: Big Brother Bart to the rescue. He wore a sheepish smile but was clearly elated to see his sister. Beatrice fell on him in joy and gratitude. He embraced her, crutch and all, in a sturdy hug. "So what's the other guy look like?" he asked.

"Damn, you're a sight for sore eyes – and legs. What the hell are you doing here?"

"Well, you may be Wonder Woman, BB, but I figured you could use a ride anyway. No, you're not renting a car. I borrowed an Explorer from my neighbor, who almost never drives anymore, the old fart. And in case we get nasty weather, you'll have four-wheel drive. Besides, I don't think an econobox rental would make for gentle entry or egress in your condition."

"Bless you," she said, clumsily patting his shoulder.

"So, no introductions? Surely, this cannot be the girl you told me about? This one must be at least a senior in high school, the way she's muscling that luggage around."

It was corny but effective, appealing to Clara's work ethic. She ventured a small smile. Bart pulled off his gloves and clasped Clara's small hand in both of his.

"Nice to meet you, Mr. Desmond," she said, looking up through her eyelashes.

"I'm Mr. Desmond only to people I don't like. And to doctors, which is pretty much the same thing, I guess. You, I think I'll like. Call me Bart."

"You're seeing doctors?" Beatrice interjected, frowning.

"Isn't that like asking if Lucy is crowding Schroeder?"

"Enough with the comic strip references! Are you okay?"

"I'm terrific for a sixty-five-year-old. For a twenty-five-year-old, which is how I feel by noon on a good day, my blood pressure and cholesterol are less than terrific, which is why ridiculously young doctors prescribe ridiculously named pills. 'Ask your doctor about Vista, and you'll never die.'"

"Don't ever die."

"I promise." He squeezed his sister's shoulder. She swatted his arm. Clara suppressed a giggle.

"The young upstart finds us risible," Bart said, glowering down at Clara, who recognized the bluff.

"You all sound like my Daddy and Uncle Ben. Except with weird accents."

Brother and sister guffawed.

“Oh, honey, you ain’t heard weird yet,” Beatrice laughed. “And up here, you’re the outlander with the accent. Be afraid. Be very afraid.”

Brother and sister guffawed again. Clara affected a knowing laugh but looked warily from one adult to the other.

FORTY-SEVEN

Sunrise and Cream Cheese

Addie's tail etched a fan in the dusting of snow that had fallen the night before. Sitting alertly about five feet from Bart's bench, she kept a close eye on the two Canadas bustling self-importantly about the little pond. She no longer chased geese but still didn't like their bossy, raucous ways. She owed this to her human, who could be too kind for his own good. She had even witnessed him tossing crumbs to the filthy birds. Addie's vigil was interrupted by the occasional thump of her tail, a sign that she felt good about being of service to her human.

Bart was feeling good, too. As usual, he had risen at 5 a.m. He figured his little sister, an irredeemable night owl, would be sacked out for another two or three hours. His memories of Martha's teenage years told him Clara would probably be down for the count for a while yet, as well. He recalled some scientific study showing teenagers needed ridiculous amounts of sleep to compensate for those growth spurts.

Although he was delighted to have the company, Bart was happy to have the morning to himself—and Addie. He liked to watch the sun come up over the little pond a few blocks away. Ancient hemlocks obstructed some of the magenta and lavender clouds, but Bart was happy to coexist with the venerable trees. He had been raised to show deference to his elders.

When the weather cooperated, like today, Bart would take Addie on a brisk walk to that pond, the central feature of a little park. At this time of day, he and Addie were the only sentient beings in this green space, for that was precisely how he thought of his Lab. Well, there was that jogger, with wires coming out of her ears and the annoying habit of placing two fingers on her neck to monitor her pulse. Bart did not count her among the sentient. He objected to the garish colors of her coordinated running outfit, complete with iridescent strips on arms and shoes. She clashed with the quiet beauty of the sunrise.

Bart wondered if such thoughts made him a cranky old goat. No. He basically liked himself, or would if he bothered to stop and think about it. Unlike his sister, he rarely picked at scabs. In the past decade, his ability to appreciate a good moment and live in the present had improved considerably.

In his younger years, he had chased after the future. Given the difficult economic circumstances of his childhood, that was the prudent thing to do. Poverty was no crime, his mother used to say, but it was damned inconvenient. The Desmonds were not exactly impoverished, but times were often scarily tough, thanks to a series of layoffs and strikes at the shipyard. So Bart chased after an education, chased after Betty, chased after a job, chased after loans for his business, chased after the investments that would pay for his daughter's education and eventually allow him to retire.

He enjoyed much of the chase. He was good at it. But somewhere along the line he realized there was a whole lot more past than future. Chasing after the future now seemed a lot like chasing after death, so at a certain point Bart stopped running. He could be as frantic as anyone else about the cares of the day, but he no longer obsessed about the possibilities of tomorrow. He understood this new Zen version of himself would have been a lot harder to achieve without the financial cushion he had accumulated and without the healthy constitution he had lucked into. But he wasn't going to turn up his nose at his blessings. When life was good, he had every intention of enjoying it.

With the pale, lemony sun now shining on his face, Bart called to Addie, "Life is pretty good, old girl, isn't it?" She wagged her agreement, spotted a likely stick, picked it up, and plopped it in Bart's lap. She had no real interest in a chase but couldn't come empty-flewed. With a sigh, she settled by Bart's bench and laid her head over his shoes. Contentedly.

Bart wondered if Beatrice ever felt contented. She didn't appear to. Her life had developed some troubling complications lately. Thinking of her problems saddened him, but he realized he could not uncomplicate her life or magically transform her into a carefree child of the universe. He could, however, arrange a little treat. That idea banished the brief flash of sadness.

"C'mon Addie, we have breakfast to make."

Bart remembered how fond he and his sister were of French toast—but only the way their father made it: accompanied by salt and cream cheese and an ample supply of crisp bacon. Bart had all the ingredients at hand. Having lost both his mother and his wife at young ages, he was a competent cook. The prospect of having an appreciative audience turned him into an enthusiastic chef.

Beatrice almost undid his plan. He was shocked to see her in the kitchen when he and Addie returned from their walk. Fortunately, there was no sign of breakfast yet, only a cup of tea parked beside her open laptop.

"Who are you and what have you done with my sister?"

"I was worrying about how I'm gonna handle the ex-wife interview this afternoon. Couldn't get back to sleep once the sun came up, so I figured I might as well do some work."

"How's it going?"

"I'm actually more on top of the subject than I realized."

"Surprise, surprise, Miss *Semper Paratus*."

"Yeah, well sometimes I over-plan things … oh, shut up!" she said, tossing a kitchen towel at her brother, who was rolling his eyes in mock disbelief. "Over the phone, Patty didn't strike me as someone with poor verbal skills. So maybe the best thing I can do is listen and see where things go."

"Sounds like a plan to me. And I've got one, too. How'd you like French toast, the real way?"

Clara padded in, wearing a sweatshirt, jeans, and heavy wool socks with no shoes. "What's French toast the real way?"

"With salt and cream cheese," Bart said, taking half a dozen eggs out of the fridge.

"Yuck. Do you put syrup on all that, too?"

"Beatrice, you are harboring a Philistine." He began whipping the eggs with a fork. "No, my young Southern friend with the Southern sweet tooth. Just salt and cream cheese. But I do have some maple syrup, the real Vermont kind, somewhere in that cabinet right there." He pointed above Clara's right shoulder.

"Could I try it both ways?"

"The true spirit of compromise," Beatrice mumbled, still hunched over her laptop.

"Now that sounds like a plan," Bart agreed.

Thirty minutes later, Clara was setting the kitchen table with two plates per person. Man, woman, and child were seated when suddenly Bart bolted up, raising an index finger and saying, "Oops, forgot something."

He returned with the newspaper, a good old-fashioned hard copy of *The Boston Globe*. Although Internet savvy, he did not number among the hordes who had abandoned inky fingers for electronic media. His news came with a thud against the front door every morning. He flipped through the sections until he found what he wanted. "There you go," he said, handing one folded section to Beatrice, who cracked a wide smile. "My baby sister, BB, you see," Bart said turning to Clara, "would never eat breakfast without doing the crossword puzzle. In less than five minutes. We got into a few set-tos over it, because the crossword was in with the funnies, and I couldn't do breakfast without Li'l Abner."

"What are the funnies? Who's Lill Abner?" Clara asked, looking from one adult to the other.

"No daily paper in Seneca County. No funnies," Beatrice explained.

"No soul," Bart nodded cheerfully.

"I'll catch the crossword later. How about we eat?"

"Something else takes priority," Bart admonished sternly, whereupon Clara guiltily bowed her head. "Grace," Bart pronounced solemnly.

"Molly, Blackie," Beatrice responded with equal solemnity. And then she and her brother burst out laughing.

Clara spun her head around in utter confusion.

"Grace and Molly lived in our neighborhood when we were kids. Blackie was their dog. Inside joke. So stupid, but it still cracks me up," Beatrice explained through giggles.

Still bewildered, Clara stuffed a salted piece of French toast, topped with a dab of cream cheese, into her mouth. "Weird."

"Think that's a comment on breakfast or us?" Bart asked.

"Both," Beatrice replied, her mouth filled with cream cheese.

FORTY-EIGHT

Ruling the Roost with a Twisted Hand

Beatrice made a mental note to thank her brother on several counts. First, he volunteered to take Clara on a tour while Beatrice headed for her Quincy rendezvous with Patty Scanlon. On today's agenda were The Freedom Trail, lunch at Faneuil Hall Marketplace, and feeding the flying rats on The Common. But Beatrice suspected the highlight for Clara would be riding on the smelly T.

Second, Bart's choice of the Explorer as a loaner was inspired. In a small rental, Beatrice would never have had the courage to brave the Southeast Expressway. The Explorer not only gave her some height to anticipate all the seventy-mile-an-hour feuds playing out up ahead but also gave her some hope of surviving a collision with one of those duelists.

Her heart was still thumping when she pulled up to the Scanlon residence. The pulse rate was unlikely to moderate anytime soon, she thought, as she regarded the seven-foot-high chain-link fence surrounding the modest two-story house. The house occupied a corner lot that was unusually large by Quincy standards: more than half an acre. The property was hard-looking but also hard to stereotype.

Two huge bloodhounds, rounding the left side of the house, did not soften the landscape but lent an air of slightly menacing whimsy, as they effortlessly levitated onto their hind legs and inserted the bony knuckles of their front paws through the links in the fence. Beatrice estimated they stood close to six feet tall, certainly taller than her. After assuming that height, they both let loose with precisely two bays. Then each raised its head skyward while puffing air in and out through prodigious flews. The visitor was being sussed out.

The sheer size of the beasts was intimidating, especially in Beatrice's impaired state. So she began talking in soft, low tones, as she closed the car door. She avoided direct eye contact and tried to walk as confidently as her single crutch permitted to the front gate, where she noticed a small buzzer near the latch. By the time she reached the gate, one of the hounds had climbed down and gone into an alert-sit, its meaty tail concussing the sparse grass. Beatrice put the back of her right hand against the fence, and the wagger leaned its nose toward the hand and inhaled deeply.

Striding from the side door was a raw-boned woman with a short mop of white curly hair, so thick it looked like it should belong to some platinum-blonde Scandinavian goddess. But the leathery wrinkles around the eyes and mouth suggested the goddess was closer to sixty than thirty, as did her choice of clothing: low hiking boots, wool knee socks, a plaid wool skirt, and a cardigan. Everything about Patty Scanlon screamed "practical!" Everything except her smoke-colored eyes—eyes that had seen a lot and had compassion for what they had seen.

As soon as Patty appeared, the hounds padded adoringly toward her. A casual chop of her right hand put the beasts on an attentive sit-stay, as Patty opened the gate for Beatrice. "Welcome. Don't worry about the boys. They won't knock into you."

The handshake was predictably firm, dry, and warm. Beatrice instantly liked her hostess. Patty Scanlon looked like someone who had always known exactly who she was and had zero interest in experimenting with new personae. This was not someone suited to accompany Tanner Fordyce through his multiple reinventions of himself.

The interview began in Patty's kitchen nook, over coffee (for Patty) and tea (for Beatrice). As the women warmed their hands on the cups, Patty asked somewhat warily if the discussion would be recorded.

"No," said Beatrice. "I don't like hearing myself sounding like a doofus on replay. Besides, the recorded word isn't as accurate as the impressions I put to paper."

"How come?"

"What people say isn't always reality. It's how they look. How they move. We all say things we're supposed to say to be polite, fit in, whatever."

"I don't."

"Well, maybe not, but I still trust my legal pad more than any recording."

"And you don't suffer fools gladly. Neither do I. Okay, I'm in. Whaddya wanna know?"

With such a practical subject, Beatrice started chronologically and learned that Patty and Tanner had grown up in the same neighborhood. He was shyly enamored of Patty's younger sister Gerry, who was in his class at St. Mary's. Gerry, who would break many a boy's heart before her fourteenth birthday, had no intention of encouraging young Will's fantasies but felt sorry for the tall, skinny lad. The Scanlons—all thirteen kids, as well as the parents—were one of those huge families that attracted strays. It wasn't long before Will was part of the crowd gathered round the TV for the late-afternoon cartoon hour on weekdays and even for the old movie one Boston station showed every Saturday afternoon. Over Bette Davis, Will and Patty bonded.

"Yah, I know, that sounds like Will was gay. Not a chance. He just liked grit … and class. Bette always had both. I liked her because she was a take-no-prisoners woman. Ya gotta remember, this was back when women were supposed to bake cookies, have a bazillion kids, and faint at the sight of a spider. I never could figure out how a woman who could go through labor a dozen times would blanch at a spider. My ma wouldn't blanch. Bette wouldn't either, and she wore better clothes.

"Will modeled himself after those old movies. He could do a drop-dead impression of Ronald Colman. He could also reproduce my pop's brogue precisely, differentiating one county from another. What an ear!"

"You were born in Cork, right?"

"I was the last of the Irish-born siblings. My family crossed the pond so many times we got whiplash. Blame Grandma Scanlon. Her husband got himself killed in one of those endless risings, and she got herself twisted up with the cops. So she became a big believer in putting the Atlantic Ocean between the family and trouble. My old man was born right here in Boston. That was when Grandma Scanlon was dodging civil war conditions in the Auld Sod. And when she got wind of World War II, she got an itch to revisit her Irish roots, before Pop got drafted. But I'm a U.S. citizen. Had to choose between the two when I came of age. I'm no dummy."

"Do you think Tanner thought of your family as exotic?"

"Exotic?" Patty erupted in laughter. "No, we were like the Atlantic Ocean."

"Come again?"

"Keep up with me here, Beatrice. We were safe harbor."

"I'm confused."

"The Scanlon clan was Will's buffer against that hell he came from."

"What kind of hell?"

"The hell where your father, that worthless piece of shit, tuned out shortly after you came into the world. The senior Berrigan was a decent enough provider, but he abdicated all parental duties. Old Lady Berrigan ruled that roost. With one twisted hand."

"Translation?"

"She beat the crap out of Will, all while quoting one goddamned saint or the other. A daily communicant was she."

"I've gathered Tanner is less than sold on organized religion."

"Oh, he can play the game if need be. But he also knows faith doesn't equate with sadism. He knows his mother was not the norm. Still, it's a wonder he didn't become a serial killer."

"Lots of kids have abusive parents and don't become violent themselves."

"Not so many kids experience what Rita Berrigan dished out."

Beatrice let the silence hang. After a few sips of coffee, Patty sighed and continued. "Old Rita could have taught that Nazi concentration camp doctor a trick or two. Medical treatment was a lovely vehicle for torture. She never met an enema bag she didn't like. Obviously, there was a sexual twist. Will zoned out for the worst stuff, I gather, but ... let's put it this way. It's amazing he was able to father a son. It was even more amazing he was able to keep his mind intact."

"Jesus!"

"Yeah, Jesus. I'm not sure it serves any purpose telling you this." For the first time, Patty looked nervous. " What are you gonna do with it?"

"I haven't a clue."

Rory, the younger hound, dolefully spread his velvety flews across Beatrice's lap. Declan, the elder, deposited his great bony head on Patty's lap. The women automatically stroked the long ears ... and welcomed the grounding effect.

FORTY-NINE

TMI

A heavy silence muffled Patty Scanlon's kitchen, as she opened a drawer and pulled out a pack of menthols. "Ya mind?" she asked, waggling the cigarettes.

Beatrice shook her head.

After several puffs, Patty reopened the conversation. "Will wouldn't like that I told you so much. There was always a part of me that wanted to shout from the rooftops what that old harridan did. I would have liked to see that pious bitch exposed, shamed. I think I was angrier at Rita Berrigan than he was. And not just for me—not just because her warped soul didn't do our marriage any good, even from the grave. I think a good clearing of the air would have done Will more good than harm. Maybe if it all spilled out, he wouldn't have felt the need to keep so many secrets, to tell so many lies, to play so many roles. Maybe he never would have manufactured Tanner Fordyce. Ah, hell, what do I know? Maybe there never would have been a Harvard education, either. No wealth, none of the honors, none of the travel. And when you get right down to it, Will seems pretty happy as the Fordyce four-flusher. Would he have been any happier as plain old Will?"

Now Patty was pacing, leaving a contrail of cigarette smoke. She reminded Beatrice of Bette Davis in *All About Eve*, just before Margo Channing mouths off at her sycophantic assistant.

"I was bitter for a while. It's no secret there were some affairs. The cheating didn't bother me so much as the lying. Like I was too stupid not to know what was going on. That hurt my pride a lot more than the thought of him with some bimbo. You ever been married, Beatrice?"

"Yes."

"It sucks, doesn't it? It's one damn compromise after the next. It's getting tuned out when you feel like talking. It's waking up every time he flips in bed. It's not being able to put asparagus in the salad, because he hates asparagus, even though you love asparagus. Maybe if you were crazy, batshit in love with each other, those little annoying things wouldn't bug you so much. But batshit love never lasts. Not sure we ever had it in the first place. Will kinda started out like another kid brother I could boss around. Then those feelings got all muddled, as he got to be so damn tall and smart-mouthed and great-looking. Vice is nice; incest is best."

Patty sighed, shook her head, and smiled sadly. "You have any kids?"

"No."

"You didn't want any?"

"Couldn't have any."

"That's rough."

"Maybe it was a blessing. Maybe I would have been bad at it."

"Bullshit. The dogs like you, and they're never wrong."

"So, were you as good with your kid as you are with your dogs?"

"I was wondering when you were gonna bring Tim up."

"Is he supposed to be a secret?"

"In a way, yah. I think sometimes Will needs to keep secret the things in his life that are most important to him."

"That speaks well of you, then."

"I never thought about it that way. Maybe you're right. As messed up as our marriage was, we always cared about each other. Always will."

"So where's Tim Fordyce now, or is it Berrigan? And what does he do?"

"It's Tim Scanlon. Will wanted it that way. And no, not because he lacked paternal feelings. I think Will never felt good enough for Tim. So his name wasn't good enough for Tim. I kind of get that. Tim was this perfect little human being. It was like he only got the good parts of both of us. Best thing we ever did."

Patty sucked deeply on her cigarette. "Be right back." She darted into the living room and returned with a framed photograph, which she handed to Beatrice. "This is Tim."

Beatrice saw a tall young man wearing unattractive black sunglasses but flashing a killer smile. He was draped over an easy chair; an English White Retriever was draped over him.

"That's Bessie. What a pair they made. She was one of the few service dogs that flunked her course. Tim's course. He normally had a genius for recognizing dogs that would be great with the blind, the cerebral palsy folks, the MS patients, the PTSD victims. But he let his heart override his head with Miss Bessie. And in a quirky way they did work pretty well together, even if she almost broke his leg a few times. That's what Tim did. He had his own company that trained service dogs and trained the humans he matched them to."

"Do you mean Tim's blind?"

"Almost since birth. A freak infection when he was an infant."

"That must have been tough on the marriage."

"Funny thing is, it wasn't. We were on the same page about Tim. Determined to give him a normal childhood. All the opportunities we could. And independence, too. We were lucky. First, Tim was such a sunny child he made it easy for us. And Boston is one of the best places you can live if you want to mainstream a kid who can't see. Me having a nursing background came in handy, too, because I knew where to go for the best physical, occupational, vocational therapies. Because of Tim, I got into PT myself. And I guess it was partly because of me that Tim got into dog therapy."

"Sounds like a real glass-half-full group. But how do you manage that with a globe-trotting husband? Will … Tanner must have been an absentee father much of the time."

"He was. But he made damn sure he stayed in close touch with Tim. That wasn't so easy in the days before e-mail, especially since Will spent a lot of time in some real dirt-bag countries. And truth be told, I kind of liked being the primary parent. With Will gone, I didn't have to compromise my ideas about raising a kid. As the middle child in a big family, I knew a thing or two about raising kids and felt up to the task."

"How old was Tim when you guys divorced?

"Twelve. But by then, the divorce didn't change much. It helped, I guess, that Will had already made a bundle, and money was something he was more than generous with. Will paid my way through PT training, paid for the roof over my head, provided the seed money for my kennel and for Tim's service-dog academy. He wasn't so generous about sharing himself, though – his real self, that is. But Tim never seemed to mind. Spending so much time training dogs and handicapped humans made him tolerant. Can't say the same for me. Tim was always able to accept people the way they were, warts and all."

Only then did Beatrice absorb how many times Patty used the past tense when speaking about her son.

"What happened to Tim, Patty?" Beatrice asked softly.

"He died five years ago. He died saving his neighbor's dog. Fitting, huh? Bessie started barking when she smelled smoke coming from next door. Tim figured out what was up and called 911, because he knew the Bonannos had gone out for the evening. Which meant Sophie, their scruffy little terrier, was home alone, trapped inside the house. So Tim wouldn't wait for the fire trucks. He went in himself. Got Sophie out okay. Then he remembered the Bonannos had an old cat, too. He went back in to get her. Turned out she had already escaped through a loose window screen. The smoke got Tim. When the firemen carried him out, they thought he'd be okay at first. No burns. But it was too late."

"I'm so sorry."

"I hated that cat. Not even Tim liked her. But he felt a responsibility to her."

"How did Tanner take it?"

"He shut down for a while. Went off to Afghanistan to do good deeds. Maybe that was his way of honoring Tim. I got real mad at him. I needed him. I needed to connect to the Tim in him. I was a real bitch when Will got back to the States. I feel a little bad about that now. I needed to be a brat about it all. I wanted Will to be a brat, too. But he was as well-mannered as always. So I accused him of not caring. That was wrong."

Patty held Beatrice's eyes a long time as if searching for absolution. The only thing Beatrice could think of to say was, "That was human."

Beatrice limped away from Patty's house with a headache. She had learned far too much about Patty and Tanner and Bessie, who had mourned herself to death; and Caitlin, Tim's fiancée, who drank her way into rehab after Tim's passing.

Beatrice wondered darkly if the Cosmic Chuckle ever spared anyone.

FIFTY

Notes from a Sad Pepys

Dear Diary,

I'm confused. I was excited about flying. Excited to see a new state. And Mr. Desmond was very nice today. He took me to a big garden, although not much was in bloom. He took me to a bunch of historic places. Stuff from the Revolutionary War. One Protestant church looks pretty much like another, tho'. He took me to a fancy restaurant, but there was lots of fish. Not my favorite. And the waitress laughed at the way I said "fire." What was she laughing at? She was the one who sounded weird. She said the shrimp was grilled over an open "fie-yah." Two syllables! Who uses two syllables to say "fire?"

And when she asked me where I was from, she laughed.

The subway was way cool. Noisy, a little scary. But cool. Except it smelled a little like when the llamas pee on their dung pile. Does that mean people pee there? I wanted to ask Mr. Desmond but was too embarrassed. Why would anyone pee on a wall?

There were a lot of different looking people on the subway. Black people and Chinese people and people who spoke foreign languages. I couldn't even guess where they came from. There was one person who looked like an old-fashioned nun. Except only her eyes showed. Mr. Desmond said she was a Muslim woman. Some of them won't show their hair or their face or anything, because they think that's sinful. He didn't seem to like the idea much, even though he tried not to show it.

The ice cream place was awesome. But I was definitely not going to order the "Raspberry Lime Rickey." Beatrice said her brother was "addicted" to the stuff when he was a kid. I ordered a sundae. I let them put something called "jimmies" on it, because Mr. Desmond said they were like little chocolate chips. They were okay. To be nice, I took a sip from his drink, but it was sour and fizzy. Not much taste.

It's just that things are too different here. Even the trees look different. At least it isn't real cold. Early April here isn't much different than back home. It could be warm and sunny. It could snow. There was a little bit of snow on the ground the first day.

I don't think anyone knows it's my birthday tomorrow. Tomorrow Beatrice is gonna take me to where she went to college. The way she talks about it, it's some big deal. I never heard of it. I'd like to go to college, but to be so far away from home would be scary. I can't imagine living up here, where I feel so different, where nobody knows my family and people think I talk funny. I talk funny? I have trouble understanding THEM! They sure have a weird way of saying words with an "r" in the middle. Like "heart" sounds like "haaaht." And they say "O" funny, too. Like the word goes on and on. Kinda like "Mawwwwm" instead of "Mom."

I wonder if Daddy knows I'm here. Beatrice said it was okay with Ben for me to come here. Maybe Daddy has forgotten about me because he's so busy in Virginia. I wonder if he'll remember it's my birthday tomorrow. But even if he does, would he know where to call?

I think Mr. Desmond knows I feel a little out of it. He asked me to help him make a fire when we got home. That was nice. He said I was a good fire-starter. And his dog is awesome. Addie. She likes Mr. Desmond better than me, of course. But I think I'm winning her over. Except she wouldn't sleep in my room. She sniffed my hand before I went to bed, but then she went back to Mr. Desmond's easy chair. I wonder if Ralph feels lonely. He likes Beatrice better than me, but he likes me.

I wish someone liked ME more than anyone else, Dear Diary. I guess I'm not supposed to complain and say things like that out loud. Like when Beatrice asked me how my day was. At first she was okay. We laughed about "Bart" and his Raspberry Lime Rickey and how I didn't think it tasted all that great. But then I had to go say the waitress in the other restaurant was snooty. I said the subway smelled. I said people talk weird. And then Beatrice got weird. She didn't seem mad really. More like sad.

She said she had an odd day too. She said she learned a lot of sad things about Mr. Fordyce and his family. She didn't say what things. And I didn't ask because she froze up. Meemaw used to say sometimes, when bad things happen, they can make a person's blood run cold. That's the way Beatrice looked. So I knew I shouldn't ask. I wanted to, tho'. Sometimes, the things

I imagine are worse than what really happened. I hope that's true with Mr. Fordyce, because the stuff I imagined happening to him was pretty bad.

Then Beatrice looked me really close in the eyes and said bad things happen to most of us, at least some of the time. She said it was okay to feel sad about it. But she said the worst thing you could do is let the bad stuff "warp" you. Like you shouldn't murder someone because someone murdered someone close to you. I get that.

But she also said something funny. She said it was bad to be a victim. Aren't we supposed to sympathize with victims? Weren't all those saints who became martyrs the same thing as victims? But Beatrice said being a victim doesn't do anyone any good. Victims are a burden to other people, she said. That sounds mean, don't you think, Dear Diary? Then she said being a victim is often an excuse. She said some people spend so much time griping about the tough things that happen to them that they don't recognize when good things happen. They don't take advantage of the good stuff that falls right into their laps. And people like that, she said, get too "self-absorbed" to do the hard work it takes to make their way in life.

Anyway, Beatrice was getting real fired up. Oops, would one of those snooty Boston people laugh at the way I said "fired up" in my head? But something about this whole victim thing sure got to Beatrice. Then she seemed to think maybe she went too far and I might cry or something. No, Dear Diary, I was NOT about to start crying! But I did feel like my head was spinning.

Anyway, Beatrice suddenly put her arm around me. It felt a little awkward. She said, "I know hard things have happened to you, Clara." She said it wouldn't be healthy to pretend the bad stuff didn't happen. And she told me not to push the bad things down deep inside. She asked me to promise her something. "Promise me you won't let the bad breaks paralyze you."

I didn't promise anything. I just asked her what she meant. I won't say something just because she wants me to! But I was also curious.

She said sometimes the bad stuff can have a positive effect. For instance, if you were poor as a kid, and hated being poor, you can work really hard in school and in your job and make sure you're never poor as an adult. I think she was talking about herself as a kid. Although her brother sure isn't poor now. And Beatrice, although she doesn't have a big house like he does, isn't poor either.

Then she said if it bothers you when people are mean to you, you can make a point of being kind to people who are nice. She said kindness can be just as infectious as meanness. She said you don't have to fake friendliness when you don't feel it. And you certainly don't have to be all smiley to someone who's being mean to you. But she said good manners help spread kindness. Saying please and thank you, just like you were taught in kindergarten. She said being thanked for a simple kindness makes you feel special and more likely to be kind in the future.

Her brother is kind. Kinder than Beatrice. I think he's a good example of what "gentleman" means. It doesn't mean snobby or high class. Or it shouldn't. It should mean a gentle man. Momma would probably say a gentle man is a wuss. She's wrong. I'd rather be around Mr. Desmond than any of the men Momma brought around.

I said some of that to Beatrice, about her brother anyway. She hugged me. She said her brother was one of the best men she knew. And then she got sad again and quiet.

I don't understand these people. But I don't always understand myself. Tomorrow I'll be 14. Maybe I'll understand more when I'm 14.

FIFTY-ONE

Diverse Thoughts

Jane Lowell looked exactly as one would expect a Jane Lowell to look. Which is to say she was one scary WASP. She might have been Beatrice's contemporary, but Ms. Lowell brought to mind every authoritarian nun, teacher, or prison matron who had ever crossed Beatrice's path. That path included serving as translator when one of Wolfgang's puffballs interviewed one Frau Metzger. The interview was part of a study on the mellowing process of incarcerated leftist terrorists from the 1970s and 1980s. Beatrice had no doubt even the most violent Red Army Faction anarchist would have morphed into a meek schoolgirl under that German prison matron's flinty eye.

But Frau Metzger had nothing on Jane Lowell. The other people occupying the Admissions Office at Wellesley College appeared to be perfectly nice, friendly women, quick with a smile, eager to make a visitor feel comfortable, ready to answer any and all questions about the college. It was just Beatrice's dumb luck to pull Ms. Lowell when she called to see if she could arrange a (very) preliminary interview for Clara. She had explained Clara was years away from applying to college. She also explained she wanted to see how Clara might compensate for the limitations of a Seneca County education, in the hope of getting into a top-flight college. Ms. Lowell agreed to meet, separately, with Beatrice and Clara.

Beatrice was not encouraged by her meeting. As Ms. Lowell studied the list of subjects covered in Clara's eighth-grade class, the woman's steel-blue eyes narrowed menacingly. The admissions officer had taken the liberty of researching Seneca County's school system and said it was woefully substandard – in terms of the educational level and experience of its teachers, in terms of student scores on standardized tests, in terms of the colleges that accepted those relatively few graduates who applied. When Beatrice asked what Clara could do in the next four years to compensate for those failings, Ms. Lowell clipped, "Absolutely nothing. She'll be lucky if she gets accepted by WVU."

Meanwhile, a cheerful student employee at admissions had taken Clara under her wing. She offered to give the youngster a guided tour of the campus, while Beatrice conferred with Ms. Lowell. Because the tour guide and Clara were late getting back to Green Hall, Ms. Lowell was unable to interview her. As she marched for the door, while ushering Beatrice ahead of her, she suggested Clara might speak with a Mrs. Cunningham. The implication was that Mrs. Cunningham was of no import and thus had endless amounts of time to waste on hopeless girls from Appalachia. Or so Beatrice inferred, as the chip on her shoulder began digging into her trapezius.

Mrs. Cunningham was a plump thirty-something who might be called voluptuous, if her chosen style had not been Academic Drab. On her desk she maintained a crystal bowl filled with wrapped Ghirardelli chocolate squares, which she offered to Clara. Mrs. Cunningham refused to accept the inevitable, "No, thank you, ma'am."

But as friendly, cheerful, and maternal as Mrs. Cunningham was, Clara quickly deduced the admissions officer thought the interview was a waste of time. Perhaps it was because Clara was fed up with Bostonians making fun of her accent. Perhaps it was because Beatrice had preached about the folly of victimhood. Perhaps it was because she felt she had nothing to lose. But suddenly Clara, who was only going along with this Wellesley tour to please Beatrice, decided she did not like being perceived as unworthy to consider this particular college. A switch she hadn't even known existed snapped softly inside her cerebrum.

Instead of listening mutely to Mrs. Cunningham's recitation of the stiff competition applicants faced – from graduates of the best prep schools with straight As and flawless standardized test scores, from students who spent their summers with Habitat for Humanity, tutored inner-city children, played violin with small-city orchestras, exposed corrupt city councilmen, and patented apps for Bill Gates – Clara decided to see if Wellesley would pass muster with *her*.

"How many of your students are from West Virginia?" she asked.

She learned there were none.

Mrs. Cunningham bubbled about how many different countries were represented within the college community. Clara asked how many of the girls from foreign countries were poor. Mrs. Cunningham wobbled briefly then said some of the girls from Asia, Africa, Europe, and Latin America benefited from partial scholarships. But she acknowledged they probably would not be considered poor by the standards of their home countries. Then Mrs. Cunningham launched forth about a recruitment campaign in poor U.S. urban areas. As a result, she beamed, African-American enrollment was up five percent over the previous year.

"Well, what about country kids?" Clara asked.

"I've never been asked that before." Mrs. Cunningham paused. "I suspect, Clara, there is less interest."

"*I'm* interested. Wouldn't girls from Appalachia make for variety too?"

At a loss for words, the admissions officer laughed awkwardly. "If the applicant from Appa-*latch*-a, as you call it, used the logic you just wielded, I imagine she could carve out a very nice academic career here. Have you ever thought of going to law school? And yes, a diverse college community probably should include students from rural West Virginia."

"Ma'am, I don't expect Massachusetts folks who live in Quin-zee would much like to hear they were wrong for not calling their city Quin-cee, the way it's spelled. In Appalachia we call it Appa-*latch*-a," Clara said, speaking as Southern Highlanders have for centuries.

"I stand corrected. I guess I don't know very much about where you come from, and that's to my discredit. I hope to see you applying here in another few years, Clara. In the meantime, explore any supplemental educational opportunities your area may offer. Get involved in as many extracurricular activities as you can. Volunteer. Explore your own talents. If you have a knack for music, take guitar or piano lessons. If you can't afford that, try out for a local band or chorus. Look at the clubs in your community, where you can learn from people with unique skills and interests. Amateur radio, star-gazing, bird-watching, whatever. Lots of them will happily accept younger members. Embrace eclectic, interesting hobbies. They look great on an application. In other words, compensate for what your school system lacks by educating yourself—making yourself an interesting human being."

Clara did not want to admit she didn't know the word "eclectic". She would look that up later. But she had an idea what Mrs. Cunningham meant. And she had an idea that perhaps she already had a few options.

"I helped with a difficult llama birth. And I'm learning how to spin llama fiber. Would that kind of hobby count?"

"Llamas? Well, that's a new one. You could become the college community's resident expert on fiber arts and certainly on all things llama. Yes, Clara, that would indeed be helpful."

From the waiting area, Beatrice was puzzled to see the different expressions worn by Mrs. Cunningham and Clara, as they walked out of the office. Clara looked deep in thought. Mrs. Cunningham was beaming. She walked purposefully to Beatrice. "That was one of the most enjoyable interviews I've had in a long time. Clara is quite a remarkable young woman. I hope to see both of you back here in a few years."

Later, Beatrice nudged Clara and said, "You aced that one, kid."

"Did I? I just got a little mad, so I didn't really care if she liked me or not."

"Good for you. I wish I'd gotten mad at the old witch I talked to. See, sometimes standing up for yourself is the best thing you can do."

"Who'd a thunk?" Clara said, shaking her head, not realizing she had just borrowed an expression from Beatrice.

"I'd a thunk, birthday girl."

Clara looked up from under her eyelashes. "You know it's my birthday?"

"Of course I know, and once we blow this joint—after I show you where my dorm was—we'll celebrate properly."

From the car window, Clara noticed for the first time how pretty the campus was. Used to the lush wildness of southeastern West Virginia, Clara was not floored by the extensive acreage and greenery. The campus would probably be spectacular in a few weeks, as the rhododendrons and dogwoods exploded in pastel fireworks. Yet, even now, the subtle blue of violets was advancing over some gentle hillsides, softening the stark Gothic outline of the academic quad.

Maybe I COULD like a place like this.

FIFTY-TWO

Insiders, Outsiders

Addie skidded on the tiles in the front hall, as she greeted Beatrice and Clara but tarried only long enough to sniff both humans' proffered, empty hands before dashing to the kitchen. The new arrivals followed to see what the attraction was.

Before they reached the kitchen, they were enveloped by the unmistakable aroma of basil and oregano and sautéed onions. Evie was grating mozzarella into a big bowl while carrying on an animated conversation with Bart, who was stirring a huge pot of marinara sauce. Bart flipped an edge of the kitchen towel, draped over his left shoulder, to acknowledge his sister and young charge. Evie hastily wiped her hands on her apron and strode, arms outstretched, toward Beatrice. Witnessing the hug, Clara felt like an outsider.

Then Evie turned to Clara, curled the girl into her arms, and squeezed vigorously. "Hey, birthday girl!" Evie shouted happily. "I hope the hell you like lasagna, because that's what's on the menu this evening. I wanted to make my world-famous Chicken Kiev, but Bart said lasagna would be a safer choice. No teenager, he said, would ever turn up her nose at lasagna or pizza. And what do I know about teenagers? So he won that argument. But it will be his only win for the day, I guarantee."

Clara nodded that she liked lasagna. She leaned in toward the pot Bart was tending and took a deep whiff. "Yum!" she approved. Seeing the kitchen windows fogged over with steam from the marinara sauce and the furiously boiling lasagna noodles, she was suddenly transported back to her grandmother's house. She remembered Meemaw "worrying" a huge pot of chili or spaghetti sauce or chicken soup. The windows would steam up in defiance of the wintry blasts outside and make Clara feel secure and cozy inside.

Bart gave the back of her neck a gentle squeeze with his free hand.

"Happy fourteenth, kiddo!"

"The dessert is not my first choice, either," Evie continued. "But the Apple Charlotte I wanted to make was just too time-consuming. My flight landed only a few hours ago."

Clara felt herself slipping away from the conversation, which cheerfully discussed the best cakes for birthdays, the best bakeries in the area, the best birthday celebrations of years gone by. She suffered a sudden attack of homesickness, oddly deepened by the realization there were precious few memorable birthday celebrations in her own past.

At the same time, she realized all three adults were going out of their way to make her feel at home. Still, the kitchen cheer, a bit forced, made her withdraw into herself.

Her shyness increased, as Evie, done with the grating, turned her full attention to Clara's campus tour. "So, do you think that college is someplace you might be interested in attending? What advice did the admissions people offer?"

Despite Clara's mumbled responses, Evie pressed on.

"Hey, give the girl a chance to catch her breath," Bart interjected. "Why don't you guys grab a drink and catch up on business out in the living room, while I put my sous-chef to work. Here, Clara, you stir the pot while I drain the noodles."

Evie rolled her eyes in annoyance but complied, fishing the bourbon bottle out of the cabinet. Beatrice noted the sureness with which her friend knew the layout of Bart's kitchen. "We have been dismissed, Beatrice," Evie complained. "Don't work the kid too hard," she called over her shoulder.

The kitchen noises, now audible, comforted Clara: the thick bubbling of the sauce, the slap of the noodles hitting the colander, the rumbling of the refrigerator's compressor, the soft hiss of the gas oven, and Addie's rhythmic panting from the nearby corner, where she lay out of the way but ready to vacuum the floor free of dropped morsels.

Clara was genuinely interested in the architecture of lasagna, which, in her experience, was something that came frozen and got nuked. Not a believer in make-work projects, Bart accorded Clara a substantive role. She was to wield the ladle spreading the meat sauce over the noodles while he, using his naked hands, applied the cheese layers.

Once he placed the concoction in the heated oven, Bart announced that the next job was to prepare the salad, which could sit undressed in the refrigerator until the lasagna was done. As each cook manned his and her own cutting board, the sounds of chopping filled the quiet kitchen.

"You're really fast," Clara observed. "My father is pretty good in the kitchen but not as good as you."

"Well, my wife died when our daughter was still quite young. So it was sink or swim. Cook or go hungry. And I like to eat well."

"How old was your daughter?"

"A little younger than you. Twelve."

"What happened to your wife? I mean, if you don't mind?"

"Breast cancer."

"I'm sorry."

"Me too. But Betty is a constant. I talk to her all the time."

"So you still miss her?"

"Hmmm, I wouldn't say I miss her exactly. She's been dead for more years than we were married. But she's part of me, part of who I am."

"Then she must have been nice."

Bart smiled to himself and kept chopping. "That college you saw today, that was probably the first place where BB – I mean, Beatrice – was happy."

"Really?"

"She loved it. She was such a good student she loved the challenge of it. But she also loved how pretty it was. Where we grew up wasn't so pretty. I suppose to someone like you, coming from the countryside, the campus is not remarkable. But Beatrice just loved the greenery, the open spaces, swimming in Lake Waban, sledding down the snowy hills."

"She wasn't happy before she went to college?"

"Nope."

"How come?

"Stuff."

Clara decided she should not ask for an explanation, but her imagination went into overdrive.

"Just because Beatrice loved Wellesley doesn't mean you have to."

"You don't think I'd belong there?"

"It's up to you to figure out what you want to do with your life. And it's not too early to start doing some serious thinking."

"The lady in the admissions office acted like I wouldn't belong there. Or that's what she thought at first."

"And that ticked you off."

"Yeah." Clara said, attacking the carrot on the board before her.

Bart erupted in laughter. "Some old dragon lady told BB very much the same thing. It made her so mad she resolved to prove her wrong. Before that interview, I don't think BB was all that interested in Wellesley. But being made to feel like somebody's poor white trash relation got under her skin. From then on, Wellesley was the only place for her."

"She felt like white trash? In Boston?"

Bart paused his chopping. "Do you know what a Yankee is?"

"A Northerner."

"To a Southerner, that's what a Yankee is. To the Boston Irish working stiff, at least when we were kids, it meant a White Anglo-Saxon Protestant with a pedigree going back to the Mayflower. A Yankee has breeding, money, privilege, and contempt. We were most definitely not Yankees."

"At least people didn't call you hillbillies."

"That they didn't. But we had no shortage of colorful terms – terms applied to us and terms we applied to others. Politically correct we were not." Bart chuckled to himself.

"Mr. Fordyce calls Beatrice 'Hillwilla.'"

Bart laughed again. "Mr. Fordyce has a sense of irony. It has been my sister's curse – and her blessing – never to belong anywhere, to straddle several different worlds, identities. Hillwilla, I take it, describes someone who walks the walk, but doesn't talk the talk?"

"She doesn't exactly fit in, I guess."

"There are worse things than being an outsider."

Clara wasn't so sure. But she was sure tonight's diary entry would be a long one.

FIFTY-THREE

A Red-Letter Day

Clara's latest diary entry would indeed keep her from sleep for quite some time. Even though the party broke up at a reasonable hour, shortly before eleven, the evening was filled with surprises.

The first came at eight as garlic-laden air hung heavily over the diners, taking a breather in anticipation of the birthday cake yet to come. The front door chimed. Bart and Addie tended to the call, while Evie and Clara began clearing the dinner table.

Beatrice crutched into the living room. En route she caught a gust of cold air, scented by Chanel No. 5.

Uh, oh. Martha.

It was indeed Bart's daughter, announcing she had just finished checking out a potential client's disastrous décor in nearby Sherborn and realized she could squeeze in a quick visit with her father on her way back home. "But I didn't realize you had company. I hope I'm not intruding, Daddy," Martha said, maintaining forward momentum into the living room.

Martha very well knew Bart would be playing host this night. Bart could not have missed her fib but showed no sign of annoyance. Bussing Martha on the cheek, he said, "Always happy for an opportunity to see my ginger-haired daughter."

Having paused at the small mirror in the hall to primp her auburn hair, Martha began scanning the living room for the target that most interested her. That target was not Beatrice, who merited a "Well, if it isn't my favorite aunt," along with an air kiss.

Beatrice was about to reply she was Martha's only aunt, but her niece's attention was already elsewhere, focused on Evie, who was entering the room wiping her hands on a towel. "Well, this must be the ladyfriend who has been such a good fashion influence on my father," Martha cooed, waiting for Evie to approach and accept the proffered hand.

Evie, flashing a wolfish smile, first at Bart and then at Beatrice, moved in close to Martha, swatting away the younger woman's right hand and then embracing her in a bear hug. "For gracious sake, my dear, not a handshake. I've heard sooooo much about you, you feel like family already. Here, give us a kiss."

Only slightly put off her game, Martha kissed Evie's cheek. Whereupon Evie kissed both of Martha's cheeks and led her to the couch. "Let's find out all about you, dear," Evie said sweetly. "But, oh, my goodness, I think I forgot something first. Just a minute dear. Oh, Clara!" Evie called back to the kitchen. "Could you bring me my Piaget? I believe I left it by the sink."

With that, Evie shot a heavy-lidded, cow-faced stare at Beatrice, who quickly averted her eyes, lest she drown in giggles. She risked a look at her brother, nestling into his easy chair. She was certain he knew Martha was here to scope out his ladyfriend's virtues, especially the ones she reported to the IRS. He also knew Evie knew Martha's agenda. As long as everyone appeared to be playing nice, he was content to sit back and watch the theater. For a while, at least. Bart's sufferance was not unlimited.

He reached that limit after half an hour, during which Evie, after slipping on the expensive watch Clara had plucked from the kitchen counter, blocked every one of Martha's fact-finding queries by expressing enthusiastic interest in Martha's business, educational background, activities, etc. Martha ended up doing most of the talking. She actually seemed charmed by Evie's interest in her. Although no awkward scene appeared imminent, Bart reminded everyone the birthday celebration was not yet ended and invited Martha to stay for cake.

Martha agreed but soon lost interest. She lasted through extinguishing the candles before pleading the press of the next day's business. She let Bart wrap up a piece of cake for her and extricated herself with a minimum of fuss. After Martha's departure, the living room felt like the aftermath of a sudden cloudburst, with startled leaves exposing their whitish backsides but only minor limb-fall littering the ground.

During Tropical Storm Martha, Clara watched the two principal players attentively. She seemed particularly fascinated with Evie, who was, after all, acting more like the Queen Mum than her usual irreverent self. The kid had better work on her poker face, Beatrice thought, as if planning to incorporate that mental note into some future conversation. Beatrice was suddenly startled by her own presumption – the feeling that Clara was hers to educate.

It was Evie who breathed air back into the party. She ducked out of the living room and reappeared with a festively wrapped box. "This is for Clara, to thank her for taking such good care of my crippled friend here, for shoveling llama shit, for putting up with Beatrice's dark view of life. You may have to live like a hermit at chez Beatrice, but at least you won't have to dress like one." Evie plopped the box onto Clara's lap.

The girl was genuinely surprised. She stumbled out a thank you but just sat there, looking at the box.

"Rip into it, for Chrissakes," Evie urged impatiently.

Tearing off the fancy gift-wrap, Clara found a shoe box. With a quizzical look, she popped the top and fished out, by its sling-back, a ridiculously expensive, ridiculously high heel. A big-girl party shoe if ever there was one. A red party shoe.

"I understand red is your favorite color," Evie prodded.

"Oh! My! Gee! Wow! They're beautiful! And they're my size! And yes, I love red! My momma told me I shouldn't wear it, because my hair is reddish brown, and I should stick to blues and greens. But I love red. I don't have much red clothing. I certainly don't have red shoes. But I do now. Wow! How did you know?"

"Every girl needs some fancy shoes. And if we left it up to Beatrice here, you'd spend your life in Wellies and maybe a smart hiking boot or two."

"Just don't break an ankle in those things," Beatrice laughed. "We don't need two crips on the farm."

After Clara hurled herself at Evie for a hug, Bart retrieved two more packages from behind the couch. "The first one is from Beatrice. She sneakily ordered it online before you guys left and had it delivered here."

The package was awesomely large. Clara looked at Beatrice with wonder. "What could it be?"

The size was deceptive because of all the packing materials, which Clara, growing more impatient, now ripped through. Inside she found a laptop. With a red cover. Her jaw dropped open. "Really?" was all she said.

"Well, I know a lot of kids, even in Seneca County, have their own computers – for schoolwork as well as the Internet. This one doesn't have quite all the bells and whistles for playing games. But unlike a lot of laptops, it has first-class word-processing software. I figure it will come in handy for school and all the writing you do on your own."

Trying to master the lump in her throat, Clara choked out, "But it's too much!"

"No, it's not. You've helped me a lot these past few months. And if this helps you out, then I'm happy."

Clara, still struggling to keep from crying, nodded slowly, her head down as she looked at the happy debris on her lap.

Bart stepped into the vacuum by dropping a small box beside the girl. As she opened it, he explained, "You admired my orchids the other day, when we were in my little greenhouse. I know you can't take one with you on the plane, so this is just a small wrist corsage to enjoy here. Meanwhile, UPS will deliver a living version of your own to Beatrice's farm. It's a vanda. And it's almost red."

Clara buried her nose in the fuchsia-colored corsage. "It's beautiful! And it smells beautiful, too. Thank you so much! All of you."

"Ah, but there's more," Bart added, handing over several envelopes. They contained birthday cards from Eltie, from Vaughn, from Ben, from Uncle Virgil, from Clara's father. "Your father called today when you were out. He said he has a present waiting for you back home. Couldn't get him to drop a single hint."

The final envelope was larger than the rest. Clara didn't recognize the return address. Inside were brochures from The Marlboro Academy for Girls. Clipped onto one was a heavyweight piece of notepaper embossed with "From the Desk of Tanner Fordyce." Having difficulty deciphering the scribbles on it, Clara solicited help from Evie and Beatrice. The three deduced Tanner had "learned" that the academy offered one scholarship a year to a worthy Seneca County girl. The scholarship was Clara's for the taking, if she was interested.

Simultaneously, Clara and Beatrice said in shock, "Who'da thunk?"

Evie added, "What the fff… udge?"

FIFTY-FOUR

Crawlspace Blues

Ben would have preferred spending the first weekend in April on Gurney Mountain. Now that the weather was tolerable, even at four thousand feet, the myriad chores involved in restoring the old Buckhalter homestead seemed manageable, despite its lack of running water, central heating, and electricity. Just a few months ago, Ben was wondering if the restoration project wasn't a lost cause. But three successive days with sunshine and temperatures approaching seventy, after weeks and weeks of gray, cold gloom, have a way of resurrecting confidence. Once again, the project looked doable – in time to infuse new life into Ben's marriage and rescue Clara from an uncertain future.

Instead of focusing on the Gurney Mountain property, however, Ben was fixing up his brother's cabin in the northwestern corner of the county. With Mike in Harrisonburg through the winter, problems were inevitable. On two occasions, storms had shut off electricity for nearly a week at a time in the area, one of the county's most remote. If someone had been in residence, to build a fire in the fireplace or turn on the gas oven, the cabin probably would have limped along without damage. One thawed pipe was currently weeping water into the crawlspace. Another had sprung a major leak within the north wall on the upper floor. The pipe needed replacing, which also meant replacing the drywall damaged by the dripping water. The constant demand for water, thanks to the constant drips, had burnt out the pressure tank. Ben was not looking forward to squeezing his large frame into the crawlspace to get at the tank.

He consoled himself with the realization he could soon pass the torch on to Mike. His brother was in the process of extricating himself from his contract in the Shenandoah Valley without incurring any lawsuit. In fact, he was getting a separation bonus and a cheerful recommendation. He had spotted a potentially disastrous construction flaw in one of the four-thousand-square-foot homes he was turning into a showcase for his woodwork. Although remediation would be costly, catching the problem at the current stage would be much less serious than farther down the line—and infinitely preferable to a reputation-shattering lawsuit. Most important, Mike had been circumspect in sharing his news. He thereby minimized the potential embarrassment for the developer and for the county inspectors, who had already signed off. Mike suspected the bonus was more in the nature of hush money, but his conscience was clear. He had seen evidence that the flaw would indeed be fixed.

Mike agreed to finish the work on one specific house. After that, he could head back to West Virginia. If all went well, he and Clara could move into the cabin in July, thus well ahead of the start of the school year. He had no shortage of connections in Seneca County and surrounding areas, and he anticipated steady work. It would not, of course, offer the challenges of the Virginia job. And it would mean a huge drop in income, a development that would set back his dream of devoting himself to handcrafting beautiful musical instruments for some of the country's top performing artists. But he was painfully aware his daughter needed him now. Besides, he was astonished at how much he had been able to save during his months away from home. Having zero social life on the other side of the mountains, and often camping out in one of the developer's houses, Mike had minimal expenses.

It also helped, Ben thought sourly, to have a brother who would work for free. Although they always had a close relationship, Mike often exasperated Ben. It was not that Mike was irresponsible. He was a dreamer. And his dreams didn't always have a firm basis in reality.

Charyce was a case in point. Mike actually believed the incredible lust that had fired their relationship for a few years was something more complex and lasting. On the day he and Charyce married, Mike confided in his best man, big brother Ben, that he considered his bride his soul mate. Ben was hard-pressed to suppress a guffaw. Not half an hour earlier, Charyce had made it perfectly clear she would not be averse to a little slap and tickle with the best man. Even if Ben were still single, even if Charyce's new husband were not Ben's brother, the idea would have been appalling. Some men would have eagerly sampled Charyce's wares and then beaten a hasty retreat. But Ben knew the woman was trouble with a capital T; trouble that was not worth even the most mind-altering sex.

Mike should have known that, too. Tall and well-proportioned since his mid-teens, Mike had ample experience with girls and women. And growing up under the practical guidance of Mary Buckhalter should have schooled Mike in reading people. But Mike was a dreamer, which meant sometimes he saw what he wanted to see.

Even though he knew Charyce had been unfaithful before the end of the first year of the marriage, Mike "saw" that motherhood would change his wife for the good. The child would bond the pair, give them a common mission in life. Mike did not know Charyce had made an appointment with an abortion clinic in Charleston. She canceled only because a girlfriend had made a compelling case for the financial opportunities of motherhood. She could extort all sorts of gifts from her husband, who seemed invested in the fetus from the moment the pee-stick turned blue. If he was so psyched about fatherhood, Mike could change the diapers and handle the pre-dawn formula feedings.

When motherhood did not turn out to be quite the bargain Charyce had anticipated, she fell back to Plan B. She would get divorced, dump the child on Mike as much as possible while still maintaining the fiction of shared custody, and collect child support. Maybe she could collect welfare payments, too, she thought happily. But before she implemented her plan, Charyce knew she had to get her figure back to become a marketable commodity once again. And she had to get her tubes tied, lest the Buckhalter sperm proved too potent for her IUD. So, for a while, she played dutiful Madonna.

During those months, Mike envisioned the domestic bliss the couple would share—not only with tiny Clara but with several more children. Mike found Clara a truly enchanting being. Playing out the domestic Eden in his mind, Mike happily changed diapers and walked the floors with a colicky infant draped over his shoulder. He played endless rounds of peek-a-boo, briefly hiding his face behind his rough carpenter's hands and then beaming with wide-eyed cheer when his daughter's face morphed from anxiety to bubbly joy at rediscovering Daddy.

But the reality of fatherhood fell short of the dream of fatherhood.

Although Clara was a sunny infant, for whom a minimum of positive attention went a long way, life intruded. When Mike was with his daughter, he was really with his daughter. When Mike was away from home, however, his daughter was not much on his mind. He told himself he needed to get more income to raise a family. So he began taking more and more jobs in other counties and spent endless hours on the road and would often agree to work from sunup to sundown to help the main contractor make up for weather delays. Until he drove the last nail into the last piece of framing, Mike focused only on the job. He was not worrying about whether Charyce had left Clara with some meth-smoking girlfriend, so she could take a breather from motherhood.

While Ben regularly popped antacids, he knew his brother would never get an ulcer. Ben sometimes envied Mike's ability to be in the moment. He sometimes envied his younger brother's ability to dream big. And he genuinely hoped the dream of making guitars for Nashville would become a lucrative reality.

But Ben doubted a Buckhalter guitar would become the twenty-first century's version of a Les Paul electric. He also wondered how much Clara would see of her father once he moved back across the Alleghenies. Ben wondered how much time Clara would actually spend in the cabin he was currently fixing. Would she end up back with Charyce? Would his niece yet again run afoul of Rodney? Would there be new Rodneys to worry about?

Wedged between pressure tank and water softener, Ben had difficulty accessing the breast pocket on his flannel shirt. He finally succeeded and popped the last Mylanta Chewable into his mouth.

FIFTY-FIVE

Getting to the Heart of the Matter

It was good to be home, where people pronounced the letter "r" and didn't regard Clara as if she was the product of sustained inbreeding once they learned she was from Appa-*lay*-sha, a place she had never heard of. As she trudged down the hill to the llama barn, the girl stooped over a bloodroot straggling from the edge of an unmown section of hillside. She savored the redness staining her thumb as she plucked the stem. Farther up the hill, hundreds of the white flowers brightened the shady corner. "Welcome back," Clara whispered, happy the familiar but short-lived flowers had returned with the warmer weather, happy that spring seemed to be one reasonably reliable miracle, happy she was back home in Seneca County.

With those thoughts, the teenager experienced a shiver—a rabbit running over her grave, as Meemaw would put it. Shaking it off, Clara focused on how comforting it was to see Ralph again, ebulliently determined to sniff out every fold in her jeans, every pore in her skin, as if he were taking nourishment from the mere smell of his human. But I'm not his human, Clara corrected herself. And the curly-locked fuzz ball, who now pronged sideways up to her, might have hair almost exactly the same color as hers, but Buck wasn't hers, either; nor she his, even if she had midwifed him into the world. She briefly crooked the baby llama's neck in her elbow, before Buck dashed off in response to a worried hum from Reine.

"Hey, llamas, are you glad to see me?" Clara called, wishing she knew the answer. Several herd members inched shyly forward for a nose-kiss, motivated mainly by curiosity.

Leaning into her knees and hiking back up the hill, Clara admired the pumping action of Ralph's head, as he sprang ahead of her up that same path. He looked back several times in mid-pump and appeared to be nodding at the girl, encouraging her to follow him to the house. To his home, not hers.

Clara gazed at the smiling dog, at the slowly greening hillside, at the still-naked trees, at the small farmhouse. It was all so familiar and alien at the same time. It was not home. But the realization did not upset her nearly as much as the suspicion that the apartment she shared with her mother or the cabin she shared with her father or the doublewide she shared with Ben and his family did not constitute home, either.

She had felt so alien in Boston. And now she realized she still felt like an alien back in West Virginia.

Slipping off her boots in the mudroom, Clara called out, "The baby looks fine. All the llamas are okay. I changed the water and set out fresh hay."

"Thanks, Clara," said Beatrice absent-mindedly, as she sorted through nearly a week's worth of mail at the kitchen table. She paused over one envelope, bearing the now-familiar image of an acorn superimposed over the paler, ghost-like outline of an ancient oak tree. It was the logo of The Marlboro Academy for Girls.

It was one of two envelopes addressed to Clara, care of Beatrice. The second was small, fat, and square. The back flap was embossed with some kind of vine erupting with hearts. The return address was that of Ms. Charyce Trask and Mr. Rodney Madsen.

"Uh-oh!" Beatrice blurted inadvertently. She considered hiding the tacky thing, but she didn't. She regarded both the vine-hearts and the stylized acorn and suspected she was looking at a fork in the road. In Clara's road.

"What's the matter?" Clara asked, as she entered the kitchen.

"I just realized Bart's present must have been on the doorstep for a day. I hope it's okay." Without missing a beat, she scooped up the nearby UPS package and handed it to Clara.

Even though the girl knew what was inside, she felt a surge of excitement. She had never received an orchid before, unless you counted the severed one that had adorned her wrist a few days earlier. Clara also felt a surge of belonging. If she was receiving packages at this address, maybe she was home after all? She tore into the birthday gift from Bart.

"It looks a bit tired, but this pamphlet says that's normal, and I should give it a little water and let it rest in the shade a few days," Clara mumbled, looking from the pamphlet in her left hand to the slightly droopy vanda in her right.

As Clara brought the plant to the kitchen sink, Beatrice tried to sound casual. "You also have mail."

Clara spun her head around. "You're kidding!"

"See for yourself."

Child that she was, Clara reached for the larger, fatter envelope first. Then she set it back on the table and patted the acorn logo nervously. "I guess Mr. Fordyce wasn't joking?" she asked, trying to read Beatrice's reaction.

"I don't imagine Tanner would joke about something like that."

Clara reached for the envelope again, hesitated briefly, and then ripped it open. After a few moments of sorting through the contents, she squinted skeptically. "They're thanking me for my application and congratulating me on my school record. I didn't send them any application. I didn't have the school send them my grades."

"Don't look at me," Beatrice replied. "But I bet I know who did."

"Mr. Fordyce? How?"

"One of Tanner's minions, I expect. As for the 'how,' I haven't a clue, except he has enough swagger to pull off just about anything. Did he write an admissions essay, too?"

"It doesn't say anything about an essay. But there's something here about a scholarship fund set up in the 1960s by a woman named Marvela Hornsby. It says she grew up in Seneca County and then became rich and famous. No, wait; she married someone rich and famous. And then she died, and her husband donated money so other girls from here could get a good education. But it doesn't look like Marvela went to Marlboro herself. Nope, her daughter did. And one scholarship a year goes to a Seneca County girl, just like Mr. Fordyce said. They want to give next year's ninth-grade scholarship to me."

"And do you want to accept it?"

"Could I?"

"Well, you should at least consider it. And figure out if it's right for you."

"But it's in another county."

"So what? Marlboro is probably closer than Seneca High School, which is in the northern part of this county."

"But the northern part of the county is where Daddy's cabin is."

Beatrice paused. She didn't want to hit the girl over the head with an unkind truth. But after all this time, Beatrice had no confidence that Clara and her father would be living in that cabin when the new school year started in late August.

With a jolt, she wondered just where Clara would be living.

God! Will Clara still be here with me?

Then she realized that, by suggesting the relative nearness of Marlboro, Beatrice was thinking Clara would indeed be on hand, come late August.

Clara filled the pause. "Well, I guess I don't know if I'll be living at the cabin next year, do I?"

Beatrice could only shrug. "Why don't you decide first of all whether you'd like to go to Marlboro Academy? And if you want to, then we can figure out how you get there." She wasn't ready to offer long-term lodgings, not just yet. There were times she sorely missed her solitude, even in her current gimpy state and needing Clara's help.

Beatrice noticed her choice of pronouns. "We" would figure out the transportation options. Beatrice was automatically assuming responsibility for facilitating the girl's education. She shook off her confusion. "Why don't you look over the brochures carefully first? We can visit the campus. So you can have the info you need to make a decision."

"Okay," Clara said thoughtfully. She put the big envelope aside and picked up the smaller, embossed one and opened it wordlessly.

Beatrice watched a range of expressions on the girl's face: first curiosity, then surprise, then just the hint of a sneer. Finally, a coldness composed Clara's features. She reinserted the heart-festooned invitation and a hand-written Post-It note into the envelope and pressed down on the back flap as if trying to quarantine the contents.

"Momma and Rodney are getting married in June," Clara explained calmly. "She wants me to be her maid of honor."

"How do you feel about that?"

The indecision Beatrice had seen in Clara's eyes as they discussed The Marlboro Academy for Girls was gone. The teenager fixed Beatrice with a steady gaze and said evenly, "I'd rather choke."

FIFTY-SIX

People in Walmart

Amanda Buckhalter could think of better ways to spend a balmy day in mid-April than immersing herself in the claustrophobically stacked shopping lanes of the Marlboro Walmart. Amanda suspected all Walmarts were embarrassingly tacky, but the West Virginia versions were surely among the worst. She had once fielded an e-mail forwarding those widely distributed photos featuring the "People of Walmart." She was pretty sure she had recognized two locals among the photographic subjects, complete with tattoos, wattles, and trashy clothing. The e-mail had embarrassed and angered Amanda, particularly because the forwarder was one of her husband's business contacts in Virginia. It was yet another example of how people beyond the mountains sneered at West Virginians.

But Amanda was having difficulty stifling a sneer herself, as she regarded her fellow shoppers.

Why must they dress that way? Why must they talk that way? Does anyone really want to see the naked belly of an already overweight woman who is eight months pregnant?

Amanda mentally scanned her own appearance. She was dressed appropriately, without having incurred undue cost. Thanks to exercise and dietary discipline, she was still slender, even approaching middle age. So why couldn't her fellow Walmartians manage a fraction of similar decorum?

For maybe the billionth time, Amanda reflected on the tough work it had taken to "get above her raisin'." But fear undercut the satisfaction she derived from her achievements. Could she maintain her hard-won status, surrounded as she was by so many negative examples? Amanda worried about slipping back. Getting fat. Getting lazy. Cutting corners. Taking the easy, low road, as many within her own extended family had done. She would feel more secure if she could just put more distance between herself and the human wreckage around her. But here she was, cheek to jowl with it yet again, trying to shake off her sense of vulnerability.

Amanda aimed her cart toward one of the checkout counters. She groaned inwardly, noting the outrageously black dye job on the (overweight) sixty-something clerk. Then she caught sight, two counters over, of a familiar figure—a very trim albeit curvy figure, which is why the woman stood out. Amanda immediately bent over one of the scandal sheets beckoning impulse buyers trapped in the checkout lane. She tried to look absorbed by the latest celebrity rehab/DUI/eating-disorder saga. She was embarrassed to be seen reading one of those dreadful rags, but she desperately wanted to avoid a conversation with that piece of trailer trash Charyce Trask.

The ploy failed. The customer ahead of Amanda was collecting her bags of Cheetos and beef jerky, along with two six-packs of lite beer, so Amanda had to move forward. As she did, she could not miss Charyce eagerly waving. Amanda also could not miss Charyce's Wonderbra-fortified breasts bobbling with each wave. The customer in back of Charyce noticed the undulations as well and stared open-mouthed, first at Charyce's cleavage then at the target of the wave. Disappointed with the latter, the bandy-legged man with the shaved head and snake-tattooed left forearm returned his full, reverential attention to the energetic Charyce.

Amanda nodded curtly, hoping the acknowledgement would suffice. But Charyce kept waving, pointing to the ring on her left hand. Then Charyce yelled—cheerfully but at full volume—that Amanda was not to leave the store before they had a chance to chat. Amanda felt a red wave sweep from her face to her chest. Talking to Charyce was the last thing she wanted to do, but the skank would probably cause even more mortification if Amanda tried to slip away.

The black-haired old biddy scanning Amanda's items smirked when she asked, "And how are you today, sweetie?"

Amanda replied tightly, "Quite well, thank you." But she feared her blushing had undone the regal nonchalance she was trying to convey with her grammatically correct, well-modulated diction. Nevertheless, the response choked off any further exchange of amenities, even if it failed to wipe the smarmy expression from the clerk's face. Amanda briefly fantasized about slapping the woman, which made her feel somewhat better.

She took more time than usual to check the carousel to make sure she had not missed any of her bagged purchases. Despite the line of customers waiting to check out, the clerk paused to watch Amanda carefully examining the carousel. She crossed her arms over her stout chest and glared. Amanda glared right back before spinning around and muscling her shopping cart out of the checkout lane. She thought she heard a snigger exchanged between the old biddy and the next customer. That snigger would obsess Amanda later in the day.

But right now her energy was focused on Charyce, who by now had pranced over to her. Amanda's eyes darted down to the woman's feet.

Hooker shoes. Ridiculous! But isn't that exactly what Charyce is? Hooking up with an affluent man she doesn't love, trading sexual favors for material possessions?

"How you doin', girl?" Charyce exclaimed cheerfully.

"I'm doing well, Charyce," Amanda replied leadenly.

"I suppose you've heard the news by now," Charyce continued, flapping her left hand. "Rodney and I have set a date. June fourteenth. He is just the most impatient boy. He could not wait to reel me in. So here I am, rushing around making all these arrangements at the last minute. Men have no idea."

"Last I heard, the wedding was off," Amanda said bluntly.

Charyce narrowed her kohled eyes for an instant then resumed her bubbly demeanor. "Oh, I just bet my ex was spreading nasty rumors. He is sooooo jealous. But I'm surprised Ben would believe anything his little brother says about me. Ben is one Buckhalter who always had his shit together." Charyce winked knowingly.

Amanda winced but kept silent. There were many things about her husband that annoyed her mightily. There were many things about the whole Buckhalter clan she found trying. But Amanda never, not in her most insecure moments, doubted her husband's fidelity. Nor did she doubt for a minute Ben's ability to see right through his former sister-in-law.

"Now, hon, I know a lot of water has grown up under our feet since Mike and me split. But you was always fair with me. And I hear you didn't go swallow all that trash Mike's dyke cousin's been spreadin' about my Rodney. That's yesterday's newspaper. I always figured you and me had a lot in common, puttin' up with all that Buckhalter nonsense. You're kinda like the sister I never had."

Charyce paused to scrutinize the other woman. She saw the constipated expression Amanda so often wore when she was in disapproving mode, which was nearly always.

Damn, that girl needs to get laid more often. Big Ben looks like he should be hung like a horse, so you'd think Amanda would be wearin' a smile from ear to ear. But poor old Ben probably has a tough time gettin' it up when he looks at that sour schoolmarm face and that skinny, flat-chested, tight-assed body. What a waste of a good man.

Not really knowing how to read Amanda, Charyce charged ahead.

"So we was hoping, Rodney and me, that you and Ben would come to our wedding."

Amanda's eyes widened in incredulity. She sputtered, "You want us at your wedding?"

"Well, hon, I want *you* at our wedding. I don't have no momma around, and I figure I'm gonna need a little womanly help on the big day, what with the morning sickness and all." Charyce's right hand caressed her abdomen. Her lower abdomen, Amanda noted.

Feeling slightly ill herself, Amanda realized pregnancy would be the perfect ruse to get Rodney to trot down the aisle without Clara as his prize. The pervert might even be hoping the baby would be a little girl.

But, of course, Amanda knew there was no girl baby. There was no pregnancy. One of Amanda's talkative former classmates worked at the Charleston hospital where Charyce had gotten a tubal ligation a decade earlier. Charyce had apparently thought going so far out of town would prevent anyone back home from learning about the procedure. But Charyce had underestimated the broadcasting power of the West Virginia grapevine.

Amanda knew pregnancies were not unheard of after a tubal ligation, but the odds were slim, all the more so given the markedly reduced fertility of a woman closing on forty. She imagined Charyce had one of her karaoke BFFs pee on a stick, which would later be waved under Rodney's bulging eyes. She imagined Charyce had been tickling her uvula every morning before Rodney went off to work.

Right now, Charyce was standing with pelvis thrust forward in an effort to simulate a baby bump. She continued to rub her lower abdomen. Amanda bit her lip. Rodney was just stupid enough to buy the act.

Men are hopeless!

But not all men, Amanda suddenly realized, as she came up with a new reason to bless Uncle Virgil. June fourteenth, she remembered, was the day Uncle Virgil was having back surgery. With lugubrious glee, she explained the scheduling conflict to Charyce. She even managed to congratulate the future bride. "I'm sure you and Rodney will get everything you deserve out of life together," Amanda added – with just a hint of a smirk.

FIFTY-SEVEN

Fellowship on a Foggy Deck

Living in, but not on top of, mountains constituting a non-tropical rainforest means not seeing those mountains for a good chunk of a spring morning. Even at the start of a day that will eventually be bright and warm, thanks to the temperature differential, the fog is particularly opaque.

But that reality did not deter Clara. As soon as she spotted a thin shaft of sunlight penetrating the dense white curtain, she dashed onto Beatrice's deck and stretched out on a chaise lounge. With middle-school graduation approaching, Clara and her schoolmates were supposed to sit for class photos, and Clara was determined not to look like a "pasty-faced hillbilly" in hers. Even though the temperature was barely fifty degrees, Clara bravely exposed her face and neck to the soppy air.

Amused, Beatrice joined her. Wielding only one crutch, Beatrice had no problem taking a cup of hot tea to the shivering teenager.

"Not that desperate, yet," answered Clara through chattering teeth. "But if you had a hot cup of coffee...?

"That stuff will stunt your growth," grumped Beatrice, settling into an adjacent chair. She had failed utterly to instill an appreciation of tea in Clara, but she persisted, even if coffee was now a staple on the weekly grocery list. "So good. Soooo warming," she murmured, sipping the steaming liquid.

"How come you're having breakfast this early? I thought you couldn't handle the idea of food until nine."

"Tanner is finally back from his business trip. He was gone so long the book project is badly backed up. I needed to grab him at the first available opportunity. He has some appointment later today, so early morning was the only time he could see me."

"On a Saturday?"

"Desperate times call for desperate measures."

"I'm gonna be rich and famous, so I won't have to work Saturdays."

"When you're rich and famous, you'll probably be working every Saturday."

"Okay, then I'll settle for comfortable and halfway well known."

Ralph erupted from the side of the house and barreled onto the driveway, where he let loose with three sonorous barks issued from a completely vertical throat. A joyous baying from the road, several hundred feet from the house, echoed in response. Ralph had apparently sensed Gertrude, riding shotgun in Tanner's Hummer, long before the boxy vehicle crackled onto the driveway gravel.

Clara sat up in response to the canine duet and watched the spectacle of Gertrude trying to disembark without taking out one of Ralph's eyes. He snuffled her bony knuckles, poised for a dive off the running board. Beatrice, now yelling at Ralph to back off, empathized with the older dog's care in planning her imminent landing. Tanner solved the problem by coming around in back of Ralph and nudging the setter's rump with his knee. Diverted from Gertrude, Ralph focused on a new target of veneration and wiggled in happy circles around Tanner while shoving a wet nose in places where well-bred dogs should not go.

"I hope you feel properly welcome," yelled Beatrice from the deck.

"Dang," interjected Clara softly from the chaise lounge. When Beatrice turned to learn the reason for the exclamation, the teenager shrugged and whispered, "You know, for an old guy that dude is not bad." Clara returned to baldly staring at the "old guy," who was more or less leading the boisterous pack up the fieldstone path linking driveway to deck.

Beatrice turned her attention to Tanner, as well. His white, ribbed, cotton crew-neck sweater showcased pectorals and biceps. He had acquired a tan, which contrasted nicely with the sweater, the thick crop of expensively scissored hair, the bleached teeth. He smiled nonchalantly, basking in female admiration.

"Look sharp, Ms. Clara!" he shouted and tossed something at the girl.

The toss went high, but Clara snagged the prize with insouciance. In her hand she found a clear plastic cube containing an iPod Nano – the newest, smallest model. The girl looked from her palm to Tanner, with just the hint of suspicion on her face.

"Every time I come to this benighted corner, I am appalled at the technological backwardness. You have no cell phone reception. Your 'high-speed' Internet provider should be shot for false advertising. Your landline is in jeopardy of going down with a good blast of wind or an errant shot by a feckless hunter. But I will not tolerate – nay, I cannot abide – seeing a young woman in the prime of life bowed down by the unfashionable weight of that ridiculous thing you use as a music player. Come over to the twenty-first century."

"Why does that sound like something Darth Vader would say?" asked Beatrice.

"But…" Clara said, looking for guidance from Beatrice, who just shrugged. "Gee, thank you, Tanner."

"*Ne za shto,*" he replied, adding, "Ask your keeper if I got that right. My Russian is rusty."

"Clara and her keeper have some other things to thank you for – and interrogate you about," Beatrice said. Clara was already engrossed in the tiny instruction booklet included in the cube. "Well, maybe not both of us," added Beatrice. "Go play with the new doodad, Clara. I'll grill Tanner about the Marlboro Academy myself."

Still reading the booklet, Clara nodded and left. Beatrice called after her, "Hey, will you fire up the coffee machine, please?"

"Doodad? Coffee machine? As impolitic as it is to refer to a lady's age, I have to wonder just which century you were born in, Hillwilla."

"The wrong one."

Settling down on an Adirondack chair, Tanner laughed good-naturedly. "Quite right. I think I should have come of age in The Restoration, myself."

"A little lace at the throat and cuffs would suit you. But it would be a crying shame to cover up that hair with a wig."

"You don't say?" he asked innocently. "But you would be better suited, I think, to an earlier century. You strike me as a late-Renaissance woman."

"No, earlier. The twelfth or thirteenth century. But only if I was rich and extremely healthy. And lived far enough away from other people to avoid the plague."

"In other words, pretty much the way you live today."

"You forgot I said 'rich.' One simply must have servants and a few well-muscled minions to keep the riffraff away."

"Yes, but there's still the bother of cold drafts, lice, and bedbugs. Even the finest castles had them, you know."

"That's the trouble with fantasies. They dead-end in reality. Well, maybe I could at least have a hot spring on the castle grounds, so I could bathe away the bugs."

"That would certainly help. Maybe you should reconsider the milieu. Maybe you could be a rich Roman matron. Some excellent baths in that era."

"No, thanks. Whatever century I pick, I'll be a man, thank you very much. There weren't very many women's lives I would care to live in bygone centuries."

"What a pity. But I take your point. Even Lucrezia Borgia had a rough start to adulthood. Still, you'd be quite fetching in Renaissance gowns."

Awash in historic fantasy, Beatrice was surprised to realize she was actually enjoying the banter, perilously close to flirting. Beatrice Desmond did not flirt. Not normally.

Tanner jumped up, index finger raised. "I assume I was the reason for Clara turning on the 'coffee machine'? I've yet to see you drink anything but tea. And it looks like you could use a refill," he said, before snatching Beatrice's cup and disappearing into the house.

Beatrice didn't know whether to be annoyed her territory was being violated by yet another interloper—or charmed by the casual familiarity. She decided to remain in her chair and enjoy the now-warm sun on her face. Closing her eyes, she felt something remarkably near contentment.

Beatrice's eyes fluttered open with Tanner's return. She sensed him rather than heard him. He leaned forward, delivering her tea with his right hand. His left hand caressed, ever so briefly, the bare nape of her neck. The warm touch sent a shiver from her scalp all the way down to her toes. The shiver was not unfamiliar, even if Beatrice had not experienced its like in years. It made her feel unsettled, young, and just a little wonderful.

FIFTY-EIGHT

That Dorchester Chip

As quickly as it surfaced, the pleasurable aftershock from Tanner's ephemeral, almost electric touch faded. But the blush remained on Beatrice's face. Her heart continued to thud at nearly twice its normal pace, and the soaring pulse now suggested a panic attack more than an erotic reawakening. The walls she had so carefully constructed, brick by brick, during her late husband's slow descent into madness wobbled ever so slightly. Could she survive without the protection of those walls?

She had planned to brace Tanner on the subject of Clara's sudden invitation to the Marlboro Academy. Suspecting he was behind the letter, Beatrice was already annoyed by his presumption, however well-intentioned. Now that annoyance intensified in direct proportion to this newly perceived threat to her *modus vivendi.*

She flashed on all the little encroachments on her turf. During the weekly sessions in her office, she tired of weaving around Tanner's long legs and Gertrude's massive frame, whenever she wanted to fetch a book from the shelf or tea from the kitchenette. And now Tanner was bulldozing his way into Clara's life, as well. In the process, he was not only intruding on Beatrice's delicately crafted guardianship of the girl but also trespassing on the sensitivities of the extended Buckhalter clan.

"You can't keep doing this!" Beatrice snapped, as Tanner settled back into the adjacent Adirondack. His grin, evoked by her blush, fell instantly away.

"Getting you a cup of tea?" The smile made a crooked effort to return.

"Playing Fairy Godfather with Clara. Today it's an iPod. And the other day, I assume, yours was the hidden hand behind her application to that fancy school."

"You're objecting?"

"Yes, I'm objecting. You couldn't consult me first? It didn't occur to you that her family might feel insulted? That your intervention might send the kid a skewed message about values?"

"Couldn't you have used a boon or two growing up in grim old Dorchester?"

"That's not the point."

"Why not? Are you and I really better for pulling ourselves up by our bootstraps? It was one helluva long pull."

"You're saying the lessons of self-reliance are bad?"

"Only that you can overdo self-reliance. The fire that makes good steel can also forge one mighty chip on the shoulder."

Beatrice's nostrils flared. If she were a llama, her ears would have flattened against her head.

"I was actually talking about myself, Beatrice," Tanner continued gently. "I spent far too much time trying to prove something. That I deserved a good education, for one thing – right next to all those Richie Riches. I imagine you know how that feels."

"And wouldn't Clara feel as out of place at Marlboro as you did at Harvard? At least you earned your way into Harvard academically."

"Just because I had Krupp use her considerable powers of persuasion on Clara's principal to forward Clara's grades to Marlboro doesn't mean those grades weren't the real deal. Every bit as real as the writing sample sent along with Clara's application."

"Come again?"

"Marlboro wants an example of a student's writing ability – and not necessarily one of those dreadful essays about 'why I want to be a preppy.' There was broad latitude. So I included that wonderful piece Clara wrote putting herself in the mindset of the pregnant llama. Oh, don't look so shocked. I simply made a copy of it in your office."

Beatrice squeezed her eyes shut and gritted her teeth – in anger and a sense of violation. How did he find Clara's essay amid all the litter on her desk? What else had he snooped about in her office?

"Yes, yes. I understand your nose is out of joint, Hillwilla. But your annoyance is no reason to deprive Clara, is it? You know she'll look for your approval before accepting that scholarship. And you know she'll have a much better chance of getting into a good college, getting a decent start in life, if she graduates from Marlboro, as opposed to Seneca County's pitiful high school."

"Did you buy her the scholarship, too?"

"Absolutely not. Any Seneca County girl automatically becomes a contender just by getting accepted. As it happens, no other county girl even applied for the next academic year. The local kids are just too cowed by the idea of trying for a place like Marlboro. Mustn't get above one's raisin'. Stupid, stupid, stupid! Here, let me retrieve the scholarship brochure. I have it in my glove box. Meanwhile, you can simmer down."

Tanner rose and began to walk toward the Hummer.

"Do not patronize me, dammit!" Beatrice slapped the arm rest.

"Well, it's either that or shake some sense into you," Tanner retorted. He sat back down and fanned his hands in frustration.

"Fine. Get the goddamned brochure, then. And just give me a chance to think."

He shrugged and rose once again.

For all the fury she felt toward Tanner, Beatrice did not want to deprive Clara of a genuine opportunity. Her job was to guide Clara, not make the girl's decisions for her. Besides, the responsibilities of guardianship weren't the only factors coloring her take on Tanner's intervention.

Beatrice thought back on her own start in life and acknowledged the large chip she had carried on her thin shoulders back then. Would Clara be served by a similar chip?

Beatrice liked to think she was a better person for her humble beginnings. But there was no getting around the occasional bleakness of her childhood. Back then, she knew some children had things far worse, just as she knew her own troubles could get even worse. Beatrice had never been envious of children who appeared to have easier lives. She always figured if she wanted something badly enough, hard work might make it achievable. And when a prize fell to her grasp, the sense of achievement was invigorating.

Nevertheless, Beatrice always felt a tad off balance. Maybe it was that heavy chip on her shoulder. She hadn't realized how unbalanced she was until she met Kate in college. She didn't believe Kate was real. But try as she might, Beatrice couldn't find any flaw in the roommate miraculously assigned to her. By the end of freshman year, the girl with the Dorchester chip on her shoulder surrendered and let Kate be her friend. Kate was smart and beautiful and funny and popular and incredibly kind. She made Beatrice feel like she actually belonged.

Kate, of course, never once questioned the why of their friendship. She simply treasured it. Kate was balanced enough to accept the good things in life. Kate was balanced enough to appreciate the good without feeling somehow weakened by it – as Beatrice still did.

Clara would be far better off to turn out like Kate than like me.

Walking slowly back to the deck, Tanner eyed Beatrice with concern. Without saying a word, he sat down and laid the brochure on the arm of her chair.

Beatrice scanned it distractedly. Keeping her eyes on the flyer, Beatrice said, "I'll let Clara decide. I won't urge her to look a gift horse in the mouth."

Tanner reached for Beatrice's hand. It flinched away, but not in time. Holding her fingertips in a strong grip, Tanner said, "This isn't just about Clara."

Beatrice shook her head slowly. "No, it's also about work. About our being able to work together. At least, long enough to complete this book project." She reclaimed possession of her hand and defiantly returned Tanner's gaze.

"Just Boswell and Johnson, then?" he asked.

"Yes, Boswell and Johnson."

"You're a piss-poor liar, Hillwilla."

"I am what I am, Tanner. And not likely to change."

"We'll see."

Tanner leaned back on the chair, stretched his legs out, and crossed them at the ankles. He cradled his head in his interlaced fingers and looked up at the clearing sky. A thoughtful smile briefly lit up his face, as he followed the wisps of dissipating fog.

"This isn't over. Not by a long shot."

FIFTY-NINE

Gaudeamus Igitur

The east-facing slope of Gurney Mountain was erupting in trilliums. Every now and then, Ben would pause to admire the white triangles hiding amidst the dappled shade of fat, green leaves. As his eyes absorbed the calming hillside palette, a wood thrush poured out an achingly melancholy paean. If this were a Hollywood set, no movie viewer would believe all that visual and auditory beauty concentrated in one sweet, simple moment. But of course, that kind of synchronicity could be found in real life – in the deep mountains of West Virginia. In Appalachia. In spring. On Ben's ancestral homestead.

Ben savored the uncomplicated pleasure of working his property all alone. It made him hopeful to be moving so concretely toward the goal of a happier family, with him and Amanda and Uncle Virgil and Clara all under one large, rainproof roof. Except he suspected that dream would never come true. For all he knew, by the time he finished fixing up the old log home, Uncle Virgil would need nursing care. Amanda would hate living so far away from town. And Clara? Clara wasn't much acting like a Buckhalter these days.

At least, that was Brother Mike's take on recent developments. The other day, Mike had called his daughter to share the good news about coming back home in July. His announcement was met with silence.

"Clara has never been a moody kid, Ben, you know that," Mike told his brother the next day. "But she had a real pout on. When I asked her what was wrong, she said nothing. No enthusiasm. She didn't seem much interested in talking. She sure didn't seem happy to hear we could go back to the cabin in a few months."

Ben had already heard about the scholarship to the Marlboro Academy. He didn't know exactly how Clara got it in her head to apply, but he was glad she did. He was happy she was acting like she was worth something, especially after all that had happened lately.

Mike was less than happy when he finally prodded Clara into opening up and disclosing her educational plans. Incredulous, he shouted into the phone, "What do you want with a snooty school like that, where people will make fun of you?"

Ben listened to his brother's narrative over the phone.

Way to go, Mikey. Nothing like undermining the budding confidence of a fourteen-year-old.

The wood thrush resumed its aria. Ben knew people who spent a lot of time in the woods and had never heard that rapturous sound. It wasn't that they had hearing problems. Some people were just closed off to the beauty around them. He couldn't imagine his own brother could be one of them, not someone who crafted exquisite musical instruments that made such glorious sounds. But why couldn't Mike see the little jewel—hard, but with so much light inside—that was his daughter? How could he not want the absolute best for her?

Maybe, Ben thought, it was easier for him to see the potential in his goddaughter, because he would never have a daughter of his own. You often take for granted what you already have. Most days, it bothered him not at all that he would have no progeny, no one who would carry his unique genetic code into eternity. He knew childlessness was part of the deal when he married Amanda. But still… Nevertheless, Ben was not all that sure he could have lived up to his ideals about fatherhood. Such a failure might have been hard to live with.

Although he never suffered any abuse at the hands of his father, the senior Buckhalter was not the best role model for parenting. Carl, unlike Mike, probably never spent an overnight apart from his children when they were growing up. But Carl's presence in the household was purely physical. He was in the house—not in the family. Fortunately for Ben and Mike, Carl's lack of interest was counterbalanced by The Incredible Nails. It was interesting, Ben thought, that the verb "to father" meant little more, in colloquial usage, than donating sperm, while "to mother" conveyed a much longer-term commitment. Ben would have wanted to be a totally committed father. Could he have lived up to that goal? Or would he have proven as detached as Carl? Life had a way of diluting ideals, watering down the best intentions.

As he returned to scraping the mullions on the homestead's old but spectacularly crafted windows, Ben wondered if he was being too judgmental about his brother's parenting flaws. Hadn't he, Ben, ranked Clara below Amanda, when the child was in desperate need of a safe haven? Sure, Clara was not his child. Sure, he had tried to bulldoze Amanda into accepting Clara into their home on a permanent basis. But Ben was actually relieved when Eltie concocted the solution involving Beatrice. Without that Hail Mary save, the truth was Ben would ultimately have chosen his wife over his goddaughter—not for noble reasons about upholding his marital obligations but for selfish reasons. His life would be a wreck, emotionally and financially, if he lost Amanda. By comparison, losing his goddaughter's trust was something he could live with.

Of course, not without sadness. And not without some resentment toward Beatrice, who had stepped, however unwillingly at first, into the large gap in Clara's life. That outlander woman was becoming more important than any Buckhalter to the youngest member of the clan. It was only a matter of time before Clara would start acting less like a Buckhalter and more like a Desmond. Whatever that meant.

If it meant grabbing for the gold ring, however, Ben was glad. And he experienced some malicious glee at the shock Mike was feeling over Clara's new show of self-assertion.

During the phone call with Clara, Mike had apparently tried the stern approach. "It's too goddamned bad my cabin is too goddamned far away from the fancy-pants school. You can go to Seneca County High School like Ben and me did. It was good enough for us. It will be good enough for you." He was yelling by the time he finished.

Mike told Ben he thought maybe Clara would sniffle a little. Maybe she would whine and try to punish her father for not being around much this past year. But eventually, he figured, she would relent and want to be with her daddy.

Mike was totally unprepared for Clara's response. It was a simple, calm, "No."

"Whaddya mean, no?" Mike had demanded of his daughter.

"No, I'm not going to SCHS. No, I'm not going to live in the cabin, except maybe for a month or so in the summer. I want to live with Beatrice."

"Why would you want to live with a stranger instead of family?"

Clara paused and then said, with the first sign of a quaver in her voice, "Because Beatrice was there when I needed her."

She got you there. Got all of us.

Ben couldn't help admiring his goddaughter for standing up for herself. The Incredible Nails would have been proud. Maybe Clara wasn't acting much like a Buckhalter, but she was doing a good impression of a Moriarty.

According to Mike, the conversation ended in a stalemate; no firm decisions reached. Ben suspected Clara had already made her decision and would not waver. And he wondered if his brother might not ultimately be relieved. Being a full-time, single parent might prove far more difficult than Mike could handle.

A sliver of wood suddenly dug into the meaty part of Ben's thumb. As usual, he had begun his tasks with heavy work gloves. As usual, he had removed them, because he regarded them as more trouble than they were worth.

As he sucked on the wound, he again surveyed the landscape surrounding him. Contrasting with the hard crenellations of the mountains to the north were the gentler curves of Gurney acreage, carpeted by hardwoods whose fuzzy contours looked like an impressionistic painting—their leaf buds and flowerlets pregnant with promise and having a surprising range of hues, from soft red to yellow-green, to the most vivid green imaginable. In another week or so, the greening on Gurney Mountain would become so intense it would almost be painful for retinas to absorb.

In Sunday school, Ben had heard the old stories about the average mortal being unable to survive looking on the visage of God. He didn't know whether that was true. He didn't know whether there was a God to look at. But he knew he was never so aware of his own mortality, his human frailty, as when he allowed himself to breathe in the overwhelming glories of nature. The experience made him feel simultaneously insignificant and exalted. It was more profoundly religious than any Catholic mass he had ever attended.

For all the family drama, Ben realized a deep sense of peace in his solitude on Gurney. Here, in the mountain cathedral, he suddenly felt everything was on track. His godchild was starting a new journey, one that certainly would have pitfalls, but one that held high promise. And he was right to be working on the family homestead, which might just provide some healing for the Buckhalter clan.

At very least, his labors were helping to heal him. Splinters and all.

SIXTY

An Irrational Cosmos

A business update was the pretext for Beatrice's call to Evie. For fifteen minutes, she briefed her friend on the status of the Fordyce project. Beatrice explained her reasons for incorporating only selected biographical information supplied by Patty.

"There's so much interesting stuff in his life that I see no reason to dredge up the most depressing details. We don't want to look like a tabloid with all that Mommie Dearest stuff. The economic hardships of his early years will give a good enough feel for how much he's overcome, how much he's reinvented himself. You know, it's a wonder he's as well adjusted as he is. With that background, someone else would have turned into a psychopath. You gotta admire the guy, even if he's a royal pain in the ass."

"You admire him now? Since when? Has something happened Mother should know about?"

"Oh, shut up! It's just that … for all his obnoxious qualities, he's maddeningly hard to dismiss… Oh, shut up!"

"I didn't say anything."

"No, but I could hear the wheels whirring."

Beatrice then launched into the latest Clara saga. She told Evie all about the Marlboro Academy "application," the scholarship offer, and Clara's nervous interest. Beatrice said Tanner had advised her to encourage the girl to seize the opportunity. Nevertheless, she admitted, she was unprepared for the consequences of that act of encouragement.

"Clara seems to think the only way she can go to the academy is if she lives with me."

"How's that?"

Beatrice explained the geographic realities. Commuting from northern Seneca County, one of the largest in the state, to the next county south would be an enormous drain on the girl. It would not leave much opportunity to participate in extracurricular activities. Which would be important selling points when Clara got around to applying for college.

"I understand all the points she made, Evie. But, Christ, I didn't exactly sign on for the long term here. Come to think of it, I didn't sign on for anything."

"No, but it hasn't exactly worked out badly. For either of you."

Beatrice was surprised by her friend's reaction. Evie was hardly a woman oozing maternal sentiments.

"Funny you should point out the practical advantages. Because that's exactly what Clara did. She reminded me of the knee-replacement surgery I will supposedly need, once I've healed up from the break. 'How will you manage without me? Who'll feed the llamas? Who'll walk Ralph? I'll come in handy.'"

"The kid has a point."

"Oh, I suppose, but I can't imagine her family going for the idea. She insisted she would deal with her family. And Clara just might have the moxie to pull it off. But I don't know..." Beatrice trailed off.

"What don't you know?"

"I like living alone. Sure, sometimes it gets lonely, even overwhelming. But I'm much more comfortable by myself than having people around, day in, day out."

When that confession failed to elicit any sympathetic response, Beatrice reminded Evie of her own quirks. "It's like what you said about your relationship with Bart. Are you really ready to give up the life you've shaped, your independence, to marry him?"

"Well, yeah, but stuff happens."

"Oh, my God! You're about to become my sister-in-law!"

"Down, girl. That's not what I meant. But I am kind of testing this togetherness business."

"Details, please."

"Well, Bart and I are going out of state on vacation this summer. A couple of weeks."

"I am almost as thunderstruck by that news as I would be by a wedding announcement. Getting my brother out of Massachusetts is a huge undertaking. He has yet to visit me in West Virginia. And it was like pulling teeth getting him to visit me those few times in Virginia. How in God's name did you manage that feat?"

"It all started with him musing about how he'd like to go to Newfoundland, to do some family research. I gather some knuckle-dragging ancestors of yours used to choke herrings up there?"

"You're going to Newfoundland? I can't see you in a heavy wool sweater and brogans."

"What are brogans? No, of course I'm not going to Newfoundland. But the interesting thing is he suggested I join him. It wouldn't be fun for him to go there alone, he said, the sweetie. So I proposed he do the genealogical research on the Internet, with my assistance. Then I added I'd be happy to go on vacation with him in a coastal area – like the Bahamas."

"I can't see Bart snorkeling in the Bahamas."

"That was just the opening gambit, dumbass. We compromised. We're going to Miami."

"Some compromise."

"Well, it is, once you learn Bart wants to drive there. So he can take Addie."

"You have lost your mind!"

"No, I figure a road trip is a real good test of compatibility. Also, we can break it up by visiting you. But, wait, it gets better. We want to bring you with us."

"What, as a chaperone?"

"No, we'll already have that in Shirley. I have some business in South Florida and need Shirley's help. Besides, it will be a nice reward. She says she wants to go clubbing in South Beach."

"The cosmos no longer makes any sense. So, is Shirley planning on entering a wet T-shirt contest while she's there?"

"Hey, with her rack, she'd probably win. But don't interrupt. We'll spend part of the time housesitting for a friend of mine who lives right on Biscayne Bay. Then we're going to rent a house on the Keys, where Bart can do his nature walks – with Addie, of course – and he can get his fill of all sorts of subtropical flora. I also got him a membership at the Fairchild Tropical Gardens, so he can get lost in orchids and bromeliads, even while we're in Miami."

"Yeah, that might work. But why do you need me?"

"Bart thought you could use the R&R after such a tough winter. Get a little salt air and sunshine. Get a break from the farm. Get a little break from playing mother. And you'll need that break all the more if Clara's going to be a permanent fixture. Plus, from what you've just told me, this will all mesh nicely with her plans. She'll probably be visiting her father's cabin when we head south."

Beatrice bit her tongue to avoid laughing over the nonsense about taking a break from the farm. Farmers didn't take breaks – at least not breaks lasting several weeks. The llamas needed to be fed and watered and medicated and watched for heat stress. After a few weeks, the grass would be hip-high, supporting colonies of insects that would make Beatrice's and Ralph's lives miserable for the rest of the summer. And then there was the slight matter of her job. She was already pushing Wolfgang's tolerance levels by spending so much time on the Fordyce book.

But all Beatrice said was, "That's Bart's reasoning. What's yours?"

"Martha."

"Huh?"

"It seems Bart casually mentioned the vacation plans to his daughter during one phone conversation. She immediately exclaimed about this client who lives in the Boston burbs but has a winter home in Miami. The client was so 'ecstatic' – Martha's adjective – about the job Martha did on the Boston townhouse that he wants his Miami digs done over, too. So, of course, Martha sees this as a 'perfectly serendipitous opportunity' – once again, her words. I could kick Bart in the shins for blabbing."

"It's a perfectly serendipitous opportunity to check you out some more, you mean."

"Exactly."

"Well, I'm not getting into that mess. As you well know, relations between Martha and me are tense. So schmoozing with her would be less than restful for my weary bones. Nope, girlfriend, if you need a buffer, it ain't gonna be me. Besides, Shirley should be more than up to the task."

"I hate you."

"Is that any way to talk to your future matron of honor?"

SIXTY-ONE

Serendipity After All

The strange hum had been going on for a while.

Ralph, knowing he was not allowed up on any bed, risked an indiscretion. He laid his head, flews splayed, on the bedspread and stared intently at the lump that was his human. Unsuccessfully.

Ralph padded down the hallway to check on the girl. She was already up, but humans had a way of appearing and reappearing without much purpose to their movements. It wasn't like they tracked scents or marked territory, or focused usefully on the myriad things that moved about inside the house: the ubiquitous moths, the sly spiders, the annoying flies, the whining mosquitoes. Not that Ralph knew any of those intruders by name. But he certainly could distinguish them by scent and sound.

The roots of both ears stiffened, as he heard the strange hum again. Ralph bustled downstairs to find the girl. The girl would surely be on alert. Young humans had keener senses than their pack leaders.

The girl was in the kitchen. She was humming, but hers was not the hum that had alerted Ralph. Hers was an aimless, carefree human hum. Ralph, all business, sat down abruptly in front of her and thumped his tail on the tiles to catch the girl's attention.

"What's up, furry face?" she asked absent-mindedly.

Ralph dashed to the outside door but paused before exiting through the dog panel. He looked over his shoulder to see if she was following. She was merely watching him without moving from the kitchen counter, so he barked once and then ducked through the panel.

The girl followed. Ralph ran purposefully, without his usual springs and wiggles. Looking toward the barn, he parked his butt and barked again.

The noise startled a great blue heron, stalking a rivulet formed by mountain runoff. The girl's and Ralph's ears were buffeted by the fwoop, fwoop, fwoop of the ponderous takeoff.

"Oh, it's just a heron, Ralph. Chill." Clara knew Ralph was obsessed by all large birds.

She turned back toward the house, but Ralph stayed put. He would maintain his vigil until one of the humans understood.

Clara returned to the kitchen and heard the familiar thump of Beatrice's single crutch. The woman was already dressed in jeans and sweatshirt, but her face was still pleated by the pillow, and her hair was disheveled. Hung over, Clara decided. The previous evening, Beatrice had announced her intention to celebrate the successful conclusion of a particularly onerous work week. When Clara went upstairs to bed, Beatrice was already nodding off on the sofa with a half-finished drink on the side table. Her "celebrations" had become less frequent, Clara thought, with a touch of curiosity.

"What's with Ralph?" Beatrice asked, as she filled her teapot.

"Heron."

"Ah. He hates herons."

Looking out the kitchen window, Beatrice followed the direction in which Ralph's long nose was pointing. Six of the llamas were clustered together, looking somewhat nervous, although not enough to impede their occasional grazing. Standing apart from the group was old Tess. Nothing unusual there. Tess was a loner. Especially when it came to her toilet habits, which appeared to be her current focus. Except Beatrice could not see any dung pile nearby. Yet there Tess was, assuming the position: tail up, rear legs spread wide, really wide.

"Oh, my God! Clara, I think Tess is in labor. Meet me in the pasture. I'm gonna fire up the lawn tractor."

By the time the two humans converged outside, a large gray lump was on the grass by Tess's feet. The old girl turned and sniffed it. The other llamas drew closer. When Buck boinked a little too close, Tess clucked banefully and shot a bolus of partially chewed grass right into his face. The little llama stopped in his tracks and began shaking his head, mouth open, trying to avoid inhaling the vile odor of Tess's spit.

The lump shifted into an approximation of a kush, with tiny feet tucked neatly underneath. The heavy knob at the end of the long neck was not yet a match for gravity and lolled on the grass. By the time Clara and Beatrice came within reach, the little gray cria was bobbling its heavy head into a vertical position, more or less.

Beatrice knew she should fly off on a million tasks. The umbilical cord would need to be dipped in iodine. Tess would have to be watched to make sure she passed the placenta. The placenta would need to be buried, lest it attract coyotes. Mom and cria would need watching to make sure nursing began and progressed normally. But for now, Beatrice just wanted to savor the moment.

"How?" interrupted Clara, pointing at the baby.

"I guess Tess got bred when Graf escaped from his pasture, back in Staunton. Arthur only saw the breeding with Reine, but that doesn't mean anything. Apparently, the outing was more eventful than we realized."

"But Reine delivered a month ago. Why didn't Tess have her baby then?"

"Llamas are weird. A textbook pregnancy is eleven-and-a-half months, but I've also read some llamas carry for over a year. Which must be the case with Tess. I'm just amazed she could still get preggers at her age."

Clara was admiring the big llama, who sniffed at her baby and alternated between emitting soft hums and clucking a warning at the humans and the herd. Then Tess began humming more loudly. Turning abruptly, she waddled away from the gathering in apparent discomfort. A good distance away, she assumed a straddle position once again, gave forth with a long, low moan, and promptly delivered the placenta.

"Good girl!" Beatrice called in appreciation. Tess, as if responding, walked more sedately back toward her baby and sniffed Beatrice's head. The woman had awkwardly settled onto the grass beside the baby.

The sniff might have been born of nervousness, but Tess did not seem too disturbed by the humans in such close proximity to her cria. Clara, sitting cross-legged beside Beatrice, risked reaching out a hand to touch the baby's soft, wet curls. Tess briefly pressed her ears back, but sensing no threat, she began looking for grass to graze—all the while keeping a watchful brown eye on the scene.

"Oh, it's so soft! His wool is just beautiful."

"Her wool is just beautiful," Beatrice corrected, pointing as the baby flipped its tail up over its back, in submissive response to a sniff from Tess.

"A girl? Maybe we can breed her! Isn't her color unusual? Imagine the babies she could have!"

Beatrice smiled. Clara's sense of ownership and feeling of inclusion were endearing. Beatrice found Clara's projection into the future comforting. Or maybe Beatrice was absorbing a progesterone high from Tess. Or maybe it was the warm sunshine on her face or the sweet, pungent smell of the wild onions the llamas were nibbling. Or maybe it was the way the violets fooled the eye. One minute their blueness would provide a startling contrast to the spring-green grass; the next minute the violets would blend coolly into the shadows of the blades.

For a change, Beatrice was not focused on her broken leg or her off-track knees. She was not obsessing about how long she could keep on keeping on. She was not worried about money. As she sat on the warm grass and watched the perfect little creature struggle to its feet, Beatrice thought of all the unexpected things that had happened in the past thirteen months, beginning with Kate's death. And not all of them were bad.

"I know what to call her!" Beatrice announced abruptly. "Serendipity!"

Clara winced at the big word.

"No, no, no! Really, it's perfect! This baby is a shining example of how serendipity can come into our lives. She came into my life. So did Buck. And so did you."

And so did Tanner, dammit!

Beatrice smiled at Clara.

"I know spit happens," she said, a knot growing in her throat. "But so do good things. Good things like you."

Beatrice squeezed Clara's hand. Clara squeezed back.